THE SPIRES AS THEY ARE SEEN FROM THE RAILWAY

Margaret Gillard

THE SPIRES AS THEY ARE SEEN FROM THE RAILWAY

THE BODLEY HEAD
LONDON

ACKNOWLEDGEMENTS

The author and publishers wish to make the following acknowledgements:
Extracts from 'The Banks are Rushy Green' and 'King's Cross, what shall we do?' from *Nursery Rhymes and More Nursery Rhymes* by Eleanor Farjeon reproduced by kind permission of Gerald Duckworth & Co.
Extract from 'The Love Song of J. Alfred Prufrock' from *Collected Poems 1909–1962* by T. S. Eliot reproduced by kind permission of Faber and Faber Ltd.
Extract from 'Afternoons' from *The Whitsun Weddings* by Philip Larkin reproduced by kind permission of Faber and Faber Ltd.
Extract from 'Morning has Broken' from *The Children's Bells* by Eleanor Farjeon reproduced by kind permission of David Higham Associates Ltd.
Extract from 'New Year's Eve' by Gordon Bottomley reproduced by kind permission of Roger Lancelyn Green.
While every effort has been made to contact the copyright holders, the publishers have been unable to trace all owners of copyright material reproduced in this book, but will be happy to make suitable acknowledgement in any future editions.

British Library Cataloguing
in Publication Data

Gillard, Margaret
The spires as they are seen from the railway.
I. Title
823'. 914 [F] PR6053, R35
ISBN 0–370–31046–2

© Margaret Gillard 1987
Printed in Great Britain for
The Bodley Head Ltd
32 Bedford Square, London WC1B 3EL
by Redwood Burn Ltd, Trowbridge, Wilts

For David and Gregory
and for
Brigid, Cynthia, Peter,
Maggie and Sarah

I
September 1983

I

On the first day of the autumn term, when Richard stopped the car at the top of the side street which led to the school gates, Clare saw that the corner shop, which had sold sweets and crisps to the children, and refused to sell them cigarettes, stood empty. CLOSING DOWN, said white-wash capitals across its windows. ALL SWEET'S AND BISCUIT'S ½ PRICE.

Richard said, 'Are you sure you feel up to it?'

'No, to be honest,' said Clare. 'It's got to be done, however.'

Across the lowered car window they kissed, more than the usual goodbye dab of lip to cheek. Of course, two girls, in parodic versions of the school uniform — coloured leg-warmers and skirts slit up to the thigh — chose that moment to walk past. Clare pulled back and waved Richard on, but their catcalls followed her.

'Hey, miss!'

'Is he yer feller, miss?'

The concrete was still unnaturally free of litter and blown dust, but the usual gas-fitters' hole, pegged around with red and white plastic bunting, was there in the drive-way. During the six weeks' holiday the hole had moved down from the old bicycle stands to a point directly in front of the staff entrance. She paused at the edge. One of the workmen looked up, eyed her legs indifferently.

'Good morning,' said Clare. 'Is this hole going to be in front of the door all term?'

'Nah, miss. We're just waiting for some parts.'

If he had been a pupil she might have asked 'Parts of what?', but she resisted the temptation. 'Oh, I see.'

'Mind, it'll all have to come up again over there. Whole place is falling down.'

'Quite. I often feel like giving it a helping shove.'

She went through the double doors. Disloyalty, Mrs Baylham, she said to herself in the headmaster's tones. There is such a thing as obligation ... Of all the people who worked in those buildings, only Kettleby could use words like 'duty' and 'obligation' without any air of self-mockery. Behind her, from the gas-fitters' pit, she heard a faint wolf whistle. That might have been heartening, except that she suspected it was meant ironically: *Bitch*. It takes the whole holiday, every summer, to get out of that way of talking to people, and then only two seconds to get back into it.

The two main buildings, facing the road, were architectural mirror images of one another, inside and out. In the front lobby of each was a brass plaque recording the fact that the Lord Lieutenant of County Durham and the President of the Board of Education had been present at the opening of the two schools on such-and-such a day in 1908. In what was now Middle School there was an additional plaque, the wood so darkened that it took a conscious effort to read it. *In memory of the masters and pupils of the Stanburn Boys' Grammar School who* ... those first pupils must have finished their Higher School Certificate just in time to put on a different uniform. *Abbott, J.F., Durham Light Infantry; Adamson, W.R., Royal Flying Corps:* Clare had never seen anyone else but Colin so much as glance at that appalling register. Sixty names: two classes full. What did you do in the Great War, Daddy? I made the world safe for comprehensive schools, my son.

There was a powerful first-day-of-term smell of disinfectant and polish that did not quite obliterate the smell of doubtful plumbing. Clare gulped back a second's-worth of nausea, and walked firmly down the corridor, glancing through the internal windows of each classroom as she went. Start as you mean to go on. One or two children were in already, swinging their legs from the desks or tilting backwards on the chairs, but the noise had not started yet. She pushed open the connecting door to the new building, shoving her briefcase ahead with her foot.

The new building which the Education Authority had promised had been very grand indeed, with new classrooms, a sixth-form block and a sports block, and a staffroom and assembly hall which would hold the combined populations of three schools merged into one. The reality which went up was a tiny staffroom, glass-walled on three sides, offices for the Headmaster and the secretaries, and a hall that would hold only the fifth and sixth forms. So the prefabricated buildings on stilts, which had gone up to house the post-war 'bulge' that was Clare's own age group, stayed on; and the old secondary-modern buildings half a mile away in Tenter Street, dating from the 1870 Education Act and sentenced to demolition years ago, stayed on too.

In theory, if you fancied carrying piles of thirty or sixty textbooks several times a day from one building to another, you had a choice of half a dozen staffrooms and the company in them. In practice you were confined to wherever you had a shelf. Kettleby had discovered long ago that the allocation of shelves was a means of breaking up dangerous alliances. This year Clare was sharing the glass-walled staffroom with two scientists, an RE specialist, a 'home-economist', and the member of her own department with whom she had the least in common. Still, as things had turned out she was glad of it.

The letters TGIF, Thank God It's Friday, had been embossed by someone, last term, in drawing pins on the cork notice board. Every time the door opened, the incomer would look at the message, laugh more or less hollowly, and sit down. No one exchanged actual greetings. There was a newcomer, a tall girl with fuzzy hair; very young, almost certainly a probationer, which was something you saw less often these days. It did not look as though anyone was going to make an introduction. Clare remembered her own first day: Lucy Knowles taking her round, introducing everyone by name, making sure for weeks that Clare was included in conversations . . .

'Hullo,' she said. 'I'm Clare Baylham, from English.'

'I'm Gillian Newfield. I'm going to teach RE.'

'I didn't know we had a new post in RE ... sorry, I mean welcome to the Alderman Cassop.'

'The job advert only came out last month,' said the girl. 'I thought I was going to be unemployed. I've been really lucky getting this.'

'I hope you still think so by half term' said Clare. 'Look, this is Alan Carr, Head of Maths, and Bob Murray, Head of Geography. The reason they don't move or speak unless you kick them is that they've been here since they were about eleven.'

'Ninety years, man and boy,' said Alan. The door opened again. The latest arrival looked at the drawing pins but failed to laugh. 'And this,' said Clare, 'is my colleague Janet Waldridge, also from English.'

'Hullo,' said Janet. She picked some drawing pins out of TGIF, and put a notice on the board.

Alan said, 'Does that bit of paper say "Mr Carr is made redundant on full pay", by any chance?'

'It's about the new tutor groups,' said Janet with her back still turned. Janet never saw jokes, even of the most limited kind.

'When I were a little lad,' said Bob, sliding from his natural accent into a stage Yorkshire one, 'us used to call them things "classes", not "tutor groups".'

'That just shows how long it is since you were a little lad, Robert.'

'I'm sorry to say,' said Clare to the newcomer, 'that this is all too fair a sample of the staffroom wit of this school. Your Head of Department should have warned you. Where *is* Ted, by the way — has anyone seen him?'

'I haven't met my Head of Department yet,' said the girl.

'What — at twenty to nine on the first morning of term? That's not like him. But you do know where you're supposed to be for the first lesson, at least?'

'No,' said the girl. 'I haven't got my timetable yet. Nor a syllabus. The Headmaster said I'd get them through the post, but nothing's come.'

Would she just have sat there, waiting for someone to attend to her, until the bell went? The first wave of the comprehensively educated hits the teaching profession. Clare said, 'That's fairly typical of the administration of this place.'

'The secretaries have to have holidays too,' said Janet.

'Well, Kettleby knows that as well,' said Clare. 'He ought to have seen to it himself, even if it meant licking his own stamp.' *Disloyalty, Mrs Baylham* ... 'Look — Gillian — I don't know where the RE books live these days, but we've got a pile of Bibles in the English cupboard, which we used to use for stylistic analysis in the days when sixth-formers could do such things. That'll give you something to fall back on for the first lesson. Then we'll try and find Ted Auton.'

As they came round the bend of the stairs towards the book room there was a scuffle of feet. Clare decided not to investigate. Gillian said, 'Is that the Mr Auton whose job I got?'

'No, can't be. I told you, he's your Head of Department ... wait a bit, though — if he *has* gone, I suppose they'd be bound to replace him with a probationer and keep it cheap. And that would explain why it was advertised late.'

'It was definitely a Mr Auton. The Headmaster said something about early retirement.'

'Well, I wonder how Ted pulled that off. I'm sure he's only in his early fifties. He can't possibly have worked out his notice, either. Look, here are the Bibles. I think there's still more or less a full set.'

'Oh ... these are the Authorised Version.'

'Well, yes. You couldn't do much stylistic analysis with the Revised Standard Version, could you?'

'No one teaches the Authorised Version now. I mean, it's very kind of you, but ...'

There had been a time when Clare had perfected the icy schoolma'am's stare: but from increasing lack of effectiveness it had fallen into disuse.

'Well, it's all I can suggest. If you can think of something else—' Someone still had to find the wretched girl's timetable, too. In the small of her back a tightened muscle began to throb. The bell, deafeningly recharged during the holidays, rang over their heads; an outside door began to bang rhythmically, and shouts and hooting noises rose from below. An adolescent male voice sang loudly, 'We don't need no ... education ...'

A small bespectacled man with a shiny face, vaguely familiar from one of the other staffrooms, was puffing along the corridor towards them.

'Is this my new young lady, by any chance? His Nibs chose to wait until ten minutes ago to tell me I'm acting Head of Department.'

'I hope he offered you a Scale 3 to go with it,' said Clare. 'I'd been Deputy Head of English for two years before I got a penny out of it, and that was only because Colin Rowsley went and made a scene for me.'

'Hell-as-like he did. I got a lecture about the cuts instead. You'd think our salaries were being paid out of His Nibs's own piggy bank. Welcome aboard, Miss Newfield. Mind you don't drown.'

'What's happened to Ted?' asked Clare.

'No idea. Cut his throat, perhaps.'

Clare said hastily, 'Help, I must rush. Have a good morning, Gillian. See you at break, I expect. Don't give the kids an inch.' She clattered down the stairs. A voice yelled 'Taken short, miss?'

She passed Bob and Janet coming out of the staffroom. Alan was still inside, sitting with his feet stretched out in front of him. Clare dropped on to a seat and reached for her briefcase.

'Not going to sing to your Maker this morning?' said Alan.

'Yes, I am. But I simply must have a mouthful of coffee first. I wish that blessed architect hadn't had a mind above electric sockets: I'm sick to death of not being able to boil a kettle in here.' She took out her thermos flask. Alan, always on the verge of becoming the parody of a schoolteacher, got out his pipe.

'I take it you haven't come round to the joys of prayer in the holidays, Alan?'

'I tell your Head of Department,' said Alan, 'that I was turned off religion for good when we were both young lads by having to drag him feet first out of Assembly after he'd been on a Lenten fast, or something. Came down with such a crash we thought they'd dropped the Bomb at last.'

Clare grinned in spite of herself. 'I've heard that story. Mind you, Colin's version of it is that his was the reaction of a soul in a state of grace — having to stand next to you, you see. What it is to have a shared adolescence with one's colleagues.'

'Pity we didn't know Kettleby in those days. We could have arranged an accident in the chemistry labs and changed the course of all our lives.'

'Quiet,' said Clare. 'For all we know he's had the room bugged over the holidays. Anyway such lost opportunities don't bear thinking about.'

If you could go on talking in this staffroom idiom for long enough it cut everything else down to manageable proportions. She swallowed what was left of the coffee. 'See you, Alan. Give 4B my love.'

She pushed into the hall just as the Headmaster, up on the stage, was arranging the folds of his gown. Academic dress was banned for the rest of them — divisive, and insulting to those who had none.

As she had planned, there was no room except at the back among the prefects. She had made up her mind that she would not look to see whether Colin was there, but her eyes found him at once: the thick straight mousy hair, and the flash of his spectacles as he turned, hearing the door swing. Carefully she did not look in that direction again. Oh, God ...

'Our Father,' intoned Kettleby, 'which art in Heaven, hallowéd be thy name ...' To be appointed to a headmastership in that county it undoubtedly helped to be Labour and Methodist, and Kettleby professed to be both: all the same, he had the *vox Anglicana* to perfection. The first time we heard that 'hallowéd', thought Clare, Colin and I set each other off laughing, and didn't dare to look at each other ...

She was conscious of a small sharp pain, as real as the one in her back but unrelated to it. Or at any rate, not directly related to it. It was a pain she was going to have to get used to. Come on, there are more immediate things to think about. Today's teaching, for instance — and Deborah. I'd forgotten Deborah.

Until the end of last term, she was the one thing I thought I'd have on my mind this autumn.

'... the power and the glory, for ever and ever. Amen.'

It's very kind of you, but no one teaches the Authorised Version these days.

Something was producing giggles in rising volume from one group of the fifth-formers. Kettleby glared down towards them and the laughter faded away. Betty McCabe, a reliable plonking pianist, struck up:

*Morning has broken
Like the first morning;
Blackbird has spoken
Like the first bird ...*

A loud fart came from the far corner of the room, echoed immediately from the opposite side. The singing faltered. There was another fart, a resounding one.

Clare's pupils tended to say, as a kind of catch phrase, 'Now yer know yer've not ter be crude with Mrs Baylham — — so be-*yave*'. Still, her squeamishness was not usually such as to make the room go out of focus in this particularly sickening way. She muttered something to the nearest prefect and struggled through the swing doors again. Alan, mercifully, was no longer in the staffroom. She sat down, poured herself another cup of coffee, and found that her hands were trembling. Probably not enough to show. Come on, you silly cow, you can keep them occupied for one lesson. One lesson at a time, that's all there is to it. They can't *do* anything: this isn't the kind of school where you get beaten up. Not yet, anyway.

Doors began to bang again. Janet came back. She was a small, squarely-built girl, with fair hair cropped short: the type that women's magazines wish would make more of themselves. 'All right, Clare?' she asked, without much interest.

'Fine, thanks. I just felt dizzy for a second. Must be the shock of coming back to work.'

Janet said, not unkindly, 'I imagine you're not much looking forward to this year.'

'Not a lot, no.'

'I do have a certain amount of sympathy for you this time. I even have a certain amount for our revered Head of Department.'

'Do you always *have* to be so nasty about poor Colin?' said Clare. That, at least, was still permissible.

'Poor Colin my foot. He always seems to me to be so thoroughly willing to wound and yet afraid to strike. Oh, by the way, he told me to ask you if you can manage a quick Department meeting at four?'

'All of us?' asked Clare cautiously.

'As far as I know. I think it's just to discuss the mechanics of running the Department with him over in Tenter Street nine-tenths of the time.'

'It's going to be practically impossible, is the short answer to that.'

'It should demonstrate some interesting truths,' said Janet. 'You may find that we can manage perfectly well *without* a hierarchy.'

If Ted Auton really were not going to come back, then Janet would from now on be the only person in this staff-room with whom it was possible to hold any kind of sustained conversation: which made it rather a pity that their conversations were nearly always politely hostile. Bob and Alan, whose natural loyalties were much closer to Clare's own, were good for a predictable laugh; but in conversation they always operated that cutout, between the inner and the outer parts of the personality, that men are inclined to think is their greatest asset and strength. Clare was too apt herself to bring down that shutter to feel able to damn anyone else for doing it: but to be able to have the sustained conversation, the self-revelation (however partial), and the jokes, all with the same person, had meant the end of being alone.

Keep occupied. Go and see Kettleby now, in the form tutors' period, instead of sitting here.

Outside, three girls were just tiptoeing past the door.

'About turn,' ordered Clare. 'And I'll have the cigarettes, please. Is there anyone else in those lavatories?'

As always, 'lavatory' proved to be the funniest word they had ever heard.

'No, miss.'

'Well, we'll just go in and see, shall we?'

Ceremonially she turned on a tap and shredded the cigarettes under it. Strands of tobacco and filter paper gathered in the plughole. 'This is just to show you,' she remarked 'that I'm not confiscating these in order to smoke them myself.'

'Ee, *miss*, cigarettes cost money, y'know.'

'I do know. *I* certainly can't afford to pay anyone money for giving me cancer.'

'Miss, that's all lies about cancer. Me dad says so.'

'Your father can do what he likes. You can't, just yet.'

'Yer can't stop us, miss.'

Colin Rowsley, still out of breath from his rapid transit between the main school buildings and the annexe at Tenter Street, pelted up the stairs to the staffroom like a late schoolboy. As soon as he opened the door there was silence.

The room was already full of cigarette smoke, and all three bars of the electric fire were glowing. In the sudden heat Colin's spectacles misted over, and all he could do — all he had time to do in any case — was to smile blindly round the room, say 'Good morning', pick up his class register and go. As he closed the door he heard a murmur start up again.

You had only to stand in a doorway and utter two words to classify yourself. As clearly as though it were hanging round his neck, his label read *Grammar school master. One of that lot*. Even after five years of being the other thing.

Come on, he said to himself, go and do your worst with 3N. At least they won't know why you're there teaching them. He took off his spectacles and polished the lenses so as to be able to see where he was going. This year is going to be hell. But there are other things.

The Headmaster was ostentatiously busy on the telephone, and kept Clare standing. After a couple of minutes she decided to sit down anyway. Kettleby always underestimated the security of those who had nothing to lose:

it was why, although he terrified the well-behaved out of their minds, he never had the same effect on the delinquent fringe.

'You had a pleasant holiday, I hope, Mrs Baylham?'

As pleasant as you could make it. 'Very, thank you.'

'What can I do for you? It is a busy day, as you can see.'

'I wanted to let you know, Headmaster, about my plans for a pupil of mine.' (*Don't* appear to ask permission — speak as though you took permission for granted.) 'Deborah Robson, in this year's Upper Sixth. I intend' (yes, good: 'intend', not 'hope', or 'should like') 'to put her in for the Oxford Entrance exam. This autumn.'

'Deborah—?'

'Robson.'

'And you wish to enter her for which examination?'

'The Oxford scholarship exam. She's an exceptionally able pupil.'

This style of speech was catching. What Clare had meant to say was something like 'She's particularly bright'.

Kettleby moved the papers on his desk, picked them up, shuffled them, put them down again. Partly, no doubt, in order to keep her waiting; but also, she judged, to give himself time to work out whether there could be some obscure but immensely sinister motive behind her approach.

'Mrs Baylham, may I ask why you have selected this particular pupil?'

'I've just told you, Headmaster. She's particularly bright.'

'You've been giving her some special attention in class?'

In a good cause, Clare could succeed in keeping her temper. 'If you're asking whether I neglect the rest of her group, no, I don't think I do.'

'But you *are* proposing to give her special attention from now on?'

'She'll have her ordinary class work to do, and I'll mark it to a higher standard than the rest of them — without making it obvious to anyone else, of course. Apart from that, I propose — provided that she agrees, of course: naturally I'm mentioning it to you first — to give her at least a couple of hours a week extra tuition on her own. More if we can fit it in.'

'In her own time?'

'Naturally, Mr Kettleby. And in *my* own time, too.' Or is it a mistake to admit that I have any?

'On school premises?'

'If you agree. The upstairs classrooms are nearly always empty during the lunch hour. If that's not acceptable, obviously I'll have to arrange something else — at my house perhaps.'

That did it, as she had thought it would. If it were going to take place anyway, much better for it to be on the Headmaster's doorstep where he could keep an eye on it. No harm in a potential Oxford place to impress the governors with, so long as you could show that you'd done nothing out of the way to bring it about. *Intelligent children will fulfil their potential in any educational system.* Kettleby's biro came down on the pile of papers.

'Very well, Mrs Baylham. I shall have to check from time to time that this is not interfering with the girl's other work, but I see no objection in principle. And of course you understand that it must not be allowed to interfere with your other teaching.'

'Of course not.'

'I refer particularly to the low-ability classes you are teaching this year.'

'I know you do.' Let him work out whether that was an offensive answer or not. She got up briskly — too briskly: for a moment she felt dizzy again.

'Thank you, Mr Kettleby. I'll ...'

'One other thing, Mrs Baylham.'

The *quid pro quo*.

'Yes?'

'Since you are obviously free at the moment, I take it that you are not in charge of a tutor group this year?'

'No, that's right. It's my turn for a year off.'

He ignored this. 'You have heard that Mr Auton has left us suddenly? His departure has left me with a good deal of rearranging to do. I still have to find a tutor for 3F: have you any suggestions to offer?'

Clare said '3F is one of the Tenter Street classes, isn't it?'

'It is.'

'In that case, Headmaster, I don't see how I can offer to help. All my teaching is over on this site, and as you know, I don't drive a car ...'

'I confess I had forgotten that.'

No reason why you should remember, except that it's not like you to forget anyone's weak spot. I was supposed to jump at the offer of Tenter Street, wasn't I? An interesting bit of reaction for you to store away and use some time.

'I'm sorry not to be more help,' she said. Learning to recognise a trap at last, Clare Elinor Baylham. And not before time, at thirty-two.

'Sir,' said Melanie Turner, in a confidential whisper designed to carry just as far as the front row, 'Sir, can I be excused?'

'Not during a lesson, no,' said Colin. 'You can wait another ten minutes. Now try this sentence ...'

'Sir, please,' said Melanie. 'I think I've come on.'

Odd phrases from earlier centuries lingered on in their language: phrases that would have rung true in Shakespeare's or even Chaucer's time. To 'come on' was to start menstruating: Colin, whose own children were boys, made the mental translation a second too late. 'All right,' he said hurriedly.

'Sir, what did she say, sir?'

'That's Melanie's business, Andrew, not yours.'

'I know what it was, sir: she ...'

'That's *enough*,' said Colin, with a sense of already having begun to mismanage the situation. 'Since you seem anxious to make your voice heard, Andrew, perhaps you could read out the sentence on the board.'

'Miss, this is *stupid*. It's *boring*.'

'Really, Tracey?' said Clare. 'I asked you all to write something about yourselves and your life. Most people find themselves quite interesting.'

'Miss, I don't know what to write!'

'Miss, *I* know what to write!'

'I'm glad about that, at any rate. Get on with it, and I'll look forward to reading it later. Now, Tracey, just think back to what you were doing yesterday, the last day of the holidays ...'

At mid-morning break she looked at the two essays on top of the pile.

Every day during the holdays my neice samantha came round becuase my sister gos out to work, when samantha comes she allways gets all of her own road ...

In the sumer hollidays i had grils, i can get grils by just snaping my fingers ...

How very nice for us grils. What was that about recognising a trap?

At the end of the morning she looked into the Upper Sixth classroom. She had slung a large shopping basket over one arm, in case anyone thought of waylaying her. 'Is Deborah anywhere around?' she asked.

'Which Deborah, Mrs Baylham?' It was quite true that half that age group seemed to be called Deborah, in one spelling or another.

'Robson.'

'I think she's on cloakroom duty, Mrs Baylham.'

There was a time when this would have been followed by an offer to go and find her. Still, it was something to be addressed by name instead of as 'Miss'. Clare had her own reasons for not wanting to hang around the building. She said: 'Well, I'll be back just before the end of break. Could you ask her to come and see me then? She'll know what it's about.'

'Bob,' said Colin. 'Is Clare anywhere around? There was something I wanted to check with her.'

Bob Murray, in the act of opening his sandwich box, looked up.

'Hullo, Col. Thought we'd seen the last of you for a bit. How's Tenter Street?'

'Tenter Street is all right. It's the people in it ... *have* you seen Clare?'

'I fancy I saw her heading off with that enormous shopping basket.'

'Damn,' said Colin with admirable calm. 'Oh well, I'll see her after school. It can wait.'

'Glad to see you're still alive, anyway, after the first morning.'

'Give it time' said Colin.

It would not have seemed in the least odd if he had sat down in the staffroom which had been his territory for years, to pass the lunch hour with a colleague and contemporary. But this perfectly innocent cover story did not occur to him until he was halfway back to Tenter Street. The staffroom there was empty: presumably all those games-playing types went to the pub at lunch time. Unused to having no one to talk to, he looked around for something to read. He was not entirely surprised to find nothing but a six-week-old copy of *The Sun*.

'I don't want to put pressure on you,' said Clare. 'But did you have a think, over the holidays, about my idea?'

Deborah, a solidly-built girl with long brown hair which had no shine, looked down at her fingernails and said indistinctly, 'Yes. I'd like to have a try, if it's still all right.'

'Good,' said Clare. 'I really am pleased.' She was managing to sound pleased, too, she thought. Not over-enthusiastic, not pushing: just pleased. 'And the Headmaster says we can use one of the classrooms; so there's no reason why we shouldn't start right away. I'm afraid it means you won't have much free time this term. Do you think you can cope?'

'It's all right,' said Deborah. 'There's nothing much to distract me at home. And we never get any peace at break anyway, with the fifth year bursting in and out all the time. I'll be glad to have something sensible to do.'

'That's fine, then. Well, I'm obviously not expecting you to have written an essay for me by tomorrow; but can you find Larkin's poems in the library? There are three volumes, and they're all there, I've checked. And I'll write to your parents tonight. Are they reasonably happy about this?'

'They don't really know what to think. But it'll be all right once they've had your letter.'

*

Colin looked up to see a tall, nervous-looking girl standing in the doorway. 'Hallo,' he said. 'Can I help?'

'I'm new,' she said. 'I'm supposed to be teaching in Room 14 after break, and I can't find it. It doesn't seem to be anywhere near Room 13.'

'How innocent of you to think it might be,' said Colin. 'Would you like some coffee before I show you? Have my mug — it is clean.'

She was not an appealing girl, but she looked and sounded thoroughly miserable. 'That would be nice,' she said flatly. 'I didn't get any lunch. I found I had to walk over here for the afternoon lessons, and I was afraid of being late.'

'Didn't anyone offer to bring you over and show you round?'

'No. No one seemed to be expecting me here at all.'

'What are you teaching — sorry, I don't know your name? I'm Colin Rowsley. I'm alleged to be the Head of English here.'

'Gillian Newfield. RE. I'm Mr Auton's replacement.'

'His *replacement*?'

'Everyone seems to be terribly surprised,' she said. 'He's taken early retirement, or something.'

'That's *very* odd,' said Colin. Some warning bell was ringing a message somewhere in his head, but he could not think what the message was. 'Ted's one of the pillars of this place: in fact he was my form master at one stage, if you can imagine that far back.'

The five-minute bell rang. She jumped.

'It's all right,' he said. 'You've got a minute or two: finish your coffee.'

'I met someone from your Department, I think,' she said. 'Over on the other side.'

'Who was that?' What magnificently elaborate unconcern.

'Mrs Something. She helped me to find some books to teach with.'

'Quite small, rather pretty, with reddish hair?'

'I think so.'

'That's Clare Baylham, my deputy,' he said. There were some rewards for speaking kindly to strange probationer teachers after all. 'Be sure to ask her for help if you need it. She's very nice.'

'I thought she was a bit frightening,' said the girl.

'Clare frightening? Don't you believe it.' This time the warning bell was telling him quite clearly to stop. 'Perhaps we *had* better go and find Room 14 now, so that you can be there before the kids are. I'm in the room next door, as it happens, so bang on the wall if you have any trouble with them.' She looked alarmed. 'Joke,' he said, smiling at her: though he was not sure whether it had been a joke or not. As he held the door open for her, a figure in football shorts swept through, ignoring them both. He opened his mouth as though to make an introduction, then shut it again.

It was not often that anyone but Deborah disturbed the Literature section of the school library. Sometimes when she looked at the rows of cloth spines — the dark green of Macmillans, the navy blue of the Oxford University Press — she let herself wonder what it would have been like to go to a school where you were not always the odd one out.

She walked home, the books she had chosen in a big hessian bag slung over one shoulder. They made sharp projections that banged against her as she walked. Her parents lived in one of the Edwardian terraces — outside the centre but before you got to the newer housing estates — that were the town's lowest form of owner-occupation. Deborah thought that living there had only one compensation, which was that it spared her having to travel on the school buses. On the school buses, if you were a prefect, you had two choices. You could try without support or assistance to control the shouting and singing, the scuffles and the flying drink cans and exercise books, and so spend each day in a state of tightening tension as home time came nearer; or you could opt out, sit looking out of the window or down at a book, and pretend not to react — and so lose whatever minimal authority your badge brought you at other times. It was better not to be part of it, even though that meant you were alone at the end of the day too.

Walking in her flat school shoes made her ankles ache. One day when she no longer had to wear uniform it might be worth the effort of doing something about the way she looked. At least she had got past the stage of spots now, but she had neither the money nor the skill to do anything about her hair; and she was still more than a stone overweight. The shops she passed were full of end-of-season summer clothes, in sugary pinks and yellows and greens: all with nipped-in waists and cut-away sleeves, and Deborah could not have worn any of them.

Still, when she thought about the books in her bag, and tomorrow's session with Mrs Baylham, her heart lifted. The only problem at the moment was what line to take with her parents. She passed the Co-op and the Yorkshire Bank and was out into the suburb. Should I make a big thing of it, or not? she asked herself. Which would be better, if it doesn't come to anything?

Clare had hoped to be last into the Department meeting, so that she could sit near the door and make a fast getaway. But the only seat left empty was right over in the corner. Colin was not there yet either: she had not reckoned on the time it would take him to dispatch his last class in order, and get over from Tenter Street.

She recognised his light, uneven step in the corridor. 'Here he comes,' said Dave Bowburn. 'Our lord and master.'

She took care not to be looking towards the door. 'Sorry, everyone,' he said. '4H detained me. Need I say more?'

Colin's was the physical type that never puts on weight; but he was heavy-boned, inclined to be awkward in his movements. As he sat down someone snatched a metal ashtray away from his feet. He said, 'As you see, I haven't got any more graceful over the holidays.'

For six weeks and a day she had been imagining what it would be like when they met again. All she could think of now was that she had forgotten how he always tripped over things.

'Sorry to keep you all from home on the first day of term,' he said. 'Only things are going to be unbelievably difficult this year. I think if you can all bear it we're going to have to work out some contingency plans.'

'Sir's using long words already.'

'Just to show,' said Colin, 'that my command of the vernacular is as good as yours, Dave, I will enquire whether everyone's heard about the great timetable cock-up?'

Everyone, even Dave, looked at the floor. Someone made a sympathetic throat-clearing noise.

'I see everyone has,' he said. 'Well, the first thing we'll have to do is to keep a record of where I'm going to be, and where Clare's going to be, at any given time. If it's one of the times when I'm half a mile away, then take whatever the problem is straight to Clare. But remember she's got plenty on her plate already.'

She dictated her own timetable: copied down the record of his, with everyone else. She would have to know where *not* to be, at least for a few days. For her notice to take effect in December she would have to hand it in by the end of this month; and if she were going to hand it in she would have to tell him first; but she could not tell him anything until she knew whether or not there was something to tell. Even though she was sure by now.

'Apart from that,' Colin was saying, 'has anyone met a problem yet? Human or otherwise.'

She got up, fastening the belt of her raincoat. 'I'm sorry, Colin,' she said. 'I'm afraid I've got to vanish — someone's waiting for me. The others can tell me if there's anything important. 'Bye, everyone.'

And at last he looked directly at her. His eyes, greybrown behind their screen of glass, sent her some momentary message which she could not decode but could guess. I'm sorry, Colin. I'm not doing this for fun.

She went out, across the playground, towards the road. In one hand the shopping bag hung heavy; in the other, the briefcase with the empty thermos flask and the term's first batch of exercise books to mark. The plane trees along the railings at the edge of the playing field were still green; but already there was autumn in the air. In another six or seven weeks they would be going home in the dusk again.

She was still wearing her summer sandals. Her feet on the pavement made scarcely any noise.

It was a long, straight road from Stanburn to Pelworth, and Colin took it automatically. He had, after all, been doing the journey for eighteen years: for many of them not in a car but on draughty buses. Only in those days it had scarcely ever occurred to him to feel tired, or sorry for himself. Amber, green. He put his foot down. As he pulled out of the Market Place he wondered briefly about Ted Auton. Something odd there — telephone this evening, perhaps.

One of his left-over scrupulous habits on the journey home was to think back through the teaching day — a sort of survey, or secular examination of conscience. Well, better than the other kind at the moment. He thought of the Melanie Turner episode and flinched at the retrospect. No, forget about that.

All right. The staff meeting.

What did I expect, in a room full of people?

I don't know, but I expected *something*. If she'd given any sign, I'd have recognised it.

Would you? Does it really work like that?

Why did she hurry away like that?

Oh, shut up. There's bound to have been some good reason for it.

He pulled off past the green motorway sign and up into the housing estate: link-built houses arranged in tiers and crescents, grandiosely named after Durham landowners: Percy, Neville, Shafto, Lambton. When the houses were new to match the married couples who lived in them, the size of the mortgage had seemed terrifying: now it was mercifully tiny, left years behind by inflation. Only another seven years till the brick-and-glass box belonged formally to him and Judith rather than to the building society.

And yet in those days we were happy, weren't we? Even though we couldn't afford a stair carpet for years, and the children arrived sooner than we'd meant them to? I used to look forward to getting home, not just to getting out of school. And didn't have to watch my tongue all the time. Or what was going on inside my head.

Why didn't she stay and at least say something?

He stopped the car at the end of the road. Across miles of dead ground rose the grey finger of the Cathedral, foreshortened by distance and height to look as though it came soaring straight out of the fields. He got out to open the garage door, and felt the first passing breath of unmistakably cold wind. It reminded his body, for the first time since the spring, of faint arthritic twinges in shoulder and hip.

Clare, finding herself on the long cross-seat of an empty bus trundling steadily up to the highest point in the county, furtively took off her sandals and put her feet up on the hard cushions. What would the kids think if I did that in class?

Colin does, she thought, when he's reading to the first form. He sits on the teacher's desk and puts his feet against the edge of the one in front. When he does it, it's just a device to make a friendly atmosphere: when Dave Bowburn does it, it's a political statement. Or is it just that Colin's political statements are more indirect?

But there was no one now with whom to share this idea. The pale fields and the dark villages rolled past. Oh, I'm going to miss you ... it was not what she still had to do: it was what she had already done.

II

When Clare and Richard were first married, Richard was still a student and Clare the breadwinner: so to start with they lived in two rooms. Then when Richard had his PhD, and a job in industry, at a salary that soon left Clare's behind, they lived for some years in an estate house very much like Colin and Judith's. The young mothers on either side of them would look at Clare in the mornings with a curious mixture of envy and pity. But unlike Colin and Judith, Clare and Richard, with two salaries and no children, had been able to move on again, to a stone cottage high up on the edge of the village of Gatelaw: 'gate' meaning goat, and 'law' a barrow or high ridge. The study of Anglo-Saxon at an impressionable age leaves its mark.

Gatelaw was the only gentry village for miles in any direction: once a cell of the Abbey of Durham, it stayed in the hands of the Church instead of the hands of the coal owners, who built a ring of dismal pit-rows around the base of the law. So it stayed pretty for the commuting middle classes who arrived there in the mid-century when the era of coal was over.

Clare loved the cottage with a passion that astonished her, since she had always thought before that a house was merely a place you lived in. The journey involved two buses and then an uphill walk, but there was hardly ever a time, even at the end of term when she was almost too exhausted to crawl up the lane, when it did not seem worth it. As soon as she got inside the front door and put her bags down in the hall her back stopped hurting: nothing to worry about. Probably mainly tension in any case.

She sat at the kitchen table to slice some mushrooms and onions for a flan. These days she had a food-processor which would have done the mechanical part of the job in seconds: but Richard would not be home till six, and it was soothing. She liked cooking, but she was not adventurous: she always followed recipes with absolute literalness, feeling real guilt if some shopping oversight forced her to use cornflour instead of arrowroot, or white pepper instead of black.

Colin felt a reluctance which he could not explain about getting down to the business of telephoning Ted Auton. He spent some minutes sitting at the bottom of the stairs, carefully looking up the number which he was fairly sure he knew in any case. Judith, going backwards and forwards between the kitchen and the dining room, stepped over his outstretched feet three or four times, and then said with only slightly exaggerated patience:

'Col, do you absolutely *have* to do that now? Apart from

anything else, sitting in that draught isn't going to do anything for your poor old bones.'

'Poor old bones yourself. All right, I'll do it later. I suppose Edmund *is* doing his homework in there?'

'*Prep*, Col, not homework — remember? No, I told him to wait until after supper. Sorry, but he'd only have had to interrupt himself.'

'That really would have broken his heart.'

'Don't worry,' said Judith. 'He'll do it. It's physics and maths night, so I'll check that he's done it properly. You couldn't pick Francis up from orchestra practice while I do that, could you? He said the eight o'clock train, unless he rings.'

'Yes, fine. Thank God for one child who can see further ahead than the next two minutes.'

This domestic programme, added to the evening's marking and preparation, safely ruled out the possibility of making any delicate or protracted phone calls. *How all occasions do inform against me.* But in spite of this masochistic bit of prodding, the curled-up guilt inside him hardly stirred.

Richard Baylham drove up through the open gateway and parked neatly round by the side of the cottage. He would have liked a garage, but neither Clare nor the county planning authority would let him build one. Richard sometimes had the impression that his mind worked in a completely different way from those of all the people he knew best, outside work: but he was not a man to spend time brooding over deficiencies he could do nothing to remedy.

He got out of the car, taking his first breath of the thin clean air, driving out the fumes of Teesside. He was only just over five foot eight, a fact which had bothered him in adolescence but hardly since then. He had dark hair, and a round face with high but not very detectable cheekbones. He was three months younger than Clare, a fact he never played upon except in mockery.

She was sitting at the kitchen table, peeling cooking apples. 'Are you all right?' he asked.

'Fine. You?'

'Yes. Can I do anything useful?'

'You could grease a dish for these apples. And then pour out some sherry?'

Richard got an earthenware dish down from the cupboard, a butter wrapper out of the refrigerator. Then — because it would go on hanging over him unless he did — he asked, with a careful mixture of lightness and solicitude:

'What sort of day did you really have? Was it awful?'

'Not really. They were still pretty subdued.'

'Perhaps it won't be nearly as bad as you thought.'

This said more about Richard than it did about anything else. But there was never any point in doing battle with his optimism: being cruel to be kind is not very far removed from simply being cruel.

'I also braved the Headmaster about Deborah,' she said.

'Deborah? — oh, yes, sorry. How did he take it?'

'Remarkably well. He must be saving something up.'

'Oh, for goodness' sake — he probably just knew he owed you a good turn.'

'Your trouble is,' said Clare, 'you think everyone's like you.'

Richard, his duty done by Clare's working life, kissed the top of her head and went for the sherry. Later, when he brought the plates out, he found her glass, almost full, still standing on the draining board. He took it through to her. She was sitting down, just in the act of balancing a pile of exercise books in the angle between armrest and chairback. 'Did you forget this?' he asked.

'Oh, sorry. No, I started it, but it didn't taste right. Like acid.'

They looked at each other almost shyly.

'Do you think ...?' he said.

'It does rather look like it, doesn't it?'

Richard sat down on the arm of the chair, next to the books: he laid his hand below the waistband of her dress. 'When will we know?'

'I'm a week overdue now. I could go for a test in about another week.'

'A *week*?'

She put her hand over his. 'Well, after ten years, surely you can wait that long?'

Ten years ago she had started the job at Stanburn Girls' Grammar School: it was already under sentence of change for some date in the future, but she was expecting to be there for only three or four years at the most. Ten years ago she had shaken hands with Colin in the hall of the boys' school, and asked, 'Before I drink this tea, are you a Leavisite?'. It was poignant, but not surprising, to remember that bit of nervous showing-off when so much else had gone.

Gail Fox was drumming her fingers on the desk. The look on her face told Clare that this was no mere absent-minded twitch. This was a challenge. In response to it the muscles in her back set up a renewed vibration.

'Gail,' she said. The drumming stopped.

'All right,' said Clare. 'Now look at the sentence that I'm going to write on the board, and let's see who can be the first to tell me where the punctuation marks should come.'

A touch of the Joyce Grenfells there. Careful.

All the classrooms in the old building were the same: square, high, with a wooden platform for the teacher's desk, and the blackboard along the wall behind it. She half-turned to write: 'The two gangsters who carried sawn off shotguns and bags marked swag got on a number 64 bus they had striped jerseys and black eye patches ...' *Never turn your back on a class*, the textbooks said. *Perfect the overhead reverse scrawl.* But then no textbook teacher ever used the blackboard anyway, having nothing to do but make out worksheets in advance; and no Head of Resources to say that this year paper consumption must be cut to the minimum.

The drumming on the desk began again. Clare finished writing and turned back. When she looked towards Gail Fox it stopped; as soon as she looked away it started again. Then the chorus:

'Miss, this is *stupid*.'

'It's *boring*.'

Dave Bowburn would have said, 'That's right, it is'. But

then Dave Bowburn would not have been doing it in the first place. Clare said:

'Gary — where should the first punctuation mark come in that sentence?'

Gary drooped at his desk.

'Come on,' said Clare, filling her voice with cheerful confidence.

No answer.

'Well, would you put a punctuation mark after the first word?'

'Nah.'

'After the second word?'

'Nah.'

'Linda,' said Clare, pretending not to be defeated, 'Where would you put the first punctuation mark?'

'Miss, can't we do something else?'

Outside the window, in the gas-fitters' pit, the workmen were leaning on their picks. Gail Fox was looking out at them, waiting for one of them to look round so that she could ogle him.

'Gail,' said Clare.

'What?'

'Keep your eyes on the board, please. Now, *you* answer the question for me.'

The ponderously slow-witted, like Gary, somehow engendered the response of patience that was needed. It was the stirrers, like Gail, with adequate intelligence that they would use for anything except learning, for whom good will was not enough. *And who gave her that attitude?* said a catechetical voice in Clare's head. I didn't, at all events. To know all may be to forgive all, but it doesn't tell us what to do after that.

'What question?' said Gail.

It was Clare whose glance flickered. Gail, without shifting her gaze, began to drum her fingers again.

Clare did exactly what she knew she should not do.

'*Gail!*'

Only the slightest of titters from the class: but enough to signal a goal.

'You'd better read the sentence on the board aloud,' said

Clare. 'Then I think you'll be able to see where the natural pauses come. That's what punctuation is for — to show us how to read a sentence.'

Not precisely silence: but no answer.

'Come on, Gail – read what I've written on the board.'

'Can't read, miss.'

'Really?' said Clare. 'Well, you'd better learn how to in the next five minutes — or you'll find yourself doing it after school.'

'Can't stay after school, miss. I've got to babysit.'

In the staffroom Betty McCabe was sitting at the table: in front of her was an ashtray full of stubs. Clare felt her stomach flutter ominously for a moment and then subside.

'How's it going, Clare, pet?' said Betty. Of the full range of accents heard from time to time in that room, Betty's was the most unadulterated Wear Valley.

'I'm afraid I've just had the first confrontation,' said Clare. 'And come off worst.'

'Yer've not to let that lot get away with anything, yer know. They'll not respect yer for it.'

'I made the most utter pig's ear of it,' said Clare. 'You'd think I'd never taught a class before in my life. I can't see why it should ever get any better.'

'Yer just not used ter that kind of class,' said Betty soothingly. 'Yer'll soon, like, learn how ter handle them. A clever lass like you.'

'Thank you,' said Clare. 'I hope you're right. The trouble is — really I suppose I don't *want* to get used to them.'

She poured herself some coffee. It tasted horrible: bitter one minute, sickly-sweet the next. She put the cup down furtively. One means of support the less. My vices are being struck off the list one by one.

Colin put aside all thoughts of trying to chase Clare up again this lunch time. It wasn't fair to risk drawing any more attention to it. There was bound to be a chance in the next few days.

Fortified by self-denial, he made up his mind to ring

Ted Auton right away: but when he reached the coin box in the Tenter Street lobby there was already a group of girls in possession of it.

'Come on, girls,' he said. 'Out.'

'Sir, I've got ter ring me Nan!'

'And I've got ter ring the hospital, sir!'

A certain natural fair-mindedness had at one time worked to Colin's advantage as a teacher. More recently it had been as much of a disadvantage as anything, since he was liable to say, 'Oh, yes, I see', in circumstances where it was taken as evidence of weakness. 'All right,' he said. 'But I shall be back in a few minutes. Mind you're outside by then.'

In the surprising brightness outside he screwed up his eyes. There were telephone boxes in the Market Place. He pressed in his tenpenny piece, and curled his hand round the receiver to shut out some of the traffic noise.

'Mrs Auton? I don't think we've ever met, but I'm a colleague of Ted's. Colin Rowsley. Would this be a convenient moment to have a word with him, if he's there?'

There was a pause. 'Well ... he's much better, but he's resting at the moment. I'd really prefer not to bring him to the telephone. Is there some message?'

Colin understood at once that he had known from the beginning there was something wrong.

'I'm sorry — I didn't realise he'd been ill. I just heard that he'd decided to take early retirement.'

'The Headmaster didn't make any announcement?'

'Nothing at all. I'm afraid that's the sort of thing we've come to expect here. I'm very sorry to hear Ted's been ill. I hope it wasn't too serious?'

'My husband's had a coronary thrombosis, Mr ... Rowsley? ... Visit? Well, I'll have to go and ask him ...'

In her absence the pips went. Mercifully he managed to find another coin in time. When she came back there was a distinct thaw in her tone. 'Edward would like to see you very much, Mr Rowsley. He told me he'd like to see you *particularly*.'

Gratifying as that ought to have been, what Colin actually felt was a minor surge of apprehension. He stepped out into the Market Place, where a grim-faced queue had formed outside the kiosk.

On the ledges of the Town Hall and the old parish church, birds were gathering in shrill lines: but the air still felt like summer. A small child in a romper suit, ice cream cornet held against its face as though it were smelling a flower, staggered past with its hand in its mother's. In spite of his tension Colin found himself smiling. It was the kind of afternoon that coaxed all suppressed misgivings into the light and made them seem ridiculous.

The science labs were kept locked at lunch time, but Clare had lifted the key from the secretaries' office. She had made a half-hearted attempt to find the Head of Chemistry to ask his permission, but he was not to be found. The science staff, lords of the last corner of education that still yielded jobs and status, came and went as they liked. They even had their own staffroom. 'What do you suppose they talk about up there?' she had once said to Colin. 'The higher science?'

'Football, at a guess,' Colin had said. 'Or last night's *Dallas*.'

'You appalling snob.'

'I sat through their conversation for years, you may remember, before the reorganisation. And I used to have to stagger round the soccer field under Chris Simpson's direction in our mutual youth. He's the furthest thing from an intellectual you've ever met.'

Clare shut the door behind herself and Deborah, and locked it. The blackboard, one of the rolling kind set on a frame, began to rotate at a ghostly pace among the motes of chalk.

'Did you remember to bring some lunch, Deborah?'

'Yes, Mrs Baylham.'

'Good. Well, we'll get straight on with it, then. Oh, how did your parents feel about it?'

'They're a bit doubtful,' said Deborah. 'But they'll believe you if you say it's worth it.'

'Of course it's worth it. Now, how did you get on with Larkin?'

*

When Clare got back to the staffroom, a safe five minutes before the bell, she found Gillian Newfield, sitting twitchingly upright, knees well together under plaid skirt. She wore a yellow crocheted top the same shape as a T-shirt, which was not the most becoming of garments if you were as tall and thin as that.

'How's it going?' asked Clare. 'You did eventually get a syllabus and some books, I trust?'

'Yes, thank you. I've got some *awful* classes, though.'

'Oh, dear, have you? The Headmaster *keeps* doing that to new teachers — he doesn't seem to be able to learn. Does your Head of Department realise?'

'There seems to be a lot of muddle about who *is* my Head of Department. I've met yours, though — he came and disciplined one of my classes for me.'

'Did he?' said Clare. 'Well, I'm glad he was on hand. He's got some pretty appalling classes himself this year — so have I, come to that. But at least we're not trying to get through our probationary year into the bargain.'

'He's nice,' said Gillian. 'No one else has said a word to me yet over there.'

'Yes, he is. And I'm sure he'll do anything he can to help, so don't be afraid to ask him. As for the rest of that Tenter Street mob, you'll just have to wait till they've got used to you, I'm afraid. Teaching takes some people that way — they like to watch other people going through the hoops.'

At the window behind Gillian's head a leering face appeared. Clare made a threatening movement, and the face vanished. 'God knows where the architect of this building can have been to school,' said Clare. 'What have you got next, Gillian?'

'A CSE class,' said Gillian. 'Do you think they'll be all right?'

'Well, the thing about CSE classes is to keep them really hard at it during the lesson, but not expect them to do much on their own. Don't set them more homework than you can help, because half of them will never do it, and then you'll have to take endless detentions to make them do it, and the whole thing will turn into one long battle. It took me ages to learn that, so you may as well have the benefit of my painful experience.'

'Thank you,' said Gillian humbly, so that Clare felt an unexpected stab of conscience.

'Good luck, anyway,' she said. 'I mustn't lay down the law too much. We're all at sea here.'

Only, Gillian had probably wanted the simple certainties: this-is-how-you-do-it. She had, after all, just finished her teacher training, and that was a world of soaring moral assurance.

'Quite good,' said Clare, when her pupil had stumbled to the end of a paragraph. 'A very good try. But if you find there's a word you don't know, don't just stop and wait for help. Try working it out letter by letter. Then if you still can't get it, try a sensible guess. Think what it's *likely* to be.'

She looked down at her seating plan. She had ruled spaces to represent the rows of desks, and they had filled in their names. If none of them had thought of the trick of pretending to be someone else, she should be able to attach a name to every face by the end of the week. 'Right,' she said. 'Next ... Dean, isn't it? Will you read on, please?'

'Can't read, miss.'

'I've heard that already today,' said Clare. 'Come on, get started.'

Dean elbowed the boy beside him. 'Miss, let *him* read.'

'But you see, I've asked *you*.'

'Miss, I don't like reading.'

'We all have to do things we don't like,' said Clare. 'Now I'm not going to change my mind, so will you please just get on with it.'

'The,' said Dean, and stopped. Clare, registering some alarm instinct that had not yet put itself into words, said more kindly:

'Come on, Dean. The what?'

The word was *kestrel*. 'The,' said Dean, 'The k—'

'Yes?'

'Crisps?'

'Do you spell "crisps" with a *k*?'

'Please, miss, let someone else read.'

They were all waiting for her to back down, show alarm, put the first foot wrong. *Yer've not ter let that lot get away with anything, yer know.* 'We'll get to the end of this sentence, Dean, at any rate,' she said. 'Then we'll see. Now think — what *is* that word? We've had it several times already.'

'K ... car?'

'Look, Dean, there are seven letters in this word. So it isn't "car", is it? Now what is it *likely* to be?'

'Cat?'

This desperation was the real thing.

'Miss!' said someone, far too late. 'Miss, he really can't read.'

'Let him off, miss!'

'We'll have to come back to it another time, Dean,' said Clare. She had meant to sound kind, but even to herself all she sounded was patronising. Below the rim of the desk her hands were trembling again. 'All right,' she said. 'Now — Lorraine — let's hear *you* try.'

Ted Auton and Colin had been first master and pupil; then senior and junior colleague; then, since age gaps cease to matter after thirty, equals. But they had never been, as Colin and Clare had been from the beginning, on family visiting terms. The Autons were not like that.

Their house turned out to be a nineteen-thirties semi on the edge of Stanburn Moor. The garden looked dispirited, but the inside of the house was unexpectedly smart, with up-market floral covers and curtains: rather at odds with Colin's normal image of the house's owner.

Mrs Auton said firmly, 'I'll leave you two men together. Shall I make a cup of tea, Edward, or will you offer Mr Rowsley something stronger?'

'Something stronger, of course. Remember where he's come from. Help yourself, Colin, will you? I'm forbidden the stuff, needless to say.'

A flatter and duller voice than before. Ted in an armchair, with a blanket — trimmed with incongruous satin binding — over his knees. A grey face, its expression heavy, slow to change. Much thinner, and somehow shrunken, so that Colin, who just topped six feet, felt gross and indecently clumsy, a tactless giant pouring himself an inch of someone else's whisky.

'Sit down, boy,' said Ted. 'Or I'll make you stand on the desk.'

'Now I know you're getting better, Ted.'

'Do you?'

Richard, at the last of the Teesside roundabouts, waiting his turn, thought deliberately, for perhaps the fiftieth time that day, of the secret process he and Clare had set in motion. There couldn't really be any doubt about it, could there? The cells already dividing and multiplying, the bloodstream nourishing them. He could picture, without any effort of the imagination at all, the scene next spring. Clare plump and smiling — because once she had been forced to let go of that frightful school she would learn how to relax, wouldn't she? — and himself in the driver's seat; and the carrycot strapped into the back. You sentimental so-and-so, he thought; but felt, also for the fiftieth time that day, a rush of what he was not too self-conscious to name as joy; and kept bursting into ridiculous smiles all the way home.

Colin came out with his prepared lines.

'I was shattered to hear about ... what happened, Ted. I know the others will be, too. None of us had heard anything about it.'

In the silence the little carriage clock on the mantelpiece struck a quarter-hour.

Ted said: 'I'd been in that place thirty years. Longer than anyone else.'

'Yes, I know.' Colin looked down into his glass, tilting the liquid and swirling it around.

'It's as though I'd never existed. Even bloated capitalists *notice* when their employees leave.'

When words fail, men are not allowed to touch each other, as women are.

'How old are you, Colin?' said Ted abruptly. 'Invalids are allowed to ask these rude questions.'

Colin looked up with relief. 'Forty-three, I'm sorry to say.'

'I shouldn't be too sorry. You don't look it, particularly. It's because you've still got your hair. I've almost forgotten I ever had any.'

'I can remember you with hair,' said Colin.

'Yours must have been one of the first classes I taught.'

'Yes. Alan Carr and I were in the same form, and Bob Murray was the year below.'

To Colin's further relief, Ted smiled.

'Carr was always a pain in the neck in Scripture lessons. An intelligent pain in the neck, though, I have to grant. One of those "But surely, sir ..." boys. I've often wondered what's happened to his brain since then.'

'The same thing that's happened to mine,' said Colin.

'How is it I seem to remember teaching you? You must have been withdrawn from Scripture lessons, surely?'

'You took us for Latin,' said Colin. 'Just for a term. And had great fun with my ecclesiastical pronunciation.'

'As in *a-cheepit* for *accipit*?'

'I can still hear you saying "All right, Rowsley, now we've had the Vatican version, can we hear you say it in the tongue of the ancients?"'

Ted said, 'They'd have a teacher court-martialled these days for talking to a pupil like that. Did I warp you for life?'

'Warped I may be,' said Colin. 'But I hardly think it can be because of that. Why were you having to teach us Latin anyway?'

'I've been remembering about that,' said Ted. 'The regular master — what was his name? — a middle-aged chap with a war wound ...'

'We used to call him Syngman Rhee,' said Colin. 'But that can't possibly have been his real name, can it? I'd forgotten all about him.'

'Who the devil was Syngman Rhee?'

'Wasn't he one of the leaders in the Korean War?'

'Your memory's certainly better than mine,' said Ted. 'Anyway, whatever his name was, he failed to appear at the beginning of one term. All we were told officially was that he'd been "taken ill", but what the grapevine said was that he'd had a colossal nervous breakdown. He never did come back — I suppose he had a disability pension of some sort, poor bugger — so in those days of the teacher shortage anyone with some pretensions to a classical education had to chip in. You couldn't let Latin drop then. I must say I'm surprised you boys didn't pick up any rumours.'

'I think there was some story that Syngman Rhee had punched the Headmaster on the nose, or been found blind drunk in the bogs,' said Colin. 'I don't think adolescents knew about nervous breakdowns then.'

'They do now,' said Ted. 'They see them coming before the victim does. But then it was always the occupational disease of teachers, wasn't it, even in happier times? The thing I've been remembering about that chap, whatever his name was, is that he was a very serious Christian. And in those days I was naive enough to wonder why that hadn't been enough of a support to him.'

'We all expect too much of religious belief,' said Colin — and then regretted it.

'Quite,' said Ted. He fiddled for a moment with the satin edge of the blanket, and then looked up. 'Mine vanished some time ago.'

After a minute, knowing that the silence must be broken, Colin said: 'Ted, I'm sorry. I don't really know what else to say.'

'Not particularly attractive, is it?' said Ted. 'Given the nature of my job. I suppose there are RE teachers all over the country without a shred of anything you or I would call religious faith, but presumably they don't think it matters. Unluckily for me I can't see it that way. I did my degree in Theology, not interpersonal relationships and social concern.'

'There is a connection ...'

'Well, of course there's a connection. There's a connection with English Literature too, isn't there? But they're not the same thing, and none of them is a substitute for any of the others. You of all people ought to know that.'

'I'm only making a feeble attempt to be fair,' said Colin. 'You know I agree with you. I try to keep off the whole subject, except with the sixth form. Not that they're particularly quick to grasp it.'

'I don't know why they should be, when one's colleagues aren't. Carr's never learned the first thing about it, has he? And Murray may be a lay reader, but he knows less about theology than my right boot. The only one who ever struck me as having the faintest idea what it was about was little Clare, who I take it is a thoroughgoing agnostic.'

'She calls herself a Deist,' said Colin, rationing himself carefully. Still, Ted had introduced her name, so that much must be allowed.

On a September day like this one, in the first term after the two schools merged, Colin, a brand-new Head of Department, had pushed his way into the brand-new staffroom with two armfuls of books, cursing his predecessor meanwhile, in all-male-company vocabulary, for having left them in the wrong cupboard. And encountered not only Bob, Alan and Ted, but a slightly astonished-looking Clare. Only a friend and new colleague then.

'Oh, my God,' he had said. 'I am sorry. I'm afraid I'd completely forgotten we were in civilised company now.'

'Don't mind me,' said Clare. 'I might want to do the same once I've met some of your boys.'

'You'll have to behave yourself from now on, Col,' said Bob. 'Some of us need the restraining influence of ladies more than others.'

'I might have shown more restraint just now,' said Colin, 'if Arthur Powell hadn't celebrated his farewell to state education by leaving our stock of books strewn over the entire school. I still haven't found everything.'

'You'll just have to say a prayer to the Virgin Mary,' said Alan, deadpan.

'I shouldn't dream of asking Our Lady to tidy up after Arthur.'

Alan rolled his eyes; Bob looked vaguely shocked. Ted and Clare laughed.

'I take it,' she said, 'that you're an Anglo-Catholic?'

'Nothing so exotic,' said Colin. 'Just the ordinary Roman kind.'

'But we try not to encourage him,' said Alan.

'Most of the time,' said Ted, 'I'm glad to be rid of it. The whole burden of obligation: and having to believe against all one's instincts that everything's got a purpose and a pattern. Top yourself up, Colin, by the way, unless it'll make you incapable of driving home.'

'I'd better not, thanks.'

'Up to you ... what was I saying?'

'Religion. Being free of it.'

'There are still times,' said Ted, 'when I envy people who can make it hold together. You, for instance.'

'Could I change my mind about that drink, perhaps?' said Colin. (*That can't have touched your throat*, she had said.) No, too difficult to start redefining yourself now. Even to someone who knew you before you picked up the protective habit of irony and the social poise to carry it off: someone who first knew you when you were an anxious, clumsy adolescent with the wrong pronunciation of Latin.

'How are you in yourself, Ted?'

'Dying,' said Ted briskly. 'But only in the sense that we all are. I'm told that if I sit round like Patience on a monument my chances are quite good. Apparently I'm doing rather well to be as much like a human being as this after only six weeks.'

'Six weeks ... so it happened right at the beginning of the summer holidays?'

'The end of last term was quite a drama for several of us, as I remember it.'

'Ted — I was in such a state of fury at the end of last term, I never thought ... did Kettleby come down on your teaching timetable as well?'

'He did. I found myself being made personally and solely responsible for the teaching of RE to the low-ability groups all the way up the school. The O-level work and the bright junior classes were parcelled out amongst the rest of them.'

'But you're the only member of that Department with a degree at all!'

'Quite so. Your grasp of the situation is almost as good as Kettleby's.'

'You never said anything ... but I suppose I was doing enough ranting and raving for everyone, wasn't I?' said Colin.

'I dare say it's that temper that keeps you sane and healthy. After all, *you* can't run off and have a coronary, can you, with your responsibilities? I just seethe and fume inside, with the results you see. I dare say having a heart attack was my alternative to going the same way as our friend Syngman Rhee. Somehow it's a more socially respectable way of going to pieces.'

Colin looked out of the window, at the rusty heads of the chrysanthemums, the blank white-curtained windows of the houses opposite. 'Ted,' he said, not turning round, 'I take it you do *want* to retire? Because if you don't, I don't know, but there *might* be a strong enough case to call this professional harassment.'

'I can't see you turning into a barrack-room lawyer at your stage of life.'

'They keep telling us we've got to learn new skills.'

'It isn't worth it,' said Ted, 'is it? The job's filled. And even if it weren't, can you imagine what it would be like to go back on those terms? And with the kids watching me, waiting for my lips to turn blue? Don't think I'm not grateful. If I had children and a mortgage I might be forced to it. But the house is paid for, and I shan't need my car any more. Phyllis enjoys her job, and we can live well enough on what she earns and my pension.'

'If you're sure,' said Colin. 'But if you want me to take it to the union — which one are you in? AMMA?'

'I believe you're shocked that I'm planning to live off my wife.'

This was not quite true, but it was near enough to the truth. 'It isn't that,' said Colin, but he did not say what it was instead. He was not even sure himself.

'Thank you for coming,' said Ted. He looked down at the satin edge of the blanket. 'If you could face coming again, from time to time ... I find I miss masculine conversation rather badly.'

There were still three feet of space between them. Colin said:

'Of course. I miss it too, particularly with you. In fact, human converse is generally a bit lacking in Tenter Street.'

Ted looked up. 'Of course, you're over there this year ... you'll be missing little Clare too, then, I dare say?'

It was true that the top of her head was level with his shoulder, but he was not accustomed to thinking of her as 'little Clare'. He said calmly: 'Yes, I do. But come to that, I even miss bloody Janet. After only a couple of days, I find myself thinking quite affectionately of all that left-wing rectitude.'

'She always made me feel,' said Ted, 'that my shabby moral compromises were laid bare before her. Paranoia, of course.'

'Do you think so? She makes me feel like that too.'

'Then you're paranoid as well. Hardly surprising in that place, but watch it. Whom the gods wish to destroy they first make mad. Can you still put that into Latin?'

Colin's car, an ancient Morris Traveller in faded bottle green, stood parked by the kerb outside Ted's garden gate. Even when Colin had more money to spare than was the case now, he had always driven battered old cars. It was, if not precisely an affectation, certainly a piece of public image-making: shabby, high-minded, scholarly grammar-school master. He found himself looking at the car with dislike. Kevin Colin Rowsley, the well-known fraud.

Before he unlocked the driver's door, he looked back. The white outline of Ted's face at the window, like the face of an imprisoned child. He lifted his hand.

He knew who it was he wanted to talk to. But they had promised, hadn't they, not to telephone one another at home? It wouldn't have been fair.

One of the strongest themes, wrote Deborah in the deserted school library, *in Larkin's poems is the theme of disappointment. In 'Next, Please', he writes of the way in which human beings are constantly hoping that the next event, or the next arrival, will be the thing that they have been waiting for all their lives, which will change everything for the better. In 'Deceptions' he writes of the betrayed girl, but also of the sense of futility and letdown felt by her* seducer when he has 'ruined' her, and 'burst into fulfilment's desolate attic'. In 'Afternoons' Larkin identifies the disappointment which is felt secretly by the contented families whom he might be expected to envy: 'Something is pushing them/To the side of their own lives'.

As she looked up to focus her thoughts, a crop-haired figure materialised outside the window. It appeared to be pulling itself up over the sill. As soon as their eyes met, the face and its owner vanished below the sill again. A minute later a hail of small stones hit the window. 'Go to hell,' said Deborah absent-mindedly, turning back to the essay.

Curiously, she wrote, *there is a kind of satisfaction about this disappointment. Anything else, Larkin makes us feel, would open up unbearable possibilities.*

She looked again at the last sentence. It sounded mature, and she felt sure it was what she had meant to say; but she was not altogether sure what it meant.

Clare got home at half-past five on the Friday evening and went straight to bed. 'I *can't* eat, Richard,' she said — firmly, though she did not feel firm. 'I'm not hamming it up, I'm simply too worn out. I'm sorry, you'll have to look after yourself tonight.'

She woke up when he came to bed. He was trying to move quietly, without a light. 'It's all right,' she said. 'You're not disturbing me.'

He switched on one of the bedside lamps, but tilted the shade forward to keep the light out of her eyes.

'I'm sorry,' he said. 'I didn't understand how bad it was going to be. I'm sorry not to have had more sympathy.'

'It's all right,' she said. 'How could you know? I don't suppose it'll go on being like this. It's just a matter of getting used to it. Other people manage, after all.'

Richard said, 'With luck, it'll only be till Christmas, anyway.'

'With luck.'

'Will you go for that test on Monday? You said a week.'

'Yes. I will.'

'How long does it take to analyse?'

'Forty-eight hours, I think. I'll have to stay late for the

parents' meeting on Wednesday, anyway. I'll go along and learn the worst at evening surgery then.'

'The *worst?*'

'Oh, you know what I mean.'

He got into bed beside her and switched out the light. 'How are you feeling now?' he asked.

'Perfectly all right.'

'Are you sure?' He put his hand out tentatively, over the opening in her nightdress.

'Quite sure.' She guided his hand inside. He took the nipple between his thumb and forefinger, and she drew in her breath.

Later he said 'You're sure it's all right for us to do this? Now, I mean?'

'Of course it is.'

'If you find you feel different about ... you know, if you don't want to, you must tell me.'

She tightened her arms round him. 'I do love you.' And in spite of what he had said, at the right moment she gave a little cry and arched her body underneath his.

In the dark, when he was asleep, she thought about next Wednesday. And Colin, although she was going to have to learn not to think about him. An end to running away.

Colin woke up before dawn, suddenly and completely. It was not something he was used to. When the children were small, he had taken some pride in being able to do his share of feeding and changing, or comforting after a nightmare, without ever totally waking up; and being able to go straight back to sleep afterwards.

Without his spectacles, all he could see of the bedside clock was a luminous fuzz without hands. If he moved, he would wake Judith.

The voice that had woken him up said again, inside his head:

She's avoiding you. She doesn't want to be with you.

I know.

And he acknowledged that he had known, all week.

Far away outside, on the distant main road, the night-time traffic went on, rumbling out of nowhere back into

nowhere. As the light began to grow, the objects in the room gradually took on recognisable shapes: a picture on the wall; a shelf with books and a potted plant; a chair, with the sleeve of a blouse trailing on to the floor.
She was playing with you. Or being kind.

II
July 1983

III

Two weeks before the end of the summer term, the Headmaster had sent out what Bob Murray called a Yellow Peril. A Yellow Peril was a notice, Gestetner-ed on to yellow paper: this one summoned all the full-time non-science staff to a meeting on Friday evening. The only significance of the colour was that it indicated a three-line whip.

'You might as well be warned, you two,' said Janet. Janet's aggression, though constant, was as a rule curiously impersonal, and in that respect markedly different from Dave Bowburn's. 'The word is that there's a plan to de-stream English and various other subjects right up to the beginning of the fourth year.'

There was silence for a moment. Colin said, more surprised than shocked 'We went into all that at the time we were reorganised. There wasn't a single Head of Department who agreed to put off streaming beyond the second year. Kettleby can't think we've changed our minds.'

'He doesn't actually have to have your permission,' said Janet. 'The only people he's obliged to consult are the governors.'

'I'm well aware of that. But I never dreamed he'd bring it up again. To give even Kettleby his due, he's always been fairly good about the need to get habits of work going at an early stage.'

'That's an extremely loaded way of putting it.'

Between Colin and Janet, Clare often found herself propelled into the uncharacteristic rôle of mediator. She said: 'Honestly, Janet, you must admit, whatever mixed-ability teaching might be like in ideal conditions, if you try to do it in a class of thirty, with not enough money for textbooks, and in a tiny little room where you can only just get between the desks anyway, everyone ends up getting less done.'

'Only if that's what you want to happen.'

'Despite your undoubted powers, Janet,' said Colin 'I can't imagine how even you could do the best by everyone in a class which contained both Melanie Turner and someone working up to 'O' Level.'

The one small table in the glass-walled staffroom was piled with manila folders. As soon as the last batch of school exams had been marked, there were report cards to fill in. Once, the staff had been able to rely on each other for school plays and concerts and sports matches to take pupils away occasionally and leave them some free time. None of the extra-curricular activities had survived the demands of the four o'clock buses which took the children home, or the demand for something which *everyone* could do, failing which nothing must be done at all. These days the report cards had somehow to get done during break. Clare had vowed never again to write 'Could do better' or 'Always tries': but it was difficult to think of other observations that would fit into the space on the form.

Outside the window, distractingly, some of the younger boys were taking it in turns to enact a death by machine-gun fire. Ted Auton sat by the window, staring out at them. They did not seem to notice.

'I'm not saying it wouldn't be difficult,' said Janet. 'But it's something we ought to be doing, no matter what the arguments on the other side are.'

'The categorical imperative' said Ted, not looking round.

'I've always meant to ask you, Ted,' said Colin, 'why it's "categorical".'

Bob, hitherto absorbed in the crossword, looked up.

'Because it's not dog-egorical, of course.'

'Oh, shut up, Bob' said Colin. 'If you're a product of selective education I may be forced to see Janet's point. Ted?'

'Sorry. What?'

'The categorical imperative. Why is it "categorical"?'

'Ask me some other time, Colin' said Ted. 'My brain feels like cold mashed potato at the moment. Which is another way of saying I don't know.'

Colin said hurriedly 'Sorry, Ted. It doesn't matter anyway. Get your own back on me some time by asking me about Structuralism. I mug up on it about three times a year and its always gone again by the next morning.'

'Like me with Existentialism,' said Clare.

'Perhaps,' said Janet 'if you'd been less crammed at school, and had learned to work more on your own — which is what would happen to people like you in a mixed-ability class — you'd be able to absorb knowledge of that kind.'

Clare was too taken aback for immediate anger. 'That's a bit priggish, isn't it?' she said.

'Janet,' said Ted from the window 'you're breaking the rules.'

Colin began slamming his books together into a pile. 'Janet's doing her best not to answer the point that mixed-ability teaching wastes time and energy and prevents the better pupils from getting on. It can't fail to, and she knows it.'

'For someone with your particular background, Colin,' said Janet, rising to the bait at last 'you've got the most uncontrolled Protestant work ethic I've ever come across.'

'I don't give it any moral significance at all,' said Colin. 'Protestant or otherwise. I find it hard to be patient with the kind of child who spends more effort dodging the work than it would cost to do the work in the first place — but before you tell me that's a class prejudice, let me tell you one of my own children is that kind. It's not a religious attitude, just a practical one. I don't look to my work for moral significance.'

Clare expected Janet to say 'Then you should.' She asked: 'Janet, where did this bit of information about the de-streaming come from? Is it reliable?'

'I got it from Dave,' said Janet. 'I don't always believe everything he says, which may surprise you, but he generally seems to know what's going on.'

'Dave gets selected to know what's going on,' said Colin.

'So I suppose that must mean it's true.' Clare knew that his simmered-down tone meant an apology to Janet as well as the beginnings of genuine anxiety: she hoped that Janet realised. The pieces of her own anxiety were falling into place.

'Does it mean anything that it's only the arts people? And only the full-timers, which means none of the Germanists? All the subjects that don't matter, according to Kettleby.'

'French seems to be included' Janet pointed out.

'Didn't you know? French is an effeminate language useful for nothing but literature and diplomacy. Whereas German is associated with commerce and other purposeful activities.'

'It's also a major language of poetry' said Janet, quite mildly.

'Do you imagine Kettleby thinks of that?'

Janet picked up her nylon holdall and slung it over her shoulder. The weight of books and folders pulled her whole body down awkwardly on one side.

'I really could almost feel sorry for you two. You see persecution lurking in every corner. You'd do anything rather than give something new an even chance.'

When she had gone Bob said: 'Us would never have dared to speak to w'Head of Department like that, would us, Col?'

'She's not under any obligation to agree with me' said Colin.

Ted said, his back still to the room: 'You can't have the attitudes of a conservative and the temperament of a feeble liberal: not in this job. That way you can't even go down fighting.'

The meeting was in the new assembly hall. Like the new staffroom, it had one wall entirely of glass, looking on to the sports field with its fringe of plane trees. By half-past five the meeting was still haggling over the control of pupils who went home for lunch, and the timing of school trips. Whenever the subject looked like being exhausted, Kettleby would invite some further member of staff to give an opinion. Next to Clare, Colin began to fidget and look at his watch.

Finally he whispered 'Clare, I'm sorry, I'm going to have to go soon. Can you cope?'

'Colin, you *can't*! You know that's why he's doing this — he's talking the opposition out.'

Kettleby was looking at them: whispering in class. Colin tore a page out of his diary, wrote on it, and handed it to her. Is passing notes in class any better?

I've got to meet Edmund off a train. He's been on a school trip too! I shouldn't have said I'd do it, but I never dreamt we'd be this late.

She wrote: *If you're not there, won't he ring home? Or wait for you?*

Francis would. Ed's idiotic enough for anything.

Isn't there a bus?

Not after six. I'm rather worried he might try to hitchhike. Sorry, I really will have to go. You can do it just as well as I can. Ted and the others will back you up.

Kettleby was looking at them again. Clare turned her back on him, got up, and mouthed to Colin: 'Stay there — don't go till I come back. I'll be as quick as I can.'

Up on the main road she shifted from one foot to another outside the telephone kiosks. In one of them an old man stood, not talking to anyone, merely standing with the receiver to his ear. After a few minutes she opened the door of the kiosk an inch, and heard the ringing tone.

'Excuse me, but if you aren't managing to get through, could I use the telephone, just quickly?'

'Eh?'

'Could I just make my call, quickly, since you aren't getting an answer?'

'She's not answering.'

'No, I can hear that. So would you mind if I just used the phone for a minute?'

'Eh?'

At that moment the orange-haired youth in the next box was heard to say 'See ya, then,' and put the receiver down. Clare flung open the door. 'Cool it' said the punk, stepping out.

51

'Richard, thank the Lord you're back. Listen, we're absolutely stuck at that meeting: we simply mustn't either of us go before the end. You couldn't possibly go and pick up Edmund from the station, could you?'

'Colin's boy? Hell's *teeth*.'

'Yes, I know: I'm sorry. It really is important. I'll explain later.'

'All right. Will I recognise him?'

'Bound to; he's the image of Judith. Dark hair, round face: usually looks as though his school uniform had been thrown at him. And *quickly*, Richard: all right?'

'Yes, miss.'

'You are a love. See you later.'

It would have been good manners to ring Judith too, but there was no time. At any rate it would save the Rowsleys the cost of a transfer charge call.

As she came back into the Hall, Kettleby was saying: '... not a final decision, one way or another, but to examine the state of opinion amongst my staff.'

Colin, half out of his seat, was looking round anxiously. She made what she hoped were reassuring gestures. Kettleby looked at her unwaveringly as she made her way back up towards her seat; she stared back. What's making me so brave all of a sudden?

She added to the scrawled-over bit of paper the words: *Richard's gone to collect E.*, and passed it back to Colin. He looked at her, mouthed 'Thank you', and got to his feet.

'Headmaster' he said. 'I'd like to start off the discussion if I may. From my point of view nothing's changed since the last time this was talked about. I accept the arguments for mixed-ability teaching in the first year; but after that, whether we call it streaming, setting, banding or anything else, I think it has to be done if we're to hope to teach with any degree of success at all.'

Kettleby said 'May we hear another opinion?'

At the back, Janet stood up.

'Mr Rowsley knows my views on this matter, and he knows this isn't a personal attack on him. I feel that we not only could but should extend mixed-ability teaching up the school – right to the top, as far as I'm concerned.'

'I support that,' said Dave Bowburn. For Dave that was a surprisingly formal and correct turn of speech. Janet's respect for other views was genuine; Dave's was strategic. Clare found herself on her feet.

'I do realise this doesn't involve only the English Department,' she said. 'But since we seem to have people on both sides, I want to record my agreement with Mr Rowsley. English needs teaching in different ways for different aptitudes, quite as much as any other subject does. Whatever kind of lesson it is, the result is the same if you try it — — all the attention goes to the disruptive ones; the bright ones may or may not get something done on their own; and the pupils in the middle get nothing.'

Kettleby said with remarkable mildness 'Someone from another department, perhaps?'

A nervous silence. Come on, you rotten lot.

Bob Murray: 'When would this be happening, Headmaster?' A nice safe noncommittal one there. We need Alan Carr, thought Clare — he doesn't know what it is to be intimidated by authority. But of course no one would ever try to de-stream a subject like Maths.

Kettleby: 'This is all still so hypothetical, Mr Murray, that I shall have to ask you to bear with me on that point.'

Colin said out of the side of his mouth to her: 'Is he going to give this the chance to turn into a proper discussion, or is he going to go round the room letting everyone speak once?'

'What do *you* think?'

'*Right.*' Colin stood up again.

'Headmaster: if no one else is ready to speak, could I amplify what I said earlier?'

Kettleby looked around the room. No response. 'I had hoped that all members of staff would contribute to the discussion' he said.

'I wish I thought we could operate a mixed system, so that Miss Waldridge and Mr Bowburn, and anyone else who feels enthusiastic about the idea, could teach mixed-ability classes as an experiment and prove to the rest of us that it could be done — or not. But obviously we couldn't even work out a timetable on that basis, let alone conduct a year's teaching. I know some people here feel committed to the idea for moral or political reasons, but I think it's up to those people to show us in detail how anything so difficult or so contentious could work in real life.'

He spoke well in public, Colin — always had since she had known him. He had an easy control of his sentence structure, and the kind of voice that carries without being raised. But it was a pity about the last few words: they introduced an emotional and rhetorical note which gave the game away. 'Well done,' she whispered. He pulled a face, and held up for her inspection a pair of visibly trembling hands. What *is* it about Kettleby that does this to people?

Janet was saying: '... a pointless hypothesis to say in detail how things would be achieved from day to day. A lot can be done with individual worksheets and group projects: it's a matter of the will finding the way.'

'I think I must ask someone else to give us a view,' Kettleby said again. His gaze settled on Brian Ludworth, the Head of French. No response. They all want to get home for their tea, of course. Leave us alone and the threat will go away. Then Ted Auton got slowly to his feet.

'I'm well aware,' he said 'that Scripture — I beg the meeting's pardon: RE — tends not to command a great deal of respect. But at one time even those of us who taught it were expected to be able to pass on some form of rational knowledge to our pupils.'

Stop it, Ted: this just puts people's backs up.

'It may be that all our pupils are equal in the sight of God, but I don't feel that it's part of my duty to anticipate this state of affairs on earth. It's not my business to turn my pupils into Christian believers, but it is my business to teach them what it's possible to believe, and why. For some of them that means the first steps in philosophy: for others it means telling them fairy tales.'

There was a perceptible shock wave. The difference between a myth and a fable — but Ted's audience had not understood that. Ted underestimated the low-key non-conformist orthodoxy of many of his colleagues. It was that, after all, which kept people like Bob Murray going.

Better, no doubt, than drink, or despair. The Valium of the people.

'Mr Auton, I think ...' began Kettleby, but Ted overbore him. 'Perhaps someone would like to suggest how, in the same lesson, I could teach one child the doctrine of transubstantiation whilst the child in the next desk is breathing heavily over a drawing of the tares coming up in the wheat? Or perhaps that's not what it's about anyway — perhaps I ought just to be telling them to be nice to each other? If that's so, then it's a pity I didn't know before I spent my life doing it the other way.'

Clare, who never cried, found tears coming unexpectedly to her eyes. Dave called out 'Do Mr Auton and his kind know the amount of human misery they're causing —— or do they just not care?'

Kettleby said: 'I'm afraid we must begin to think about the time.' The caretaker was at the back of the room, standing and pointing at his watch. He was the one person to whose priorities Kettleby always deferred. 'I'm disappointed, I must say, that such a small number of people have felt called upon to speak. Perhaps in answer to Mr Auton's point it is only necessary to say that in some schools, teachers have found it possible to overcome the problems he so movingly describes.'

The last sentence might or might not have been intended to be as insulting as it sounded. Colin stood up again.

'May I ask, Headmaster, whether we are to expect any changes as a result of this meeting?'

'I think I shall have to report to the Board of Governors, Mr Rowsley, that only a few members of staff have any definite views on the matter.'

Colin persisted. 'I feel sure that in fact there are a number of people who haven't spoken, for one reason or another, but are quite clear in their minds about which system they would prefer.'

'You consider yourself an expert on your colleagues' opinions, Mr Rowsley?'

Colin's hands came tightly together in front of him. Clare found herself on her feet.

'Headmaster,' she said. 'I'd like to propose that we take a vote. If the principle becomes clear, then we can surely discuss details at another time on the basis of that vote.'

'This is not a trade union meeting, Mrs Baylham.'

'It seems to be the only way of finding out what people actually think. I should have thought it would be to everyone's advantage.'

'Is it, then, the wish of this meeting that a vote be taken?'

Clare could not move to look and see whose hand went up: but evidently it was enough.

'Will a further show of hands be good enough, Mrs Baylham, or do you wish to propose a secret ballot as well?'

Colin whispered urgently 'Let me do that'; but this time Ted got there first. 'I should like to propose a secret ballot' he said. 'That doesn't prevent anyone who wants to from standing up and being counted.'

Brian Ludworth said 'I second that.' Clare, knowing at last exactly what was meant by a cold sweat, sat down. Kettleby spoke, loudly and pointedly, across the room to the caretaker.

'I'm afraid that we shall have to delay you by another few minutes, Mr Armstrong. It seems to be the wish of the meeting. I can only apologise. Mr Auton, Mr Ludworth, will you please be as quick as you possibly can?'

The caretaker said 'I yav ter lock up, mind. Nobody said anything to me about a late meeting.' Absence of fear is only a matter of how you see things.

The slips of paper read thirty-seven against detreaming; eight for; three abstentions. Kettleby said calmly: 'Of course the Board of Governors is not bound by this decision. However, I accept it as a clear indication of the wish of the majority. I can only repeat that I should have found it more useful if people had been prepared to voice their views publicly. Please will you now leave as quickly as you can, so that we give no further trouble to Mr Armstrong?'

They stood up to file out — better ordered than their pupils. Colin put his hand under her elbow. She was vaguely surprised: Richard was a great toucher and embracer of his female acquaintance — Colin wasn't, usually.

'That caretaker is the real boss of this school' she said.

'It's a pity he isn't' said Colin. 'I'd back his judgement against the Governors' any day.'

Brian Ludworth came over to them. 'Well done, you two.'

'We could have done with your help a trifle earlier, Brian,' said Colin.

'Fair comment, I suppose. I somehow got the idea to start with — quite wrongly, it seems — that he'd made up his mind already. I just didn't feel like being crucified for nothing.'

'Anyway,' said Clare 'it's worked out happily in the end.'

Colin said 'I'm not convinced he was ever going to do it in any case.'

'Then why on earth have a meeting?'

'That's what's worrying me. It may be something quite simple like having a defence to put up to the governors for not doing the trendy thing. Let's hope it stops there.'

'Anyway' said Brian 'all credit to you two. Whatever he may have had in mind, he'll find it difficult to get round this in the future.' He wandered off.

'Nice man, Brian,' said Clare.

'The road to hell is paved with them.'

'You're very sour in your hour of victory. Talking of hell and kindred subjects, where's Ted gone? He deserves his share of thanks.'

Ted had disappeared. Even his car had gone from outside.

Clare said 'I thought he seemed in a bit of a state.'

'Oh, I don't think so. No more than usual for the end of term, anyway. He's always had a rather theatrical style in public ... look, may I just open up the car for you, and then ring home to make sure Richard found Edmund all right?'

Clare sat in the front passenger seat, leaned back and closed her eyes. The evening sun came red through her eyelids. The idea of a large gin and tonic presented itself to her, but it would be tactless to voice the idea to Colin in his penurious state.

She heard his steps outside the car, and opened

her eyes. He smiled at her. 'I thought you'd gone to sleep.'

'Everything all right back at the ranch?'

'Yes — thanks to the Baylham family. I've been told to bring you back for something to eat. Richard's there already.'

'Oh ...'

'Look, if you're doing something else, then of course ... but if you're being tactful, please don't be. I should hope we can still offer our friends a meal from time to time. It's a small enough return for this evening.'

'Oh — gerraway. All right, that'll be lovely, but we must stop and let me get a bottle somewhere.'

'I certainly shan't refuse to let you do that.'

'In that case,' said Clare 'let me get *two* bottles. We've got something to celebrate for once.'

Judith Rowsley had the round face and pink cheeks which were reproduced in her younger son. She had also, until recently, had very dark brown hair, which had suddenly gone grey. Since her face still looked young, the effect was startling but not unbecoming. It said something about Judith that she had neither dyed it nor had it permed, but had simply let it grow until she could put it up in a chignon. On Judith, moreover, the chignon stayed put: Clare had never been able to keep her own hair pinned up for more than ten minutes.

Without apparent panic Judith had turned cassoulet for four into cassoulet for six. Clare was a respectable cook herself, but outside the summer holidays she relied on recipes in which expensive ingredients made up for a shortage of preparation time. Time, on the other hand, was just about all that Judith had to spare.

'I make great lakes of the stuff, Clare,' she said. She sat on a cushion on the floor, Colin in an armchair behind her. She held her glass of wine in both hands and leant back against his leg. 'The blessed freezer costs even more to run if I let it get half-empty. You wouldn't believe the number of variations on the basic bean that you'd find under that lid.'

'We really ought to sell it,' said Colin 'but that would spoil my fantasy about keeping the Headmaster's dismembered remains there.'

'And sending them through the post to the Chairman of Governors, a limb at a time' said Clare.

'They're off again, Richard,' said Judith. 'What shall we talk about while they're at it?'

'I'm sorry,' said Clare. 'We really oughtn't to bring it home with us. Can I make amends by clearing the table for you?'

'Certainly not. But I might feel more inclined to go and make the coffee if you came and talked to me while I did it.'

The kitchen was even smaller than Clare remembered it. 'You can imagine,' Judith said 'what it's like in here with both Col and Francis. I spend my entire life stepping over legs. Edmund's going to be just the same when he stops growing.'

'It is a bit staggering to see your Francis so grown up' said Clare. 'He gets to look more and more like Colin, too. I still think of him in short trousers, sitting in the front row at *Iolanthe*.'

'It was a pity the school stopped doing those G. & S. productions — they were good, weren't they? Was that the first time we met?'

'Yes. Colin was always the only person in the boys' school who ever introduced anyone properly to anyone else.'

Judith grinned. 'Oh, he knows how to behave like a gentleman, I'll give him that. Some of the other men at that place are a bit on the oafish side, aren't they?'

'I'm afraid we all pick it up a bit. The other day we were at the Theatre Royal, and during the interval the Ladies' was full of people smoking; and I only *just* stopped myself from booming "Right, we'll have all the cigarettes out, and everyone into the corridor!" And sometimes I find myself ordering people out of the way in supermarket queues.'

Judith spooned the coffee into the top of the percolator, and said, without looking round: 'Col's lucky to have you at that school. I hope you know how much he values you. For all his pretty manners he's not always very good at saying what he means.'

Clare felt uncomfortable. She did not get much practice these days at female conversation.

'It does work both ways, you know. I've been incredibly lucky with my Heads of Department. When the merger happened and Lucy retired I never thought anyone could replace her.'

The coffee began to bubble. Judith, perched against the edge of the sink, said suddenly: 'I wish now I'd encouraged Col to make a move when that place went comprehensive. I feel a bit responsible that he stayed on and now he's stuck there.'

'I've never heard him blame you.' This was not strictly true, but it came out automatically.

'He only comes out with it when we're having a flaming row about something else.'

The idea of Colin and Judith having flaming rows was disturbing. When Clare and Richard quarrelled the row was always conducted with a deadly restraint.

'I'm sure he doesn't mean it, Judith. I know he does let fly a bit when he loses his temper. But I distinctly remember his saying years ago that he thought comprehensive education ought to be given a chance.'

Judith looked up and smiled. 'You can come here any time, Clare,' she said. 'You're good for my spirits. I'd almost forgotten he once held views like that: frankly I think he's forgotten it too!' She swung herself off the edge of the sink and opened a cupboard.

Clare said: 'You couldn't really move now in any case, could you? With the boys coming up to 'O' and 'A' level?'

'No. We're tied to this area until Edmund's finished, really. But five years ago we could have tried another part of the country. Only my parents were still alive then, and I didn't want to be hundreds of miles away from them. At least that's my excuse. But I suppose really it was just the Durhamite's typical reluctance to cross the Tees.'

'Richard's got a terminal case of that too,' said Clare. 'And he's not even a native — he just did his degree here. Even so he seems to have taken root.'

'Would he be able to move if he wanted to?'

'I shouldn't think so — not now. Where he is at the

moment his job's as safe as any job is these days: if he were the new boy somewhere else he'd have redundancy hanging over him all the time.'

'You've never thought of striking out on your own, and having one of those long-distance marriages? I sometimes think it's what I'd do if there weren't the children. Or at any rate encourage Col to do it.'

Clare fielded the question. 'You still haven't had any luck on the job scene, I take it?'

'None at all,' said Judith. 'Damn, hang on — I haven't heated the milk. No — at the moment no one needs to contemplate taking on a forty-two-year-old who hasn't worked for years. They tell you you're lucky to have a husband who can support you. Which is true, although demoralising: but it doesn't look after two sets of school fees.'

'Has Francis still got his sights on Oxbridge?'

'Yes — which means an extra year, of course. Typical of our luck that Oxford are introducing this fourth-term entry business the year *after* it's Francis's turn.'

'It's always been possible to do it without an extra year in the sixth form,' said Clare. 'I did, for instance, from a perfectly ordinary grammar school. In fact there's one of my present Lower Sixth that I'm hoping to put in for it next term. Couldn't Francis have a try this year?'

'Music is different from English, alas. He couldn't possibly cover enough of the Harmony and Counterpoint by this autumn.' The milk foamed up in the saucepan. 'Enough of my moans,' said Judith. 'We'll survive. I hope you haven't been too bored.'

'Of course not. I think you're both marvellous the way you put up with it. Just when you might have expected to be a bit better off if there were any justice.'

'I don't suppose I'd complain such a lot if Col didn't go on and *on* about that school so much. I know it probably is pretty awful. But I've said I'm sorry a hundred times — he seems to want me to say it all over again every day.'

Clare held the door open for Judith with the tray. A burst of loud orchestral music came floating down the stairs. 'Fran*cis*!' yelled Judith. She had a powerful contralto voice, something that would be useful in teaching. 'Tone it down a bit, would you? ... Thanks.'

'You must admit it's a very superior form of adolescent noise' said Clare.

'Oh, I know. I just wish sometimes he'd hurry up and grow out of the Romantics. What I like is a nice crisp bit of Scarlatti.'

'What I like,' said Richard, getting up for Judith to move a table 'is a nice crisp bit of Rod Stewart or Donna Summer, but Clare turns her nose up at it.'

'I like pop music,' said Edmund from the corner. His voice had not finished breaking, and he sounded perpetually hoarse. 'Do you like Frankie Goes to Hollywood?'

'Edmund,' said Colin 'have you done your homework — I mean prep?'

'Haven't got none.'

'Haven't got *what*?'

'Any.'

'Are you sure?'

'Yes.'

'Well, in that case, will you go and do some washing-up for your mother?'

'Do I have to?'

'Yes, you do have to. And did you ever thank Dr Baylham for picking you up tonight?'

The pale beams of the headlights chased in front of the car towards the glimmer on the horizon. Even after all her years in the north Clare was surprised afresh every summer by the nights which never become completely dark.

Richard said: 'Old Colin leans a bit heavily on that boy, doesn't he?'

'On Edmund? He could do with a bit of leaning on.'

'He seems pretty harmless to me. A sort of *Just William* type.'

'Oh, I think he's harmless enough. But crude.'

'Every fourteen-year-old has the right to be crude. I remember it well.'

'Your education wasn't making such a big hole in your father's pocket.'

'I don't know ...'

'Oh, come off it, Richard. There was a sliding scale of fees in direct grant schools, remember? Anyway your father wasn't on a teacher's salary.'

Richard said unexpectedly: 'That's not the point anyway. People shouldn't expect their children to repay them. It's not what you have children for.'

This was dangerous ground. Clare knew they were not really talking about the Rowsleys.

'I do see what you mean,' she said. 'But Colin and Judith changed Francis over to an independent school when St Laurence's did away with 'A' level Music. Then they did the same for Edmund because it didn't seem fair not to. I agree Colin probably ought to be more patient with him, but the whole thing's going to be such a burden to him for the next few years that you can understand why he isn't.'

Richard slowed down to let an express coach overtake them. He said 'It's Judith I feel sorry for.'

'Well, so do I, of course. I'm just saying I think Colin has a rough time too. Family life is one long drain on people, isn't it? Why does anyone do it?'

'Some people seem to think it's worth it,' said Richard obstinately.

Normally the timetables for the autumn came down from the computer unit at least a week before the end of the summer term. This term they had still not arrived by the last morning but one. Clare knew more or less what to expect for next year; but almost always the computer would pick up some inconsistency or sheer impossibility in what the various Heads of Department had worked out, and it was irritating to have to leave the readjustments till so late.

In the middle of the no-man's land between the two buildings Colin stopped Clare and said: 'You haven't forgotten about the North Yorkshire conference this weekend?'

'No, I haven't. In fact I've already drawn up a comprehensive — if you'll pardon the word — list of instructions to Richard about feeding himself.'

'Surely he can manage to look after himself for forty-eight hours?'

'I doubt it. If I didn't leave specific provision for every meal he'd spend all his time eating toasted sandwiches in the pub and pumping his arteries full of cholesterol. He probably will anyway, but at least I've done my best.'

'I've just had the car MOT'd, at enormous cost, so we should be able to get there, if you feel you can trust my driving.'

'Oh, well, that'll be fun. Even if the conference is deadly, we can have a splendid weekend talking treason.'

'The only thing is,' said Colin 'that even in its revived state I don't think the old rattletrap will do more than about thirty over the Moors, so I can't guarantee that we'll get there for dinner. I don't suppose for a minute that Kettleby'll let us go early. Perhaps we could stop at a pub or something?'

That would not do. He would feel obliged to pay for her.

'Why don't I do a picnic instead? With booze. Then we can stop and have it looking down on Whitby or something equally civilised, and take the journey as slowly as you like. I don't imagine it matters if we miss the first lecture.'

'Well, if you're sure that's not too much trouble ...'

'Of course it isn't. See you tomorrow, then, if not before.'

At the beginning of the lunch break one of the prefects put her head round the staffroom door.

'Mrs Baylham, Mr Kettleby said to tell you that the new timetables are ready, if you want to go and check yours.'

'Not before time. Thanks, Maggie. I'll go and see which of the 'O' level groups I've ended up with for my sins.'

The print-out was lying on the table in the computer room. She folded it backwards and forwards until she found the sheet with her name at the top.

5N, said the sheet; 4Y; 3T. No, this can't be right. She looked again at the heading. *Baylham, Mrs C E: English*. Must be for someone else all the same ... hell, that would take hours of sorting out, with only one day of term left to do it in.

But Colin would never have given *anyone* a combination of classes like that: not even to Dave Bowburn, who professed to revel in the 'less-able'. She looked at the rest of the spaces. 3F — a future CSE group: she'd agreed to take that one. And Upper VIa: Deborah's group. Those were the vestiges of what she'd worked out with Colin.

No chance at all of its being meant for someone else.

The facts-and-figures part of her brain registered it. Nothing else in her had yet come round to believing it.

The message had come direct from the Headmaster.

There was nothing describably different about Kettleby's face. All the same, she knew at once that he understood why she had come; and that he would wait for her to make the running.

'Headmaster' she said.

'Mrs Baylham?'

She had been rehearsing to herself, all along the corridor, the line, *I'm sure you know why I'm here*. But habits of respect to authority go on twitching long after death. What she said was: 'Mr Kettleby, I feel sure there's been some mistake. I've just been to check my timetable for next year ...'

He cut in at once. 'Your timetable is surely a matter for your Head of Department.'

'I discussed it with Mr Rowsley in detail, weeks ago. If he'd had to make any major changes he would certainly have told me.'

Kettleby's eyes had healthy whites; their irises were like pale blue glass.

'Let me get this clear, Mrs Baylham. Your timetable for next year is not as you had expected it to be.'

'No. And the changes in it are ...'

'I'm sure that you appreciate the problems caused by the size of the school, the need to arrange the timetable by means of the computer instead of in the cosy old way ...'

'I know the computer sometimes picks up the need for some minor rearrangements, but ...'

What *am* I doing?

'Look, Mr Kettleby, this isn't, even allowing for any kind

of computer adjustment, the timetable that was arranged for me.'

'Naturally you have already discussed this with Mr Rowsley?'

'He's not in school this afternoon: he's at ...'

As, of course, you very well know. Who was it who so uncharacteristically urged a Head of Department to take time off to go to an Education lecture?

'Well, I'm sorry, Mrs Baylham,' said Kettleby. 'It's with your Head of Department you must take the matter up.'

She was — she really was — about to say 'Very well, then' and leave the room.

'Mr Kettleby, you know perfectly well that this has nothing to do with Mr Rowsley. This simply isn't a suitable timetable for ...'

'You are a teacher of some years' experience.'

'Exactly.'

'You would prefer the low-ability classes to be taught by an inexperienced teacher?'

'Certainly not. It's a very skilled and specialised form of teaching. That was one of the points I was trying to make at the meeting last week.'

'The point I remember your making, rather forcibly, was that you felt that streaming by ability was absolutely essential. Am I representing your point of view fairly?'

'So far as it goes, yes.'

'You have always seemed to me to be a clear thinker, Mrs Baylham. If you regard streaming by ability as essential, then it follows, does it not, that some of those streams will be of low ability? And that the children in these streams must be taught by someone — preferably, as you say, by a teacher of some experience and standing?'

The key in the lock.

'My qualifications ...' she began.

'Qualifications' were the password of her age group: the badge of the meritocracy, the flag of Harold Wilson's England, the deferred gratification you swapped your adolescence for.

Kettleby brought his hand down on the desk, hard.

'I told your Head of Department an hour ago, Mrs

Baylham, and I'm telling you now: if you feel that your qualifications place you above the level of the rest of us in this school, then I shall put no difficulties in the way of your leaving us. I blame myself only for having allowed the situation to get to this point.'

Oh, God, don't let me start shaking in front of him.

'So you *have* seen Mr Rowsley about this!' she said.

'Mr Rowsley has already been to see me, in a state of agitation as great as your own. Am I really to understand that these two visits were not coordinated?'

'I haven't seen him since this morning. I've only just found out about — all this. You sent me a message through one of the prefects.'

'Then no doubt you and Mr Rowsley will be discussing this later. But I am afraid that the timetable is now arranged: I see no reason why, merely because you and he have the good fortune to be graduates of the ancient universities ...'

'Wait a minute,' she said. 'Does that mean Colin ... did Mr Rowsley come to see you on my account, or do you mean that you've done the same thing to him?'

'You and he will have comparable amounts of teaching in the low-ability classes. It has meant considerable re-arrangement, but —'

'You've publicly overturned a Head of Department's arrangements for his staff?'

'*My* staff, Mrs Baylham. You would do a great deal better to remember that.'

Outside Kettleby's window the sun trailed out from behind its cloud, and promptly vanished behind another. Her voice, with its carefully-pitched 'carrying' tone, the prissy accent that came out under stress, was saying: 'Look, Mr Kettleby, never mind about my timetable. But please consider Mr Rowsley's again. You can't humiliate a Head of Department in front of his colleagues like that.'

Kettleby watched her. He smiled, not saying 'Can't I?'

Well, she thought. There was no room for anything but surprise and recognition. Well, so that's it.

There are all sorts of reasons for putting the interests of others before your own — out of a sense of duty, for instance, or even in order to be thought well of. But there is only one human condition where to put someone else's interests before your own is not only easy but a source of delight in itself.

Kettleby picked up his biro, balancing it delicately between forefinger and forefinger.

'You'll be surprised to know,' he said equably 'or perhaps you won't, that Mr Rowsley made exactly the same offer in respect of you an hour ago.'

You've given yourself away, an unpleasant voice inside Colin's head kept saying. *You've given yourself away.*

The lecture room looked down a steep lawn to the riverbank, and across the water to the old Durham racecourse, bright green in the mid-afternoon. At the first post-war Durham Miners' Gala, in 1946, his six-year-old self had held his father's hand down there, at the edge of the crowd, and been lifted up to see the speakers' stand: Mr Attlee with his horseshoe-shaped hairline, and Nye Bevan with his heavy eyebrows. The wind blew most of what they were saying away, but no one seemed to mind. Later on there were roundabouts and swings and toffee-apples (where had the sugar come from?) and his father's friends. *Is this yer lad, Colin? He'll be Prime Minister tae, won't yer, bonny lad?* Then there was the train journey home, with the other children and the other responsible fathers. The pubs had been open all day: *It'll not be nice for bairns soon.*

You've given yourself away.

Colin's father, another Colin, had in his time won a scholarship to Stanburn Boys' Grammar School. Scholarship or no scholarship, what had it cost a miner's family to keep him there, as prices doubled and trebled during the Great War? He must have stood in the Assembly Hall when the names of Abbott, J.F., Durham Light Infantry, and Adamson, W.R., Royal Flying Corps, were read out. Too young for one war, too old for the next: at least the grammar school had meant he could escape the mines and go into 'business': first a commercial traveller, then a sales manager. A shy, dignified man who never really enjoyed trying to make people buy things; a prudent man whose only impulsive gesture in a lifetime was to marry a Dublin store buyer he met on his sales trips in the thirties. *No leaving school at fourteen for you, bonny lad. College: that's the way to get on.* And if ever the little Colin came out with a piece of Wearside speech — *Mam,* or *schoo-ul* — either or both of his parents would be sure to say 'That's not the way to talk, is it?'

The visiting lecturer today must have been a good ten years younger than Colin. Which made him Clare's age... old-fashionedly trendy in appearance, with Castro beard and pebble-lens spectacles. But what he was saying seemed to be mild, almost sentimental: 'In spite of everything, it is still possible for dedicated teachers to create a caring atmosphere...'

You've given yourself away.

Why should I be ashamed? It's only a feeling: I've never done anything about it. It hasn't done anyone any harm.

It hadn't, until now.

To take his mind off what Kettleby had done to him, all he could think of was Clare; but when he thought of Clare he could see Kettleby, balancing the biro between two fingers, and smiling.

Your chivalry does you credit, no doubt, Mr Rowsley: but I think Mrs Baylham is very well able to look after herself – don't you?

He shifted in his hard seat. Even in good weather, his stiffening shoulder and hip gave him trouble if he sat too long in one position. *Another few years, and you'll be walking like an old man...*

It was ten months, an entire school year, since a morning in the high-windowed bookroom in Middle School. He had not been thinking of anything in particular except the colour of the set of books he had come in to fetch. She was kneeling on the floor with her back to him: head bent, books spread out in piles in front of her. Wearing a terracotta-coloured dress with a print collar; a wisp of reddish-brown hair, too short to fall forwards with the rest, lying in the hollow at the nape of her neck. Her arms below the short sleeves of the dress were brown from the end of summer; the back of her neck was white.

What went through his body then was an acknowledgment of something that must already have been there for a long time. The impulse to kneel down beside her and put his arms round her was so strong that it seemed for a moment as though he had already put it into action: but he had not moved, and never would move to do that. Plainly, there was nothing to be done about it. The lady in the high tower. No one need be damaged by it, not even himself.

Of course it had not been enough merely to go on thinking about her. And it had been absurd to feel so much pain at not having what you had never expected to have. Unsatisfied desire dies away in the end, from lack of sustenance: he knew that. But he had not wanted it to die.

The lecturer's voice rose in finely-tuned passion.

'... but whoever are to be the victims of these savage and repressive cuts, it *must not* be the children ...'

Now, whenever she looked at him, there would be an undertow of caution, or pity. No gift so embarrassing, so much of a burden, as unasked-for love. Kettleby would make sure she knew.

What else could I have done? I wanted to protect her.

They would be serving their sentences apart. Tenter Street was as good a place as any in which to hide, whether from her pity or her resentment.

'... we must not only wait, but *fight*, for the changes in society that will bring about the schools we want. And whilst we fight, we may be sure that our care and our anger will communicate themselves to our pupils. We *shall* overcome.'

Perhaps the audience were supposed to rise to their feet, nineteen-sixties style, and burst into song. They shuffled and cleared their throats, not knowing whether or not to applaud. A long time since *you* occupied an ordinary teacher's place, my friend. Well, look where all my valuable practical experience has got me.

Outside, the sun was still straggling in and out of the clouds. It was warm and damp. In the car park people sighed, wiped the backs of their necks. 'Oh, well, better than teaching, I suppose,' someone said to Colin.

He put the car keys back in his pocket, climbed stiffly and carefully over the low retaining wall, and set off on foot down towards the racecourse. Revisiting the past; or just putting off the moment of going home.

The stuffy Gatelaw bus could not make Clare feel any warmer. The pale stencilled lettering of the computer print-out: 5N; 4Y; 3T. Sprawling bodies on too-small chairs; hooting voices. *These children must be taught by someone* ... And some people have to fight as conscripts in hopeless wars where the casualty lists have long since outweighed the limited justice of the cause. *Abbott, J.F., Durham Light Infantry; Adamson, W.R., Royal Flying Corps* ... Dave Bowburn during the Falklands War had shouted: 'If it wasn't for unemployment there wouldn't *be* any troops!' School leavers who would once have found apprenticeships went into the Army now because there was nothing else. For those the Army would not have there was nothing at all. But apply your arguments to us, Dave: how many aging ex-Grammar School teachers would still be in comprehensive schools if there were somewhere else to go? *Which is the justice, which is the thief?*

The bus began to climb, up between the steep fields with their thin grass, into a one-row village and out at the farther end. Whenever she put her heart to the test, it obliged by repeating that dissolving, squeezing sensation. Really the heart: not a metaphor.

I must have felt like this about Richard once. It doesn't last: you only think it will when you're young. I love Richard in every sense that really matters.

Colin. I love *you.*

Schoolgirls and silly undergraduates fall in love with married men. But I was never a silly schoolgirl or undergraduate, was I? I was level-headed, well-organised, self-disciplined. Never a moment's worry with Clare: she'll go far.

I could have had my adolescence, my fun at the right time, for all the good it's done me.

Sooner or later Kettleby will pass it on. Colin's embarrassment, or his revulsion — does it matter which?

Anyone else could manage to be happy, at least for a few hours, just being in love.

On Gatelaw Green the bus stopped. She was the last passenger left: the conductor and driver waited for her to get off so that they could turn the bus round and set off on the miles downhill again. She picked up her briefcase and shopping bag and stumbled hurriedly out. 'No smile today, pet lamb?' called the conductor after her.

'You never know,' said Richard. 'It might not be as bad as you think.'

Clare jerked the baking tray of quiches out of the oven. Her hand caught against the hot bars of the shelf, and she did not bother to yelp with the pain or to hold her hand under the cold tap.

'Richard, don't you *understand*? Those are children who can hardly write their own names. Their concentration span is about three minutes on a good day. You need a vocation for that kind of teaching — I've never pretended it was something I could do.'

'Surely it just means doing the same thing at a slower pace?'

'No, of *course* it doesn't. Children like that learn in quite a different way. When they learn at all. We haven't got a remedial section or a disruptive children's unit any more, so all the delinquents and all the slow learners get bundled together preventing each other from doing anything. Do you think *that's* what I went to Oxford for?'

'Someone's got to do it. Surely it's better if it's someone bright.'

'Some people are trained to do it and want to do it. Teaching intelligent children is what I do well. I'll only be able to do this badly, and suffer hell at the same time.'

'You do exaggerate,' said Richard. 'Can't you try to see it as a challenge?'

'No, I *can't*. It hasn't been given to me as a challenge, it's been given to me as a punishment; and that's what it is.'

'Well, then, if you really feel like that, make a big union thing of it. That's what would happen at our place if we started pushing the work force around.'

She had her back to him. She began to slice a green pepper: stripping the seeds out, slashing away at the flesh with her knife. Richard came and stood beside her.

'That isn't what the teaching unions are *for*' she said. 'Haven't you learnt anything about my job over all these years? The unions look after your salary and stop you being unfairly dismissed and pay your legal expenses if you get into a court case. What you teach and whom you teach are up to the school.'

'Watch your *fingers*, Clare.'

'It doesn't matter what I do to my fingers.'

'Aren't you making rather a song and dance about this?'

'How would you like it if you'd suddenly been told you were one of the salesmen instead of one of the research team? Would you care for it if I pointed out that the firm had to have salesmen and it might as well be someone who knew what all the products were about?'

'I don't really think it's quite the same, is it?' said Richard. 'Your job's not our bread and butter, when all's said and done. If you feel that strongly about it, just give in your notice.'

'With three and a half million unemployed? I'd never get another job in my life if I walked out of this one without something else to go to.'

'I can't believe that.'

'That doesn't alter the fact that it's true.'

'You think it's true in the mood you're in at the moment, that's all. Would it really matter that much anyway? Perhaps someone who really needs a job would be glad to have yours and make a go of it.'

Clare shovelled the strips of red and green peppers into a Tupperware bowl, then set about an onion in the same way. If she had cut her hand and real blood had flowed, Richard would have been all concern and she would have been all calm and level-headedness.

'Richard, have *some* sympathy, can't you?'

'Well, I'm sorry you're upset, of course. But you never know, this might turn out to be a blessing in disguise.'

She went on slicing. But for you I'd never have been a schoolteacher. But for you I'd never have ended up here, in this county where there are no second chances and no remission for good conduct. But for you I'd have had a career, not just a job ...

It was impossible to say the words. Other people could say the unforgivable and find they had only cleared the air. Other people could do things regardless of the consequences and still escape. No moment's recklessness had ever been allowed to her without long leisure to repent. Colin ...

'I don't know whether I can take it,' she said abruptly, looking down at the piled onion rings.

She had never said anything like that to Richard before. Only she knew what she could take. It had always been *I can manage; it can't be helped; I'll try again another time.*

'You'll feel better about it tomorrow,' said Richard. 'In the morning it'll all look quite different. Why don't you leave all this cooking stuff now and go and get changed ... you hadn't forgotten the firm's summer dinner, had you? You could wear those new earrings I bought you.'

Clare knew she had had too much to drink. Normally she stayed clear of gin except when when she was feeling cheerful (*oh*, like after the staff meeting ...): knowing perfectly well that when she was not feeling cheerful it brought out her reserves of belligerent self-pity. Tonight she had not felt like denying herself anything that she might happen to want. Going home through the summer night — horrible rerun of that other night, coming back from the Rowsleys' house two weeks ago — her head was still throbbing to the bump and thud of the disco. People in their thirties and forties pretending to be teenagers. And her own voice: penetratingly, drunkenly articulate.

'The whole thing's a complete disaster. It's been wished on us by people who don't have to live with the consequences.'

'Well, you know, I don't think I can entirely agree with you there ...'

'Do *you* have to live with the consequences?'

'We've got three kiddies ...'

'At a comprehensive?'

'Well, no, but only because ...'

'Oh, well, there's always some reason, isn't there? It'll always do for *other* people and their children!'

Richard changed up into top gear with a jolt. He was normally such a smooth driver that it meant something when the smoothness failed (Colin always changed gear clumsily, wrenching at the lever as though he expected it to resist him ...)

Richard said: 'You might have *tried* not to be so bloody aggressive.'

'I'm not feeling conciliatory tonight.'

'No one at that party was to blame for what's happened.'

'No one's ever to blame for anything, are they? You live in a very pleasant world.'

Richard jerked the wheel. The car went flying round the corner with an ugly noise of brakes. She said: 'Watch *out*. I don't want to be killed just yet, thank you, even if it would solve a problem or two.'

'Will you just *shut up*? If you want to know, you were thoroughly embarrassing.'

'Oh, terribly sorry. But don't worry: *your* talents are appreciated all right. Several people told me what a splendid career you had ahead of you.'

'Just as well in the circumstances, isn't it? I earn enough to keep us both perfectly comfortably. You can give up that damn job any time you like. As you very well know.'

'How nice and simple.'

'Well, why not? You didn't enjoy it all that much even before this, did you? What's the *point*, for Christ's sake?'

And indeed, what was the point — what had ever been the point? She hated her voice for shaking, and Richard for hearing it shake and being annoyed instead of sorry, and herself for not being able either to prevent it from shaking or to keep quiet.

'You haven't got the faintest clue what it's like to have given years to something and then just have it stamped on ...'

'Do you think I've never been disappointed?' said Richard.

'In me, I suppose?'

'I didn't say that.'

Clare said 'I don't grudge you your good luck. I just grudge the fact that you won't admit good luck is what it is. You're determined not to admit the existence of anything that doesn't fit into that lovely little world of yours. Well, *I'm* outside it, in the cold.'

'You don't have to be. You know what I want for you.'

'I know what you want for yourself, you mean. But it isn't just up to you, is it?'

'No. All *right*.'

In silence, in the dark, they went on home. Clare felt tears sliding down her face, running down her neck and into her hair, falling on to her dress. Richard, his mouth tightly shut, looked ahead of him at the skimming road. The tears would not stop; and whether she let them go on falling, or tried to wipe them away, it would look like asking for pity.

IV

On the last morning of term Colin found himself confronted, at five minutes' notice, with the job of conducting Assembly. He had never had the chapter-and-verse familiarity with the Bible that someone like Bob Murray could produce, so the text would have to be something literary. The mood he was in that morning would have suggested something like 'Howl, howl, howl, howl!'; but the book room yielded an old edition of George Herbert. When had the time been that sixth-formers were able to handle *that*?

Someone in the middle of the hall was throwing paper pellets. By end-of-term standards this was mild; but today he could not think of any strategy at all except that of pretending to ignore it. Normally he merely felt rather foolish standing up on the platform: this time he felt isolated and exposed, like the man going over the top: fixed in the cross-hairs of someone's sights.

No Clare this morning. The end of so much, or so little. In the middle of the room Bob Murray was bearing down on someone, and the paper pellets stopped.

Betty McCabe launched into the hymn. On this day,

immemorially, it would have been 'Lord, dismiss us with Thy blessing'. For whatever reason, even such small traditions as that had gone:

> *Forth in thy name, O Lord, I go*
> *My daily labours to pursue:*
> *Thee, only Thee, resolved to know,*
> *In all I think, or say, or do.*

Religious experience as something not sent but chosen. 'Loss of faith' was finding no more grounds for choosing it.

'George Herbert,' he said to the hall at large 'was an Anglican minister in Wiltshire just before the time of the Civil War.' Today he was not going to give the dates of the Civil War, or explain what an Anglican minister was, or where Wiltshire was. 'This is a poem called *The Collar*.'

> *I struck the board, and cry'd, 'No More!*
>   *I will abroad.*
> *What? shall I ever sigh and pine?*
> *My lines and life are free; free as the road . . .*

Ah yes: but free to do what? In my case it all comes a bit late.

> *Is the yeare onely lost to me?*
>   *Have I no bayes to crowne it?*
> *No flowers, no garlands gay? all blasted?*
>   *All wasted?*
> *Not so, my heart: but there is fruit,*
>   *And thou hast hands . . .*

But the power to lift them and pick . . . Herbert, constructing a perfectly-prepared lesson, had only been setting up a target in order to knock it down again:

> *But as I rav'd, and grew more fierce and wilde*
>   *At every worde,*
> *Me thoughts I heard one calling,* **Childe,**
> *And I replied,* **My lord.**

Say 'Child' to some of this lot; and see what answer you get. *They* know a hollow authority when they hear it.

As soon as the pupils had got out their unenthusiastic Amens, the Headmaster began to climb the steps on to the stage. An end-of-term pep talk, presumably. Colin moved to one side.

I always used to think my faith was the kind that had examined the other possibilities, and survived because it stood the comparison. But now it seems that I must have believed just because I was in the habit of believing. Theology explains the existence of evil to us, the way good is frustrated, the way our best intentions produce the most disastrous results: but it all depends on accepting the authority that offers the explanations. People who've never had religious faith imagine that it makes pain less painful. It doesn't: it just obliges you to be patient and stoical even in private. And adds to the load you carry round with you when you fail.

The Headmaster had to be allowed to leave the hall first. When Colin came out into the corridor Kettleby was just inside the door of his office, waiting.

Usually when they met, Kettleby, a much shorter man, was either standing on a platform or sitting behind a desk: it was not often that they stood at the same level.

'Just one more minute, Mr Rowsley, if you wouldn't mind.'

Oh, Christ: what more do you want?

'An interesting Assembly, Mr Rowsley. Miles above the heads of some of our friends, of course.'

Colin had nothing to lose. He said: 'I'm not going to be told how I must pray as well as how I must teach. I'll do it in the way that seems appropriate to me, or else you can exclude me from the whole business.'

'You are unnecessarily quick to scent persecution. If I were attempting to stifle alternative forms of belief, I should hardly allow a teacher of your faith to conduct Assembly at all, should I?'

'I'm sure you wouldn't want to be seen on the wrong side of the ecumenical movement, Headmaster.'

'You may believe it or not as you choose, Mr Rowsley,

but I have the greatest respect for the faith of anyone who speaks of prayer with such conviction.'

Portrait of the Headmaster as the personification of a guilty conscience. Or had it — most difficult of all to accept — been a perfectly sincere tribute thrown out in passing?

'In any case' said Kettleby 'that was merely by the way. There was another matter, concerning your colleague Mrs Baylham.'

What Kettleby had to tell Colin next rather changed the way he felt about the rest of the day.

Clare and Richard had been frigidly polite to one another at breakfast, speaking only about her arrangements for the weekend conference. When she reached school she stayed away from Assembly because, in her present state, she was afraid that 'Lord, dismiss us with Thy blessing' would make her cry again. During the lunch hour she went out into the town, so as not to have to talk to anyone, and to stay away from Colin. Four o'clock would come soon enough as it was.

Stanburn, for all its size, was not radial in shape, but strung out in one direction along the line of a single main road. The shops and the back-to-backs gave way to Edwardian terraces with minimal gardens, then to nineteen-thirties semis, and then to the post-war estates: 'private' on one side, 'council' on the other. The council-owned side had houses arranged in rectangles, with plain windows; the owner-occupied side was arranged in semicircles and had neo-Georgian windows. She walked on till the lunch hour was beginning to run out, and her feet in their pretty wooden-soled sandals were starting to hurt. She turned round.

I could always leave. At any rate, I could start applying for jobs in decent schools wherever they happened to be. After last night's performance, Richard could lump it. Plenty of married couples work apart these days.

Come to that, we don't have to stay married. We're not tied together the way Colin and Judith are.

Only I don't want to do that to Richard — I don't want

to leave *him* with the débris of the last ten years. That's one kind of love, I suppose.

Looking for job advertisements, filling in application forms, watching the post. Failure behind and ahead. *If I go away I'll never see him again* ... The price for that was the drab streets of Stanburn, and the broken partitions and the dirty floors and walls of Alderman Cassop. And 5N, 4Y and 3T. In exchange for, at best, his embarrassed kindness; at worst, his brush-off.

It was going to be too high a price. Even so, like a blackmail victim, she was going to go on paying while she could. After all, making rational and well-considered decisions had never done her much good.

Colin handed out the report envelopes. 'No, come on, 2A, it's term time for another ten minutes yet. Longer if you like.'

'Ee, *sir*!'

If you let them out before the normal hour, so the argument went, some of them would storm round the town on an orgy of shoplifting — 'going out nicking', as the phrase was. Since they were about to have a full six weeks free to do nothing else but go out nicking, it did not seem a very forceful argument. Lord, dismiss us with Thy blessing ... they pelted out over the playing field, towards the waiting buses, like stones from a catapult. In his entire teaching career Colin had never let a class anticipate the bell before.

You don't know that it meant anything, he told himself. A moment's mad generosity on her part. Or patronage.

But you don't believe that. No one offers to sacrifice herself like that just out of kindness.

I don't want anything from her: only not to have to suppress it any longer. We're both adults: we know it can't come to anything.

She walked heavy-footed towards the staff car park, and avoided looking up till the last minute. Colin was leaning against the boot of the Morris Traveller. When she looked up he smiled at her: it was only a stretching of the mouth. So Kettleby's told him.

'Hullo, Colin.'

'Hullo, Clare. Are you OK?'

'As OK as you are, I imagine.'

She got into the passenger seat and sat stiffly upright. She did not seem to be able to do up the familiar seat belt buckle. 'I'm sorry,' she said, still not looking at him. 'I'm completely to pieces this afternoon.'

He did it up for her without touching any part of her in the process. 'I'm not surprised,' he said. He did not look at her either. 'I'd give anything not to have involved you in all this.'

'It wasn't your fault. If I'd let you go off and collect Edmund that evening the way you'd arranged, instead of rushing round reorganising things, none of this would have happened.'

'And we'd have mixed-ability teaching now. Or you'd have taken Kettleby on single-handed and have been punished for it on your own. Not that I flatter myself it can be much consolation to you to have me for company.'

'It is. But it's no consolation to me to have made things so awful for you.'

He turned the key in the ignition. 'You were marvellous,' he said. 'I'll never forget it. But it was my responsibility: Kettleby had no right to take it out on anyone else.'

They turned out of the school gates and up the little side street. *My responsibility.* That, I suppose, is his delicate way of freezing me off. People don't die of humiliation, of course: they just feel as though they will. She spread her hands out on her skirt and looked down at them. The right hand was scored by puckered brown lines running from knuckles to wrist.

'You've burned your hand,' he said.

'I caught it on the oven shelf yesterday evening. My concentration wasn't all it might have been at the time. It's not as bad as it looks.'

'Good.'

He's not angry with me, anyway. Embarrassed, perhaps. If I had more spirit I'd say that was worse: but it isn't.

It was stuffy inside the car. Outside, shadows of trees raced across the bright surface of the tarmac. She said: 'What did *you* do yesterday evening?'

'A lot of cursing and swearing, apart from anything else.'

'Me too. Did it help?'

'Not in the least. It merely set a shocking example to the boys. When I'd exhausted my normal vocabulary and moved on to the kind Dave Bowburn uses, I took the car out and yelled obscenities to the passing landscape. At all of forty miles an hour.'

'I have to admit that I took to the bottle,' said Clare. 'By rights I should have had an almighty hangover this morning, but all that emotion seems to have soaked up the fumes.'

We're talking almost as we normally do. I open my mouth and the same sort of words come out.

He said 'You won't mind if I take my jacket off?' In the circumstances it was such a primly formal request that she surprised herself by laughing. 'Carry on.'

He rolled the sleeves of his shirt up to the elbow. Thin arms, long-fingered hands: strong-looking, though, not delicate. Fine pale-brown hairs on the back. It would have been the most natural thing in the world to put her own hands over them.

He said: 'I like that dress. I don't think I've ever seen you in red before.'

Richard often noticed and dutifully commented on what she wore. If Colin noticed, this was the first time he had ever given any indication of it.

'I always thought this one was too flamboyant for school. But this morning I felt it might cheer me up.'

'You seem to be wonderfully on top of everything, as always,' he said. 'I shouldn't be asking you, of all people, for pity.'

'You weren't, were you?'

'I usually am, I'm told.'

Who told you that?

'I don't think so. And it's lucky you can't see inside me at the moment, or you wouldn't say I was on top of things.'

Colin said 'My interior landscape looks as though a bomb had hit it at the moment. Last night I found myself remembering the most ludicrous old injuries. Like the fact that my mother tried to drag me off to Benediction on VE night instead of watching the bonfire.'

'How old were you then?'

'All of five. I told you it was ludicrous.'

'She didn't really, did she?'

'Well, you met my mother — don't you find it quite easy to believe?'

'Colin, she was charming: even Kettleby used to be entranced by her.'

'Oh, yes, she was. And don't get me wrong: we got on very well most of the time, particularly after the children were born. But when I was a child she had my soul to defend against all the heretics of the Wear Valley. And it wasn't her war, of course.'

'Did you miss the bonfire?'

'No: my father put his foot down for once. The only other time he ever did that was over my going to Stanburn Grammar School. If you're looking for an explanation of my warped personality I'm afraid it doesn't stem from VE night.'

'If my parents could hear that story,' said Clare 'it would confirm all their darkest suspicions about religion in general, and the Church of Rome in particular.'

'I've never met your parents. You don't talk about them much, do you?'

Clare said: 'We're very cordial together when we do meet. But we aren't close: I don't think we ever have been. They seem to be on much easier terms with my brothers than they are with me. They've never really known what to do with me.'

Each of us the child of our parents' middle age. Did we send out some signal to one another, all those years ago, when he offered me a cup of tea and I said, 'Before I drink this, are you a Leavisite?' I don't understand sign language. In spite of all my literary training, the surface meaning is the only one I ever see. I wish I understood your sign language, if that's what it is.

Grey-green land on either side of them cut out a wide V-neck of sky ahead. Sheep stared from the verge. 'People wouldn't believe this was the industrial north, would they?' she said.

'If we get down past Teesside as quickly as we can, we can go entirely by the scenic route after that.'

'You wouldn't rather go the quick way? You must be tired.'

'Not really: just splenetic. And going over the Moors – particularly in your company – will probably do something to cure that. I expect they'll send out search parties if we go missing. Richard would send one out for you, at any rate.'

'I'm not sure he would,' said Clare. 'I'm not all that popular with Richard at the moment.'

I turned to Richard and he turned away from me. It wasn't so very much to ask for, between husband and wife, but he wouldn't give it. Or couldn't.

'I'm in the doghouse too,' said Colin. 'In my stupid way I'd actually expected a bit of sympathy. But people don't like having a death's-head around the place. It reminds them of what might happen to them if they lost their footing.'

Clare said 'There was a little church outside Oxford, on the road into the Cotswolds. It had a sort of cautionary wall painting: three kings, out hunting, coming face to face with three skeletons wearing crowns.'

Colin said "*As you are, so were we once; and as we are now, so shall you be.*' I don't know the one near Oxford, but have you seen the wall paintings at Pickering?'

'No. Richard's not madly keen on churches. Or on the Middle Ages, come to that. It's so easy to drop out of everything you can't do as a couple.'

'We could go to Pickering today,' said Colin. 'It's only a few miles off our course, and it won't be dark till late. Would you like to?'

'I'd love to. What about the conference, though?'

'Bugger the conference. Sorry.'

'You don't still think you can't swear in front of me, do you? Bugger the conference, indeed. Why did we sign on for it in the first place?'

Beyond Guisborough the road began to climb up towards the Moors. When they had left the trees behind, there was nothing but the grey road bobbing ahead of them, and the bracken stretching out to the horizon on either side.

Clare unpacked the contents of her picnic basket and spread them out on the rug. Suddenly it all looked embarrassingly elaborate.

'I'm afraid this is what you'd call a *Guardian*-readers' picnic' she said.

'I dare say I can overcome my scruples. Did you really do all this last night?'

'It was about the only sensible thing I *did* do last night. I'd have been much better employed cooking than making myself obnoxious to Richard's colleagues.'

'You'd every right to be upset. I'm sure Richard understood.'

'He bloody well didn't. All he could think of was how it was upsetting *him*.' The memory of last night's tears threatened to produce more of them. At no cost was she going to complete her failure by crying in front of Colin. 'I'm not being fair,' she said. 'But he told me I was being embarrassing...'

'If Richard said that,' said Colin 'then he's got a harder heart than I'd ever have given him credit for.'

'Not really. He was just frightened. I do know that really. But that doesn't change the way I feel about it.' Stop it, for God's sake. You don't usually talk like this. You don't usually even *think* like this.

Colin sat with his hands clasped round his knees. He looked down at his own fingers, spreading them out.

'Judith listened to me patiently for about five minutes. Then she suddenly said she was sick to death of my endless complaining, and I should try leading her life for a bit.'

Clare said 'That wasn't very kind.'

'No, it wasn't. I dare say I was asking for it. Her life is pretty grim, I suppose; and she's been fed up with me lately anyway. But just at that moment ... well, it didn't help, to say the least.'

She looked down at the red skirt spread in a circle around her knees.

'Richard did his usual thing, trying to make everyone

out to be in the right, saying it wouldn't be as bad as all that, and so on ... he wanted me to say yes, that was right – – in order to make *him* feel better. And he was angry with me because I couldn't, not sorry because I felt like that.'

'Judith said she was sorry about you. I ought to say that for her.'

'I'd rather she'd saved it for you, if it's in such short supply.'

Colin put his plate down beside him. 'Clare, I'm sorry, I'm not doing justice to this food. After all the trouble you went to, as well ... I'm sorry: tension always goes straight to my guts. At least I hope *you* understand I'm not trying to be melodramatic.'

'I know you're not. I haven't got much appetite either. Let's keep it for tomorrow, shall we?' Her face was scalding hot. Without looking up she began to pile the food back into the basket. Colin gathered up a handful of cutlery. At the rim of the basket their knuckles touched. They both pulled away at once. 'Sorry,' they said simultaneously. Colin got up and stepped back across the rug. He did not move forward again till she had put the lid back on the basket and taken her hands away.

In the car he put out his hands and rested them on the steering wheel, but made no move to turn on the ignition. On the bracken at their side two green-white butterflies circled each other.

'Colin,' she said, staring straight ahead of her. 'I gather I owe you thanks. You tried to take the whole Kettleby thing on yourself.'

'I have to say the same to you, then, don't I? He wasn't supposed to pass that on to you, you know. It was done to try and change things, not to impress you. Or to embarrass you.'

'I know that,' said Clare. 'Kettleby knew it perfectly well too. I just made everything worse.'

'Of *course* you didn't. Look ... when Kettleby told me — what you'd tried to do — I *did* feel humiliated. I'm not proud of that, but it was only for a moment. It was what he'd wanted me to feel, that's all. But then I thought, she's much younger than I am; and she hasn't got any responsibility towards me as I have to her; and yet she offered to do this ... My bloody self-regard was a bit beside the point in the circumstances. The only good thing about all this is seeing that he hasn't brought everyone down to his level. Especially not you.'

She said, absurdly, because nothing else came to mind, 'Thank you'.

Colin, apparently beginning to say something, switched on the ignition instead. He let in the clutch, missed the take-up point, and the engine died again. 'I get more incompetent by the minute.'

This was, unmistakably, self-pity as well as humility. But she was already saying 'Of course you don't. The only thing you're incompetent at is keeping one ahead of Kettleby. Which is something to be proud of.'

He reached out his left hand, jerkily. She thought he was going to touch her hand; and perhaps he was, but what he did instead was to feel for and find the knob of the gear lever.

Whitby lay below them. From the semicircle of beach the town climbed steeply up to the Abbey: golden-blue evening light through its gaping arches. There once the Roman Church trounced the Celtic Church, and sent the monks fleeing westward; and Caedmon the pig-herd sang the first poem in the English language; and eventually, German destroyers sailed up to the harbour bar and sent the twentieth century hurtling in on the town. So that afterwards people always spoke of the past as 'before the bombardment'.

After they took the turn inland again, the horizon, fuzzed with warm air, showed them from time to time the four white globes of the early-warning station at Fylingdales. Then the road began to drop: dry-stone walls, a few trees again; and at last, beyond the Moors, the sloping triangular marketplace of Pickering. Down a side street a lonely motorbike revved endlessly.

They got out of the car, aching from the hard seats, and leant against the bonnet, looking out across the street. The air was cooler and drier than it had been; and at last, there were the first intimations of darkness in the air. The outlines of houses and trees were sharp against it.

'It smells different, doesn't it?' said Clare.

'Yorkshire *is* different. More money, for one thing. Better soil. Better communications with the rest of the country.'

'In the Middle Ages, you had to be very brave or very determined to take the road north from York. That was where civilisation and safety stopped, until you got to the Bishop of Durham's patch. The forest of Galtres came right up to the gates of York.'

'When — Chaucer's time?'

'Earlier than that really, I suppose. But I think Malory mentions it somewhere.'

Across the marketplace were a cobbler's and a stationer's shop side by side: each with the wooden window frames and small glass panes of a shop in a Beatrix Potter book. In Stanburn, old shops were scruffy and paintless, and new shops flashy with plastic.

'It's a shame you can't teach all that mediaeval literature' said Colin. 'You ought to have stayed on at Oxford, you know, and done research and tried for an academic job, while there were still some going.'

'I did want to,' said Clare. 'But when I didn't get the degree I'd hoped for, I just wanted to get away from the place for a bit ... and then I met Richard, so it never happened. Didn't you ever want to do anything like that?'

'Not really. Ironically enough, I actually wanted to be a schoolmaster. Is that girl of yours any good at Chaucer?'

'Deborah? She's not bad. She's a bit impatient with the courtly love business, but she can handle the conventions well enough. We've been doing the way Troilus slips into passionate love one stage after another, and for someone of that age she was really very perceptive about it ... Colin, I know I started this, but can we positively not talk about school again today? Are we going to see these wall paintings?'

'Let me just lock up — not that any Yorkshireman would be daft enough to steal this rust heap. I hope the paintings aren't going to disappoint you.'

'How old are they?'

'Um ... early fifteenth century, I think. Not all that much pre-Reformation anyway. I suppose it's something of a miracle they weren't scraped off either then or later. They were just plastered over, and then some antiquarian vicar in the nineteenth century had them restored. It's very subtly done, though — they haven't been Victorianised at all.'

'Your lot would have covered the place with bleeding Sacred Hearts and simpering virgins instead, wouldn't they?'

Colin straightened up. 'None of your agnostic lip here, madam. All the same, I'm afraid you may have a point.' He put the car keys in his pocket. 'Shall we go?'

'I'm not an agnostic, Colin, I'm a sort of Deist. I believe in God — at least I think so. But if He did anything more than just to wind the mechanism up, then He's got a lot of explaining to do.'

'I thought the last Deist had left this wicked world about a hundred years ago,' said Colin. 'Why did I never know that about you before?'

There was a steep narrow flight of steps up to the churchyard; set in the angle of two houses. As they went up he reached out and joined hands with her. His fingertips just barely laced between hers.

The dragon was orange-red. It lay on its back above the Norman arch with claws extended, while St George's horse bestrode it: as the Saint's lance rammed down its throat, its tail in a last frenzy had whipped around one of the charger's hooves. St Christopher strode between formal bluish-green waves: over one of his bare feet curved the enquiring head of an eel. Herod and his court, in fifteenth-century caps and wimples, sat around a table graced with the head of John the Baptist on a plate: overhead the heavenly host crowded to the ramparts of a mediaeval walled city to gaze down at the scene. Above the last arch, nearest the chancel wall, was King Edmund, his pale body lashed to a tree and bristling with arrows. A black-letter legend ribboned out of the mouth of one of the archers: *He sall haue heuene to his mede.*

'Your son's patron Saint,' she said. 'But I suppose you never did the legend of King Edmund in Anglo-Saxon.' Her voice came out too loud.

'Not at *Cambridge*. Anything before Chaucer was a special option for eccentrics, and I was too young and ignorant to see the value of being eccentric.'

'You've missed something.'

'I know.'

On the south wall were the Passion and the Harrowing of Hell. The sudden light from low down in the west window made Colin screw up his eyes. She moved closer to his side. From the fanged red mouth of the Beast stepped the newly redeemed dead, Adam and Eve emerging side by side, Adam holding up the apple to Christ in Majesty. Their bodies were white, androgynous, innocent: behind the stiff, awkward arms with which they covered their nakedness was nothing that needed shame or forgiveness: their childish sins long ago paid for.

Clare was suddenly conscious of a sharp pain across the back of her hand. By the time she realised it, she had already winced, and at once it diminished. She looked down: at the same moment, so did he. He had loosened his hand, but the pattern of red and white marks across the back of hers showed her where it had been: Colin's wedding ring, pressing into her scorched fingers.

'I was wrong,' he said. 'That picture of the three kings meeting their dead selves isn't here.'

Coming out of the church they walked separately, side by side; but at the top of the steps he stopped, took off his spectacles, then put his hands on her shoulders. 'Clare,' he said: then leant down and kissed her — a quick awkward kiss between closed lips.

'Sorry. No, I don't mean I'm sorry: I mean I hope you don't mind.'

None of the possible inflexions of 'I don't mind' was any use. She put her hands on his shoulders in turn, stood on tiptoe and kissed him back. Her feet felt so unsteady under her that in those impractical sandals she missed one of the steps altogether and nearly fell.

When they drove along the lee of the cliffs to the conference building, it was fully dusk at last. It was a nineteen-sixties College of Education: a complicated arrangement of interlocking brick polygons. Opposite the drive was a craggy line of sand dunes: when they got out of the car she could smell the invisible sea.

From now on, I shall never be able to smell the sea again without remembering. Teachers once more now: never such closeness again.

They went through the swing doors. The lobby was deserted and almost dark, but facing the entrance was a long table on which lay a few little cardboard discs. Clare picked one up.

'Badges,' she said. 'Look, different colours for different parts of the region. How sweet. Pale yellow seems to be County Durham. Here's mine, and here's yours, Mr K.C. Rowsley.'

'I loathe wearing badges,' said Colin. Her fortitude began to trickle away.

The strip light overhead flickered into life. A neat blonde woman emerged from a side door.

'Well, you're late, aren't you?' she said. 'I can't let you go into the hall now, I'm afraid. It's not fair to interrupt the speaker.'

'That's quite all right,' said Clare. 'Perhaps we'll go in for the questions afterwards, if that's all right. Can you just tell us where to put our luggage?'

Colin carried her case to the door and then set it down. Clare looked at the cardboard nameplate. '*Ruth Colby*,' she said. 'What a nice sensible name.'

Colin said 'Do you really want to go in for the questions?'
'Good God, no. Do you?'
'What I actually feel in need of,' said Colin 'is a drink, but I don't suppose they'll open the bar up till the session's finished.'

'They wouldn't want wicked characters like us to have somewhere more entertaining to go to.'

'Are you going to call it a day, then? Or could you face coming for a walk?'

'Of course. But aren't you tired? You seem to have been driving for hours.'

'No, just stiff. Old age, you know.'

For the first time that day they actually laughed together; and if there was a certain amount of nervousness in it there was also a good deal of relief. 'Oh ... go and jump off a cliff' she said. 'Come to that, let's both go and jump off a cliff. There's one right up above us.'

'See you downstairs, then.'

The room had white walls and a blue cord carpet; and, bizarrely, a teak-plank ceiling. It was enough like one of the rooms she had had as an undergraduate to stir a faint, apprehensive nostalgia. But the view from the window was not of the trees and mild brick of the Banbury Road: it showed the same line of dunes they had seen from the driveway.

At that age she had had National Gallery and Ashmolean postcards on her walls. Miss Ruth Colby evidently went in for posters. The one over the bed had a treescape with the setting sun, and the legend *Thank you for the world so sweet.* The other one, on the opposite wall, showed a ginger kitten peering round the edge of a half-open door. *When God shuts one door He opens another.* Does He indeed? Perhaps God is a ginger kitten, then.

The red dress was crumpled now, but to change it at this stage would be too self-conscious. She found her hairbrush at the side of the case. What stared back at her from the looking glass over the washbasin was not in the least flushed or bright-eyed: it looked watchful and, if anything, paler than usual. Damn you, won't you ever learn the trick of letting go when you want to?

On the dunes the spiky wooden heels of her sandals sank in at once. 'Hold on a minute,' she said. 'I'm going to take these stupid things off completely.' She held them, bunched together by the straps, in her left hand, to leave the other one free. Without her high heels the top of her head was just level with his shoulder. The sand was firmer under her bare feet. Yorkshire sand is yellow and cohesive; Northumbrian sand is white and granular: no use for building castles. As they moved along the beach he held her hand more firmly. They walked from one breakwater to the next, further and further, listening to one another's breathing. *All we need for a bit of pathetic fallacy is the tide coming in. Colin, I don't want to be like this for the whole of my life. Change it for me.*

On the ground floor of one of the polygons a row of windows poured light out on to the path. Where the gravel of the drive began again, she had to stop to put her sandals back on. To lean against Colin while she did so seemed a desperate gesture, stagey and kittenish; but to have made a point of not doing so would have been worse. After she had put the sandals on, the two of them stood for a long time in a patch of shadow, out of range of the windows, with their arms round one another: not tightly, but close enough for her to hear his thudding heartbeat. Her own was slower, but no less violent. At last Colin said: 'You'll get cold in that dress. We'd better go in.'

In the big lit-up room all the tables were littered with glasses. At the far end, a group of men whose cardboard badges were dark green were talking one another down. 'So I told him he could play or not as he chose: he's no sodding Kevin Keegan when all's said and done . . .' Only the regular bursts of guffawing showed that it was not a fight going on.

'Colin,' she said. Her voice came out small and breathless. 'That bar looks horribly shut. There's some wine in the picnic basket: I even remembered a corkscrew. Shall I go and get it?'

'I'll get it. You find us somewhere to sit.'

We've got to drink it down here. If I asked you upstairs you'd have to say either yes or no.

One corner of the room, in the angle of the bar, was completely deserted. There was a round white table, a sofa and some chairs. On the wall above the sofa was a handwritten poster. *Boy George concert – sign up here for end-of-term trip.*

She gathered the glasses and ashtrays off the table and carried them over to the bar. She wiped the spilt ash and sticky ring marks off the table with her handkerchief and then threw the handkerchief away. Real little middle-class housewife you are, Clare. But it mattered very much not to finish the evening in public squalor.

The sofa had a white-painted frame and armrests, and plum-coloured cushions. The foam rubber inside was not thick or springy enough: student furniture.

Colin was walking carefully towards her — though she had been the one doing all the tripping-over today. He held the bottle in one hand, glasses and corkscrew in the other. The humble domesticity of it made her heart perform its melting act all over again. Love makes you do stupid things: it makes you promise what you can't perform and ask for what no one can give you. But we're not asking or promising very much, are we?

He put the glasses on the table and sat down beside her. He put the bottle down on the floor, steadied it with one hand and pulled the cork smoothly with the other.

Clare said 'That was very professional.'

'There are some things I can do.' He sounded subdued and breathless like her. 'Things that don't involve co-ordinating the feet.' He handed her one filled glass, took the other and gulped from it. 'That can't have touched your throat' she said. Clare, will you for God's sake just *shut up*. She swallowed from her own glass.

His arm lay along the back of the sofa behind her. The noisy group with the dark green badges was beginning to break up. ''Night, Bill. 'Night, Reg.' From another corner a couple got up and drifted off through the swing doors into the dark. Easy for some. No one at all was watching. His arm settled round her shoulders.

'Some more?'

'Please.'

His hand moved along her shoulder: stroking, testing. *If one should say: 'That is not what I meant at all; That is not it, at all'* ... She had not sat like this, waiting for the next move, for more than a decade. One wrong word now, and you'd turn cold and polite, cut me off, never make contact again.

His hand moved along: first the thin fabric of the sleeve, then the bare skin of her arm where the sleeve came to an end. And at last moved up again, just momentarily, to touch her breast. All right, Colin. Then he lifted his hand away altogether. He picked up his glass, swallowed what was left in it. He pressed both his hands, palms together, between his knees and sat looking down at the floor.

Colin. Don't say *I'm sorry.*

'Clare.'

It was her turn to make the move: it was only fair. She sat up close against him and put both hands together on his knee.

'I don't know how to start this,' he said. 'I wouldn't have got started at all without the drink, but that doesn't mean it's the drink talking.'

He took off his spectacles, folded them and put them on the table in front of him; looked down again at the ground.

'Now ... even if I looked at you I wouldn't be able to see your face properly. So you don't have to pretend anything. I want to make love to you. That's no reason why you should want to, and if you don't, I'll never mention it again. Only I hope you won't be angry.'

He began to tremble. He did not look up.

After a minute she could feel the trembling begin to slow down under her hands. He was expecting to be rejected, already preparing his retreat. It was not taking anything away from Richard.

She made one false start, her voice coming out this time as a croak.

'Yes. All right.'

He took a long breath.

'Are you sure?'

'Yes. Sorry, I couldn't ...'

'Really sure? Don't let me ...'

'No. I want you to.'

He picked up the bottle again and divided what was left between their two glasses. He said: 'Do you remember what you said earlier about emotion soaking up the fumes?'

'Yes.'
'It does seem to.'
She drank the wine quickly and stood up.
'I'll go up now. Can you give me twenty minutes?'
'Of course.'
'Do you remember how to find me?'
'Yes.'

All the eyes in the room seemed to be on her: a woman in a red dress going upstairs to wait for her lover. But when she turned at the door of course no one but Colin was watching.

She took off her clothes without once facing the looking glass. No use wondering now if her body would do ... she felt better once her nightdress was on: pseudo-Victorian, with a high, ruffled neck. Come on, Clare, you're not a little bluestocking virgin now.

She looked around the room. Those posters might be making some witty and ironic comment, but since she could not tell what effect they might have on Colin, she took them down, carefully peeling the Blu-Tak from the wall. She made a neat roll of them and put it on the top shelf of the wardrobe. Miss Ruth Colby must surely have been meant to take them down at the end of term anyway. A pale girl with flat shoes, perhaps: a future teacher anyway, poor fool.

Her discarded clothes lay on the chair: she bundled them up and rolled them into a corner of her suitcase. She switched the bedside lamp on and the overhead light off. In front of the glass at last she wiped off what was left of her make-up. Without all that careful shading and blending her face looked childishly pink and round.

Unable to think of anything else to do, she stood in the middle of the room in her bare feet, waiting.

Colin, tying the cord of his dressing gown with a steadiness of hand that surprised him, caught sight of his wedding ring. The sight produced no faltering of intention at all. Tomorrow, probably, I shan't know what to do with myself for guilt: Kevin Colin Rowsley, the adulterer. Whoever thought courtly love could lead to anything else?

There was a defensive half-line which kept running through his head: *Who's injured by my love?* Byron? No, Donne.

Judith doesn't want to hear about what happens to me: she won't hear about this either. I've missed most of the chances that were offered to me. Not this one too.

The absurd noise his heartbeat was making was perhaps not all sexual excitement. But if any of it was fear, it was fear of failure, not of punishment. The celestial clock-winder, if He existed, had never intervened in real life to kill dragons or pull the saved away from hell: He was the wish fulfilment, the fear embodiment, of an obedient child. *Now I am become a man, I put away childish things.*

She tried saying 'Come in', but the sound that came out could not have carried more than a few inches, so she had to go and let him in. He looked pale, and without his spectacles, vaguely startled. She shut the door behind him and put her arms up around his neck. He was taller than Richard, and it felt awkward and unfamiliar, her head and hands in the wrong places.

If it were left to him, it might never be done, even now. She pulled the nightdress over her head and let it drop on to the floor, resisting the impulse to pick it up and fold it, and the other impulse to cross her arms over her breasts and pubis. Clumsy with the buttons, he took his own clothes off. In spite of his aroused state the haste was clearly the haste as much of embarrassment as of desire: he must not leave her naked alone.

He had a white pre-NHS vaccination crater on one arm; the hair on his body was darker and more vivid than the hair on his head: almost the same colour as her own. *Unaccommodated man is no more but such a poor, bare, forked animal as thou art.* She found herself beginning to shake: not in any delicate maidenly way, but violently. He sat down beside her on the edge of the bed and put his arms round her, but the shaking broke his grasp. After a moment he picked up his dressing gown from the floor and put it around her. So that she was covered and he defenceless.

'No,' she said. 'It's not that, I'm not cold. I'm being stupid.' She pushed the dressing gown away, put her head on his shoulder and closed his arms round her again: the shaking did not stop. Her breasts pressed against him.

'Look' he said, muffled, above her head. 'You mustn't feel you have to do this, just because you said yes to start with. I knew I was pressuring you.'

'You weren't. I'm not a schoolgirl: I could have said no if I'd wanted to. What I want is to stop quivering like this.'

'Could we just lie together for a bit?' he said. 'I mean literally, not ... nothing else need happen if you don't want it to.'

In the narrow bed, the lamp shining just above their faces, they lay side by side. He put his arm behind her neck, curving it round so that his hand rested on her shoulder. The trembling began to subside at once. The teak-plank ceiling reminded her of something. A voice, not Richard's, saying impatiently, Come on, Clare, *respond* a bit.

After a minute he said tentatively 'This feels right, doesn't it?'

'Yes,' she said. 'Yes, it does.'

Under the covers she reached out her hand, cupped it under his testicles, because that was what Richard liked. Colin moved his body sharply.

'Don't,' he said. 'Please. Not unless ...'

She turned on her side towards him. 'It's all right,' she said. 'It's all right now, really. I'm sorry I was such a fool. I just needed time.'

He turned his face away from her and said: 'I don't mind if you don't let me start. I never really believed ... only if you let me begin to make love to you, and then you don't want me to go on ...'

Whatever choice was made, was made in Kettleby's room yesterday. We can never be the same again now. Colin, stoically unsatisfied, making his way back through the darkened corridors: sharing his bed with the guilt, without having had the pleasure.

'I shan't want to stop you' she said.

So long as he was touching her face and breasts, it was all right: little waves of sensation went spreading out through her. But as soon as his fingertips found the clitoris, the current of feeling cut itself off, as it always had. Disappointment so entire and yet so expected that it made way almost immediately for adaptation. Colin, I'm sorry, I should have known. I did know, only I wanted you to change me. I wanted not to be the same. I wanted to be kind. I wanted comfort too.

'Is this all right?' he said 'I'm not hurting you?'

'Yes, it is. No, of course you're not.'

So far as she could judge, he was skilful enough: accustomed, clearly, to give pleasure as well as to receive it. But not experienced: a faithful husband going astray for the only time in his life. She knew he would look at her face as he entered her, so she was prepared for that: and after that it was not difficult to pretend.

III
September—October 1983

V

On the Wednesday evening of the fifth-form parents' meeting, Clare spent forty minutes talking to Deborah about Joyce's *Dubliners*, and trying to get Deborah to talk back; then she put on her raincoat and set off to collect the results of her test.

In the Market Place the town hall clock was still showing only ten to five. All right, Clare, here's a test of another kind. She turned the corner into Tenter Street.

If he's there I'll get it over. I'm practically sure anyway. It'll give us both a graceful way out.

She pushed open the double doors. A cleaner was pushing a mop along the floor of the entrance hall.

'Do you know if there's anyone upstairs in the staffroom?' asked Clare.

'Don't think so, miss.'

'Would you mind if I take a quick look? I won't mess up your clean floor.'

On the coconut matting she stood first on one foot, then on the other, to pull off her shoes. The wooden-heeled sandals were standing at the bottom of her wardrobe at home now.

She went up the stairs, opened the staffroom door. It was empty, but someone had left the electric fire on. She went across the darkened room and switched it off. Which is his chair? Oh, stop it. Grow up.

It was a new doctor, one she hadn't seen before: a middle-aged man with dark hair shading tastefully into grey. Under the smooth professional accent were the perceptible spiky vowel sounds of County Durham.

'The results of your test were positive, Mrs Baylham. I imagine that wasn't too much of a surprise, was it?'

'No. I thought they would be.'

'So the first question is what you want to do about it?'

'Sorry?' said Clare. Then she realised what he meant. 'Oh, I see. No, I don't want to do anything about it, thank you. Apart from just letting it take its course.'

'Good. Only I thought, since you obviously haven't wanted to be pregnant up till now ...'

'Yes, I understand. But I'm quite happy about it.'

And I suppose that's true. There's something I can do right, at any rate.

He said 'You're a bit older than the ideal, of course. But as far as I can see you have excellent health ...'

'I always have had,' said Clare. 'Disgustingly so.'

'And you're feeling reasonably well at the moment?'

'I can't stand up for too long without getting dizzy, but there are ways round that. I get a bit of backache sometimes. But I'm not being sick or anything.'

He laughed at her. Better get used to being patronised.

'It isn't compulsory to feel sick, you know. Plenty of mothers don't. Are you going to keep on with your job?'

'No, I don't think so. I'll pack it in at Christmas.'

'In that case I don't think I need to see you again for a month or so. How do you feel about drinking milk?'

'I loathe the stuff. But it's all right, I know that's beside the point.'

Outside on the steps of the surgery she looked again at the town hall clock. Most of the time since she last looked at it had been spent not with the doctor but in the queue. A whole lifetime signed, sealed and delivered in less than an hour. She set off down the main street, past the darkened shops. Do I feel any different? Well, not 'radiant' or 'fulfilled', certainly: but calmer; or resigned, whichever it is.

The middle-school assembly hall was pure 1902-Education-Act in design, with classrooms opening off three sides of the rectangle, and a corridor running parallel to the fourth side. Upstairs, on the second level, was a gallery, with more classrooms, and book rooms. It was always bitterly cold in the building, whatever the weather was like outside.

She picked up her cardboard identity badge from the end table. I'll never be able to forget about cardboard badges again either ...

Her eyes picked him out at once. Of course she could pick him out in any crowd: probably always would be able to. He was sitting at the far end of the hall. It must be only the light reflecting off his spectacles that gave that blankness to his stare. There was a difference between the pain of loving something and not being able to have it, and the pain of loving something and giving it up. Not mine to give anyway ... but it still hurt, physically as well as emotionally. She sat down behind the nearest empty table. There would be time enough later: an endless amount of it.

He looked away, didn't he? Obviously he's been dreading this too. Tied in knots with guilt, if I know him: wanting to finish it off without anyone's getting hurt. Well, in that case I'm making it easy for him.

The parents who brought themselves to meetings were always those whose children caused you no worry anyway — or sometimes even whose children you could hardly remember. The parents you would have liked to meet almost always failed to appear.

Half a dozen of Clare's fifth-form group were taking CSE Mode III. That should have made sessions with them less pointless, less purely custodial. But it was no use expecting the other twenty-five to be quiet or to concentrate: so each lesson had to be a series of attempts at discussion or explanation, broken up after two minutes by a belch, or a guffaw, or a chair being kicked over. Even ten years ago, pupils of that age would have been at work, allowed to become the young adults they were ready to be.

'Miss, our Tracy's ever so worried about her work.'

'Really? I am sorry. I'm afraid you can't always tell in class.' The last thing on the mind of the amiable Tracy seemed to be work.

'She's that worried, miss, because you haven't given her enough copying to do.'

'Enough *copying*?'

'Last year she had some teacher, who gave them ever such a lot of copying to do. Our Tracy had some really nice writing in her file. It does upset them, you know, when they have to change teachers.'

This was constantly claimed, but Clare had never noticed it to be particularly true, either in her own schooldays or now. 'I'm sorry that Tracy's worried' she said. 'I'll try and see if I can put her mind at rest. But you see ... I know they like copying, and it would be easy enough for me to give them more of it, but those files for CSE are meant to be their own work, something they've produced themselves.'

'So can I tell our Tracy you'll give her some copying to do?'

Clare wondered whether to find out which member of the department had let Tracy and her group spend a whole year copying. But what on earth would she do with the knowledge once she had it — take it to Kettleby? Tracy had had a year of contentment, and the illusion that she was doing something praiseworthy and constructive.

'I'm Mrs Burton, sir. Darren's mam. We don't usually, like, come to these meetings. His da doesn't see the need. But when we heard you'd brayed our Darren, I was that upset ...'

'I'm sorry you were upset,' said Colin. 'I really don't go in for using the cane very often. But I'm afraid Darren just pushed his luck too far this week.'

'The da was all for coming straight up to the school and having it out with you, sir.'

'Did Darren tell you what had happened, Mrs Burton?'

'He's no trouble at home, sir.'

'Well, shall we just say that he was coming out with a stream of words that you usually only see written up on walls? I don't just mean once or twice, in a fit of annoyance, though frankly I think that's bad enough in the classroom. But this was quite deliberate. It was to see what

I'd do about it; and in any case I'm still old-fashioned enough to think that it's particularly important not to let that sort of thing happen in a mixed class.'

Not that the girls in the class, some of them at any rate, hadn't loved it. No one too sensitive to wield a cane could possibly have survived twenty-two years in teaching: if you couldn't use the cane you had to go in for verbal brutality instead, and the Darrens of the world were often as good at that, in their way, as you were. All the same, as he brought the springy end of the cane down on the boy's hand, he had been able all too easily to see the scene from outside — a dried-up schoolmaster, humourless and authoritarian, imposing middle-class habits by force on a working-class victim; taking out the frustrations of his private life on the underprivileged young. To strike a pupil is an admission of defeat. What can you do with a defeat other than to admit it?

'He doesn't swear at home, sir. The da'd bray him if he did.'

After about eight no more parents came to Clare's table. The parents of the ambitious and the industrious queued up to see Janet, and Dave Bowburn, and the others. It was a bit like being the last to be picked for a team game. At the other end of the hall, the one time she dared to look, Colin also sat bleakly idle.

You haven't done anyone any harm. No one's been hurt except you: and you ought to have had the sense to expect that. But if you'd gone on someone would have had to get hurt. Too late now anyway.

Outside in the corridor the caretaker began to walk up and down, rattling his bunch of keys. The most potent walking-on part ever devised. She remembered the staff meeting in the summer: the de-streaming victory.

The parents were leaving; members of staff were standing up behind their tables, collecting their notes and registers together; sighing, running hands over hair, clicking briefcases shut.

Colin's chair was empty, pushed neatly in under the table. The relief, however temporary, was overwhelming.

She pushed her arms into the sleeves of her raincoat. She would have to telephone Richard to meet her at the bus stop: he did not like her to walk up the lane in the dark. Still, he would not mind anything now.

In the darkened and now deserted corridor Colin was waiting for her, leaning up against a radiator; white-faced and tight-lipped. It needed no effort at all to remember when and where she had last seen him looking like that.

'I'll give you a lift home, Clare.'

Stupid prevarication, as well as cowardice, to say 'No, thank you, it's all right.'

'You needn't worry,' he said. 'I shan't force my unwanted attentions on you.'

They walked through the dark, over the asphalt towards the car park. *When have I ever been at a loss for words before?*

In the passenger seat she bent forward suddenly, rested her forehead on her knees. 'Sorry,' she said, muffled. 'I felt a bit dizzy. It'll go off in a minute.'

He fastened his safety belt. He neither spoke nor touched her. *He thinks I'm playing for sympathy.* She sat up again. 'I'm all right now.'

She had had her speech worked out for days. Across the traffic lights, down steep Stanburn Peth, she arranged and rearranged the words she did not say. *For someone who's never learned to drive, it's ironic how many of my big moments seem to take place inside a car.*

The road from the bottom of the Peth was a dual carriageway, with a wide verge. Cars passing on the opposite side sent bars of light through the windows.

She took a deep breath and looked ahead of her. 'Colin' she said. 'I shall be leaving at Christmas. I'm going to have a baby.'

Headlights coming towards them on the other side of the road dazzled Colin for a moment. Two great chrysanthemum-heads of light. One was horror; the other was relief.

'*Clare!*'

There was nothing melodramatic about the way he signalled, slowed, began to pull towards the verge. All the same, his movements sent her a message about something that should have occurred to her before, except that whatever was happening in her womb had done something disastrous to her reactions.

'Colin ... not yours. Richard's, not yours. You needn't worry.'

One of the chrysanthemum lights went out; then the other.

After a while he said 'Are you sure?'

'Quite sure.'

'How? I mean ...'

Stolidly she said: 'I had three days' worth of pills left that weekend. I finished that course and didn't start the next. Sorry, but you did ask.'

'I should have asked about ... that, at the time, shouldn't I? I just ... Clare, are you all right? I mean, is it going as it should?'

'I'm fine.'

'That'll be why you felt dizzy, though. It does something funny to your sense of balance. I remember Judith couldn't reach up to a high shelf for anything.'

Colin, I wish I *didn't* know with such certainty it wasn't yours. I wish I had left myself with that.

As the car moved forward into the road he said: 'I'm sorry, I should have said how glad I am for you both. I take it congratulations are in order, not commiserations?'

'Colin, I should have got all this out earlier. I am sorry, really. Only I didn't expect it all to happen so quickly. I thought there'd be time to talk first ... and then it just seemed too awkward and difficult until I was sure.'

'You've only just found out for certain?'

'Only today. Richard'll be over the moon.'

'Yes. I expect he will.'

The drive would end some time: it would have to. Then he could stop holding his eyes wide open and opening his mouth and hearing words come out of it.

'I'm sorry if I gave you a fright,' she said. Her voice was small and uncertain.

'Well, I'm glad it's all right ... and you're happy about it.'

The words were all right, but he knew the tone was not. What did I want, what did I expect? She lay underneath me: her eyes went wide and blank before she cried out. She held me as though she were drowning, and her body arched up under mine... I never said 'I love you': I said 'I want to make love to you.' Afraid to make what might look like a claim.

He said 'You aren't... Clare, I'm sorry to go on about it, but you aren't trying to take everything on yourself again, are you? I mean, shielding me because of Judith, or — ?'

'And letting Richard think it was his when it wasn't? Do you think I'd do that?'

'No, I'm sorry, I didn't mean — look, Clare, all I'm trying to say is, don't punish yourself, if that's what you're doing. If it is — if it *had* been my child, I'd do whatever you wanted. Do you believe me?'

Given the ultimatum, the unalterable facts, wouldn't I have said, and with what regretful relief, *My responsibility is to Clare now*? But my responsibility will never be to her now.

She said 'Even if I'd wanted an abortion?'

'*No!*'

The headlights swerved in front of them. *Who's injured by my love*? A two-month foetus thrown into a hospital incinerator. Does a dead faith jerk and scream like that?

'I suppose that sounds thoroughly hypocritical,' he said. 'Adultery, but not abortion. I say I'll do anything you want, and then immediately say not that. But there is a difference: I could explain...'

'I didn't mean to upset you,' she said. 'I'd never have thought of it, only the doctor tonight was clearly working his way up to suggesting it... it was a stupid thing to say to you, though. I don't know what I'm doing half the time at the moment: my hormones must be running riot.'

'It's all right. My fault anyway.'

'I feel just the same as you do about abortion. I always have.'

'I said it's all right.'

She saw the church spire of Gatelaw take shape through

the darkness. Home, and Richard, and an end to saying the wrong thing every time I open my mouth. Colin, what I want is forgiveness: not just the words of absolution; the sacramental forgiveness, the impossibly clean slate. Everything I love I do harm to. Everything I've ever wanted, and got, has come to pieces in my hands. You're better off without me.

On the gravel at the foot of her garden path she said: 'You won't come in?'

'I won't, Clare, thanks all the same. Good night — give my congratulations to Richard.' The Morris Traveller dug an arc in the gravel and shot back down the lane. She watched the rear lights disappear. As she turned towards the house, the front door opened into a rectangle of light, with Richard outlined in it. She had something to tell him, hadn't she?

There's more than one kind of love. Richard, I wish I had remembered that earlier.

The beams and patches of sodium light flashed past, crossed and re-crossed, veered away and back. You're driving too fast, you bloody fool. You've got a wife and family, remember? In front of the patches of light, inside the car with him, inside his head, was a picture, detailed and obscene. Clare with her narrow waist and small firm breasts — well, *they* wouldn't last much longer now, would they? — her smooth unmarked thighs, her triangle of reddish-brown pubic hair ... Clare and Richard in the act of sexual intercourse. You bastard, he's her *husband*. His own voice was saying something, again and again. As he slowed down, up the hill to his own road, he heard himself: his measured, modulated schoolmaster's tones, coming out with all the obscenities and blasphemies for which he had taken the cane to Darren Burton.

He stopped the engine at the top of the hill, cruised along to the spoon-shaped end of the road. Well, that was a thoroughly pretty exhibition, wasn't it? Disappointed love is one thing: a dignified, even a respectable emotion. Sexual jealousy is another: a foretaste of hell. Clare, you haven't left me with *anything*.

He got out, stood in the roadway staring across to where the ghostly finger of the Cathedral rose up into the night; the pattern of lights stitched around it, miles away across dead ground.

The quick blaze of shock and anger was already dying down: it had sprung up to protect him from his loss. He knew he had not even begun to feel that yet.

Ordinarily, Richard only found it hard to sleep when something was worrying him. The last time had been that night in the summer when she had got tiddly and gone on and on about the lowest streams and the awfulness of comprehensive education. She had cried in the car, and then again in bed, and neither of them had referred to the fact; and he had lain awake, listening to her pretending to be asleep, knowing he ought to try to show some feeling, and unable to show the right kind.

Tonight, she had fallen asleep almost at once. Flaked out, poor old Clare. All those years ago, it was the controlledness of all her reactions that had attracted him. By her restrained standards she had been almost hectically excited tonight. If I'd had any sense, thought Richard, I'd have insisted on her getting on with this years ago. We always agreed we'd have children when we could afford them.

Gently he switched on his lamp; turned his head on the pillow to look at hers beside him: as he used to do when they were first married. Her face was almost hidden from him, the silky reddish-brown hair fanned out over the pillowcase: one hand half spread out beside her cheek. Ten years: almost a third of a lifetime. *My child.*

'Col,' said Judith, sleepily dutiful. 'Shall I make a hot drink?'

'No, don't bother.'

'It's not like you not to be able to get to sleep.'

'I'm all right. Just go to sleep yourself.'

'Chance'd be a fine thing. Are you not feeling well?' What she meant was 'Is something bothering you?'

'Not particularly.'

'Would you like an aspirin?'

'No.'

The tight-lipped response was a weapon he seemed to use on the slightest provocation or none at all.

'Well, there's not much I can do, then, is there?' she said.

'I'm sorry. Perhaps you'd like me to go and sleep in the grate.'

She sighed and turned her back on him: soon she was breathing peacefully. Lying still in the dark, Colin pieced together a world in which no building he ever entered, no street he went down, would contain Clare.

'Mrs Baylham,' said Deborah. 'Could we do some Gerard Manley Hopkins next? I know you said read some Coleridge, but I'd really like to do Hopkins.'

'Well, of course,' said Clare. 'Coleridge was only a suggestion. It's much better if we can concentrate on things you feel enthusiastic about. Hopkins is a bit of a special taste, that's all.'

Deborah said: 'I don't think I really understand some of his religious stuff: but I think I ought to *try* to understand it.'

'I used to have the impression that I understood it,' said Clare. 'Whether or not I really did will appear, I suppose. Colin Rowsley would probably do it better.' Well, why not the Christian name? — it gave her comfort to say it, and it would make Deborah feel like an adult amongst adults.

'It sounds awful,' said Deborah. 'But I'm a bit afraid of Mr Rowsley. I don't think I could work terribly well with him.'

'Good Lord,' said Clare. 'Offhand I should have said he was the least frightening person I know. Except with bad boys, possibly.'

'When he taught me in the fourth year, there were some really silly, noisy people in the class. I couldn't concentrate on anything, because I was always sure there was going to be trouble ... when he *did* get angry, it was much worse than it is with someone who shouts all the time, like Mr Lodge ...'

'Watch it,' said Clare. 'You never know where the hidden microphones are. Seriously, Deborah, I think he'd be very worried if he thought that he intimidated someone like you.'

'I expect it's just me,' said Deborah. 'I know the other sixth-form group think he's a pet, though I don't think they know what he's on about half the time.'

'That probably says more about them than it does about him,' said Clare. 'Anyway, Deborah, let's find out what you know about Hopkins. Which philosopher do we associate with him?'

'Someone called Duns Scotus ... one of the poems I read was called *Duns Scotus's Oxford*. Do you know that one, Mrs Baylham?'

Clare said, surprising herself:

'Towery city and branchy between towers:
Cuckoo-echoing, bell-swarmèd, lark-charmèd, rook-racked,
                                river-rounded;
The dapple-eared lily below thee; that country and town did
Once encounter in, here coped and posèd powers ...

I'd completely forgotten that one.'

Deborah said 'It sounds wonderful when you say it aloud. I know this isn't exactly literary criticism, but it really made me *see* Oxford ... I'd always thought of it before, you know, as a centre, for scholars and things, but not a *place* ...'

Remorse. On this small scale at least she could do something about it.

'Deborah' she said. 'That really is an indictment of me. Look, I've had an idea. I was thinking, as a matter of fact, of going down to Oxford at half term ...'

She had not been thinking of any such thing. Over the last ten years she and Richard had stopped in Oxford two or three times. The centre of the town belonged to everyone, and was nearly without painful association. Being driven along streets where you once walked, pointing landmarks out to Richard — Carfax Tower, the Martyrs' Memorial — seeing the changed shop fronts — Elliston and Cavell transmuted into Debenhams, the old Cadena Café vanished so completely she could not even reconstruct exactly where it had been — might have been poignant but was not. Oxford in August was a place her undergraduate self had never known: Japanese with their cameras on the steps of the Taylorian, German guided tours in the front hall of Bodley (in all her time there they had been sluicing-down the front of Bodley, turning the grime back to yellow; it had never been possible to get into the front hall). When people asked her the way to odd places like Summertown, or Mansfield College, she knew where to point them. She was an MA of the University, a British subject: she had a perfectly normal right to be there. To her own Oxford, that leaf-and-Cotswold-stone wedge between the Woodstock and Banbury Roads, she had never been back. Materially, at least, that Oxford still existed. You can't go on hiding for ever.

'Would you be able to come with me?' she said to Deborah. 'My treat, of course.'

Deborah seemed not to know where to look.

'Yes,' she said, in a tight little voice. 'I think that would be all right.'

Clare understood. If you don't show that you want something it may be less likely that it will be taken away. It's a pity, she thought, that I'm not so quick on the uptake with other adults.

'Well, then,' she said. 'I'll write to your parents. And I'll write to my old College to see if they've got any guest rooms free. Now, can you get started by doing a practical criticism of one of the short poems? Not the final sonnets, leave those: something like *God's Grandeur* or *The Starlight Night*.'

'Yes, Mrs Baylham.'

'Between these four walls,' said Clare, 'I think you might start calling me Clare. Only don't let it slip *outside* these four walls, for pity's sake.'

When Deborah had gone she realised she had not thought about Colin for a full ten minutes. It's not so difficult. You keep busy; you give yourself small things to look forward to. A train journey to the gentle Thames Valley in autumn, out of the north-east winds.

No more bursts of independence like that soon. No more money of my own; having to depend on other people for the smallest bit of freedom. Like my life before

Oxford, but with responsibilities. At least now I know the advantage of having outside circumstances to blame.

No one else in the Tenter Street staffroom seemed to feel the blast of the electric fire. I don't have to sit here at lunch time any more, thought Colin. She won't be avoiding me any more. I could go over there and sit in my old place and at least pretend to be a human being for a bit. Fifty school days to the end of term. Fifty school days left to see her.

I can't. Not today, not yet. I'm being a fool: she wouldn't snub me; I could behave myself decently in public. It's not that. I'm afraid of feeling my own pain, that's all. It's not going to go away; I'm just going to get more used to it.

He looked around him, at the discarded tracksuits, the pair of plimsolls on the floor weighing down a folded copy of the *Daily Express*. Here at least there were no tender or long-standing associations.

Richard put a cushion behind her back and brought her a cup of tea. 'At least bring me the chopping board and a knife too,' said Clare patiently. 'The meat won't cube itself.'

'You mustn't get too tired' said Richard.

'This isn't work, this is therapy. This piece of meat is Gail Fox, and that one is Andy Reid. I'm going to cut them up into small and extremely symmetrical pieces.'

'You really are mad,' said Richard. 'I think I'm very clever, getting you out of that place.'

'I think you're quite clever too,' said Clare. Her hair was hanging forward and he could not see her face.

'Have you given in your notice yet?'

'I have tried a couple of times, but Kettleby's avoiding me, I suspect. It'll have to wait till next week now.'

'Well, make sure you do it.'

'Don't worry. The end of September is the deadline anyway.'

'I bet he won't be pleased.'

'He'll be torn between pleasure and fury, I imagine.'

'He's been lucky to have had you all this time,' said Richard firmly. He could afford to be firm now.

*

Clare seldom dreamt at nights. When she did, it was almost always a variation of the same theme. She would be trying desperately to catch a train; in an effort to stop her, roads would grow wrong turnings, paving stones spring up into the air, gates and barriers grow up out of the ground. But eventually she would reach it; and then find that it was the wrong train, going the wrong way. It streaked through station after station without stopping; and every station had a name more sinister and incomprehensible than the last. The point where she tried to force a way out of the train had always been the point at which she woke up. But this time, against all expectation, the train stopped. On the platform someone was waiting for her, holding out his arms. He had no face, but she ran towards him, because this was what she had been travelling to. Then as his arms began to fold round her, she understood they were the wrong arms, and tried to pull free. Behind her, the train pulled out, taking with it her coat, her shoes and bag.

Usually the mere fact of waking up was enough, so that she could fall asleep quite soon, and have no more dreams that night or for some time to come. This time she found herself bitterly cold and hardly able to move. She would have liked to turn to someone, to another body for warmth and comfort - was it in order to have someone to cling to that she had committed herself to sharing a bed for life? But it was Richard beside her, breathing deeply and peacefully: was it Richard she had tried to run from in her dream?

She lay awake on her own. Slowly her limbs relaxed: some warmth came back to her skin.

I've always been afraid. Without knowing it, half the time, which makes it worse. I'm not afraid of the dark, or of childbirth: but I'm afraid of almost everything else.

'You have been entrusted with an 'A' level group, Mrs Baylham,' said Kettleby. 'How am I to tell the parents that next term there will be no one to teach their children?'

Once, in spite of herself, Clare had been easily moved by the rhetoric of education. Not any more, though.

'In the summer, Headmaster, I understood that you found me a disruptive influence, and would be delighted to see the back of me.'

'Clearly you misunderstood me. Your imagination is perhaps rather too lively. In real life no member of my staff has ever been hounded out of a job which he was fulfilling competently. I repeat, in this matter you seem to have given no thought to anyone but yourself.'

'There are thousands of unemployed teachers,' said Clare steadily. 'It would be quite remarkable if not one of them were able to finish the year with my sixth-form group. We'll have been through the whole syllabus once by the time I go. A temporary, or part-timer, would do after that if necessary.'

'So you're now an expert on the recruitment of staff?'

Clare hit back. Wonderful how the distant sight of freedom makes you lose all fear.

'If I had a sensible and rational kind of timetable to hand on, Mr Kettleby, you'd have no trouble at all in filling my post. As it is, I dare say some teachers might be wise enough to prefer the dole. All the same I'm sure there'll be some poor mug who thinks she can improve her lot by hard work and dedication.'

He did not reply in kind, of course.

'I shall have to consider, Mrs Baylham, whether I should not remove your sixth-form group right away, if that is your attitude.'

Clare had thought of that. He could not take Deborah away from her.

'I assume you won't think this is the moment to let a non-graduate start teaching 'A' level. I doubt if the Education Authority would find that very impressive when they come round to rationalising the sixth forms in the county. So you've a choice between Janet Waldridge and Colin Rowsley to give my sixth-form group to. If you give it to Janet you'll have to take away one of her other forms and give it to someone less able, which won't be very popular with the parents. If you want to give it to Colin you've got my blessing — but I thought he was supposed to be on punishment duty like me.'

An empty offer in that Kettleby would not take her up on it. Not that she had not meant it: but it was a different kind of offer from the one she had made before. Not just because it was calculated rather than spontaneous; nor because it involved only a ten-week sacrifice; but because there was guilt in the offering. Never again that blind generosity.

Kettleby opened a drawer and began to move papers round inside it. Without looking up he said: 'That will be all, Mrs Baylham. Please make sure that you continue to pull your full weight as a teacher until you leave us.'

'I don't think I've ever done anything else.'

Her hand was already on the door handle when he said: 'Have you informed Mr Rowsley of your plans?'

'Of course,' said Clare. 'He's a personal friend as well as my Head of Department ... as I'm sure you know.'

In political matters Kettleby might be a crook, but it was perfectly possible that in sexual matters he was entirely virtuous. Had he assumed last summer that Clare and Colin were already lovers? And if so, were the powers of clock winder and puppet master to be attributed not to God but to Kettleby?

Colin walked down the long shopping street towards the main building. It was a clear bright day, Michaelmas weather. For the first time for several days, he found that he could lift his head and look straight in front of him. That's the worst of it over, he told himself. Ninety per cent injured pride in any case. It couldn't have gone on: you ought to be glad she had the strength to put an end to it. She must have loved you a bit: she's left you with that.

Long before I ever thought all that much about her body, it was her company I enjoyed. I can still have that, for the time that's left.

As soon as he opened the staffroom door, he knew, without looking round the room, that she was not there.

'Look who's here,' said Bob Murray.

'Greetings, Col,' said Alan Carr. 'We'd forgotten what you looked like.'

Well, did I expect her to sit around waiting for me?

Probably it's better to do it bit by bit. At least I've taken the step of getting myself over here.

That evening he made a conscious effort not to snap at his sons, or to answer Judith in grunts and monosyllables. The amount of effort this required made him wonder what he had been like to live with recently.

There was one double period — Friday, after Assembly — when they were in the same building at the same time. There was no more need to hide now. They would have to meet some time; and at least if it were during a free period they would have time to be more than barely civil to one another.

Surely he'll have understood, once he's got used to the idea, Clare thought. I know I did it badly. But after all, he can't really have wanted it to go on, can he? I'd have been the one to do the clinging, try to make it live after it was dead.

He'll understand. His children obviously mean a lot to him. Why should he think of seeing it as any more complicated than that?

She went up to the book room. She had meant to spend the time conscientiously in sorting out some of the 'Topliner' books for low-ability reading. There were not enough copies of anything; whilst she was rooting around for enough to make up a complete set, she found an old single copy of *Poems of Today*. Far too old-fashioned to be usable for teaching, even in her own schooldays.

> *O Cartmel bells ring soft tonight,*
> *And Cartmel bells ring clear;*
> *But I lie far away tonight,*
> *Listening with my dear . . .*

So there she was, kneeling on the floor, with her back to him: her hair falling forward, and a beam of weak September sunlight striking the back of her neck, where a wisp of hair, too short to fall forward, lay along the nape.

Colin's week of instructing himself in what he could learn to do without went for nothing.

*

She watched him put down an armful of books on the table. *Criticism and Comprehension*: mostly without their spines, and some with no cover at all.

'It's time we threw those out,' she said.

If we just make ordinary conversation, perhaps we can slip back into the way we were.

'Well, we can't throw them out. There are cuts on, in case you hadn't heard.'

'Colin — don't be angry with me. Please.'

He shut the door. He stood by the table; spread his fingers out on top of the double pile of books, and looked down at them. He said: 'I love you. I'm sorry to sound theatrical, but irony has its limitations.'

She said 'I'm so sorry.'

No matter what the emotion behind the words, it was still the same formula as the one you used when you bumped into someone with your trolley at the supermarket.

'You make it sound as though I had a disease,' he said. 'I suppose you've got the weight of English literature behind you there.'

To kneel on the floor like this and look up at him was not human. She got to her feet.

He shook his head a little, as though trying to clear it of something.

'I could tell you to the day and the hour,' he said, 'when I realised; but I don't suppose you want to know. I thought, well, at least after all these years of the English Novel I ought to know it can happen to anyone. It reminded me I was human.'

'That's easy to forget in this job.'

'Look, spare me the worldly wisdom, will you? I'd never have inflicted any of this on you, only I once got the idea you loved me too. I apologise for my presumption.'

Clare, you bloody fool, you can't start crying again. There'll be no end to it if you do. You've got to face 3T again in half an hour. They'd just love you with a shiny red nose.

'I did,' she said. 'I do. But I love Richard too, in a way, and it's Richard I'm married to.'

'Then why did you sleep with me?'

'You asked me to.'

'You had plenty of chances to call it off. Right up till the last moment. Christ, Clare, you're not a baby: you've been around long enough to have known what was happening. What were you playing at?'

'I wasn't playing at anything. I'm sorry if you think I led you on.'

'Didn't you?'

'Colin . . . it's horrible to be called a cockteaser.' *I am sure I am none such.*

His face went red. 'I'm just hitting out in all directions' he said. 'Wherever I think it'll hurt. I made all the running, I know that.'

'Please try to understand. It wasn't that I didn't want you to.'

'This is all the wrong way round, isn't it?' he said. 'It's supposed to be women who can't separate sex from emotion.'

'Colin, what did you *expect*?'

'I don't know. I ask myself that. But I expected *something*. Surely you realised it wasn't a trivial business for me?'

'Yes' she said. 'Yes, of course I did, but . . .'

'But what?'

'Oh, hell, Colin, we were both feeling miserable and angry and let down, and we comforted one another in a fairly obvious way!'

'You think I generally make sexual advances to the nearest woman when things go badly for me?'

'Look, what can I say? I really am so sorry. I imagined I was being mature and acting like an adult at last, and I was just being naive as usual.'

'I was the naive one. I know, I'm carrying on like a betrayed virgin. I know I'm making myself ridiculous.'

'No, you're not . . .'

'It doesn't matter now anyway, does it? I've already made enough of a fool of myself. I never thought Lust was my besetting sin, particularly — I always knew it was Pride.'

'Colin, for heaven's sake keep your voice down.'

'Does it matter?'

'Of course it matters.'

'Always the teacher, aren't we? Mustn't lose any authority with the kids.'

'Believe it or not, I was thinking mainly of you. In another ten weeks or so, it won't matter what they think of me.'

Colin sat down suddenly. 'I shouldn't have said any of that. I don't know what to do with myself at the moment.'

'I wish I could say something ...' Colin. Understand. Don't make me explain.

'Are you all right?' he said. 'While I've been ranting on ...'

'My back aches, that's all; and I feel a bit queasy. It's nothing to do with you: I've had it all day.'

'Yes, Judith did, all the time she ... *oh, God*. Clare, you're just going to have to try to understand. I feel as though *I'd* been cuckolded. I dare say Richard would behave with far more dignity if he knew, So would Judith, come to that.'

'Richard hasn't got your imagination. I don't know about Judith.'

'You mean Richard isn't in the habit of building up fantasies.'

'Colin, *stop* it. Even if I had meant that I wouldn't have said it.'

He got up, turned his back to her and started to take a row of books from the top shelf. They were paperbacks, with bright blue spines. He said: 'What did you mean, then?'

'Do we have to go on with this? Suppose someone came and listened outside the door?'

'We'd hear them coming if they did. Clare, from literature if not from life, you ought to be able to recognise what's wrong with me. I want to know about how Richard's mind works because he's got you and I haven't.'

She rubbed her eyes, then remembered her mascara. 'I meant ... I didn't mean he's insensitive. But if he told himself it wasn't reasonable to feel something then he wouldn't go on feeling it; and he'd find it hard to understand anyone who did.'

'I like Richard,' said Colin. He sounded surprised at himself. 'We've never had much to say to one another, but I've always taken to him. I can't truthfully say I feel guilty about him, though.'

'There's no reason why you should. You haven't done him any harm. I ought to, I suppose; but it's you I feel guilty about. It has been, all term.'

He looked down at his fingers. 'At least tell me you didn't go to bed with me out of pity. Even if it isn't true.'

Pity is what you feel for someone *less* than yourself. And my pity would be redundant when you've got so much of it already for yourself. I wanted comfort too.

'I want to try to understand,' he said. 'Because if I can understand I can probably learn to get used to it. I'm not proud of this, you know. I don't imagine there's anything heroic about it. If you imagine I see myself as Troilus and you as Criseyde you've got it quite wrong.'

'I've got it *all* wrong. I didn't know I was going to make you unhappy. Can't you just believe that?'

'Look,' he said obstinately 'you gave yourself to me — what? — three, four times, over that weekend? No, I won't pretend I don't remember exactly: four times. And if I'd been younger and could have made it more often it would have been more often. I'm sorry if I'm embarrassing you, but I don't think you have any right to be embarrassed. And I think I've got a right to know. It was fairly obvious even to my restricted experience that you hadn't made a habit of adultery. If it didn't mean anything, then *why*? Didn't I deserve any better than that?'

He keeps calling it adultery. When I told him I was pregnant all he could think of was whether his blasted religion would have let him allow me to have an abortion. Now all he's thinking is that he's committed a mortal sin for nothing. Why should I have thought you could ever understand?

If Colin's way of giving vent to anger and pain was to say whatever came into his head, hers was to say what was true, but what she would not have said otherwise.

'I had a lot of reasons, Colin. Sympathy and gratitude and ... and love. And you can believe that or not as you like. But if you must know, I also thought I might find out, just for once in my life, what it was that everyone else gets out of sex. If that sounds as though I used you, then I'm sorry. It's not what it felt like at the time.'

Then he turned round. The expression on his face did not change: only his eyes widened a little.

'I asked for that, didn't I?'

Already she could only half remember what she had been angry about. But in a few more minutes the bell would send her scurrying off again; and it was too complicated to build lies on top of truth.

He said 'And did you find out?'

The feel of his naked skin under her hands; his hair between her fingers. Lying while he slept, watching the bumpy line of the dunes riding through the night.

'It was ... nice, touching you,' she said. 'And lying together afterwards. And waking up with you. But the thing itself ...'

He waited. There was no help to be looked for there.

'It wasn't anything you did wrong,' she said. 'I realise it must be just me. I always knew it was really. Only with you I hoped it would work. And since it didn't with you, I suppose there's no reason to think it ever will. I don't mind all that much, most of the time: it's only like being colour-blind, or not having a sense of smell. Most of the time I feel far worse about not getting a First than I do about that. But with you I wanted it to be all right.'

He still had not moved. Had the histrionics of ten minutes ago really happened? Then he moved his tongue over his lips.

'But you did ... "come" is the word *Guardian*-readers use, isn't it?'

'No. I don't know what it feels like. I'm sorry.'

'Sorry you pretended?'

'Yes ... no. Sorry I didn't keep the pretence up.'

'Well ... I'm sorry, too. For myself as well as for you. I thought at least I'd ... no, what I thought doesn't matter, does it? I wanted an answer and you've given me one.'

I wanted not to be always alone. And now I'm more alone than ever.

'*Frigid bitch* is the phrase you want, I think' she said. 'Only of course you're too much of a gentleman to say it, aren't you? It's the one crime you can't be forgiven for, don't think I don't know that. Why do you think I never told anyone before?'

He sat on the edge of the table, hands dangling in front of him. He took his spectacles off, then put them on again.

'What about Richard? Doesn't he know you feel like that?'

'I don't think so. How would you suggest I set about telling him?'

He looked down; gave again the little, puzzled shake of the head.

'You don't realise ...' he said. 'You think you do, but ... you don't understand what you've done.'

She didn't know how to wail or scream. And anyway, what would have become of them if she had?

Behind him on the table stood the forgotten pile of books.

'I love you,' she said.

He jerked his head up and looked across at her.

'Then all I can say is, God help anyone who comes within range of your kind of love.'

Too late, the bell shrilled through the room, above their heads. They stared at each other — conscious of having said, like a married couple, unforgivable things to one another.

She missed her footing, slithered awkwardly down the last half-dozen stairs, but landed on her feet, wrenching the heel of her shoe half off. Her first thought was, One day you'll break your neck; the second, Damn it, that was a decent pair of shoes.

The third thought, which the other two had been busy trying to intercept, was, Now I've got nothing left at all. Nothing I want.

Was it ten minutes ago she had allowed her anger its way because she was afraid that otherwise she would weep? And if she had wept instead of telling ... well, no tears of hers should ever flow again. Degradation, an appeal for help that no one could give.

I always manage it in the end. I watch people for the first signs of rejection, and they always appear. I always make sure they do.

Love seeketh only self to please. The only source I've ever learned anything from is books; but if I've ever known anything, it's always been at the wrong time.

She pushed the heel back on her shoe as firmly as it would go, and limped off in the direction of 3T. The sudden absence of fear and resentment was an odd feeling. There was nothing they could do to her now.

'Right, exercise books open' said Colin. 'Now begin by copying this down'.

'Sir, I haven't got any paper.'

'Sir, lend us a pen!'

Inside Colin was a sense that something disastrous had happened, which if once brought to mind could never be put out of mind again.

He wrote across the blackboard 'Punctuation is a way of letting people see the *shape* of what we mean.' He had no idea whether this made sense to them or not. It merely seemed like something the new kind of teacher would say.

'Shape' he said. Some of them were still breathing heavily over the copying: but you couldn't give the quicker ones time to start looking for diversions.

'Ian — how can what someone says have a *shape*?'

'Don't know.'

'Well, when we use the word *shape*, what do we mean by it?'

'Yer knaa – shape.'

It had been the wrong kind of question, at the wrong point in the lesson, in the wrong tone of voice, the wrong cast of thought. With the first failure of the forty minutes came the realisation of what else had happened.

'All right' he said. 'Some examples. Copy these down, under the first sentence.'

'Sir, I can't see the blackboard.'

At least, so long as his back was turned to them, no expression on his face could offer them a target. His fingers were another matter – they would not coordinate:

he had trouble forming the letters. First the chalk broke; then he dropped it. The giggling began.

One of the cardinal rules was to get the children to do the menial tasks for you. But going down on all fours seemed so appropriate he did it without thinking. He pressed his shaking hands against the wooden boards of the platform. His heart had begun to thump like a road mender's drill: surely the whole class must be able to hear it?

He crouched, his fingers closing over the chalk. I'm forty-three. I could be doing this for another twenty-two years.

VI

Standing on the Middle School steps at four o'clock, the children pushing past her on either side, Clare found herself unable to swallow or to catch her breath. Then someone yelled 'Miss, I wish you would let us through!' and the moment passed. She pulled her raincoat around her. Pure hysteria: something you're not allowed. Even the word 'hysteria'— not that she had anything but a second-hand knowledge of Greek — had something to do with the womb.

In the Upper School staffroom Janet, wearing dark red trousers tucked into heavy boots, was lying back in a chair: a surprisingly decadent posture for her. As the first wave of cigarette smoke reached her, Clare turned her back hastily and began to shovel exercise books into her briefcase. Janet said across the room 'Can you spare ten minutes, Clare?'

Clare's instinctive reactions were, unfailingly, obedient ones: defiance, however often she practised it, was always a second thought.

'Well' she said 'if it *is* ten minutes. I've got a bus to catch.'

'All right. Well, it's about . . .'

'Janet, sorry — could you either put the cigarette out or let me open a window? I'm not trying to be provocative, but it's making me feel a bit sick.'

Janet pressed the end of her cigarette against the metal ashtray. 'Forgive my asking,' she said 'but you wouldn't by any chance be pregnant?'

'Yes, as a matter of fact,' said Clare. 'How very percipient of you.'

'Not all that much,' said Janet. 'If one of the older girls kept walking around with her hand in the small of her back, and felt dizzy in Assembly, and sick at the first whiff of cigarette smoke, I hope I'd put two and two together. However, in your case I imagine at least it didn't happen by accident?'

'What was it you wanted to ask, Janet?'

'I wanted to know whether you were really serious about little Deborah Thingy.'

'Deborah Robson, I suppose you mean. Serious about what?'

'This Oxford caper.'

'I'm certainly not doing it to amuse myself.'

'To be fair to you, I didn't think it was very likely that you were just messing around with her. Clare, what in *hell* are you playing at?'

Colin, I don't play at anything. If I knew how to, no one would have got hurt.

'Janet, I take it there's something you don't approve of, again. If so, I'm sorry, but I don't actually have to have your approval.'

'If it only concerned yourself, that would be one thing. As a matter of interest, I take it you won't be coming back here after you've had your baby?'

'No. One of the things *I* don't approve of is working full-time if you've got a young child.'

'Plenty of people don't have any choice.'

'I do realise that, thank you, Janet. You ought to be glad that I'm opening a job for someone else.'

'That's not the point at the moment. You're taking this girl, filling her with ideas she'd never have thought of for herself, encouraging her to cut herself off from her peer group, and then when she falls flat on her face you're not even going to *be* there.'

Clare did not think she had ever heard anyone say 'peer

group' in actual conversation before. Concentrating on being rational and non-rhetorical with Janet was making her feel better.

'Why should you suppose she's going to fall flat on her face? She's only seventeen. If she doesn't get a place this year she can try again: the fourth-term entry business doesn't come into force till next year. She'll be able to take a second chance if she needs it. She can come to me at home for private coaching, or Colin will look after her. She knows there aren't any certainties in it, but I think she's got an excellent chance.'

'Every time you open your mouth, Clare, you add to the score. I'm not simple-minded enough to imagine that Oxford and Cambridge are ever going to be made open-access, though of course that's what I'd like to see. But at least these days, thanks to a lot of people's hard work and lobbying, ordinary kids can get in on their 'A' levels and an interview. But *you* still have to go in for cramming her for that sickening scholarship examination, and falling back on the seventh-term entry if she doesn't get it this year. And this is a kid from a comprehensive school! You ought to be ashamed of yourself.'

'Janet, you've marked 'A' level scripts for money just as I have. Are you sure you always spotted the talent after you'd done three hundred of them? And what about people who are brilliant at one subject and mediocre at others — what chance is there for anyone who doesn't get four 'A's? And interviews favour the privileged far more than exams do. Maybe with your background *you* knew how to give a good account of yourself in public when you were seventeen, but I certainly didn't.'

'You've learned to give a very convincing imitation since then, in that case.'

'If I have, I dare say I learned it at Oxford. Before that, and unlike you, I went to my local grammar school, which happened to be a thoroughly undistinguished one.'

'Then I can only wonder why you hanker so much after grammar schools' said Janet.

'I didn't think we were talking about me,' said Clare. 'I thought you were concerned about Deborah.'

'I am. My point was that if she gets in by your methods it'll be a great pity. All the more so since it's the last year before they reform the system to give ordinary schools a chance.'

'In my time, "ordinary" schools didn't need the standard of entry lowered to give them a fair chance.'

'I do try to have some human sympathy with people like you, Clare. It's hard if you can't accept the inevitable. But I can't have any sympathy for the way you try to influence your pupils.'

'They can think for themselves, I suppose. Deborah certainly can. You think we should just accept being dinosaurs, and die out gracefully?'

'*You* mentioned dinosaurs. I should have thought knowing when to die gracefully would have been one of the things you admired. And who's "we", by the way? You and our friend Colin?'

Anger is a great palliative. 'In this Department, I suppose so. But the rest of them are only on your side by default, you know, Janet. They just go along with things in the way most people do. I admire the way you campaign for things that aren't going to bring you any personal benefit; but don't think the masses will like your millennium when they've got it.'

'Is it the masses you're saving Deborah Robson from?'

Clare looked at her watch, got painfully to her feet. 'I really do have to go for my bus now. I don't imagine I can save Deborah, or anyone, from anything. But if she'd been born when you and I were, there are some chances she'd have had automatically, and now they have to be fought for. That's something I think I *can* do.'

Janet picked up the extinguished cigarette, reached for her matches. If only she'd let herself smile occasionally.

'Yes. I can see you've got some kind of point there. There have to be some victims whenever we get social change, but there's room for people to defend the victims too, I suppose.'

Clare said, on what was very nearly an impulse: 'The ironic thing is, isn't it, Janet, that you and I always talk quite constructively together? Despite hardly agreeing about anything.'

'I don't know about constructively' said Janet. 'I don't see that we achieve anything. I suppose we usually manage to be quite honest with each other, if that's what you mean. I expect I shall quite miss you. But don't think that means I'm softening up on anything I said. It'll be better in every way if she doesn't make it to Oxford on your terms.'

'Not *my* terms' said Clare. 'That's not the point.'

She had to run most of the way to the bus stop, which was not easy with a full briefcase and a shoe with a loose heel. Hot-faced and breathless, she flopped into the back seat. At least it was the weekend. She was simply too tired, all of a sudden, to think back any further than what she had just been saying to Janet. Something else had happened, something desolating and final, but even if she had had the strength, what was the point? Nothing would ever change it. There never had been anything that would have changed it.

All along the bus route, the leaves were turning: in another two or three weeks one of those sudden north-easterly winds would strip them bare. This time next year, I shall be pushing a five-month-old in a pram.

She could see the picture easily enough. What she could not produce were the sensations to go with it. But at any rate she had stopped wanting to shiver all the time.

Colin still had three persistent homework skivers to keep in from the previous week. Parents had to be given twenty-four hours' notice of a detention, which was fair enough, except that unfortunately it gave the children warning too. Invariably, a number of them would fail to appear for several days afterwards: this was the first day all three of the offenders had been present. It was no good shrugging his shoulders and using the hardship to himself as an excuse for not repeating the punishment — saying they were only punishing themselves in the end. 'The end' was something no one could see; meanwhile, let three get away with it one week, and a dozen would try it the next. Let him register in their minds as a teacher who gave in when he met resistance, and he might as well give up now, for good.

He set out on the board, yet again, the work they had been supposed to do ten days ago. By now it looked almost as pointless to him as he supposed it did to them. 'Come on' he said, making no attempt not to sound weary. 'Let's get this out of the way, shall we? Then we can all go home, and perhaps from now on you'll see that it's easier to do it at the right time.'

They sulked and muttered, but at least by the time the statutory half-hour was up they had been forced to write *something* down. 'All right' he said. 'Off you go.' Of course he should have told them to bring their books up to him, but by the time he remembered that, they were already out of the room. It was several minutes before he could summon the energy to stand up, collect the books and make his own way out.

In the driver's seat he found himself suddenly quite unable to think what to do next. He sat looking helplessly at the knobs and switches on the dashboard. He was roused by a scraping, grating sound. One of the three girls was walking slowly past, her knuckles trailing purposefully along the paintwork of the car.

Colin could not normally have cared less what the outside of his car looked like; and another scratch could hardly have made much difference anyway. He found himself out on the asphalt drive, beside the gas-fitters' excavations, holding the girl by the forearms and shaking her.

If he had shaken Clare, her soft hair would have flopped backwards and forwards across her face. This girl had short spiky hair cut close to her head.

He had always been capable of raising his voice to a parade-ground bawl when he had to. 'The one idea that lodges in your miserable little minds is how to damage and destroy things, isn't it? *Isn't it?*'

'Lerrus go!' wailed the girl.

'I'll let you go when *I* decide to. Now answer me!'

'Yer hurting us!'

'Good. Count yourself lucky *I* don't go round wearing

knuckle dusters, or I might be hurting you a good deal more.'

''S only a *ring*.'

It was quite true, of course. Why bother with a knuckle duster when a Woolworth's ring with a claw setting would do the same amount of damage and double as an ornament into the bargain?

He held her wrists tightly together and pulled the ring over her knuckle. The nails were long and polished, but the cuticles were grubby and grew right up over the half-moons. Clare's hand with its small unpolished nails, the skin scored with burn-marks ...

'If you struggle like that' he said 'you'll just give yourself bruises. Don't try taking me on when it comes to brute strength. If you want this ring back, you can ask Mrs Sykes for it next week. Now get out of my sight.'

Whatever the unwritten rules were about manhandling girl pupils in the interests of discipline, he must certainly have broken them by now. Good. He let her go. She jumped back, nursing first one wrist and then the other.

'Me dad'll be coming for you!'

'Then tell him I'll be delighted to see him. And mention the damage to my car while you're at it.'

When the car roared past her at the end of the drive, she turned her head and mouthed at him, but he did not bother to stop or look back. This was the way to survive: if you can stay angry enough, nothing can crush you. Forty-three years to learn that.

One part of him was already feeling guilty and ashamed; but that was something it would have to get used to. Or that part of him could cease to exist altogether: it did not much matter which.

At intervals Clare remembered what had happened. A scraped, raw sensation from brain to gut. *God help anyone who comes within range of your kind of love.* One thing about domestic routine was that it prevented the collapse which sets in with having time to think. On Saturday evening she was clearing the table when the doorbell rang. On the path stood a plump fair-haired girl, about Clare's own age:

someone she had exchanged smiles with in the village street. Dressed at the moment, manifestly not for clearing tables, in a ground-length brown velvet caftan.

'I've come to ask the most awful thing,' she said. 'I wouldn't, only I'm absolutely desperate. My baby-sitter's let me down at twenty minutes' notice; and I knew you were a teacher. I know I've got a nerve, but you couldn't possibly come and sit in my house for a couple of hours, could you?'

'I'm sure I could,' said Clare. It was not often she had the gratification of being able to do the pleasing thing so promptly. 'But I should warn you, the children I teach are secondary age. Yours are quite small, aren't they?'

'Yes, but it'll only be the elder one. The baby's asleep already, and honestly, she never wakes up. We were going to a dinner-dance, but we'll come back straight after the dinner.'

'I'm perfectly happy to do it if you don't mind my inexperience. And there's no need for you to rush back. I've got masses of marking to do.'

'You are marvellous,' said the girl. 'Do you know which is our house?'

'One of the new ones behind the church?'

'The one at the end, with the swing in the garden. Oh, and I don't even know your name!'

'Clare Baylham. What's yours?'

'Pauline Saxtead. Look, I must dash — I've left my husband coping. I can't *say* how grateful I am.'

If that sort of gratitude came Clare's way more often, and for such a small thing ... gratitude and fuzzy good will were the only currency in which those with children could pay. And after all these years here I am joining them.

Richard said 'Wouldn't you like me to go and do it?'

She smiled at him. 'I ought to start getting some practice, oughtn't I? I'll enjoy it, I expect: if nothing else, sitting on someone else's sofa and watching someone else's telly. You don't mind, do you?'

'Not if you're sure.' Small wire hooks dragging their way down her gullet: Colin had held his palms pressed together between his knees and said *You're sure?*

'Ring up when you're ready to come home' said Richard. 'You mustn't walk up the lane in the dark. And I'll come and take over if you get too tired, or feel ill, or anything.'

She kissed him. 'See you later.' She went down the path with her bag of exercise books. From the church tower came the sound of the bellringers' practice: some squire or parishioner, hedging his bets between this world and the next, had given Gatelaw the sounds that properly belonged with a milder air and a richer soil. I shall come out on Saturday evenings, she thought: baby-sitting, or bell-ringing, or whatever harmless things people do here. I shall have my evenings free, for the first time in my life.

Every domestic or neighbourly task done — each sensible, moderate step in an orderly existence — would be another stage of healing, if she could only last it out.

Only I want it to go on hurting, because after that he'll be even further away. He thought he wanted to understand, but he didn't. Like Richard . . . only I knew better with Richard.

The new houses were tastefully and expensively harmonised with the village and the churchyard: local stone and slate, clean square lines, small leaded windows. Only the pine-and-aluminium swing in the garden was slightly, innocently out of keeping. Decent safe Habitat and Mothercare people, kindly *Guardian*-readers, living without lost causes and impossible loyalties. *God help anyone who comes within range of your kind of love.*

'This is Luke' said Pauline 'who's seven. And upstairs is Susannah, who's fifteen months. But you can forget about her.'

Luke had fair hair, much fairer than his mother's, and a pale narrow face. He turned from the television screen and gave Clare a grin filled with formalised menace.

'Luke's committed to watching this frightful old film. If you can't bear it, do make him take it into another room — that's why we got a portable.'

'I dare say I can stand it' said Clare. *I dare say I can overcome my scruples* . . . 'So long as I can blame him for it.'

'Coffee and things are in the kitchen. Lukey, when does this dreadful rubbish finish, please? . . . well, bed the *minute* it's over, then. And be civilised with Mrs Baylham, or you'll hear about it.'

Clare said 'We'll keep each other in order, won't we, Luke?'

'We must go this minute, Geoff ... Luke, be *desperately* good. 'Bye ... um, Clare.'

'Is your name Clare?' said Luke.

Outside the garden gate Pauline and her husband were getting into a brown estate car with two child seats in the back. She had wanted time to ask what to do if the baby *did* wake up. She settled apprehensively into a green corduroy armchair. The whole room seemed much less severe, as well as much more untidy, than the equivalent in her own house.

'Well,' she said 'Clare is what my friends call me.'

'I'll call you "Auntie" if you *like*' said Luke kindly.

'No, that's quite all right. I don't feel ready to be called "Auntie" yet.'

'Do you know Catherine? She's Jeremy's mum.'

'I probably know her by sight.'

'She was coming here this evening, only she couldn't, because Jeremy fell out of his tree-house on to his head.'

'Oh, dear. How awful.'

'Oh, it's all right. I don't mind having you. Haven't you not got any children?'

'Not yet.'

'Are you sad?'

It seemed like weeks, or months, since Clare had felt herself smile without prior resolution. 'I expect I'd be sad if I thought I wouldn't *ever* have any.'

'Are you going to have some, then? Have you got one in your tummy now?'

'Yes, I have.'

'Can I feel? Mummy let me feel when she had Susannah there.'

If the children at school had asked anything of the sort, she would have assumed it was either prurience or aggression. 'You can if you like,' she said.'But it's still only very small. Perhaps next time I come to sit with you you'll be able to feel it moving around.'

She knew she would feel movement in the fifth month or so: she had read that up. It had not seemed physically real before.

She had meant to get on with her marking, but she could not settle: listening for stirrings from upstairs, for cries. Several times she went to the foot of the stairs to listen. Once she imagined she smelt escaping gas, and went into the kitchen to check. Pauline had left coffee things on a tray: Clare backed hastily away from the stomach-turning smell and shut the door. There was nothing in the bookshelves that seemed to justify the effort it would take to turn the pages. Were her concentration, her mental energy, ever going to come back?

She had never in her life sat and done nothing at all. She tried the television, but the standard Saturday-evening sport and mid-Atlantic melodrama seemed marginally less appealing even than 3T's exercise books. If she had the gramophone on, she might not hear if a child cried. She resigned herself to the marking.

> *elvis presley who was cald the king was born in memphis* (rather startling in the context, that *ph*) *tennese in 1934 and dide in 1977, this is old for a pop singer, when elvis presley dide all the pop lovers in the world were sad he was the gretest pop singer that ever livd, his most fames discs were hert brek hotel and rock a hula baby* . . .

There seemed to be no sign, even after six years, that this curious necrophily would ever come to an end. She wrote at the bottom of the page:

> *I liked this, but I should have found it easier to read if you had kept your sentences short. Do you remember the lessons we had on full stops?* (Avoid rhetorical questions, Clare, you fool: they invite the answer no.)
>
> *Also, do remember that the names of people and places always have a capital letter, like this: 'Memphis', 'Elvis'. When you use the title of something, like a song or a book, underline it, or use speech marks, like this, 'Heartbreak Hotel'.*

There was little chance that her comments would have any effect. She had abandoned her already clear handwriting and taken to printing, but even so, one of them had said kindly the other day 'Yer needn't write such a lot at the bottom, Miss: I can't read yer writing anyway'. But the only individual attention most of 3T would ever get was in the correcting of their exercise books. There was no chance of giving them individual attention in the classroom: on the simple practical level, the desks were too close together for that, and there were at least half a dozen children in each class on whom she could not afford to turn her back for more than twenty seconds.

Andy Reid's book.

The person i wold like to meet is the yorksher ripper, he rapd and murderd woemn, he had the rigth hidere ...

The right *what?* She tried saying it aloud. *Idea.* Anyway, was this one to be taken to the Head of Lower School, to be ignored, or for her to deal with herself? After a minute she put a single red line through the whole page, and wrote at the bottom:

I think you wrote this mainly to see what I'd do about it. I'm not going to mark it: it's best forgotten about. You must write me another piece, this time about someone you really would like to meet (but supposing Andy Reid really would like to meet the Yorkshire Ripper?). *What are you interested in — sport, pop music, inventions? Write about someone connected with these, something that gives pleasure to people or is useful.*

How's that for imposing your values on children? If the second piece of work were ever going to be done, it would certainly mean a detention. *There have to be some victims when we get social change,* Janet had said. And Richard, *Can't you see it as a challenge?*

As she picked the third exercise book from the pile, she heard a whimper from upstairs; then another, a kind of tuning-up; then — experimentally at first, but with growing authority — a small child began to cry.

In the one room of his house which had an open fire, Colin had already spent two hours of Saturday night marking twenty books. That was only two-thirds of a set, and there were two more sets to be marked by Monday. He sighed ostentatiously, sensed Judith opening her mouth to say something and then shutting it again. Upstairs, the monotonous ground-bass thump of Edmund's latest pop record came to an end, for perhaps the twelfth time that evening. Judith went to the door and called: 'No more tonight, *please*, Ed: there's a love.'

'OK.'

Three minutes later, crashing orchestral noises, Radio 3 at concert pitch, came from the other bedroom. Colin dropped his pile of exercise books — momentarily as a nervous reaction, then deliberately. He let them skid over the carpet. Judith drew in her breath. He got up, opened the door and bellowed at full volume: 'Francis! Turn that appalling racket *off! Now!*'

The music went off. There was no further sound from upstairs, either of apology or of expostulation. He went back, picked up a single exercise book from the carpet and sat down again.

Judith's face was turned aside. Her cheeks under the smooth curve of grey hair were bright.

'Col, that was nasty.'

'I don't see why I shouldn't have some peace and quiet in my own house. I earn the money round here.'

'That's not fair. You know how hard I've tried to find something ...'

'That's right, throw it at me. I've risen as far as I'm ever going to rise, and I can't earn enough to educate our children properly and keep you in the style ...'

'Col, shut up. Just *shut up!* I'm sorry you're having a bad time at work, but *it is not our fault.* Will you please just kindly remember that the rest of us also have a right to live?'

Colin banged the door hard behind him, knowing it

would bring soot down the chimney, spraying over the carpet and the scattered exercise books. In the hallway he took the second batch of books out of his case and carried them into the dining room, which was cold. They only used the central heating now when they had to; the house, with its plasterboard walls, and nineteen-sixties' picture windows, poured most of its heat straight out on to the hillside. That must be at least partly why his hands had begun to shake again.

In the room upstairs with the night-light, Pauline Saxtead's baby was lying on her back in the cot, her wet eyes staring up at the ceiling. She turned over on to her side, stared at Clare for a second, then rolled on to her back and began her steady wailing again.

   Clare sat down on the floor beside the cot, and put her hand in between the bars. The small fingers closed round hers, but the howling did not stop, even for a second. From over the landing, where Luke was, there came a sleepy, faintly protesting noise.

   She was not sure where to take hold of the little girl or how to lift her, and when she did, it was a heavier weight than she had expected. For a moment the noise stopped, then started again: mouth opened squarely, eyes screwed up. Going down the stairs had become alarming. With Susannah in her arms she could not see where she was going, but did not dare to let go even with one hand to hold on to the banister. She sat down on the top step, one shoulder against the stair wall, and shuffled herself and the baby down a step at a time. On my backside, how thoroughly appropriate. It was unreasonable to mind about loss of dignity when there was no one else to see.

   In the sitting room she managed to jerk the television set into life with her elbow. At the sight of the newsreader's moon-face Susannah's eyes flickered. Instead of her next scream a small hiccuping sob came out. Clare propped the baby up on her lap, to face the screen. 'That's more interesting than staring at the ceiling, isn't it?' she said. The month's trade figures would not have done as a hypnotic for 3T, but Susannah's little body, at once taut and inert, began to shudder into quiet against her own.

'Were you having a dream?' said Clare to her. 'I suppose you do have dreams, do you?' And if a child of that age did dream, what mechanism could it possibly have for separating its subconscious from the huge, noisy, arbitrary scenes in the waking world?

Luke was standing in the doorway: hair tangled, eyes still half-closed. He was wearing pseudo-Japanese pyjamas, with a bird, or perhaps a stylised aeroplane, appliquéd on to the front. 'Heard Susannah crying' he said.

Clare managed to free one arm and hold it out. 'I hoped she wouldn't wake you up.'

The television screen had become occupied by an American car speeding down a freeway. As the credits appeared, so did the muzzle of a gun through the car window. 'Luke' said Clare hastily 'do you know how to turn that television off?'

"Course I do. Can't we not watch that?'

'No. It might make Susannah frightened again, mightn't it?'

'Susannah's a wally.' But he turned the television off. Susannah's eyes, as clear and fixed as grey glass marbles, lingered on the blank screen. She drew a quavering, threatening breath.

'Luke, what does Mummy do to stop Susannah crying?'

'Sometimes she changes her nappy.'

'I don't think I'm up to that' said Clare. 'What else could I do?'

Luke, thumb hovering near his mouth, curled up against her. She put an arm round him. 'Sometimes Mummy sings to her.'

For a moment Clare's mind went blank of anything except hymns. Once she had sung in chamber choirs and college musical societies, but school Assembly was the only practice she had had for years.

'Well, I can try, I suppose,' she said.

'Will you sing to me too?'

'All right. Just for a little while.'

Her voice had been mezzo-soprano, untrained and not very powerful, but accurate and sweet. It was still there: breathy at first, but soon warming up. Luke would certainly despise nursery rhymes, but the only other thing she could think of, a legacy from her own primary-school days, would be almost meaningless to a north-eastern child:

> *The banks are Rushy Green,*
> *The banks are rushy-green,*
> *And deep enough, and steep enough,*
> *To hide a runaway queen ...*

Susannah turned round and gazed at the singer. Luke's thumb settled into his mouth and his head lolled against Clare's side. "Nother one song.'

> *King's Cross, what shall we do?*
> *His purple robe is rent in two.*
> *Out of his crown he's torn the gems;*
> *He's thrown his sceptre into the Thames ...*

They were both asleep. She could carry Susannah, but not without waking Luke; and she did not dare to try to carry Luke. After a while the central heating went off, and she began to get cold. *Frigid bitch.* But that was not his kind of vocabulary: she had said it for him. *You don't understand what you've done.* I'll have the rest of my life to find out.

'Oh, Lord' said Pauline Saxtead. 'Bloody Susannah didn't wake up and yell after all my promises, did she?'

'It doesn't matter' said Clare. 'Honestly. Only I hope they haven't got cold. I was so afraid of waking them up again.'

'They won't have got cold. Small children carry their own central heating around with them. Geoff, will you deal with these monsters while I drive Clare home? She looks half dead.'

It was raining. The windscreen wipers chopped up the pattern of the headlights on the road in front of them.

'You must let me know what I can do for you in exchange' said Pauline.

Clare said sleepily 'You honestly don't have to feel like that. But if you like, in about seven months' time you can do the same for me.'

'Does that mean you're having a baby?'

'Yes. Not before time, some people would say.'

'Oh, blow some people. Are you pleased?'

Direct questions of this kind had been easier to take from Luke. 'I *think* so' she said.

'Oh, you will be when it's arrived. Are you going to carry on with your job?'

'People keep asking me that. I'm getting quite embarrassed about saying no.'

'Why the hell should you be? The minute you're free you must come and have coffee or something. And I'll introduce you to the baby-sitting circle. Oh dear, I hope you aren't feeling too ghastly — I'd never have asked you to come this evening if I'd known'.

'I'm perfectly all right. The only things that turn me up are coffee and cigarette smoke, and those are fairly easy to avoid.'

'I feel so dreadfully guilty' said Pauline.

Social guilt, drawing room guilt, is quite different from the other kind. But not necessarily to be despised for that reason. Clare, working hard to keep her eyes open, said 'Don't be, really. I've got to learn, haven't I?'

Simply in order to get out of the house on Monday, Colin rushed his sons through breakfast, dragooned them into the car, and left them at the railway station a full twenty minutes before their train was due. He arrived in the Tenter Street staffroom before anyone else was there.

No one — certainly not in Alderman Cassop, anyway — ever picked up the *Times Educational Supplement* for the sake of the articles in it. It was the section marked 'Appointments' that sold the paper to a hundred thousand staffrooms. Colin rarely looked even at that section. He was trapped, he knew that. A dizzying half of every salary cheque went into the school fees, and he had had his last promotion. Edmund was just fifteen: for three and a half years — more — financial considerations would be the only kind Colin could take into account. By the time he was free to look around him, try for something else even if it meant a step downwards, he would be forty-seven, in a profession where it would soon be possible to retire at fifty. Those three years might just as well have been thirty.

He looked at the 'Appointments' section today, though. *Anything* ... move the boys in the middle of their 'O' and 'A' level courses, shunt them back into a state school — just *get out of here.* Or at any rate, for ten minutes pretend that you can.

The school his sons went to was advertising a Scale III post in English.

Not a Headship of Department, but it wasn't the title that mattered. How big a drop — fifteen hundred? They could save half that by all travelling together each day by car. He could find the rest *somehow,* couldn't he? Nothing of such moment could possibly hinge on eight hundred pounds a year.

Children whose parents would back the school up; children who had not been brought up simply to utter a hundred variations on the word 'no'; children for whose morals, table manners, physical safety no one would hold you responsible; children to whom you could, quite simply, teach English. Children such as he and his contemporaries had been in the days when you did not have to be rich to have such chances.

Don't get hopeful, he told himself. You know that means disaster.

'I sort of rebelled aganst this one' said Deborah. '*The Leaden Echo and the Golden Echo.* I could believe all the rest of Hopkins for as long as I was reading it — you know, the presence of God in everything, and the sacraments and the Immaculate Conception and everything—'

'Wait a minute' said Clare. 'Do you mean the Immaculate Conception, or do you mean the Virgin Birth?'

Deborah paused. 'I mean the Virgin Birth, don't I?' she said. 'And I must stop saying "sort of", I know.'

'I'm not really bullying you,' said Clare. 'Only trying to get you into shape for the interview. Now this poem. How about reading it out to me?'

> *Give beauty back, beauty, beauty, beauty, back to God,*
>   *beauty's self and beauty's giver.*
> *See; not a hair is, not an eyelash, not the least lash lost;*
>   *every hair*
> *Is, hair of the head, numbered ...*

His hair: soft and mousy-coloured. *No.*

When the thing we freely forfeit is kept with fonder a care,
Fonder a care kept than we could have kept it, kept
Far with fonder a care (and we, we should have lost it) finer,
                            fonder
A care kept. — Where kept? Do but tell us where kept, where ...

'What is it you can't swallow?' said Clare. 'The verse form, or the theology?'

'Oh, the verse form's all right. It's eccentric, but the stresses and the alliteration hold it together, just about, don't they? No, I mean all this about death not being death, if you offer everything up to God, because that's where it all came from, and He'll take it anyway ... I mean, *honestly!*

'In a way I agree with you,' said Clare. 'But is it really any different from feeling you can't share Wilfred Owen's pacifism — I seem to remember some of your lot getting quite heated over that in 'O' level year when the Falklands business was happening? There are experiences we can't all share in real life, but the poet can make us share them vicariously — do you know what vicariously means?'

'At second hand. In place of the real thing.'

'Good. Anyway, although that isn't literary criticism in itself, I think it's something we have to take on board before we can make a literary criticism. We don't usually reject Wordsworth for all that soppy nature-worship, do we? Or Yeats for the magical mumbo jumbo?'

'This seems different,' said Deborah. 'I mean, I suppose,

I can't really believe *Hopkins* believes it. When the leaden echo says "Do but tell us *where* kept" the golden echo just goes on saying "Yonder — look, look yonder". But *we* don't see what's yonder, do we? Hopkins just points at the clouds and says "Look, over there" — like someone trying to distract your attention while he grabs your handbag.'

In the lunch-hour solitude of the Tenter Street staffroom, Colin set about drafting his application. *Rowsley, Kevin Colin. Date of birth: 20th March 1940.* As a schoolboy he had kept quiet about the Kevin bit: not yet a footballer's name — embarrassingly Celtic and vaguely sissy. *Education: Stanburn Boys' Gramar School, Co. Durham, 1951- . . .* Clare was born in 1951. When she started school, a little London girl with a gingham dress and her hair in bunches, he was a Wearside sixth-former, already bespectacled. Between them they just about spanned the working life of the Butler Education Act.

'Mr Rowsley . . . I'm sorry, I can see you're busy, but could I . . . ?'

It was that tall thin girl, the probationer teacher in RE, Ted Auton's replacement. I promised to visit Ted. That's one person in the world who actually wants my company.

'Yes, of course' he said. 'Sorry, I was miles away. It's Gillian, isn't it? And I'm Colin, remember?' Somehow with people he hardly knew it was still relatively easy to be pleasant.

She said 'I don't know whether I ought to be asking you, but I'm finding it so difficult to get to know anyone, and you were kind to me on the first day of term . . .'

If Colin were going to be kind to anyone now, it would have to be in a brisk businesslike way.

'What is it? Discipline problems?'

'The thing is, some of 3G had a comic in class this morning — they weren't even bothering to hide it. So I took it away from them . . . and it was really —you know— pornographic. I sort of wondered what to do about it.'

'Take it to the Head of Lower School' said Colin promptly. 'That's Fred Errington — the short one with the loud voice who does Assembly. Drop the comic on his desk, and if he tries to throw it back at you, tell him it's from me.'

'Thank you' she said humbly. 'I will if there's nothing else I can do. Only I thought ... well, it is sort of my responsibility, isn't it?'

Colin felt a dreary sense of shame. 'I'm afraid I was thinking of it just in terms of expediency' he said. 'Of course you feel you've got to try and cope with the moral side of it too, don't you?'

She said 'All we ever did at College was about respecting other people's beliefs, and caring ... they sort of implied that would solve all the problems.'

'I bet they did' said Colin. 'Look, I'm not trying to duck out of this' — he was, of course, but professional etiquette was on his side as well — 'only I haven't taught Religious Knowledge for years, and that was in a church school, where at least we all spoke the same language. Wouldn't your Head of Department be better equipped to help?'

Her pale eyes lingered on him in disappointment. 'He said he'd talk to me about it some time. He said he was sure I'd cope somehow.'

'Oh, Lord. Well, to be fair to him, he didn't know he was Head of Department till the first day of this term. And of course all those low-ability classes were meant for Ted Auton, not for you. Anyway, let me think. If it's 3G I'm afraid you won't be able to be very abstract or philosophical about it.'

'I wasn't ever very good at the philosophical bits of RE anyway.'

The philosophical *bits* ... no more than averagely bright herself, thinking at eighteen that teaching would be a safe public-spirited job; imagining her own religious faith (based on what? — a desire for order, the wish to look up to something?) would equip her to teach RE as a school subject. Taught at College that it was about being nice to people and finding good in everything.

'Have you got the comic with you?' he asked. If her idea of pornography was something bosomy in a swimsuit, then he could advise her to leave well alone.

She hesitated. 'Yes, but ...'

'I'm afraid you'll have to learn to be pretty hard-boiled, Gillian. Even quite nice children will go out of their way to embarrass you if they think they can do it. But don't worry about sparing *my* blushes. I've got two almost grown-up sons, which must prove something, mustn't it?' *Don't show it to Rowsley*, they used to say at Stanburn Grammar School as they passed round the innocuous pin-ups of their time. *He'll have to tell it in Confession.*

In an enlarged frame in the centre of the page, a naked girl sprawled on her back: breasts ballooning, knees apart. Her face was lifted in gleeful invitation; in an inset frame in the corner an erect penis and testicles pointed towards her gaping vulva. Far too obvious an onslaught to arouse the faintest quiver of lust in him now.

'I didn't know the Stanburn newsagents ran to this sort of thing, even these days' he said. 'I'm afraid that means there'll be more where this came from. Gillian, I'm sure they told you at College that you could be a force to counterbalance this sort of thing, but you shouldn't expect too much. The most you can do is to put your own point of view, and hope at least some of them get the message. Now, how many of them saw this object?'

'Only four that I know of. Two boys and two girls. I was going to tear it up and drop it in the wastepaper bin — you know, make a sort of demonstration — but then I thought some of the others would put the pieces together and see it, so I just brought it out with me.'

'Well, that showed excellent sense. You've only been here a month, and you've been thrown right in at the deep end. Any half-decent school, even these days, would have tried to give you a bit more help.'

She swallowed convulsively. Lord, I can't cope with it if she cries. Was it because of the glimpse he had given her of how things might have been? Perhaps one way of surviving was not even to expect justice or a fair chance. He said hurriedly: 'If the rest of the class didn't see it, as far as you know, then leave it like that. Some of the others will still be very innocent, hard as that is to believe. If it were an intelligent class I'd say have a discussion about it, bring it out into the open — but I'm afraid this lot would miss the point and just get over-excited. I think I'd either leave it altogether, or else just get the four offenders together privately and tell them ... well, whatever you see fit to tell them.'

She said 'If I was allowed to talk to them about God and that, and the commandments, it would be easy ...'

Would it indeed? Don't come to me for sympathy there.

'Well, if you think you'd be safer just making some general ethical point, could you try the line that pornography is exploitation? The girls at any rate might be mature enough to understand that.'

'The thing is, though ... I mean, in this picture, the girl's enjoying it, isn't she? I don't think they'd understand. I hoped there would be something you could tell me to do.'

Colin thought of his unwritten *curriculum vitae*. There were only ten minutes left before the end of the lunch hour. 'If I knew a formula I certainly wouldn't hold it back from you. But I'm afraid if you wanted a decisive answer you've come to the wrong place. I'm sorry I haven't been more help.'

'No, you have,' she said suddenly. Was she in her turn trying to be kind? 'You haven't just brushed me off. I know I've got to do it myself really. But I felt as though nobody cared at all what happened until I made a real mess of things, and then they'd all blame me.'

She was at least twenty years younger than he. Ten years younger even than Clare. It was not her fault that her ability did not match her vocation; and certainly not her fault that she was facing, unarmed and uncounselled, a test none of them might have been able to pass. The selection of classes she was teaching was indirectly Colin's responsibility: the staff meeting and the victory they imagined they had won. Ted had escaped the blow and let it fall on her instead.

'Look,' he said. 'Give me a note of whenever you have them next. They'll tell you they've got to go shopping for their mothers, or that they've got a hospital appointment, but just keep the four sinners back till I arrive. I don't know that there's really anything I can do, but at least we can back each other up. And my advanced years may lend a certain spurious authority to the proceedings.'

Some flicker in her face told him that 'spurious' was a word she did not know. He was glad, in a way, to have registered that, because it made her pathetic gratitude a little less shaming.

My dear Clare,
Yes, of course I remember you, and have often wondered how you were getting on. You have reappeared just in time, for I shall be retiring at the end of this year. No doubt you thought I must already be at least eighty at the time when you were coming to me for tutorials!

You will not find College quite the same place these days. I must confess, my dear Clare, that our new young men do tend to make less *fuss* about examinations than certain young ladies. All the same, I cannot feel quite as overjoyed about their presence as some members of Governing Body would like me to feel.

The Bursar (now male also – ô *tempora*) asks me to say that there *are* two free rooms at the moment. They are not at all grand ones, but if part of the aim of your visit is to give your pupil a taste of College life, they should do rather well. I shall look forward to seeing you again.

Yours as ever
Eunice Kennett

To be able to parody yourself as self-consciously and enjoyably as that must be one of the greatest privileges of education. Clare showed Deborah the letter. It did not raise the flicker of a smile. 'That does mean it's all right, doesn't it?' she said anxiously.

'Yes, it does.'

'Clare ... I don't know what sort of clothes to wear.'

That was something else Clare had forgotten: to be always worrying about getting that kind of detail wrong, and usually finding out when the time came that you *had* got it wrong. Unable to conceive that you might in time overcome all the hurdles in the social obstacle course, and then find your self-made obstacles left.

'Well ... nothing to make you look older than you are; and nothing that looks dressed-up. When I went for my interview my mother made me turn up in an outfit that would have done credit to a fifty-year-old — and then of course everyone else was in miniskirts. It's not that *they'll* mind what you wear: it really is that kind of free society. The point is for it not to worry *you*.'

I'm selling it too hard. Freedom makes you sick, like drink, if you have too much too quickly. You can't do it for her. You can't have your turn again.

The chrysanthemums in Ted's garden were limp and rusty: no one had dead-headed them. Ted had put the lost weight back on, but his face was as grey and heavy as before. Colin stood halfway to the sitting room door, waiting for permission to go.

'I haven't asked after Judith,' said Ted.
'She's very well.'
'The children?'
'Fine. Huge and loud.'
'And what about you?'
'Fine too. Bad-tempered, that's all.'
Ted looked up and across at him.
'Whatever it is, Colin,' he said 'whether it's just the teaching, or whether there's more to it than that — don't just swallow it down. Or you'll end up like me.'

Colin had not intended to answer. He said: 'I've got to swallow it. There's nothing else to do with it.'

'Men aren't supposed to talk to each other like this. You can put it down to my invalid state. Will you bite my head off if I ask you what the trouble is?'

Once I was contented and didn't even know it. And threw it away. The degradation of telling.

'I won't bite your head off,' said Colin. 'But there's nothing to tell.'

'I didn't think there would be.'

Ted framed by the closing door: his lips rimmed with dark blue, the same colour as the ink spots they used to shake from their dip-pens on to the floor, at Stanburn Boys' Grammar School in the fifties.

IV
November 1983

VII

Deborah, red-faced, her long hair stringy with sweat, came puffing into the station waiting room with two or three minutes to spare. All Clare's agitation and annoyance turned immediately to compunction.

'Come on, Deborah, sit down and get your breath. I knew we should have arranged to pick you up somewhere.'

'Oh, I'm sorry, the bus ...'

'Calm down. You haven't met Richard, my husband, have you?'

The mental act of going over the top, as Deborah stuck out her wrist to shake hands like an adult, was clearly visible.

Richard said: 'Hallo, Deborah, I've heard a lot about you.'

Oh, *Richard*! But Deborah said bravely: 'How do you do, Dr Baylham.' She'd even deduced, or remembered, Richard's PhD.

'I think,' said Richard, 'that for my own peace of mind I'd better get you two ladies on to the platform. Deborah, let me take that case.'

It was the old-fashioned train with corridors and compartments. Clare felt self-conscious about kissing Richard goodbye in front of Deborah. 'You do know what you're supposed to be having to eat today and tomorrow, don't you?' she said. 'There's a casserole for tonight that you've only got to heat up, and ...'

'Yes, *miss*,' said Richard. 'Is she like this at school, Deborah?'

'All right, then,' said Clare. 'Starve and see if I care. Goodbye, love: enjoy your training course. I'll see you on Wednesday. Mind you behave yourself.'

'No, *you* behave yourself. Keep her in order in Oxford, will you, Deborah?'

He gave a single, cheerful wave and then turned towards the barrier. Looking at his receding back, Clare had a momentary, hallucinatory sense of alarm. She sat down rather abruptly, and Deborah, staccato with anxiety, said 'Clare, are you all right? You're not feeling ill?'

'I just haven't woken up properly, that's all. I'm all right in the mornings, contrary to tradition. I have to watch it sometimes in the early evening: the bus ride home isn't all that good for my inside ... for goodness' sake, why on earth are we talking about the state of my guts?'

Deborah said suddenly 'It'll be funny for you, won't it, going back to Oxford, now that ... I mean, it must make everything different.'

'Being pregnant? Well, it does when I remember about it. But most of the time quite honestly I don't remember.'

'It doesn't show.'

'Well, it's only ten weeks old or so. With luck it still won't show by the time I leave, and some of my least favourite pupils can be kept in ignorance.'

'I can't imagine what school is going to be like when you're not there.'

'You won't be there much longer yourself: that's the thing to hang on to.'

On the estate where the Rowsleys lived, you had only to look through the front bedroom window to see where the postman had got to. Colin had been haunting the letter box for nearly three weeks. When the envelope with the printed address on the flap came through, he was waiting to catch it.

Dear Applicant,
    Thank you for your interest in the post advertised at this school. More than five hundred candidates, most with excellent qualifications, applied for this post. It has now been offered to ...

The lucky candidate had come down from a Deputy

Headmastership in a comprehensive school to get the post. He stood in the hall with the letter in his hand. Judith, in her dressing gown, came out of the kitchen. 'Anything interesting, or just bills?'

'I wasn't even short-listed for that job.' When the blow chose its moment to start giving pain it would be at some unexpected time when he was unprepared to cope with it. Clare, he thought childishly, Clare, I'm tired of being a good loser.

'Oh,' said Judith. 'Oh, dear. I'm sorry.' She went back into the kitchen. A minute later she put her head out again. 'I *am* sorry, Col. But you know, if you *had* got it, I don't see how we could possibly have managed.'

If he had had a serious illness, or if he had lost his job altogether, she would have been the standard good northern mother holding the family together. She had a determined, narrow courage: the squirmings of wounded pride and the hammering fists of the trapped were what she could not deal with.

He could stand just so many humiliations. He would not try again.

Deborah had been to Spain, but scarcely ever to England south of the Tees. She gazed out of the window at the Great Plain of York unrolling past them. Clare thought of the wolds to the east, the Vale of Pickering and the coast. St Christopher striding through the waves; Adam and Eve stepping out of hell. If in some remove other than her memory, she and Colin still stood side by side in the summer-evening shadows of the church, looking up at the paintings ... dazzled; everything still possible.

She had not seen him once since that final appalling moment under the noise of the bell in the book room; but half a dozen times a day she would imagine she picked him out in a crowd. Any man with a tall angular build, any pair of heavy-framed spectacles. Colin, I didn't understand: I never expected anyone to love me. What Richard loves is someone he invented, or I did. I always knew people would turn away from me if they could see.

The compartment door slid back. 'Sheffield in fifteen minutes. Anyone for Sheffield?'

'The last frontier of the north,' said Clare to Deborah, smiling across at her.

The Rowsley boys had school on Saturday mornings; their half term, invariably out of synchronisation with Colin's, did not begin till the following week. Judith was out shopping. Colin, never very skilful with his hands, was trying to double-glaze the dining room windows with cling-film. One of the PE staff had said it worked up to a point.

Outside the windows, the garden was still cheerful with the Michaelmas daisies: one clump of chrysanthemums, in a sheltered corner, was alive too. The trouble about the chrysanthemums was that they reminded him, not only of the ravaged specimens in Ted's garden, but of the pattern of rays made by the headlights of an oncoming car: *Not yours, Colin. Richard's, not yours.*

The only remedy for such a many-layered state of misery was activity. At the moment he was spending more hours on preparation and marking than he had ever spent in his life before: but that was partly because it all seemed to be taking twice as long as it used to. Often he would find that he had read through a whole piece of work without registering a word of it.

The telephone rang. Judith, to say that the car had broken down somewhere? The boys, wanting to be collected? Stiffly, cursing his awkward shoulder and hip as well as the telephone, he lowered himself from the window ledge and went out into the hall.

'Mr Rowsley?'

'Yes?' He could not place the woman's voice.

'This is Phyllis Auton — Edward Auton's wife.'

There was only one thing she could be ringing him up to tell him.

Deborah said 'Clare, were you always going to go to Oxford? I mean, was it sort of laid down for you?'

'Not in the least,' said Clare. 'Or rather, *I* had it in mind from an early age, but it took other people longer to come round to the idea.'

The railway line between Sheffield and Derby, so weakened by subsidence and old pit-workings that trains had to inch their way along it, did not seem to have improved with the years. Twelve years ago she had made this journey in reverse, coming from Oxford to Durham. *Don't do the Dip Ed in Oxford*, Eunice had said. *It's too much of a come-down*. It was only a standby anyway, because barring accidents she would be coming back to Oxford to do research ...

Deborah said 'Did your parents want you to go somewhere else, then? Or didn't they want you to go to university at all?'

'I've never worked that one out myself' said Clare. She was surprised at the ease with which she said it. 'They were always very keen for me to do well at school, but somehow they didn't seem to expect it to lead anywhere. I think they'd really have liked me to go to a teacher-training college and live at home.'

'Were you the only child, then?'

'No, I've got two brothers. But they're both years older than I am, so I suppose it was like being the only child in a way.'

'Did your brothers go to Oxford?'

'No. I'm the only one who went to university at all. Ironically enough they've both done far better professionally than I have. Actually I think that was at the bottom of it all – my parents didn't like the girl in the family to be the only one to get a degree.'

'That's *awful*' said Deborah. 'Thank goodness I haven't got any brothers.'

'I suppose it is rather awful, really. Perhaps I'm not being quite fair: I don't suppose they formulated it as consciously as that. My school weren't madly keen, either, but they did back me up, for which I've always been grateful.'

'I just assumed you must have come from the sort of family where going to Oxford was taken for granted.'

'I don't know why it seemed such an outrageous notion, really. We didn't have any money, but my father's people came from Northern Ireland, where everyone's supposed to be so dead keen on education; and he got himself an external degree at Birkbeck by working himself to death in the evenings, so you'd think he'd have been delighted, wouldn't you, that things weren't so difficult for me? Parents are funny creatures: I probably shan't do any better myself.'

She never had been able to be or do quite what they wanted, had she? Not after she had stopped being a little-girl doll for them all to play with. A pretty baby who eventually had become a pretty enough woman, but who in between had been a pudgy child and adolescent who never showed any emotion, desirable or undesirable; a clever child who was clever only at the subjects least likely to be 'useful'. Not just the only girl in the family, but so much the youngest that she was the only post-war child in it: growing up in a world suddenly full not only of goodies off the ration, but of every possible moral and physical danger to little girls: from all of which she must be protected at any cost.

'Anyway,' said Deborah 'you got there in the end.'

'Yes. I'm just rather sorry I always had to put up such a fight for everything. I suspect it all got out of proportion along the way. What about you, Deborah? Your parents were a bit apprehensive — are they reassured now?'

'I think so. I've been playing it down as much as I can — actually I think I may have overdone it. They've got the idea now that I'm just doing it as a try-on. They think I don't really mind where I go.'

That might, or might not, have been an invitation to Clare to probe further into Deborah's private wishes and fears. She would have liked to know; but she could not do it. Whether it was respect for Deborah's privacy, or fear of a snub, of fear of exposing herself, the glass wall was there between them. Sooner or later, it always was.

'What are you reading?' she asked. Deborah had had the book beside her on the seat ever since they left.

Deborah's eyes slid away from hers. 'I'm afraid you'll think this is terribly corny,' she said. 'It's *Jude the Obscure*.'

'Why should I think that was corny?'

'You know ... the poor boy trying to get to Oxford, and all that ...'

Christminster, real or miraged. No need to enquire further what Deborah felt. 'Well, you must have a better chance than poor old Jude, at least. Even with comprehensive education.'

Colin heard himself say into the telephone: 'Good morning. Mr Briggs?'

'Speaking. What can I do for you?'

The vicar of Stanburn had a carefully warm voice.

'My name is Colin Rowsley. I'm not a parishioner of yours, but I'm ringing on behalf of someone who is: Mrs Phyllis Auton.'

'Yes?'

'I'm sure you know what I'm going to say.'

'All the same — perhaps it would be best if you were to tell me in your own words?'

Write on both sides of the paper. Do not use the same material in more than one question.

'Mrs Auton's husband died suddenly yesterday, as you know.' (Ted on the floor by the bookcase. Thoughtlessly or with intention, he had raised his arms above his head to lift a book down. She found him when she came in from work.) 'I gather that she spoke to you about the burial rites.'

'Yes, she did.'

'I understand that you refused to conduct them according to Cranmer's prayer book, which both of them wished for.'

'You are referring to the 1662 prayer book?'

'You must know its date better than I do. I mean the traditional Anglican prayer book.'

'You say you are not a parishioner of this church?'

'I'm not a member of the Church of England at all. However ...'

'Then perhaps you are unfamiliar with some of the

changes that have taken place. The parish council decided several years ago that all services in this church would be conducted according to the Alternative Service Book. That's the modernised rite, and we've found that most parishioners are very happy with it.'

'That may be true,' said Colin. 'I know Mr Auton was not at all happy with it.'

'You are some relation?'

'No. But I should say I knew him as well as most people know one another. And I most certainly knew his views on religious matters.' Except the most important thing, of course. *My faith vanished some years ago ... not especially attractive, is it?*

'Then you will probably be aware' said Mr Briggs 'that he very seldom attended this church, at least in the time that I have been here. And Mrs Auton told me frankly that she herself is an agnostic. I appreciate that you are supporting her in a spirit of chivalry, but ...'

Colin knew only that the word 'chivalry', on top of the patronising manner and the pedantic speech, made him think he was speaking to Kettleby. Outside, he heard Judith backing the car up towards the garage. He allowed a deliberate fury to rip into the telephone wires.

'I'm not an Anglican; but I am, or I was, a Roman Catholic. One of the things I detest about my own Church is what it's done to its liturgy. But at least the Church of Rome has some vestigial sense that it exists for sinners, and not just for committees of the righteous.'

Judith was standing beside him, a shopping bag in each hand. 'Col, what in Heaven's name ... ?'

Mr Briggs would not relish being unfavourably compared with his brother-in-Christ down the road. 'In addition' Colin said, ignoring Judith 'I always had the impression that the Church of England prided itself on *not* being an authoritarian institution. If that's not the case after all, a good deal of English literature and history will have to be rewritten. If I have to get the Archbishop of York himself to the telephone I'll do it if it'll get Ted Auton buried as he wanted to be buried.'

Judith put her shopping bags down and closed the front door quietly.

The voice at the other end of the line said calmly 'Perhaps I had not fully realised that there were Christians to whom this kind of consideration was still so important. You may tell Mrs Auton that I shall be happy to use the 1662 prayer book on this occasion.'

'Thank you,' said Colin — not knowing what to do with his voice, since anger was no longer appropriate. 'I'll tell her, of course ... thank you.' He put down the receiver.

Judith said 'Ted?' Colin nodded. He sat down weakly at the bottom of the stairs, arms folded tightly across his stomach — partly, he supposed, for sympathy; but partly because that was where, at the moment, it hurt.

Judith sat down beside him, put an arm round his shoulders.

'Oh, Col, I *am* sorry. Poor old love, you have had an awful time this term, haven't you?'

In ways you've never dreamed of, Judith. And never must.

'Not just me,' he said. 'What about Ted?' *Unhouseled, disappointed, unanneal'd ...*

'He's out of pain now' said Judith. 'Isn't he?'

'How do you know?'

Clare said to Deborah 'There isn't much of a view coming in from the station end. But look, the Radcliffe Observatory, with the golden ball on top. The dome of the Sheldonian. And that bell-shaped tower over there is Tom Tower – Christ Church.'

In all Clare's undergraduate time, Oxford station had been faded and shabby almost beyond belief, as though proving some kind of point: peeling paint, straw blowing about in the wind. At some point in her absence it had grown a gleaming new concourse.

'I thought we'd have some lunch' she said 'and a walk round, before we go up to College. Deborah, you aren't eighteen yet, are you?'

'No, not till April. Why?'

'I was thinking about pubs ... oh, damn it, you can have orange juice if you insist on being law-abiding, but otherwise I'll buy you a drink. Let's do it properly.'

Deborah in the King's Arms, with a glass of white wine: her hair brushed back. Wearing a polo-necked black jumper and an Indian cotton wrapover skirt which disguised her heavy hips and thighs. She looked intelligent and sensible and healthy: which of course she was — all three. Of such is the kingdom of Heaven.

'Is there any particular thing you want to see?' asked Clare. 'Or will you trust my judgment?'

'I'll go anywhere and do anything' said Deborah promptly.

'There's no need to put it so dramatically. I'm not likely to suggest doing anything very rash. Well, then, we'll do the Clare Baylham guided tour, which starts outside this pub, and finishes tomorrow afternoon with Evensong at Christ Church.'

'Clare, I'm not at all religious. I didn't think *you* were.'

'I'm not — at least not in the sense you mean. I did make a brief attempt to be, while I was here: partly because it was an Oxford-y thing to be, and partly because my parents were high-minded atheists.'

'Was that your way of breaking out?'

'You must admit it's a very up-market form of adolescent rebellion' said Clare. 'But I couldn't keep it up. All the same, Anglican evensong is something no one should be without.'

A November evening in her first term, and a thick mist transforming the walk from North to South Oxford. After London, it was so silent. Only the unseen bicycle wheels whizzing past broke the quiet down St Giles, and the Cornmarket, and St Aldates. And out of the fog leapt the great golden-brown bell shape of Tom Tower.

The nave of the Cathedral half in shadow, only the choirboys' faces illuminated above their ruffs and scarlet cassocks. *If I take the wings of the morning, and dwell in the uttermost parts of the sea; Even there also shall thy hand lead me ... The mountains skipped like rams, and the little hills like young sheep.*

Deborah said 'I ought to know the Psalms and the Book of Common Prayer. I'm always finding things that turn out to be quotations from them. But in RE classes we always used that Revised Standard Bible when we used one at all. Mr Auton gave us a couple of lessons once on the Bible as poetry, though. I've never forgotten those.'

She led Deborah out to the Sheldonian; then the Bodleian, the Turl, New College Lane and Longwall Street round to Magdalen and the High. It was tourists' weather, cold and bright. Saturday: no scholars' or commoners' gowns on the street, but plenty of cheerful bicycles. The only bad moment was on Magdalen Bridge. Deborah said 'Oh, this is where Hopkins gave his pocket of pence to the cheery beggar, isn't it? Could we stop for a minute?' They leant on the edge and looked out and down along the Cherwell with its double fringe of autumn trees.

More than two years since Christ Church had reared up through the fog to greet her that night; and this time it had been a clear night; and it had been very late, because she was going to have to climb back into College when she got back there, and she did not see how she was going to find the energy. She was standing, had been standing for some time, on the bridge facing out towards the river, her hands on the parapet in front of her. And a voice behind her asked 'Everything all right, miss?'

She realised at once that the policeman thought she might be planning to jump; and she was not the kind who jumped, so she turned round at once, and said she was quite all right, and was just about to go. Her voice came out polite and composed, but tears never stopped running down her cheeks while she was saying it; and that was bad luck, because for all the tears she shed during that last year, no one else ever caught her out. But the young were, mercifully, expected to be vulnerable and highly-strung there: he only said 'Good night, miss,' and went on his way. Poor young lady, perhaps he had thought. Or silly bitch ... supposing, perhaps, a broken love affair.

> *Beyond Magdalen and by the Bridge, on a place called there*
> *the Plain,*
> *In Summer, in a burst of summertime*
> *Following falls and falls of rain ... a gift should cheer him*
> *Like that poor pocket of pence, poor pence of mine.*

'Which College was Hopkins at?' asked Deborah.

'Balliol — couldn't have been anywhere else. You've got quite involved with Hopkins, haven't you?'

'Yes. Which *is* rather funny, after what I said to you about not being religious. Where did Philip Larkin go?'

'St John's. I'm sorry to have to tell you that that and Balliol are two of the ugliest colleges in the University, but if you want to go and make your genuflections there we will.'

By the time Clare had paid off their taxi at the Woodstock Road entrance, Deborah had gone quiet. Clare said 'I've worn you out, haven't I, with all this manic energy? You should have said something.'

Deborah shook her head. 'No, you haven't. I've just got towers and spires floating in front of my eyes. It's a lot, all of a sudden ... do you know what I mean?'

Clare was going to touch Deborah's arm, but her nerve failed her. She said instead 'I think when we've found our rooms, such as they may be, you might just rest and get your breath for half an hour or so. I hope you're not expecting much more than four walls and a gas fire, because I suspect that's all it'll be.' They went into the lodge, and she tapped on the window.

The day she had arrived there for her scholarship interview she wore an ugly green jersey dress with a skirt that was too long, and a winter coat with a brooch on the lapel, as worn by a middle-aged middle-class woman on a night out. Her stockings had been splashed all up the back with mud. The porter had snapped out in cross ladylike tones 'Come on, come on, tell me your name.' Now there was something much more like the traditional Oxford porter, an elderly man with soft long-drawn-out Oxfordshire vowels. 'I didn't think anyone really spoke with that lovely accent,' whispered Deborah.

The Cotswold stone of the main building had weathered

and darkened a little. There was a weeping willow between that and the dining hall: half-grown in her time — a little dog belonging to one of the tutors used to run in circles round its trunk. Its fronds reached the ground now. The subdued hum of cars from outside the walls was louder than she remembered. At first it had seemed to her that she was living in the country: from her window she could watch squirrels in the trees, and in May could hear the cuckoo from the Parks. Now she could see that everywhere the tall Victorian houses of the neighbourhood and the fanciful towers of the science labs overlooked the College grounds. The little Clare of those days must have been very blind as well as very young.

She said to Deborah 'I can't expect you to see it with my eyes. When I was up, none of the ancient Colleges was open to women.'

When she came up as an undergraduate the College had two smart new residential blocks, concrete outside and teak inside. There had been no more new building since. The old Victorian houses were still there. They had stood there long before the College existed: Ruskin had lived in one of them. The former shapes of their gardens were still visible.

On the north side there was a terraced row of smaller houses, their long thin gardens below the level of the path. 'Down here,' she said to Deborah.

For three years she had gone up and down these steps; the first term full of a self-renewing excitement that the mere state of waking up would set in motion. Later with a certain happy familiarity; lastly with a sense that every window was an eye, every step a wall.

Their two rooms were right at the top of the corner house: ancient servants' quarters, probably. Not altogether without charm: certainly without much comfort. What sort of room did Deborah have to work in at home? The lower middle class took their lives grimly, as Clare remembered. Not enough heat, not enough light, not enough space to work in. But the young are surprisingly stoical at times, not having learnt to be anything else.

'I'll leave you in peace,' she said 'just for half an hour. I don't think this sentimental journey would be of much use to you really.'

On the way down the stairs she passed a sleepy-looking young man coming up. Outside the staircase window it was still light, but he was wearing pyjamas, and carrying a tray full of used plates and cups. Good Lord, he's not making much effort to be invisible. Then she remembered: these days they can wander round at all hours — they live here.

The same gravel underfoot, making her shoes dusty after a dozen steps as it had always done. But the tall houses, the paths, the lawns, were none of them painful to revisit: the mirage of past emotions, not even their ghost. It was the smell in the main College building that caught her unprepared, filling her throat and eyes with water. Unpainted wood on floors and wall panelling: polish, and dust, and more polish, and the smell of the wood still coming through. It looked shabbier, more kicked about — less money to spend, heftier shoes in its corridors. Some of the voices in those corridors would be deep ones now. But nothing had changed the smell. Expectations she had forgotten she ever had — next term ... next year ... and a sense of loss and failure she had carried everywhere with her, ever since.

The building was not old enough to have any independent past: it was still the echo chamber of unfinished states of mind and feeling. It had not stood during the passage of centuries, in which anything might be made good, but for only a few decades. It had as little power to soften pain with the movement of time as the pools in the Christ Church Meadow, where on the morning of the final examination she had walked, trailing the bat-winged scholar's gown along the grass. The steely surface of the water, that reflected nothing but the flat sky, and oneself.

VIII

On Saturday evening, as the dusk began to gather, and the footballers went home, Colin walked up to the high ground behind the estate. Once he was outside, the physical sense of panic he had been feeling all afternoon — the shivering, the fluttering heartbeat — subsided. The ground was spongy and the damp began to creep through his shoes. Judith, if she had noticed his going out at all, would probably have called to him to put on his 'wellies'. No doubt that was the word Clare used too.

At one time, he and Judith had often walked up here. First of all hand in hand, then with a pram, then with a pram and toddler. After that it must have become too much of an effort. You looked for a partner because it was intolerable to be always alone; you had children as the proof and celebration of being a couple; and then found you were never so much together again. Was it simply that Clare was still childless, her negatively preserved youth, that had caught him?

In his early twenties, when everything seemed to be open to a new Cambridge graduate, he had what should have been a very good job in a public school. No one had seemed troubled by the fact that his own social origins were much humbler. But after a couple of years he had found the enclosed and mostly middle-aged society increasingly depressing, and celibacy increasingly painful. He wanted — intensely, if not always in the same order of priority — domestic roots of his own, sexual companionship, and children: and had been afraid, for no good reason other than emotional timidity, that he would never have any of them.

Then his father died — only in his sixties, but even that gave him ten years longer than poor Ted — and his mother wanted him nearer home. The Stanburn Boys' Grammar School had a post in English and would be delighted to offer it to an old boy of the school. It was a social come-down, but in those days not an academic one. It seemed the obvious solution for a year or two. So he found himself back on his own side of the Tees; and in the first term, at a house-warming party of Alan Carr's, he met a tall girl with pink cheeks and dark hair. *Judith, this is Colin. He's one of your lot too . . .*

The cold and damp were too penetrating for him to go on: up here there were no trees to break the force of the wind. He turned round so that it was behind him. It's time to put an end to this: all this tragic posturing. It's served its purpose, if it ever had one. *If Death were seen At first as Death, Love had not been* ... Could the mixture of sorrow and anger he felt about Clare really be called love any longer? Perhaps she had never been more than the reflection of his desire not to decay. Ted Auton spread-eagled across the carpet by the bookcase: weak rainy light breaking over his head. Phyllis Auton would be preparing to live through her second evening of widowhood. Colin put his hands in his coat pockets and began to walk back to the crescent, strings of house lights below him.

'Are you sure Dr Kennett is expecting me too?' said Deborah.

'Just *Miss* Kennet, not Doctor. Lots of academics of that generation only have the MA. Yes, she certainly is expecting both of us.'

Without you, Deborah, I wouldn't be here at all.

Clare squirted scent at herself and pulled a face in the glass. Her hair was beginning to look lank most of the time. 'All right, if you're ready, shall we go? I think this is my staple impression of Oxford, you know — coming out of a building into the night air.'

What she had forgotten, till she felt it on her face, was the different touch at night of a south-west wind. Deborah said 'The air smells different here.'

'Yes. I used to think it was just the smell of the country, after London. But the country at home hasn't got this smell either, has it? The wind seems to take it all away.'

And different winds meant a different cloudscape. The characteristic sky above Gatelaw was either brilliantly clear, or a thick grey slab. She had forgotten these great piles of cumulus. She had called County Durham 'home', but there was only one home.

They went up the steps from the terrace and turned the corner alongside the wall. From inside the college building came the unmistakable noise of a space-invaders machine. Even in Arcadia there am I. How would she have coped with the compulsory extroversion of college life as it was now? The street-lamp shining over the wall from the Banbury Road made patterns through the half-bare trees. By the porch of the house at the far end Clare felt for a moment that she inhabited her body of thirteen or fourteen years ago: long-haired; thinner; lighter on its feet; still unaware of its deficiency.

She said to Deborah 'It does feel odd to be coming out to see Eunice without an essay under one arm.'

'*Eu-neecie*? Clare, that isn't really how you say it, is it? I always thought it was *Eu-niss*.'

'If anyone rang up during a tutorial she used to pick up the phone and say just 'Eu-*nic*-e', so that was what everyone called her. Not to her face, of course, but I imagine she's always known about it.'

In this room, with books climbing up every inch of wall space, with a bay window that looked out into the changing treetops, she had sat on the sofa every term time week for three years and read her essays aloud — interrupted every few minutes: 'Yes, Clare, but what about — ?' You soon discovered Eunice only did that with good students: if she *didn't* interrupt was the time to worry.

'Clare, dear! Well, you haven't changed much, I must say. Though I see you've cut off some of that hair.'

'And you haven't changed at all.' Short white hair, eyebrows still dark, body still slim and quick. 'May I introduce Deborah Robson? My best sixth-former ever.'

'Come and sit down, both of you. Drink? That always was my first question, you may remember.'

'I'm afraid I'd better not: but I'm sure Deborah would like one.'

'Clare, this is a sad falling away. What shall it be, Deborah? Would it be corrupting of me to offer you gin?'

Deborah, clearly knowing that she couldn't ask for sherry at this time in the evening, said bravely, 'Yes, please. I mean, no, it wouldn't be corrupting.' And then to Clare's relief 'But a rather weak one, please.'

Eunice poured. 'And you're doing the scholarship exam this month, Deborah?'

'Yes. I don't know whether it'll be any good. Or whether any of the colleges will interview me.'

'I wish I could urge you with a good conscience to come to this one,' said Eunice. 'Ten or fifteen years ago you couldn't have done better. But now we get girls who don't quite make it into the ancient Colleges, and the young men who've been displaced by the ones who do.'

'I'd be glad if any of them would have me,' said Deborah.

'You should have come back earlier, Clare,' said Eunice. 'It's been too long.'

'I'm sorry,' said Clare. 'You know how it is ...'

'One of the nicest things that happened to me last year was being visited by three generations at once; one of the first undergraduates I ever taught, and her daughter, who was here in the fifties, and *her* daughter, who's here now. When it comes to grandchildren, I count myself ahead of the Queen Mother.'

We used to feel so sorry for Eunice's generation of educated women: the ones who had to choose, right from the start, between a career and marriage. Poor old virgins, we thought, knowing we had got it much better worked out ourselves.

Some time in her first Trinity Term, in her room in that building across the path — the room with the teak-plank ceiling – her current boyfriend had said to her, *Clare, you can't say now that you don't want to — what did you think all this was leading up to?* And because she had always known that she did not understand the rules, she said she was sorry and let him go on. She could remember hardly anything about him now except that, like half the male undergraduates of her generation, he was called Simon, and she had been fond of him but not in the smallest degree in love with him. It was messy, undignified, and more extensively painful than she had expected. Everyone knew, of course, that you weren't likely to enjoy it the first time. But you only had one virginity to lose — it wasn't the same for men — and it was a pity it had not been associated with some more important state of feeling. It couldn't be helped. Level-headed philosophical Clare of those days — not so difficult when you had everything in front of you and no sense that there was anything you could not learn.

Eunice said to Deborah 'What are you reading at the moment?'

'I've been reading a lot of Hopkins. And Hardy. And Larkin, and some Joyce.'

'All nineteenth and twentieth century stuff?'

'No, Clare's been doing *Troilus and Criseyde* with the whole sixth-form group ...'

'That was mainly for Deborah's benefit, I'm afraid' said Clare.

'Why "afraid"?' asked Eunice.

'Well, it's beyond most of them, and it's not on the syllabus ...'

'I shouldn't think it is. Why should you apologise for that? Most of them'll never come near it if you don't show it to them.' Eunice turned back to Deborah. 'She always did have the most phenomenal capacity for work, you know, this girl.'

Deborah smiled, nervously and shyly, first at Eunice and then at Clare. Trying to adjust her idea of Clare to fit in with the notion of her as a 'girl'?

In this room, on this sofa, in that last term, Clare had read aloud what turned out to be her final essay, and Eunice hardly interrupted at all. At the end there had been a pause, and Eunice had said: 'Clare, that wasn't up to your usual standard. Not by a good deal. I think you've let yourself get a bit stale, haven't you? Either that or you're losing interest. Don't let that happen at this stage. You're my best hope for this year.'

She did not remember whether she had answered. If not, she must have gone very white or attracted notice in some other way, because quite suddenly Eunice had been out of her seat and halfway across the room: 'Clare, for goodness' sake, you're not going to pass out on me, are you? Come on, you can do better than that.'

She remembered shaking her head. She wasn't the kind who fainted, any more than she was the kind who jumped off bridges. But she had heard herself say, could hear herself saying now, in a strangled, stilted little voice: 'I'm sorry. I don't think I *can* work any harder. There just aren't any more hours in the day. And it's taking longer and longer for me to do less and less as it is. I don't really know whether I can go on.'

She found she had turned her head aside now, as she had turned it aside then: not to hide tears, because she had had none of them left by that time, as she had none now; but because the final self-punishment, which was to admit her weakness, had come so suddenly after being withheld so long.

'Would you say, then,' Eunice was asking Deborah 'that Hopkins' eccentric vocabulary, and the difficult rhythms, actually get in the way of what he's saying? Can a poem carry the weight of both that kind of subject matter and that mode of expression?'

'I ... I think that rather — rather feverish tone is *part* of what Hopkins is saying, isn't it? It's a deliberate excitement, a sort of elation, and he can keep it up in words but perhaps not in other ways. So that when you get the last poems, and he says himself that he's lost the excitement —'

'Or it's lost him?'

'Yes, and then you get a sort of broken-backed version of the same rhythms.'

'Let me find a copy,' said Eunice 'and you can show me what you mean.'

Clare got up, more obtrusively than she had meant to. 'Excuse me,' she said. They hardly looked up.

By the time she reached the lavatory she knew she was not really going to be sick. What was that, then — envy, or just the smell of gin? It was a small, cold room: she leaned her forehead against the frosted glass of the window. The crushed, crinkled grain of the glass, close up, reminded her of some other time when she must have done the same. I wanted to die then. Could I say that now? Not really. Not at all, really. Perhaps it wasn't even true then: it only felt like it.

She would have patted cold water on to her face, but for her make-up. She went back to the room.

'I think she'll do very well, Clare,' said Eunice. 'She does you credit. Deborah, forgive me for talking about you like an exhibit.'

'Nothing much to do with me,' said Clare. 'She could have done the actual work on her own easily enough. I've just been a sort of administrative assistant, or cheerleader.'

Eunice said, as though Deborah had not been there: 'Your trouble always was, Clare, that you never valued anything about yourself except your intelligence.'

She had valued her power of endurance too, though: her power not to be defeated by herself.

After her ignominious collapse in front of Eunice she had been fussed over, extravagantly reassured, scolded. 'Clare, you *are* a clot, aren't you? *No* one who's worked as steadily as you have needs to put herself through a régime like that. I thought I knew all the signs, but you're obviously just too bloody good an actress. Why didn't you say something months ago?'

She had owned up to all of it, bit by bit: to waking up with that sense of desolation which lifted as the day went on and then came down again with the dusk; to the loss of appetite and interest; to the noisily thudding heartbeat and the constant sense of being watched. Confessing brought her no nearer to relief. Such trite, give-away symptoms, she knew now: so unfamiliar and frightening then. Someone more used to making a scene, less ashamed of asking for help, would have known when to give in, and recovered. She knew she never really had recovered, had never again felt any degree of security that her mind or her body or both would not betray her. She sat her exams, in the Schools building like everyone else, 'tranquillised', but certainly not incapable of functioning. If she had gone to pieces more thoroughly she could have sat her exams the following year and perhaps got a First after all: but then her parents would have had to know about it. She got a good Second — considering her state, an excellent Second, if that had not been a contradiction in terms. It was the kind of degree she could have got if she had done a steady four hours' work a day throughout her time there: and had left herself space for all the other things people go up to Oxford to do, and remember it for afterwards.

Eunice said to Deborah, 'I'm sure you're having to work very hard at the moment. That's a very good thing, but you mustn't let yourself get addicted to it. Your boss here was a bit inclined to that — weren't you, Clare?'

Eunice's habit of putting people on the hook — so clearly without malice, so evidently from an objective wish to see sloppy thinking made more stringent — was what made her a brilliant teacher of the intelligent. But how would she have managed 3F? Clare said calmly: 'I expect you're right. It's the penalty of belonging to the meritocratic generation. We still can't believe it isn't possible to work our way into everything with our grammar-school wits.'

'Saving your presence, Clare, I often think now how neurotic your whole undergraduate generation was. I don't know why everyone romanticises the sixties so much: it was a low dishonest decade if ever there was one. They worry about jobs now, and the Bomb, I suppose, but at least they don't seem to worry all the time about themselves. And yet compared with you people they've got so much less to be thankful for.'

'Perhaps that was it,' said Clare. 'There wasn't anyone else to blame if things went wrong.'

'Clare doesn't seem neurotic to me,' said Deborah, suddenly, firmly.

'May I quote you, Deborah?' said Clare.

'I wasn't thinking of Clare,' said Eunice. 'She's one of the people I never think of in the context of a particular year. But I stand justly rebuked, Deborah: one shouldn't use "neurotic" as a term of abuse.' She poured another measure of gin into Deborah's unresisting glass. 'How *very* nice it is to have you both here.'

On the way back to their rooms, along the now darkened path — the lights in the main College building had gone out — Deborah, walking rather unsteadily, stumbled off the gravel and on to the grass. Clare laughed and put a hand under her elbow, as she had not been able to do earlier.

'I think I've had too much to drink,' said Deborah.

'Perhaps just a little. But if you never get any more sloshed than you are now I shall be disappointed.'

'Miss Kennett's very fond of you,' said Deborah.

'I'm very fond of her. I'd forgotten how much.'

Eunice doesn't think of me only as a failure. She remembers the whole of it — not just the end.

In the dark Colin turned on his back and lay staring up at the ceiling. 'Sorry,' he said.

Judith lifted her hand from his limp penis and let it rest lightly on his stomach. 'It doesn't matter,' she said. 'Don't worry about it. It's my fault: I shouldn't have ...'

'It's not in the least your fault. I'm a bit of a misery generally at the moment, aren't I? And today in particular ...'

'I know. Ted and everything. I do understand.'

His hand still lay between her legs. 'There's no reason why you should suffer' he said. 'Shall I — ?'

She moved his hand away: gently but firmly. '*No*, Col. It's not ... I don't want to do it that way.'

'I'm sorry. Again.'

'Oh, for goodness' sake don't take offence as well. It is up to me, isn't it?'

'Of course.'

'I've said I don't mind. Come on, let's get some sleep.' She laid a conciliatory cheek against his shoulder.

Sensible normal Judith: orgasm as the certain and natural end of particular forms of behaviour and of no others. Had he imagined that the responsiveness of her body was due to some skill of his? Clare, if only you ...

You've got to do without that from now on. For everyone's sake, including yours.

The prospect of a world without the pain of missing Clare was even worse than a world that included it. It left only the anger.

She could not remember when she had last slept on her own in a single bed. Under the sheets she put a hand over her belly. It was already unfamiliarly hard and round.

Richard could not wait for her to look visibly pregnant. The badge of his virility, the flag of her servitude? No, that wasn't fair: in Richard's case all it was was a desire to advertise his happiness. There was never any undertow to Richard's emotions. That was, after all, precisely what she had loved in him, if love was the word.

When the results had come out, and Clare had known there would be no chance of a grant to do research, Eunice had written to her from Oxford:

> I'm so sorry for your disappointment: but I do think it's highly likely we can manage to get you something for next year. It's not the end of the world, whatever it feels like now. I don't suppose that you'll find the Theory of Education terribly stimulating this year, but I think you could do with getting out of Oxford for a bit. It's a qualification after all: and in the right school I'm sure you'd be rather a good teacher, though of course it's only a safety net ...

So it was Durham after all: the mini-Oxford of the north, with all the same vocabulary and most of the same rites, except that they punted from the Cambridge end and called Schools 'Finals'. Rather sweet, really, like a model village. In everything except the long term — and Clare had to take her own responsibility for that — Eunice had been right. Once there was nothing to dread and little to hope for, Clare had got herself off the tranquillisers and antidepressants quickly enough, and that was a small victory. After the wet languid airs of Oxford the brisk north-east wind revived her. She was frightened to start with at the prospect of teaching: but in her first teaching practice at a primary school the children seemed to trust her, even though she sometimes failed to understand what they were saying ('And then we came home and had Sweet William and chips'; 'Sweet William and chips? That can't be right, Mandy — Sweet William's a flower. It's named after ...'; 'No miss, it's a fish'). Perhaps they sensed someone who, in spite of appearances, was not quite grown up.

Eunice was right about the Theory of Education, of course. It was an emotional stimulant, not an intellectual one. Being able to see the weak links in the arguments, fatal flaws at every stage, a *hamartia* for which the perpetrators were not the ones to suffer, did not make her unable to see the virtue that motivated them: her whole upbringing predisposed her to exactly that. And however conscientiously she did her homework it was bound to leave her time to live and exist, to sing in choirs and go to theatres and readings. At half term she was walking over the footbridge that links one bank of the river with another, looked up and saw the great Cathedral rising above the spiky trees, and knew that she had not after all forgotten how to be happy. And in the same week she went to an early-music concert at one of the Colleges, and shared her programme with a latecomer, a young man with a round face and dark hair who afterwards took her for a drink. A chemistry research student, of all things: Richard. 'I have a feeling you're a serious lady who goes to these things regularly,' he said as he brought her her half pint of Guinness. 'I came tonight because I used to share a room with the counter-tenor. I'm afraid my Old Provençal's not what it was, though.' And she had a quite uncharacteristic fit of giggles over her glass.

In January her main teaching practice took her to what was then still the Stanburn Girls' Grammar School. For several weeks she got the mixture ludicrously wrong — expected indiscipline and so got it; set the standard for the sixth form far too high and showed irritation when they failed to meet it — then got the measure of the job and settled to it. 'It's a pity you're not staying,' said Lucy Knowles when Clare had finished her stint. 'There'll be a job going in the autumn, and I'd have liked to keep you. Oh, well, stay in touch.'

Richard was affectionate, gentle, almost touchingly old-fashioned in his courtship. It was not until the Easter vacation that he asked her if she would go to bed with him. By that time she had been celibate for more than two years: you dropped the subjects you were not successful at. She had sometimes missed being one of a couple, sometimes missed having someone to touch or be touched by; had never for a moment missed the actual conjunction of bodies. Naked and shivering she said 'I'm not very good at this, Richard: I don't know whether it'll be any different now.'

It wasn't. 'You just need to stop taking everything so much to heart,' he said, stroking her breasts. His experience was even less than hers, but she wanted to be convinced. There would be time for everything.

Lucy Knowles was delighted when Clare approached her again. Clare wrote to Eunice:

... so I shan't be coming back next term after all. When my fiancé finishes his postgraduate work it'll be my turn, but for the moment we'll need what I can earn. Thank you for everything: I hope it won't be too long before we meet again. I find I do enjoy teaching: you were right ...

She threw away so easily what only a year before had been all-important. Soon teaching jobs became scarce, and jobs in industrial chemistry became something to be guarded, not put at risk by moving around the country. Schools started to go comprehensive. Richard did not know that her body went on being unable to respond, however hard she tried. By the time she understood what had happened it was too late to undo it. What she had felt for him was too mixed up with the forces of self-protection, and the desire to protect him, for her to extract herself from it. And if she tried to start again alone who would protect her from herself? Everything I touch I destroy. Everything I love I do harm to. Everything I have ever wanted, and got, has come to pieces in my hands.

Once during the night she woke up suddenly, only for a matter of moments. She could not remember where she was — the single bed, the small shabby room — and then when she did remember, had a second of the old familiar fear, the sense of being too late for something. This was where the train had carried her. She was back at home, and it was still home; but she did not live there any longer.

In the morning, with the bells of the city churches sounding through the wind at their backs, she took Deborah around what had been her own Oxford. If it had been a fine summer's day she could have taken her up past the tall red houses and the walled gardens of North Oxford, to the water meadows of Godstow, or up into the Cumnor Hills in search of the Scholar-Gypsy — all the things she had planned to do herself and had never made the time to do — but the grey November morning and Deborah's copy of *Jude the Obscure* made her think of the back-street township called Jericho, leading down to the Tractarian Church of St Barnabas and the canal. As a new undergraduate she had found Jericho's little streets of chequered-brick artisans' cottages all too much like what she had left at home. Deborah — too young and resilient to have hangovers — was clearly puzzled as to why they were visiting this southern equivalent of an industrial landscape she saw every day. 'It's all right' Clare told her. 'I just wanted to show you, while we're here, the place where *Jude the Obscure* comes to a climax.' The last word was worth an ironic smile at herself; but perhaps 'climax' in the other sense was so old-fashioned a euphemism that Deborah would not even have heard of it. Had Deborah any more sexual experience than she had had at that age?

'I haven't got to the end of *Jude* yet,' said Deborah. 'Somehow there hasn't been much time for reading in the last day or two.'

'It comes to an extremely tragic end' said Clare. 'Which won't surprise you. Anyway, look up at the altar cross in St Barnabas' when we get there, and remember it later on.'

These blue-and-green-and-red wall paintings, Pre-Raphaelite saints and worthies, were what she had tried to live up to. Not the Church of Rome — strenuous, foreign, unresponsive to a Cranmerian fine phrase — nor yet the Church of England, flexible and resigned. Yet Anglo-Catholicism and Utopian Socialism — hopeless bedfellows — were what had built St Barnabas'. Almost the invention of Oxford: at least as much a part of its intellectual and emotional history as the punts and bicycles and tea parties that everyone remembers. When she looked up at the cross — openwork tin-and-spangles, faith at its most desperate, and ecclesiastical tat at its flashiest — it was not Hardy she thought of, but John Henry Newman. Another examination failure, another self-exile. *I have never seen Oxford since, excepting its spires, as they are seen from the railway.*

In Port Meadow, by some trick of the angle of vision, the towers and spires of Oxford appear strung out along the skyline. Deborah said, '*Christminster, real or miraged*'. Still thinking of Hardy. She turned slowly to see the line of images from end to end: a stocky girl with long lustreless hair. No reason to see her as a victim of herself; no part of Deborah's function to have to stand by whilst Clare sorted through the lantern slides of her disappointment.

'I have to give you credit,' said Clare 'for not having mentioned dreaming spires all weekend.'

Deborah actually blushed. 'I haven't had it out of my mind for more than five minutes since we arrived,' she said. 'Or the bit about lost causes and impossible loyalties.'

'Do you feel up to a bit more walking?' said Clare. 'Now we're here, it's quite a short walk across to Binsey. There's a nice pub where we could have some lunch, and you could break the law again, if you feel like it.'

'Binsey, where Hopkins' poplars were?' said Deborah.

'Or rather, where they weren't. The very same.'

'I didn't realise that was Oxford too. Please let's see it.'

> *My aspens dear, whose airy cages quelled,*
> *Quelled or quenched in leaves the leaping sun,*
> *Are felled, felled, are all felled;*
> *Of a fresh and following folded rank*
> *Not spared, not one ...*

They sat beside the open fire in The Perch. Behind the bar the landlord was talking to a customer: 'So we got ourselves on to the A40, loike moy woife said, but as zoon as oi 'it 'ee, oi knowed oi was wrong ...' Deborah spluttered and looked down at the tilted surface of the wine in her glass. Clare, feeling her back begin to ache again after days of quiescence, put the palm of her hand against it. It must have been with the almost-forgotten Simon that she had first come here; because her summer terms, after that first one, had been filled with more desperate occupations. On the walls hung framed photographs: dead Eights crews, an all-male Oxford: straw boaters tipped down over hollow eye sockets.

I don't really want to be twenty again: not even a happier and a tougher twenty-year-old than I was. I want the sense of choice, the possibilities: not the unpreparedness that goes with them. In real life Comus took the Lady and ravished her; Gawain slept with the wife of the Green Knight and dishonoured himself and her. Felled, felled.

In the College lodge Clare wrote quickly on a sheet from her notebook:

Dear Miss Kennett (or Eunice, if I may, after all this time)
    Thank you for being so kind to Deborah last night — and to me, of course: but that's an old debt already. I hope Deborah will manage it — it's a more brutal world than it was when I was trying to see my way through it, but I think she may be a survivor. Enjoy your retirement — not that I can imagine you retiring. It mustn't be another eleven years before we next meet — I *will* keep in touch.
                      With love,
                          Clare (Baylham)

If Eunice objected to the 'with love', Clare would not be there to see it. A grateful, graceful ex-pupil who had learned to look after herself and to live with herself.

She looked back at the receding gatehouse, the half-stripped trees around it. Perhaps to have come back did represent some kind of triumph or coming-to-terms, but it did not feel much like it. For Deborah's sake it had justified itself: without Deborah it would have been intolerable. What Clare had done to herself here had left its thumbprint on everything in Oxford that had been hers. Not a grief that could be shared with anyone else: to pass it on to Deborah would be inconceivable; Richard would shrink from it.

Which left Colin: and she had done well to get through to that point in the day without directly thinking of him — though what else had the thought of John Henry Newman been about? Oh, if only I'd known you earlier ... but when she trailed her gown across the grass that final morning in the Christ Church Meadow, he was already the same age as she was now: two hundred miles to the north-east, a married man with two children.

Above the Meadow the dusk was beginning to gather. She did not feel the need to keep Deborah entertained any longer: she wasn't a child, or a parent, whose tolerance of one's company had to be bought. They walked almost in silence up to the point where, in the green and slate-grey stillness, the waters of the Isis and the Cherwell ran together. Several times they passed intertwined couples coming the other way, back to a lighted room with books. Is Deborah thinking, as I did when I came for interview, that she might never see any of this again? *Excepting its spires, as they are seen from the railway.* She looked sideways at Deborah, but the girl's face reflected nothing. Clare felt for a moment an absurd impulse to ask her 'Will you forgive me?'

'Shall we turn round?' she said. 'You've seen the best of it now, and it's getting a bit dark. And if we're going to finish with Evensong we really ought to start moving in the right direction. You must be tired.'

Whatever the Church of England had done to its other services — Clare thought of Ted Auton and his sustained and inventive attacks on the Alternative Service Book —

it seemed to have left Evensong untouched. The nave was lit, the rest of the Cathedral in shadow. The choirboys who had sung 'If I take the wings of the morning ...' that first November of her time here would be grown-up themselves now, well on their way to children and mortgages.

'Almighty God, the Father of Our Lord Jesus Christ, who desireth not the death of a sinner, but rather that he may turn from his wickedness, and live ...'

She did not believe in sin in that sense — the violation of a command — as Colin presumably did: though the Book of Common Prayer could enchant you into believing anything while it lasted. But sin as something that had been done, and should not have been; or that should have been done, and had not been ...

I feel guilty for my failures; I ask forgiveness for my failures, only since I don't forgive them myself it hardly matters who else does. But I don't ask forgiveness for my sins: not directly enough, anyway. I can't tell Richard I'm sorry: I can't help or change the injuries he knows about: the other injuries he could only forgive if he knew about them: and I must never do that again. I must say I'm sorry to someone, about something.

Even that was a rationalisation. She had to say she was sorry to Colin.

'... He hath scattered the proud in the imagination of their hearts. He hath put down the mighty ...'

Ten minutes' standing was enough to make her feel dizzy at the moment. She sat down as discreetly as she could. Deborah glanced down at her for a second; then, reassured, smiled and turned back towards the choir.

In the darkness, from the subterranean pillars of Birmingham New Street, the train rocked northwards and eastwards. As a child, she used to fit words and tunes to the carriage wheels. *And I have never seen the city since, excepting its spires as they are seen from the railway.*

'Clare,' said Deborah maternally 'you look nearly asleep.'

'I nearly am. What about you?'

'I'm tired in a way, but I couldn't possibly sleep. Not for hours. It's a good thing there's still another day of half term. I've got an essay to write.'

'One of mine?'

'Yes. The second Hopkins one, on the tragic poems. I didn't really want to start on it, they seemed so depressing, but I think I can tackle it now.'

'Is that the fruit of your conversation with Miss Kennett?'

'I think it must be. I feel as if I could do almost anything at the moment.'

In the glass of the train window, with the darkness outside, the reflections of their faces were softened and ghostly. Forgive me, Deborah, for making you want something it isn't in my power to give. Something I wasn't even able to take myself.

'Are you sure you're going to be able to get home all right? You're absolutely certain there's a bus?'

'Absolutely certain.'

'I'll stop fussing,' said Clare. 'I do remember how annoying it is. But you will ring me when you get home, won't you? And if I'm not back myself, keep ringing till I am?'

'Yes. And Clare? ... Thank you. Whatever happens. I'll always remember this weekend.'

The telephone bell dragged Clare out of a pit of sleep. The state of the daylight told her it was late; she must have slept pretty well for twelve hours.

'Clare, it's Judith.'

There was only one Judith in her present acquaintance. An injured wife.

'Hallo, Judith. Sorry to keep you waiting. I have to admit I was asleep.'

'Lord, don't apologise. I wish my lot would let *me* sleep in. How are you?'

It must be all right, mustn't it? But Judith was a lady — she would always begin politely even if the sky were falling.

'Very well,' said Clare. 'And you?'

'Fine. Clare, it's bad news, I'm afraid, but I was sure you'd want to know what's happened.'

'What?'

It can't be Colin: she sounds perfectly calm.

'Ted Auton. He had another coronary on Friday. His wife rang Col on Saturday morning — I tried ringing you then, and again yesterday, but I couldn't get through.'

'I've been in Oxford.'

'Col said you must be away, and not to spoil your half term, but I was sure ...'

'Dead?'

'I'm afraid so. The thing is, Clare, the funeral's this afternoon, so if you wanted to come ...'

'Of course I'll be there. I was going to spend the afternoon with Lucy Knowles, but I'll ring her: she'll remember Ted, she'll understand. What time?'

'Three. St Aidan's in Stanburn. Do you know where that is?'

'I think so. I'll find it anyway.'

'Can Col and I pick you up somewhere? It'll be a devil of a journey on public transport — or is Richard on holiday too?'

'Richard's away. No, it's all right, Judith, I know the journey in my sleep after all these years.'

'Are you sure? The boys and I were going down to my sister's for their half term, but I've put that off till tomorrow now, so I could easily ...'

'No, really. There are plenty of buses: you'll have enough on your minds without me. Judith ... how's Colin taking it? They'd known each other such ages, hadn't they?'

Judith did not drop her voice: Colin was not in the house, then. Not even that remote a contact with him.

'It's hard to tell. He'd probably rather talk to you about it than me. I don't seem to be able to say the right thing.'

This tight pain at the base of her throat was not just shame — humble unsuspicious Judith — it was jealousy too. Judith had the right to comfort Colin and could offer it away so easily.

'*Saying* the right thing isn't what counts, is it? Judith, thank you *very* much for ringing me. I'd have hated not to know.'

'I told Col I was sure you'd feel like that.'

*

And though after my skin worms destroy this body, yet in my flesh shall I see God: whom I shall see for myself, and mine eyes shall behold, and not another.

Judith, reaching out unobtrusively, found Colin's hand and squeezed it.

He thought, Judith treats me like an invalid. I ought to be grateful to her. For her castrating kindness.

Clare, half a dozen rows behind, saw the squeezing of the hand and felt its pressure inside her. Some of it might have been sympathy: most of it was envy.

There were only fifteen or twenty of them in the church. It was a big, Oxford Movement-style barn of a place, but the chancel and the reredos were naked-looking where the high altar had been taken away. There was a nave altar in its place: Clare thought with shock of an ironing board.

Colin unfamiliar in a dark suit: Judith beside him with a mantilla over her hair. The woman who must be Ted's widow alone in the front pew. Small and thin: wispy hair done up in an old-fashioned knot behind a dark-blue straw hat. The Autons had no children. *We brought nothing into this world, and it is certain we can carry nothing out.* Bob Murray and his wife; Wendy Sykes, the Senior Mistress, and a man who must be her husband. No Alan Carr: he would never voluntarily be seen inside a church — and which of the ordinary human emotions were still left under Alan's running self-parody? No Kettleby: probably no one had even told him. There would be a certain justice in that.

'Edward George Auton, late of this parish ...' With the other scattered mourners she knelt and rose and knelt again. *When thou with rebukes dost chasten man for sin, thou makest his beauty to consume away, like as it were a moth fretting a garment.* At the panegyric the celebrant referred to Ted throughout as 'Edward George'. Clare read stolidly through the Act for Uniformity of Common Prayer, *primo Elizabethae*, and the seventeenth-century Preface of Bishop Cosin. When Cranmer was burned at the stake in Oxford, the flames licked the doors of Balliol. Cosin's almshouses and library stood less than ten miles from Stanburn, on the green at Durham. Cranmer and Cosin were both hard and cruel men in their way, but they knew how to make both swords and ploughshares out of words. Their joy was won honestly, out of fear and grief.

In the porch afterwards she was edging to the side to make her escape when Judith caught up with her. 'I was just observing to His Lordship here that you didn't look too well, Clare, and *now* he tells me you're having a baby! *Men!*' So she had to turn round and face them.

Colin looked tired, but that wasn't unusual by half term. Unsmiling, but that was hardly surprising at the moment. She did not know what harrowing fleshly manifestation of her guilt she had expected to see. She couldn't go on looking him in the face.

He looked down at her. Her skin had been delicate and now was turning coarse; her soft hair, pinned up into an untidy French pleat, had no shine. None of it made any difference: those things counted when you were in danger of love, not once you were in it.

I could have kept those earrings, he thought. That second night, he had laughed at her for keeping her earrings on when she was naked ... 'Well, take them out if they bother you' she had said. *Colin, it's horrible to be called a cockteaser.* He had pulled the little clips off at the back of her ears, and drawn the wires out: clumsily, because Judith's ears were not pierced. The gentle domesticity of it had strengthened his desire almost beyond bearing, and yet increased the tenderness which had made him want to prolong the act of love for her sake. *I don't know what it feels like. I'm sorry.* The earrings had been still lying there next day when they were ready to leave, and he had found them at the last moment, offered them to her in the palm of his hand. I could have kept them. She'd never have known I had them. But I didn't think I'd need anything to remember her by.

Phyllis Auton was standing beside him. 'Mr Rowsley,' she said, 'I think I was rather inarticulate last time we spoke. I'd like to thank you for all this. It was what Edward wanted, and if it can't do him any good now, it's still helped me.' Not giving him a chance to answer, she turned to the two women. 'You will come to the house afterwards, won't you? I'm told the business at the cemetery only takes ten minutes or so.'

Clare said, 'Oh, I don't think ...'

Judith said 'Of course you must, Clare. You don't have to worry about transport — we'll run you home afterwards. Thank you, Mrs Auton.'

Colin said, needing something to say, 'Mrs Auton, may I introduce Judith, my wife? And my colleague, Mrs Baylham.'

The failure to give her Christian name hurt. Presumably he had meant it to.

Judith said, 'I'll drive, shall I, Col? You two go in the back and keep each other company. I don't think expectant mums should sit in front seats, Clare — sorry to be a fusspot.'

Mrs Auton, who had been poised to go, turned towards Clare. 'You're expecting a baby, Mrs Baylham?'

'Yes. Yes, I am, Mrs Auton.'

'I'm glad you came. It makes it ... easier to believe that things go on, somehow. I'm sorry: I didn't mean to embarrass you.' She turned and walked quickly away.

'Col,' said Judith rapidly, 'I think it would be a good idea if you went up to the cemetery with her. I'll look after Clare.'

Clare said, 'I really think it would be better if I didn't come ...'

Colin stopped and looked at her. 'Mrs Auton asked you to,' he said. 'I think that's all that matters at the moment, isn't it?'

Colin turned the Morris Traveller round at the foot of the lane leading up to the cottage. Pale, washed-out Clare with her too-tight dark skirt, refusing Judith's offers of help. Judith said yet again 'Shall I drive?'

'For *Christ's* sake, Judith, I'm perfectly capable of driving.'

'I didn't say you weren't. I only meant ...'

'Yes, all right.'

They changed seats. Judith swallowed nervously and looked sideways at him. Colin — *talk* about it: it's nothing to be ashamed of, to mourn for a friend. But she could not say it: she was afraid of her own lack of fluency and of his power to snub her. She said: 'Clare doesn't seem herself, does she? We had to stop on the way up to the Autons' house because she was feeling a bit sick. Was this baby an accident?'

'I don't think so. She seemed all right to me.'

'Have you two fallen out, or something?'

'Don't be silly.'

'Well, you seemed distinctly frosty with her all afternoon, I thought.'

'I just haven't seen much of her this term, that's all.'

'You certainly didn't have to bite her head off the way you did, outside the church.'

'I just didn't think it was the time or the place for her to start parading her sensitivity.'

'Col, for Heaven's sake, she only wasn't sure anyone really wanted her there.' Judith was not sure where this insight had come from, but she ploughed on. 'Even the most self-possessed people get a bit vulnerable when they're pregnant, you know. Remember the way your mother used to reduce me to tears when Francis was on the way?'

'You're making too much of it. I don't suppose Clare even noticed.'

'I think she did. Oh, well, never mind, perhaps you're right. You'll miss her, anyway, won't you?'

Colin resisted the stupid over-compensating impulse to say, 'Oh, not really.' He said, 'Yes, I probably shall. But she'll be much better off out of it.'

'I must say,' said Judith, 'I'm surprised. I always assumed she either couldn't have children, or had decided she just didn't want any. I must admit, if I hadn't met Richard I'd find it hard to believe she was even married.'

'She hasn't got an eye in the middle of her forehead, has she? Or a hare lip?'

'No, of course not, she's very attractive. Well, usually — not today. I meant she's always seemed sort of ... well, sexless, for want of a better word.'

'I dare say we'll all manage without her,' said Colin.

'In so far as anyone cares what we all do at that place anyway.'

Was that, perhaps, what he had loved? Perhaps the whole point of the lady in the high tower was that she was cold and chaste. Courtly love was meant to be a nice clean game.

Judith said wearily 'Col, I do *try* to be sympathetic. I wish you wouldn't *always* chuck it straight back at me.'

When Clare opened the front door, the hall carpet abruptly threatened to come up and hit her in the face. To avoid this happening, she lay down on it anyway. When the sound of the telephone bell made her open her eyes again she found that the hall was dark and she was cold.

It was Richard, ringing from his training course. 'I didn't ring this morning,' he said. 'I thought you'd need a lie-in after all that gallivanting. How was Oxford? Everything all right?'

'Fine.' Mentioning Ted would take more energy than she could part with.

'How are you feeling?'

'All right. I felt a bit ropey earlier on today, but I'm all right now.'

It was true: she had not meant to fall asleep on the floor, but it had put some kind of barrier between her and the afternoon.

'Well, go to bed early. And get a taxi in to school tomorrow.'

'What, *all* the way?'

'It's only two days till I get back. From now on I'm going to pick you up in the evenings as well. There's simply no sense in wearing yourself out. Clare?'

'Mm?'

'I love you.'

'I love you too.'

That was true as well. A warm, comforting presence that demanded nothing except domesticity, order and a temperate affection. And a child. Not so much to ask in exchange for a life-support system.

*

In the dark Colin felt Judith put out a hand to touch him.

Perhaps it was not a sexual approach at all, but only a gesture of reassurance; or perhaps she wanted reassurance for herself. Trying to reach him in a way that had always worked before.

He had always tried not to think about Clare while making love to his wife. But this time it was the only way he could perform the act at all. He lay over her without making any attempt to keep his weight off her; and thrust straight into her without preliminaries. He knew the responses of Judith's body as well as he knew his own: but it was Clare's body he was subduing in imagination.

He had not thought about hurting Judith or frightening her; but when he realised that was what he was doing he did not stop. 'Col,' she said. 'Col, no, you're ... Colin, Colin, *please*.' But she could not make much sound, because of the boys; and he was so much stronger than she was that he could do anything he wanted. With her body tense like this, resisting him, he must be hurting her more, not less. Then she went limp and passive, enduring it. Waiting for it to be finished.

Afterwards, since he could not say he was sorry without attempting to explain, he tried to put his arms around her: but she lay quite still, her face turned away from him. When he touched her face to find out if she was crying, her cheeks were quite dry. She twisted out of his arms.

'Please,' he said, but she did not move or answer. Kevin Colin Rowsley, the well-known failure, adulterer and rapist. On his own side of the marriage bed he lay with his eyes open. He forced himself to breathe softly and regularly, pretending sleep, and heard Judith doing the same.

Too late now to say I understand. Too late to say, I didn't understand before; I didn't want to.

It was Judith he had injured, Judith whose forgiveness he ought to ask. But now that he was a violator, he knew what it was to be violated: the act of love not bringing two people together as one, but driving them apart into their separate tunnels. Clare: oh, Clare, I'm sorry.

IX

Clare woke up reluctantly. She had done as Richard said and ordered a taxi: so there was time to lie in bed and adjust herself to the prospect of the day. Tuesday was the worst of the week, with one bad class following another all day until late in the afternoon. Deborah had to get through Tuesdays on her own: Clare felt it unimaginable that she would survive them at all if she did not get a lunch break. And this evening she would have to start catching up on the marking again.

She would not be forgiven: forgiveness was for children and for lovers. She could learn, would have to learn, to live with that as with her other losses and failures. It was only when you tried to compensate for them, and could not, that they became unbearable.

There would be only six more Tuesdays to dread before the end of term. She rested her hand under the sheet on that hard, convex part of her body and thought, I might even start to look forward to this, soon.

During the forty minutes between waking up and leaving the house, Colin failed even once to meet Judith's eyes. When he was putting on his coat she came out of the kitchen: not to see him on his way, merely to collect something from upstairs. He said, still not looking at her, 'Judith ...'

She stopped.

'Judith. I'm so sorry.'

She looked at him. 'Yes,' she said. 'I can see you are. But at the moment I'm afraid that doesn't make much difference.'

Colin went on looking at the floor.

She said, 'Don't telephone while we're away. The boys won't notice, and I want to get right away from you for a few days.'

He nodded.

She said, 'If I could begin to understand ... but it's a bit late for that, isn't it?'. She went on upstairs.

Her anger, her shock and bitterness, were her due by any standards. But there had been something else in her voice too: a kind of relief. Free now to dislike him as much as she wanted to. Colin shut the front door behind him, and set off down through the estate towards the bus stop. A woman in a red coat, hurrying two little girls into the back of a car, gave him a preoccupied early-morning smile. He found himself shrinking from it.

'Clare,' said Janet. 'Andy Reid's one of yours, isn't he?'

Alan looked up from the *T.E.S.* 'Ee, Janet, lass, we're nowt but joost back from w'holidays.' Alan always spoke stage Wearside for a day or two after a break.

'Andy Reid,' said Clare. 'The little thug who models himself on the Yorkshire Ripper.'

'Oh, you do know who I'm talking about, then?'

'Of course I do. Much as it may amaze you to hear it, I know all my pupils' names. And I spent a very distasteful ten minutes with Andy and the Ripper one Saturday evening not long ago.' The night of the baby-sitting: the night after she had said to Colin ... and now never, for the whole of her life, would be able to say she was sorry.

Janet said, 'Do you normally ask your classes to write about the Yorkshire Ripper?'

'In my folly and naïveté — and in desperation for a topic — I told them to write about a person they'd like to meet. Most of them went for Kevin Keegan or Elvis Presley, but our little friend chose to write about the Ripper.'

'If it made *that* much impression on you, why in Heaven's name didn't you take some sort of action?'

'I did. I refused to mark it and told him to write something else; and of course I had to give him a detention to make him do that. If I had as little sense of duty as you think, Janet, I'd have let him get away with it. It'd have been a damn sight easier for me.'

'I don't doubt that you've got a sense of duty, Clare. Your consciousness of it is written all over you.'

For more than a month she had been cowering, shielding herself: don't hurt me. A sudden strength came from defending herself again, from hitting back.

'Janet, look, I did *something* about it, all right? Andy Reid is one of a class of thirty which I teach for six periods a week. I've got two more classes of the same kind and the same size and I teach them for six periods a week too. And in the interstices of that I teach an upper-sixth group and a CSE group. Then in the evenings there's the marking and preparation. I think ten minutes of my Saturday evening, and then a forty-minute detention, is more than a fair week's ration for one child.'

'You spend a hell of a lot more than fifty minutes of your time with Deborah Robson every week.'

'Oh, *that's* what this is about, is it?'

'No, it isn't. Listen, Clare, what I would have *expected* you to do, from the sound of this Ripper essay, is to take the exercise book to Lower School and drop it on Fred Errington's desk.'

'I won't say I didn't think of it,' said Clare. 'But what would have been the point? I'd have queued for half an hour to get two minutes with Fred: then he'd have roared at Andy Reid for another two minutes and then given him the cane — just as he'd have done if the boy had turned up not wearing proper school uniform. Any point I wanted to make would have been completely lost. Andy wanted someone to make a big drama out of that piece of writing, and I disappointed him.'

'If you'd taken it to Fred, just *reacted* in some way, someone might have had some idea about what was happening.'

Bob said 'Why are we talking so much about this lad?'

'Correction, Robert,' said Alan. '*We* are not talking about this lad, the ladies are. What's 'e doon, then?'

'If you people lived near the school instead of racing off to your middle-class hideouts every evening ... well, listen. On Friday evening last week Andy Reid and his brother jumped out on a girl coming back from baby-sitting. Late, after midnight some time. They snatched her bag, tore her clothes and knocked her about, and then left her lying. She had to crawl all through that deserted bit of ground, down by the old docks, screaming, for about half a mile before anyone chose to stop their cars and help her. I gather the brother, who's a bit older, had done his best to rape her as well, though luckily he didn't quite manage it.'

'Clare,' said Betty, 'do you need some fresh air, pet?'

Clare shook her head. 'No, I'm all right, thanks, Betty. I'd rather not have heard that story, but I suppose that's hardly the point.'

Bob said, 'What sort of parent lets a girl walk home that way after midnight? And what were the Reid boy and his brother doing out in the streets at that hour?'

When Clare was a child, and for long enough afterwards, she had been forbidden to go anywhere on her own in the evenings. *There are some funny people around, Clare. You'll understand when you're older.* All her friends, hardened London children, went around unattended and never came to grief.

'Sorry, Clare,' said Janet. 'I forgot about ... but anyway, these things have to be faced, don't they? It's all our faults that children like Andy are the way they are.'

Alan said violently, 'Speak for yourself.' They had shared a staffroom for five years: Clare had never before known him to speak other than flippantly. 'You just bloody well speak for yourself, Janet, and not for anyone else. I've got children, so has Bob, so has Colin. *They're* not like that. Clare's kid won't be like that either. We do what we can — you just leave us out of it. You don't have to be a Tory or a Christian to believe in that much freedom of action.'

'Your children have everything going for them,' said Janet. 'For a start, Andy Reid's mother walked out on the family. All right, that happens, I know, and perhaps it was the right thing for her. Then his father set up house with some other woman who wouldn't have the kids, so they got dumped on the mother again. Now she's got a new boyfriend who doesn't want to know either, so one of the grandmothers has got them. And I need hardly add that all the adults in the story are unemployed.'

You carried the embryo around inside you, forgot about it for hours at a time, then thought about whether when it was born you would be able to breast-feed it, where was the best play group, were you ever going to smack it or would you always use reasoned argument? While the Andy Reids of this world — no, keep it manageable, the Andy Reids of County Durham — were neglected, passed around from one household to the next, discounted from the moment of conception. *He rapd and murded woemn, he had the rigth hidere* ...

Clare said, 'I didn't know about all that. I suppose I should have done. But so many of them have a broken home somewhere in the picture, don't they? It never seems to have much connection with the kind of child they turn out to be. Some of the worst of them still have both parents and a father in employment: it just isn't that simple an equation. But I suppose in this case it does explain a bit why he might want to get his own back on women.'

Janet turned and stared at her. 'Women can't be blamed for ...'

'It explains *nothing*,' said Alan. '*I* came from what you'd call a one-parent family. So did Betty here, didn't you, Bet? Her father died of pneumoconiosis and mine was careless enough to get left behind in the Ardennes. You two ladies may have been born into the middle class, but we weren't. Our mothers would no more have used that as an excuse for letting us go to the bad than they would have used it as an excuse for going on the streets themselves. You just keep your fucking do-gooders' pieties out of it. And I'm not going to apologise for my vocabulary either.'

Clare had never found herself even temporarily on the same side as Janet before. 'I know you think I haven't got any right to talk, Alan' she said. 'But some people, like you, seem to triumph over bad conditions and others are ruined by them. Anyone who could tell us the reason for *that* difference ...'

'Strength of character,' said Alan. 'Call me a fascist pig if you like.'

'Where does what you call strength of character come from?' said Janet. 'When it isn't economics, it's just luck.'

Bob said, 'You'll all shout me down. Original sin.'

'That's very theological for you,' said Janet. 'I thought it was pastoral religion you went in for. It's the only kind *I've* got any patience with.'

'Where is original sin supposed to have come from?' said Alan. 'I never got a sensible answer to that even from Ted, so I doubt if *you* can do any better.'

Bad taste, not to mention bad luck, to invoke the dead in that tone of voice. Betty said hastily, 'Talking of poor Ted, Clare, pet, did you get to the funeral? I know our Bob did, he was telling me ...'

Janet said, 'Funeral?'

There was a sudden embarrassed hush. No one else was going to fill it in, so Clare did.

'Ted died over half term, Janet. Very suddenly. The funeral was yesterday.'

'I liked Ted,' said Janet. Her voice was small and breathless. 'I hated all his ideas, but I liked him. He saw right through all of us. I'd have liked to come to the funeral. No one told me.'

Later it occurred to Clare that not one of them had gone on to ask what had happened afterwards to the girl — Andy Reid's victim, or society's, whichever it was.

Colin heard the story on mid-morning playground duty at Tenter Street. An unctuous little girl insisted on telling him. Afterwards she hung around waiting for a response. 'That's reelly awful, isn't it, sir?'

'Yes. Now go *away*.'

He had a free period after break and went into the staffroom to try and get warm. Gillian Newfield was sitting on the window seat. When Colin came in she turned round, and he saw that she had been crying. He had, of course, been meant to see it.

'What's up?' he said.

He had expected her tears to start flowing again. To her credit, they did not. She let her foot drag childishly sideways across the floor.

'I can't cope,' she said. 'I have tried. But now I've had a few days off — having to come back ... I just *can't*.'

'What makes you think the rest of us can?'

'You can.'

'I'm glad you think so.'

He sat down beside her: looked down at her frizzy, mousy-fair hair. What he ought to be feeling was pity.

'Gillian,' he said.

She jerked her head to show that she had heard.

'If you feel like packing it in — my advice, for what it's worth, would be to do just that. Let the half-wits who created this mess put it right.'

'There's no jobs ...'

'Being on the dole couldn't be worse than getting trapped in this place. And you're young' (meaning *You've got no responsibilities*): 'you could try something else, or go to another part of the country...'

'I can't just give up.'

'No,' he said. 'I know you can't. Only I'm not going to tell you to see it as a challenge, or to sit it out and wait for it to get better, because I'm not sure it will. In some schools, maybe, but not this one. It doesn't sound as though your Head of Department's being any more help than he was last time.'

'I think he means to.'

'I expect he does. But it's his job to do a bit more than just form good intentions.'

Hypocrite. Pharisee.

'He can't do anything,' said Gillian.

'He can make himself available. That's half the job anyway. It's not completely his fault that he's so much at sea, of course. Ted Auton would have done it much better.' *All right, Rowsley, now we've heard the Vatican version ... sit still, boy, or I'll make you stand on the desk.*

'I wish I was in your Department,' she said.

'I don't suppose you'd think so if you were. It's always easy to see what other people ought to do. My lot are just having to manage without me for most of the time, and I don't think they miss me all that much.'

In the doorway Dave Bowburn said: 'Ah — my lord and master.'

Lord alone knew what Dave was doing in Tenter Street. Colin looked at him with what he hoped was pointed enquiry. Dave looked calmly back.

'Can we do anything for you?' said Colin.

'No thanks.' Dave drifted round the room, looking at shelves, picking things up and putting them down again.

'Look, Dave, if you aren't actually doing anything here, could you just go for a walk or something?'

'*Sorry* — I didn't realise I was interrupting anything.'

'It's all right,' said Gillian. 'I was just going anyway. Thanks, Colin.' And slipped out of the room. Thanks for what? There was, after all, something impressive about her. *Some* people's characters improve through suffering.

'Do I scent a romance?' said Dave.

'Oh — shut up, Dave. She's having a bad time, and I was trying to provide some sympathy, that's all.'

'That's one way of putting it, I suppose.'

'For someone who's always talking about compassion and caring' said Colin, 'you have got the most unpleasant tongue, Dave. And a mind to match.'

As soon as it was out, he was sorry he had said it: not out of charity, but out of self-preservation.

'What about you and Clare Baylham, then?' said Dave, without raising his voice.

'*What* about me and Mrs Baylham?' His voice sounded amazingly steady as he said it, but there was no telling what give-away expression might have passed across his face.

'Nothing. Just if the cap fits.'

'Dave,' said Colin. If he sounded pompous, to hell with it. 'I'm not expecting you to call me "sir" or jump to attention. But for as long as I'm your Head of Department I think a certain minimal politeness is in order. And I won't discuss Mrs Baylham with you in her absence.'

Dave sat down, looked calmly across the room at him. In the second before the younger man opened his mouth, Colin recognised that facial expression. It belonged to the fifth-former who has weighed up the status of one of the prefects and counted it not worth bothering about.

'All right,' he said. 'No implication, unless you think there ought to be one. In any case, your Church wouldn't let you fuck her, would it?'

Colin found himself on his feet; but someone who has always worn spectacles knows better than to hit out physically at another man. There was even time for him to realise bleakly that when he did use his muscular strength it was always against someone weaker. He had to have an exit line, so he said weakly: 'I can see now why it's pointless to punish the kids for using words like that.'

The only place where you stood a chance of being unobserved during teaching hours was the staff lavatory. He leaned his damp hands and forehead against the tiled wall, shivering at the cold smooth contact. Look, said the sensible schoolmaster part of him, what is all this? You can hardly pretend you've never heard that word before. You've even been known to use it yourself.

Only as a curse, though: not as a description. That was what I did to Judith: not to Clare.

Without you, nothing I do will ever be any good.

Clare did not get her lunch hour after all. She spent most of it sitting at her desk in 4Y's classroom while Gail Fox wrote out a punishment exercise. Having Deborah to coach in the lunch hours had meant letting Gail get away with it all too often; and none more surprised than Gail when the axe had fallen today.

'Bring me up what you've written, Gail. If it's all right you can go.'

The first sheet was dull but adequate. *When we are at school we have to lern how to consentrate and let other peopl get on with there work, if we do we will get beter jobs when we leave ...* presumably that was what the girl thought Clare would want to read. 'All right, Gail' she said without looking at the rest of it. 'Go and get your lunch. And from now on will you save me the trouble of keeping you behind, please? You've got a good enough brain — use it.'

As she gathered up her books to go back to the staff-room Gail's sheet of paper slithered on to the floor. Clare stooped to pick it up: better wait till she was in another classroom before throwing it into the wastepaper bin.

On the second side was printed: I DO NOT WORK BECUASE I DO NOT LIKE MRS BAILAM WHO IS THE TEACHER. I DONT NOW ANYONE WHO THINKS SHE IS A GOOD TEACHER.

There was no wastepaper bin into which she could drop that; and nowhere she could put it without having to find it again later. And if she took it to the Headmaster or the Head of Middle School whom would she be punishing?

'Now you remember,' she said to the sixth-form group 'that Chaucer finishes the *Franklin's Tale* with a direct question to the audience: *Which was the mooste fre, as thynketh yow?* He's inviting them to join in the situation in the poem by asking them to take sides. Diane, do you remember what Chaucer means by *free*? ... all right, look it up. I hoped you might have remembered.'

'*Generous*. Or *noble*. Possessing the qualities befitting a free man.'

'Or free woman, of course. Because in this story the woman has her measure of heroism too, doesn't she, even though she doesn't have any power? She has moral power, at least: is that worth having, do you think, in the context of this story? Or is the freedom the men have the only kind that's worth having? Or perhaps none of them is "free" in the modern sense?'

'Um ... will you tell us which, Mrs Baylham?'

'Oh, come on, Diane, think it out for yourself a bit. Come to that, do you think Chaucer necessarily intended us to come down on one side or the other?'

It made them feel safer to be able to quote exact answers, and give labels to the views of the people who taught them. Colin and Janet were easier meat, *religious maniac* and *women's-libber* being terms readily at their disposal. Clare was more of a problem for them, she guessed, since their vocabulary did not include the term *feeble liberal*.

'Anyway, that's the title of the next essay: *Which was the mooste fre?* We have these four people in the story, who start by thinking only of what they can get for themselves: but by the end they're all outdoing one another in generosity and self-sacrifice. There are two or three sets of rules in conflict with one another here, aren't there? The rules of the Church, the rules of courtly love, and the ordinary rules of society. The Franklin comes down on the side of the Church and society, but does the story itself come down in exactly the same place? Start making some notes — I'll be back soon.'

Now that the clocks had gone back, there was darkness in the air even at half-past three. Her back was aching furiously again, and it would have been nice to sit down in the staffroom for some comforting chat and gossip: the sixth form could have been left safely enough for ten minutes. But the staffroom would be full of cigarette smoke, and all the chat would be of Ted and of Andy Reid.

She knew his footsteps in the corridor behind her. Quick steps, but uneven: he must put one foot down more heavily than the other.

'Mrs Baylham?' A neutral, talking-in-public-to-a-colleague voice. She turned round. Colin, don't go for me in the corridor. Have mercy on me.

He looked down at the floor. He said, very fast, very quietly: 'Clare. You don't have to answer. I just wanted to say I'm sorry. About everything.'

He had already begun to turn away. She did not dare to raise her voice or make any gesture.

'Oh, Colin. So am I.'

He turned back. 'There's no need.'

'Of course there is. I've got far more to be sorry for than you have.'

'No, you haven't,' he said. 'You were trying to get out of a corner, which I'd pushed you into. *I* was just trying to hurt. It's the one thing I do really well.'

There was a pressure behind her face which in a moment was going to produce disgraceful, humiliating tears. She did not think her expression had shown it, but he said suddenly, with what was very nearly a smile: 'If you cry, I warn you I probably shall too: and that really will be an end of all discipline and order!' So she had to laugh instead. Some sound in the laughter or change in the way they were standing alerted someone, because there was a volley of catcalls from the darkened landing above. Colin stepped back, looked upwards and bellowed: 'Get back to your classrooms! *Now*!' There was a scurrying noise, and then silence. Clare said shakily 'I didn't know you could yell like that.'

'I don't seem to have been doing anything else for the last month. Come back here in a year's time and you won't be able to tell me apart from Fred Errington.'

Come back in a year's time. After today, they might never be alone together again.

'Colin,' she said. 'Come home with me. Please. I mean just ... I could cook a meal for you, if you liked.'

He said: 'I can't even offer you a lift. Judith's got the car.'

'Richard's away too.'

'I know.'

'If you could face the bus ... it doesn't matter. Yes, it does.' Now she was the one to look down at the ground. 'Colin — unless you really don't want to ... please.'

She could not possibly know, could she, the significance for him of that wisp of hair in the nape of her neck? She had never asked him for anything. Except for understanding, of one thing which was not her fault, and he had refused that. Out of the few weeks left to them, he had refused his understanding for more than a month, which they would never have again.

His darkened, empty house, with its scuffed walls. *If I could begin to understand ... but it's a bit late for that now, isn't it?*

'Yes,' he said. 'Of course I want to. If you do.'

Once again the bell sounded over their heads. They looked at one another: knowing that none of the possibilities had changed; feeling only the relief and cleanness of being forgiven.

Between buses, they sat side by side at a table with a red formica top: hardly speaking, coffee growing cold in front of them. Homegoing travellers came and went around them. There was no one there who could have had any interest in watching them, but even so they did not hold hands, even under the table. Once a girl came and swabbed the table with a wet, grey cloth. *Brief Encounter*: the potency of mass-produced associations. What went through Clare's head, over and over again, was the refrain of a song from half a lifetime ago: *Well, this could be the last time, this could be the last time; it may be the last time, I don't know*. At a table on the other side of the gangway, one woman said to another 'They say in the *Sun* Princess Di isn't seeing enough of the bairn.'

'The bairn,' was not just Richard's: it was hers too. And if wishes could be stronger than genes or chromosomes, it was Colin's. Everything she had ever really wanted she had managed to lose. She had thrown away, twice, the place where she belonged. No one could ask her to do it a third time.

On the second bus, even when they were the last two people left aboard, she did not dare to put her head on his shoulder. By the time they got off at Gatelaw Green, stray flares and streaks of coloured light were coming and going in the air. 'Guy Fawkes,' said Clare. 'I'd forgotten.' 'You won't,' said Colin. 'Not after this year.'

They walked up the gravel drive to the cottage. Surely anyone seeing them would only have said 'She's bringing a friend home', not 'She's bringing her lover home.'

She switched on the hall light; shut the door behind them and drew the blind down over the hall window. Then she turned towards him.

His heartbeat had hammered against her face like this before: the sea behind them and the lighted polygons of the College of Education in front. The choice still to be made then. Or was that self-deception too?

At last they loosened their clasp and looked at one another: timorously, almost shyly. 'I've missed you so much' she said.

'I don't know what I've been doing this last month. I've been carrying on like a madman.'

'Colin — what are we going to do?'

'I don't know.'

She said 'Shall we go into the sitting room? I could light the fire.'

'I'll do that.'

He took the basket of fir cones away from the fireplace, crumpled up newspaper, laid strips of kindling wood crisscross, piled coal on top of them. When he did it in his own house it was drudgery. He crouched in front of the grate and watched the flame. It gyrated, then spread evenly. *And though after my skin worms destroy this body* ... all right, Ted. But we're still alive.

'Are you all right?' he said. 'Not feeling queasy after the bus?'

'No. I'm perfectly all right. I've been feeling absolutely terrible for the last few days, I've suddenly realised. And now it's all gone. So much for my thinking it wasn't psychosomatic.'

'You must have had a dreadful time. And it's my fault.'

She looked down at her fingernails. She said: 'Colin ... will you come and talk to me while I get the supper?'

'Of course. Indeed why don't *I* get the supper? I'm a tolerable cook if you don't ask me to do anything too ambitious.'

She did not look up. 'I didn't mean that. But there's something I must tell you. More than one thing really.'

It might be easier, laying bare the full tale of your inadequacy, if you could look down into a saucepan of bolognese sauce while you were doing it.

Her hair was limply soft under his hand, her face against his chest, her arms round him. He went on stroking her hair mechanically, watching the clock on the sitting room wall.

He said: 'All these years, you've been thinking of yourself as a failure. And I thought I knew you so well.'

She said, not looking up, 'I shouldn't make so much of it. I don't wake up every morning and think "Clare Baylham, you're a failure". And I know it's nothing to be ashamed of really: I've done my best. But knowing doesn't help.'

'I know that. Sometimes I do wake up and tell myself exactly that: "Colin Rowsley, you're a failure". But I suppose to someone on the dole, or starving, it wouldn't look like it.'

She tightened her arms round him. When he was sure she was not going to look up he said: 'Clare, the sex thing ... has that always been the same too, or did it only start happening after ...?'

'No, always. It's not that I don't want it. I mean, I can feel sexual desire. It's not very strong, but it's there. Only as soon as someone actually makes love to me — it just vanishes.'

'You said you didn't really mind. It wasn't true.'

'I don't mind all that much missing the physical experience — whatever it's like. But it's supposed to be the moment when two people are most together, isn't it? When you lose your separate sense of yourself. And there I am still alone. Most of all then.'

'It only lasts a minute, after all. It's not the most important thing. And you forget the other person as well as yourself. In a way it's *less* than being fully aware.'

'Knowing that doesn't help either. Not if you're on the outside looking in all the time anyway. I thought it would get better. I don't mean just sex, everything. I thought everyone was like me underneath — watching themselves all the time, telling themselves what to do next. But other people aren't like that. I can tell, from the way they react to me.'

He said, 'I keep wanting to say "Why didn't you tell me?" But you did try, didn't you?'

'I shouldn't have done it the way I did. I made it seem as though I was punishing you for it.'

'All I could think of was the damage to my bloody great ego. As though I'd given you a present and you'd said it wasn't what you wanted.'

'I know. But if I'd told you *before* we made love, you wouldn't have felt so hurt, but you'd still have felt rebuffed, wouldn't you? I don't think there's any way you *can* tell someone who wants you to make love. And I wanted to, as well. It's easy enough to resolve never to say anything all your life, when you've still *got* all your life. It's when you're getting older and it's still going on and on . . .'

Outside the house, on some lower spot down by Gatelaw Green, rockets went whistling up into the night.

'The ironic thing is,' she said, 'that I did tell Richard. We weren't married then, he could have made a quick getaway, but he was so sure it would get better. And then after a time, when it didn't, he was disappointed, and I could feel him thinking that he mustn't show it ... and I thought it might work out if I started pretending, sort of acted myself into it. It didn't, of course. But it seemed to fool him.'

'It fooled me,' said Colin. 'I suppose that was what hurt. I must have thought I was too good at it for that.'

'I wasn't just playing with you, Colin. Really.'

'I know that. It seems so obvious now. I must have *wanted* to believe it, in some stupid way.'

'I don't want to be like this. But I'm thirty-two — nearly thirty-three now. I used to think, in the end I'll grow up: it'll all be different next term ... next year. But I haven't grown up: I've just got older.'

'I'm much older than you. And we're here together now, aren't we? That's something that's changed.'

He found he was running his hand, again and again, from her shoulder down to her waist: as though he still did not know her body, as though he had never seen her naked. It would be different now: the first changes of pregnancy already visible. Richard's child. And now should I tell her what I did to my wife last night? But then she'd turn away from me too.

After a while she moved her head and looked up and round: not at him but at the clock. 'Colin' she said. 'I'm sorry, I didn't mean to spring a decision on you. But if you aren't going to stay, you'll have to go now. The last bus ... I've been putting off telling you. Do whatever you want.'

He said 'I can't read your mind. Everything that's gone wrong came from my thinking I could. Which do *you* want me to do?'

Obediently she said 'I want you to stay'; and began to tremble. 'Don't take any notice of this. I'm not doing it on purpose: I wasn't last time, either. You don't have to do anything about it. Stupid thing to say.'

With his arms round her he watched the hands of the clock twitching forwards until the decision had been made for him. After a while she stopped shaking, as she had done that other time.

'Clare, I can stay tonight without sleeping with you, you

know. In fact ... I haven't been having much success in that line recently.'

The formulaic words that begin a confession are supposed to make the rest easier. But to confess something indirectly, to tell it in such a way as to strip the act of its guilt, made it more difficult to give an honest account of it afterwards.

She said, 'Was that my fault?'

'No, of course not.' Amongst all the lies there might as well be one that was intended to protect her and not him. 'Would it make it easier tonight?'

'Yes,' she said. 'But it shouldn't, should it? It doesn't seem a terribly good augury, somehow.'

An augury takes for granted a future. Sometimes these things just shape themselves. He knew his previous self would have dismissed that idea as sentimental and self-indulgent: but then he had such a lot of things to unlearn.

'There'll be plenty of time,' he said. 'When you feel ready. It seemed so important before. I suppose I thought if I didn't ask for everything all at once, I'd lose it. I hadn't had any practice at adultery.'

That was the wrong word: he had made that mistake before. Her body went stiff in his arms. 'Neither had I,' she said, 'as it happens. I slept around a bit at Oxford, but not after that. I've never been unfaithful to Richard until ... Colin, if you're not mentioning it I've got to. Someone who can come out with a word like that ... what about your religion? How are you going to ... ?'

That, at least, now that the other thing had supplanted it, was an easy confession to make.

'I haven't really believed in that for years,' he said. 'I'm not particularly proud of keeping up the pretence. But I couldn't dignify it as "losing my faith" — it wasn't as rational as that. I just seemed to run out of it. And it meant — it still means — a lot to Judith, and we'd brought the children up in it — so I just let things go on. I didn't think it did any harm. It should have made me understand about pretending, though, shouldn't it?'

She said, 'I wish I'd known. I'm not trying to justify myself, but I might have done things differently if I'd known that. I thought perhaps — no, I didn't really, but it meant I could tell myself — you were just breaking the rules for one weekend because you were angry and miserable, and we seemed to be able to help each other that way.'

'And then I was supposed to rush off and get myself absolved on Monday, and put it all out of my mind?'

'No, of course not. You're not talking to Alan Carr now. I do know more about it than that.'

He laid his face against her hair. 'I'm sorry. Of course you do. You always did, didn't you? And I can't entirely have got rid of it, or I wouldn't react like that. It's just a reflex, though: I'm not cut out for the Graham Greene bit, believing it and not believing it at the same time.'

She said, 'I used to wish I were cut out for religious faith. It can seem rather attractive if you've never had it. But I find it difficult to believe in anything lasting two minutes, let alone world without end.'

'Some things last if you only let them. It'll be all right, Clare, I promise.'

Stopping every few seconds to smile at one another, gradually winding down from fear, they made up the spare room bed together. He said 'If any of your neighbours happens to be snooping, this is the perfect vindication, isn't it? The light in the spare bedroom.'

'I suppose this would be the baby's room. I keep forgetting about that.'

'It'll start kicking you in another couple of months, and then you *will* know about it.'

'You enjoyed your children when they were small, didn't you?' she said. 'I remember seeing you once, long before I knew you properly, with Edmund on one of those Spacehopper things, and Francis trying to pretend he wasn't anything to do with it. You looked such a nice family group. I don't know why I was so reluctant to have children — I suppose I just thought I'd be finally trapped when I did.'

'It can make you feel like that. I wish I hadn't lost whatever it was I had with mine when they were younger.

Clare — I'm not trying to put a thumb in the scale: at least I don't think I am. But you do know, don't you, I wouldn't make any difference over this baby? I used to think the flesh-and-blood thing was important, but it isn't. I'd love it because it was yours.'

She said 'Sometimes I think of it as yours. But it isn't, genetically. I did tell you the truth about that. I wouldn't do that to you. Or to Richard.'

Neither of them knew what to say about Richard.

Never before in her life had she deliberately avoided making plans. But then which of her plans had ever worked out as she had intended? *This could be the last time, this could be the last time. . . .*

She said 'You're sure you don't mind being in here? You're not just doing it because you don't feel it would be right in this house, or because I'm pregnant?'

'If it were a moral scruple, I could overcome it without any trouble at all. I love you: I want it because you do. We must neither of us ever pretend again.'

Colin fell asleep easily enough; then found himself once again awake and cold in the small hours of the morning. *The winter nights are coming on, and I must lie alone . . .* His mother singing to him in another small bedroom, while the heavy noise of the bombers passed overhead as they made their way down the Wear Valley to the North Sea.

Judith's patience and forbearance overlay a certain toughness which was precisely what he had once needed from her. She would not forgive him for what he had done. Perhaps it was better for her as well as for him that she should not. It did no harm to hope so, anyway. The boys were old enough, surely, not to be lastingly damaged? You could be close to your children without always being there with them. Edmund was robust and level-headed like his mother. And Francis was so much like his father that surely Colin could explain, in some way that would make sense and do no harm? Richard . . . well, Richard had his career. There must be some sort of compensatory justice in these things. Richard was far younger than Colin: he could have other children.

Perhaps it was thinking about children that made him think he heard one cry out in the dark.

This train was not stopping at all. To start with, it did not matter, because this time she was not alone. But then, as the sinister meaningless place names flashed past the window, the old panic began to take hold of her again; and sometimes she was begging the person who was with her to come too, and sometimes she was trying to escape from him.

'Clare. Clare, wake up. No, come on, wake up properly.'

Arms awkwardly round her. A voice which in a minute she would know and respond to. 'Come on, open your eyes. Clare, come on, *try*.'

An experienced father, coping with a child's bad dream. '*Colin!*'

He was kneeling beside the bed, leaning over her.

'That was a nightmare and a half you were having,' he said.

'Was I making an awful row?'

'Hardly at all. You were trying to cry out, I think, but you couldn't.'

Clare remembered. 'Yes ... that's right. But I woke you up.'

'No, you didn't. I wasn't asleep anyway. To be honest, I was wanting an excuse to come to you.'

Still not fully awake, she held out her arms. 'You're cold. Come into bed.'

There was only a second's hesitation before he slipped in beside her. 'Now you'll think I contrived the whole thing' he said.

'You might just as well say that *I* did.' With him beside her, her heart had nearly stopped pounding already. 'I can hardly hold you responsible for my dreams. Anyway, this one goes back years. It's all very boringly Freudian and obvious.'

'Do you want to tell me?'

'No, it's not that important. Some other time. Oh, love, how *did* you get so cold?' It was all right. The need, the taking, were not all on one side. She put her arms round him, stroked his shoulders and back. The naked skin was smooth, softer than she had remembered. She felt her nipples contract and harden at it: and in response felt him begin to erect against her. At the same moment he moved away. 'I really *didn't* contrive that' he said. 'I didn't think I could, at the moment ... sorry, for what it's worth. I'll go back.'

'*Stop* it!' She reached out. She knew where to touch him. He turned back helplessly: 'After all I said ...'

'That was my fault' she said. 'I'm the one who ought to be ashamed.' She took one of his hands and laid it on her breast, guided the other between her legs.

'Clare, I *can't*. That was how it went wrong before. I didn't give you any chance to refuse.'

'It went wrong before because I wasn't honest with you: it's different now. Look, would anyone believe we hadn't made love tonight anyway?'

She could feel his heart beginning to beat faster. 'You're not just inventing another way of punishing yourself?'

'Of course not.'

'I'm not going to lie on top of you — will you lie on your side and face me?' Richard had not thought of that. But then Colin had been on this journey before.

He said, 'You won't pretend, will you? You promise?'

'I promise.'

Not having to pretend might just, even now, make pretence unnecessary. His touch was so gentle, so delicate, that if anything could, that would have done it. But long before she was ready for him to enter her, her body went dead and passive.

After a moment he said 'This isn't any good, is it?'

'No. Oh, I'm sorry.'

'A few minutes ago you wanted me. I could feel that you did. I thought it must be all right this time.'

'I told you,' she said. 'It's always like this. At best. I always hope it won't be, but it never is any different. I ought to have the sense to stop asking for more. Some women would just be glad they weren't being beaten up.'

He moved away from her. 'I hate it when you talk like that. I want you to be happy and natural with me.'

'But you want me not to pretend. You made me promise. Colin, what am I to do? You don't want me to pretend, and when I don't, you're angry with me. Where do *I* come into all this?'

Outside, in the darkness of early morning, a single car wandered up the main street of the village. Its passing headlamps sent ghostly beams across the ceiling. Colin did not speak. He was lying, staring up at the ceiling.

She said, 'I love you. If you haven't got any use for that, then just leave me with it. I'm quite good at putting up with things, even if I'm not much good at anything else. Only don't treat me as though I did all this on purpose. I could probably dig up half-a-dozen reasons for it — over-protected childhood, dominant father, pushed too hard and then held back: the lot — but none of that solves it, does it? It's not something I choose — I don't blame you for not being able to change me, do I?'

Judith had turned her face away from him. He had said, 'Please,' and she had refused his plea. Clare, last night when I should have made love to my wife I thought of you instead. I wanted to hurt you.

'If I say I'm sorry yet again,' he said 'will you believe me?'

'Of course. Turn back to me. Please.'

They lay in one another's arms. He said 'Perhaps it can be overcome, you know. I've got plenty of patience. Surely if we both tried?'

'Could you bear it if it *never* worked?'

He lay still against her for a moment. 'Yes, of course I could. If *you* can put up with it, how can *I* refuse? It's not the most important thing.'

'Then finish making love to me now.'

'Clare, what are you doing? Putting me through a test? Or putting yourself through one?'

'It would be different if you didn't want to. I wouldn't blame you. But you can hardly pretend at the moment that you don't want to, can you?'

'But if I know you're only doing it to please me ...'

'Then what's the point of love at all?' she said. 'If I do it to please you, then that makes me happy. If I can't even do that ...'

'I don't understand anything, do I?' He touched her face clumsily, and came into her.

Before, he had always moved with such control, until the last moment. Now there was an awkward urgency: a consciousness that would not go away. Poor Colin, finding none of the reciprocity that was meant to take the place of conquest. It was not long before he shuddered and lay still. He said at last, already indistinct with sleep; 'I'll make it up to you somehow. I don't know how, but I'll try.'

'You don't have to make anything up to me.'

For as long as he was awake his confidence — that masculine triumph of hope over experience — strengthened her. But after he was asleep, his face against her arm — so careful, this time, not to rest any of his weight on her — she remembered that other night. Colin in her arms and the bumpy line of the dunes with the washed-out sky above it. Perhaps everything else she had thought and done that night had been a mistake, but she had been right about one thing: there were no half measures to be had. Colin's instinct, like hers, was for everything or nothing. This time most of the self-sacrifice would be on his part. But she knew, didn't she, what happened to self-sacrifice in the end? You began it so easily: for a time, virtue and delight were the same thing. And when you woke up, it was too late to go back. You turned to the other person and screamed 'I want, I want...'

Perhaps what Richard wanted was just, at all costs, *his* child; he could have that, with someone else, and perhaps be happier. But to lose a thing and then find it again did not abolish the pain of the original loss: it was no use pretending that you could take the last ten years away from Richard without damaging him.

She could never claim maintenance from Richard; but in six months she would have a baby, and she had given in her notice at Alderman Cassop. There was not the remotest chance of another job; but how could Colin support two families? His children's upbringing would have given them no preparation for being a one-parent family; Judith would not feel herself free to remarry.

Judith sitting on the floor, leaning casually back against

Colin's leg. So clearly a sexually successful marriage. Clare and Colin would have years and years in which to regret what they had done, feel the shared and separate weight of their guilt. Would he say to her, when she had no one else left in the world but him and her baby, *I gave everything up for you, and I've never had anything back*?

But she had tried once already to cut their losses. Her motives might have been mixed, she might have been brutally clumsy in the way she did it, but she had tried, and the child inside her was the result. She could not be responsible for trying again.

They woke up almost simultaneously; and lay without even turning to one another. Reluctant to break the peaceful contact of their bodies: skin against skin, hair against hair. Then Clare saw the clock.

'Colin, I must have done something stupid with the alarm! It's nearly eight: we'll have to get a taxi.'

He sat up. She remembered that: he was always wide awake immediately. 'When's the last possible bus?' he said.

'Quarter past. Even that won't get you there for Assembly.'

'Bugger Assembly. I'll get it: you have the taxi. You mustn't get up too quickly — anyway it's better if we don't leave the house together.'

The prospect of separating before they had to was unbearable; but it would give her time to remove all the evidence before she left: dishes put away, sheets bundled up for the laundry. Whatever they were going to say to Richard, he must not find it out by accident if he got home before she did.

'I'll go and get my clothes,' he said. 'Don't move. I want to look at you while I'm dressing.'

'I was looking forward to making breakfast for you' she said plaintively, to give vent to a deeper sense of pathos.

'How very unliberated of you.'

'Liberation is having the power to do what you want to do, isn't it?'

'Pedant. I love you. When are we going to meet?'

'Oh, Colin ... I've simply *got* to do something with

Deborah this lunch hour. She didn't get any attention yesterday because I had to keep bloody Gail Fox in. I really will have to play fair with her today.'

'Yes, of course. And after school you'll have to rush back for Richard?'

'Yes. For today, I think I must. You do understand?'

'Yes, I do. And Judith's not back till the weekend, so anyway we couldn't... Clare, we must work out what we're going to do, though. Tomorrow?'

'Yes. I'll think about you all the time till then.'

'So shall I. Do you think we could send each other thought waves?'

'I don't suppose I'd be any better at telepathy than I ever was at catching a ball' she said. 'Colin, you *must* go. You've got about four minutes to catch that bus.'

At lunch time — how could he possibly sit still in the staffroom today? — Colin met Wendy Sykes in the Tenter Street entrance hall. 'Bad job about Ted Auton' she said. In Wendy's vocabulary that indicated considerable sorrow.

Colin had not spared Ted a thought for about eighteen hours. 'Yes' he said. 'Good of you to come to the funeral, Wendy.'

'Wouldn't have known about it except that it's my parish church. Not that I go there as often as I should.'

'Has the Headmaster mentioned it? I haven't been going in to Assembly.'

'Not a sausage. To be fair, I think that was embarrassment rather than callousness. He does have his human side, whatever it sometimes seems like.'

It was not difficult now to find so small a measure of generosity. 'I suppose so,' Colin said. 'I admit I've never looked very hard for it. You obviously have.'

'Not particularly. Just from time to time, when you have to work with him as much as I do, it shows up for a moment or two. Not that I'm trying to defend the way he treated Ted — or you or Clare Baylham, for that matter. The trouble was of course that he wanted the three of you on his side — and you'd none of you play ball.'

'Good God,' said Colin. 'Why the three of us particularly?'

'The academic stars of this establishment, you foolish young man.' Wendy was, at most, four or five years his senior. 'That's why he didn't bother to persecute Brian Ludworth over the de-streaming business. Surely you realised that? Brian is my dearest friend, but in grammar-school days can you imagine he'd ever have got to be Head of Department? But Ted was a scholar, and you and Clare are the only Oxbridge people we've got left now. Look at it from the Headmaster's point of view.'

'I've never noticed that he looked at it from mine.'

'I shouldn't think he could afford to, could you? He's got himself up to the top of the tree, and now the whole thing's starting to shake. He wants to impress the Board of Governors; he wants to keep his sixth form; and he wants to have a reputation for being able to control everyone, from the highest to the lowest. He wants the lot, our Mr Kettleby. Still, don't we all?'

'He missed his aim a bit, then, didn't he?' said Colin. 'Ted's dead. Clare's leaving. I assure you I'd be leaving too if there were anywhere else I could go.'

'I think you might find him more amenable from now on, for that very reason. It wasn't part of his plan for you all to disappear. Not that I blame you for feeling bitter. Oh, speaking of which, I've been meaning to ask you ... I had a most peculiar visit from a parent the other week. An enraged father. He said you'd manhandled his daughter, and confiscated some piece of jewellery she was ...'

'Oh, Lord,' said Colin. He remembered the girl who had scratched the outside of his car; his own mindless rage.

'Gotcha,' said Wendy. 'Well, he huffed and puffed a lot, but I told him untruthfully that I knew all about it; and I said I backed you up to the hilt and she shouldn't have been wearing jewellery anyway, and that she'd get it back at the end of term and not a day before. Luckily he wasn't one of those parents who knows his rights. Have you still got the object, or did you pawn it for a vast sum?'

Colin fished in his pocket. The Woolworth's ring was where it had been lying for the last five weeks. He held it out to her. 'Shows how often I change this jacket,' he said. 'Sorry, Wendy. I know exactly why I didn't remember to give it to you. It was a thoroughly discreditable incident and I'm extremely ashamed of it. Do you want me to tell you the ghastly details?'

She patted his arm. 'I shouldn't bother. If you've never done anything worse than that, I don't think we'll be taking you to court just yet.'

At the end of morning school, for the first time in her pregnancy, Clare was sick. The thought of making different arrangements for Deborah made her feel worse than the thought of going on, so she went on.

'I didn't like the end of *Jude the Obscure* much,' said Deborah. 'I don't know whether that's a critical reaction or just an emotional one. I kept seeing that big flashy cross in the church in Oxford — that weird Anglo-Catholic one — and poor old Sue Bridehead spread-eagled out under it. It was ... I don't know, *brutal*.'

'Well, obviously Hardy intends it to be a very disturbing passage. The question is really whether the shock of it breaks up the balance of the rest of the book, or whether Hardy's managed to set up the situation well enough for it to seem natural.'

'Natural enough if you go along with Hardy's view of life, I suppose. I don't usually mind that, though — usually I can accept practically anything so long as I'm reading — but I *couldn't* take this one on board, not straight after Hopkins. Hardy twists your arm, doesn't he? He won't let you disagree.'

Clare thought, but could not attend properly to the critical formulation. 'You're obviously right in a way,' she said. 'We get used to the way Hardy manipulates events, because he tells us with such passion that life's *like* that. Perhaps we let him off too lightly for the way he manipulates *us*. Would that be a good idea for an essay — or do you want just to read and make notes for this last ten days?'

'I haven't done much on novels,' said Deborah. 'It might be a good idea. You wouldn't mind if it was just in note form, would you?'

'Of course not. I know you can write continuous prose. Hang on, then — I'll just work out a title.'

She stood up and reached for the chalk; she felt a

dragging sensation, heavy rather than painful, in her abdomen; and took a step to balance herself. When she looked down there was a spot of blood on the floor. No bigger than the splashes they used to shake from their dip pens at primary school.

'Deborah,' she said. Her own voice, exaggeratedly level and calm. 'Will you run and find another member of staff — a woman if there's one around? It may be nothing, but I think I might be starting a miscarriage.'

X

Janet swept across the room and knelt down beside Clare. 'I've sent Deborah to telephone for an ambulance,' she said. 'And she's to tell them you can't walk — all right? The secretaries will ring your husband at work, if you give me the number.'

'He's not there,' said Clare. 'He's at a conference — at least, he'll be on his way back by now.'

'We'll think of something to do about that in a minute. Now look, what exactly's happened?'

Clare said carefully, 'I started to bleed. I think I still am ... and I felt as though I — as though it had started to come away. So I thought I'd better lie down flat at once.'

'Does it hurt a lot?'

'It's beginning to. And I feel a bit faint.'

'That's probably shock.'

'Sheer terror, you mean.'

Unexpectedly, Janet took hold of her hand. 'Why not?' she said. 'Look, this pain — is it steady, or is it coming like contractions?'

'Steady.'

'Then there's probably a good chance it won't come to anything.'

What could Janet possibly know about it? Still, it was kind of her to try. Colin ... but that wasn't fair, that was jumping the gun. And why should he have to watch Richard's child miscarry? She felt a sucking blackness inside her head, and clutched at Janet's hand.

'Clare, if you can manage *not* to pass out ...'

'It's all right: I never have. I don't suppose I'm likely to start now.'

The floorboards were hard under her back. From where she lay she could see the splintered undersides of desks; pencil shavings and sweet papers on the floor. Then Deborah's voice from somewhere behind her: 'They've just arrived.'

Janet's voice: 'Thank God: that was quick.' Funny for Janet to say, 'Thank God'. Did fear betray you into saying what you did mean, or what you didn't mean?

Deborah's voice, wobbly with tears: 'Is she all right?' Clare wanted to answer her, make some reassuring noise, but while she was making the effort to open her mouth, Janet said: 'She's all right. Deborah, there's nothing you can do here. The most useful and helpful thing you can do is to go and find Mrs Sykes, or if she's not around it'll have to be the Headmaster. Tell them what's happened, and that I'm going with Mrs Baylham to the hospital. All right?'

'Yes.'

'Good girl. I'll see you later.'

Clare said weakly, 'You don't have to come with me ...'

'No, but I'm going to. They can just bloody well arrange cover for me. I haven't been off ill for all the time I've been here, so they owe me that much.'

Clare kept her eyes shut when the ambulance men were carrying her down the stairs: perhaps only to shield herself from the eyes of the children jostling past to the classrooms. 'Get out of the *way*!' Janet kept saying.

'Ee, it's Mrs Baylham!'

'Miss, what's up?'

'Get out of the *way*!' said Janet again.

The hospital was only about half a mile down the road: near the church where Ted's service had been (only the day before yesterday). It seemed fraudulent to be going there in an ambulance. Her eyes were still shut, but she heard herself saying to Janet, very clearly, as though to a willing but not very bright pupil: 'I think the best way to let Richard know is to look in the phone book for some people called Saxtead: S-A-X-T-E-A-D. The husband's initial is G. — or J. – and the address will be The Glebe, Gatelaw. If you asked them to put a note on our front door ...'

'Yes. Fine. Clare, stop *fighting* it. The only thing you can possibly do to help yourself is to try and relax.'

'I can't.' Without Colin I can't do anything. The only time I ever let myself need someone ... 'Yes. I'll try. *Try* to relax is a bit of a contradiction in terms, isn't it?'

'Clare, shut *up*! Just for once in your life stop talking!' Someone's hand was trembling; but it seemed to be Janet's.

They kept telling her, in a kindly, bullying way, to open her eyes; and after a while, since they were determined to go on asking her questions, and had started addressing her as 'Clare', she did so. 'Ee, look' said one nurse to another 'she's decided to come to life! That's better now, isn't it, Clare?'

'I'm sorry,' she said. 'That was a bit silly, wasn't it?'

Neither of the two nurses looked more than about half her age. They smiled at her, then at each other.

'We don't mind, do we, Donna? We get some that scream and swear at us, don't we? Now what's yer date of birth, pet?'

'30th January 1951.' An *elderly primagravida*. Not any more.

'Now we're going ter give yer a bit injection, ter help yer relax, like. Can yer just tell us, Clare, did anything, like, come away before yer was brought in, or was it just blood?'

Clare shut her eyes again quickly. 'Just blood.'

The textbooks called it, 'the products of conception,' that detached themselves from the womb. Nothing so emotive as a baby.

She had never been in a hospital bed before. Creaking, scuffling noises went on the whole time, and sometimes there was the subdued shriek of metal wheels. But she could not see anything, except the fading reflection of the windows on the ceiling, because someone had put screens round her bed. That was hard to understand, because she had always thought they did that when you were dying, and it wasn't she who was dying. All she was doing was being the host to a death. If it would come quickly, she could start getting used to that too.

It stopped, started again, stopped again. The outline of the window on the ceiling had faded completely, and the streaking reflections of car headlights had replaced it, when one of the nurses came back. 'Yer've been so quiet we forgot about yer,' she said. 'Are yer managing, pet?'

'Yes, thank you,' said Clare. 'Donna — it is Donna, isn't it? — do you know if anyone's managed to track down my husband yet?'

'Yer friend, that brought yer in, she said she'd get in touch.'

So there was nothing she dared to do to try and reach Colin.

The girl was halfway through the screen before Clare, with a desperate rush of courage, said: 'Donna. I don't want to get you into trouble, but could I ask you to do something?'

'What would yer like us ter do?'

'If my husband does come and I'm ... you know, if I'm not properly in control of what I'm saying, could you try and keep him out of the way?'

'Ee, Clare, that's not very nice, is it?'

'No, I suppose it isn't. Forget I asked. I'm sorry.'

'I've forgotten already. Anyway, yer going ter be all right, aren't yer?'

Perhaps all this desire to protect Richard had been really her knowledge that if she did not have him she would have no one else. Colin was not there to hold her hand, to tell her it did not matter, to share her guilt and her failure and somehow take away the disgust.

I didn't even think I wanted this baby all that much. It was a way out; and then it was a justification of everything else. Something that came out of me that wasn't only me. *I myself am hell.*

If you had a body that would not do anything you wanted it to do, there was no point in going on struggling against its reactions to pain and fear. 'Donna' she said. 'Donna, I'm sorry, I'm going to be sick.'

The humiliation of vomiting in front of someone else, and the extra pain of retching, brought weak tears to her eyes, and when she lay back on the pillows Donna saw them. 'There's no need ter cry, pet,' she said. 'I think it's time someone came and had a look at yer.'

Richard, coming up the motorway in the wake of a lorry, suddenly found his windscreen had become opaque and crazed with distracting patterns. The lorry had thrown up a stone and shattered the glass. He pushed the blunt pieces out on to the road and tried to carry on, but in a north-eastern November that was hopeless: soon he could hardly feel his hands or feet. At the next service station he stopped to warm up and get a windscreen fitted. There were queues for all the telephones, and he had not said he would be home by any particular time.

It was nearer seven than six by the time he swerved round Gatelaw Green. Now that the trees were half bare you could catch a glimpse of the cottage as you turned the corner by the church.

There were no lights in any of the windows.

In so far as Richard was anything philosophical, he was a scientific rationalist: but he found himself doing something fairly close to praying. There was no moonlight, and out in the country like this there was no glow from street lamps either: when he saw the sheet of paper pinned to the door he had to take it back to the car headlamps to read it.

A BIT OF AN EMERGENCY, THOUGH IT MAY BE NOTHING. PLEASE RING ME OR COME TO THE HOUSE AS SOON AS YOU GET BACK. PAULINE S. Then there was a telephone number, and an address. It took him three or four attempts to get his key into the lock, and as many more to dial the number.

Colin finished the accrued marking of two days and packed it into his briefcase. After that he made some toast and scrambled some eggs and washed up with elaborate care. He did not want to confront the moment when he would have to start doing his sums.

There was no way at all in which they would work out. In so far as he had had a rational thought at all for the last twenty-four hours, it had been that he would be withdrawing from his wife and children only his physical presence, which was a burden to them as well as to him. Without him there, everyone would be happier. But two households meant two sets of bills. Clare could not go on working much longer: in any case he could not possibly depend on her to keep them both. *How very unliberated of you*, he had teased Clare: but it was much easier to break a commandment than a taboo. In another two years — less if Francis could be persuaded not to bother with Oxbridge — the money situation would be easier; Edmund could perhaps go to a sixth-form college, and that would help too ... but there was Clare's child. There was no longer any possibility of waiting. To take possession of a child in embryo was one thing; but to separate a two-year-old and its father — was he going to end up as the kind of person who did that? Was that how Clare would end up?

He would have liked to telephone her. If she imagined that he was the one who provided strength and dependability, that might be an illusion they both needed, but it was an illusion nonetheless. He could have gained assurance, somehow, just from hearing her voice, that it was possible, because it must be. But tonight was Richard's: it would have to wait. They were civilised people, weren't they? If it could not be done without giving pain, and of course it could not, then at least they could try to do it in as careful and responsible a way as possible. Kevin Colin Rowsley, the well-known hypocrite. Guilt of a perfunctory, automatic kind, was something he had always been familiar with. This personal and particular kind of guilt was something he was going to have to get used to.

The reception hall of the hospital was dark, with a high ceiling. Someone had tried to cheer it up with a false ceiling of white trelliswork, and there was smart white panelling on the lower walls. All the effort that had gone into this only drew attention to the building's intrinsic gloom. Richard had been sitting there, amongst the coughing, the cigarette smoke and the whispered conversation, for more than two hours. He sat, not because he did not want to pace up and down in the approved manner, but because sitting down enabled him to convince himself that he was staying calm.

Couldn't she even manage to have a baby without making a Greek tragedy out of it? *My* baby — why couldn't she take care? If she took some stupid risk I'll never forgive her.

Richard was not used to violent emotion or to introspection: he did not like either of them. What he wanted was not for everything to come out right now, but for it never to have happened.

At last a doctor appeared and called him over into a corner. A short, delicate-boned Asian: his was the only coloured face in the room. He might have been any age between twenty-five and fifty. Richard got up and followed him: there seemed to be nowhere more private to go.

'My wife' he said. 'Is there any news?'

'A haemorrhage always looks alarming, but it is not necessarily very serious. But she does seem to be in a good deal of pain, and I am afraid that is not such a hopeful sign.'

'Can I see her?' It came out because it was the right thing to say. But she never had shared anything with him, had she? Not really. Was it likely she would begin now?

She was so controlled, so in-turned: but then that was what had attracted him once.

'I cannot let you see her now,' said the doctor. 'You may go home, or stay here if you prefer. I have given her a very powerful sedative, something that should knock her out for several hours. She was being very brave, but she was so tense it was quite hopeless.'

The old-fashioned vocabulary, the perfectly-formed sentences — if the doctor had been white, Richard would have cut across them. As it was he waited politely and then said: 'But do you think she'll be all right? I'm not a temperamental character: I'd prefer an honest answer.'

He saw the doctor look at him: sizing up, with an ex-colonial's detached accuracy, Richard's manner, his accent, his neatly subdued clothes.

'There is no doubt that your wife will be all right in herself. An abortion is very sad, of course ...'

'*Abortion?*'

'Miscarriage. Clinically it is the same thing. She is still quite young, and her health seems to be good. There will be no damage to that even if we cannot save the pregnancy.'

'But do you think you can save it?'

'Some pregnant women can be knocked down by buses, you know, or fall out of windows, and still bring the child to term. If she can manage to rest now, we may be lucky.'

Richard went back to his seat. Brave ... yes, she would be that all right: to the *nth* degree. But was there nothing more to life than that?

Next to him sat a young woman: younger than Clare, probably, from the rounded, unformed outline of her features; but already stout and ungainly in a middle-aged way. She had three children with her, or sometimes it seemed to be four: Richard was not sure he was seeing everything quite as it really was, tonight. The youngest child slept intermittently on her lap. The other two, or three, ran round the room, shouted, fell over, howled. Richard alternated between irritation at their piercing voices and runny noses, and a well-brought-up feeling that he ought to help. But he did not know how. He wanted children of his own, had always assumed that he liked children: but he did not know anything about them.

'Is yer wife having a baby?' the young woman asked sympathetically.

'A miscarriage. A threatened one, anyway.'

'Did yer want the baby?'

'Yes.' Richard felt his eyes begin to smart. This development was so appalling, the need to thwart it so overriding, that he pointed at the sleeping child in her lap.

'Can I take that one off you for a bit? It must be rather uncomfortable for you.'

'Would yer reelly? I can see our Wayne needs to go ter the toilet.'

Richard took the bundle stiffly. 'No, pet, like this: yer bend yer arm round, all right?'

She seemed to be gone for ages. Richard felt conspicuous and embarrassed, and ashamed of himself for it. The baby was dressed in layers of frills; a pink plastic dummy was plugged into its mouth. He knew he would much rather have been holding, not just his own child, but any tastefully-dressed dummyless middle-class child; and he did not like what this knowledge told him about himself. What was it he had wanted so much — something on a level with an estate car, a detached house, a box file of insurance policies?

The woman came back. One of the children leaned against her, the other against Richard.

'I'm reelly sorry about yer wife. Still, yer never know, pet, a "miss" doesn't always come to anything. Perhaps she'll be lucky.'

'Yes. I suppose so.'

'My eldest was bad with stomach pains at school. That doctor, the foreign one, said it was appendicitis. That's not serious, is it?'

'I don't think so. I've had it, anyway, and I'm still here.'

'I told our Tina she'd be all right, but I didn't, like, reelly know. I had ter bring them all with me, because my husband's on late shift. He's only just got the job, he didn't dare to take time off.'

Once you had children, you could never do anything unpremeditated again. Richard had not thought of that either. One way and another, it seemed, he had a good deal to learn.

It was well after midnight when a nurse — tiny, five-foot-nothing with a snub nose and broad Wearside accent — came and called Richard. The woman and her children had gone; there were only Richard, and a couple of blood-stained drunks, left.

It could not have had anything to do with what she had said to Donna, could only have been good luck, that had kept Clare alone all evening. She could remember being given another injection, and then someone had come and washed, very gently, between her legs; and that, without warning, made her vomit again, so that then she had been apologising to someone who briefly took hold of her hand

and patted it; and then, as the sedative took effect, before it sent her right down into darkness, hearing the continuing sound of her own voice. She did not know, and now presumably never would know, whether that less disciplined self had called out for comfort from a lover who was not her husband, or for mercy from an active, interventionist God in whom she did not believe. When Richard was brought in to see her she was, more or less, her familiar self again.

She was lying back on the flat hospital pillow: she was very pale, her hair was tangled, and she was wearing a hospital nightdress which fastened with tapes at the back of her neck. But she held out her arms to him, and he did not pause to ask himself whether this was to receive comfort or to give it.

'Richard,' she said. 'Richard, it's all right. I haven't lost it.'

It might have sounded as though she were talking about a missing credit card, but she knew he understood. And she understood that it would be much more difficult now, nearly impossible, to take away from him what had been lost and was found again.

Colin slept that night, an uninterrupted sleep he had not known for weeks. In the morning the arithmetic looked no better than it had done the night before. But though he had always imagined himself to be someone who took responsibilities gravely, while he was shaving he found himself humming in the most irresponsible manner possible. He would see her today, and together they would decide how to do it.

Every Friday morning his timetable forced him to spend the ten-minute break getting between the two sites, with no time for collecting his thoughts or even for a rapid cup of coffee. Nothing could put him out of temper today, though. He grinned cheerfully at his sixth-form group, perched himself on a desk in front of them and propped his feet up on the one opposite it. There was the usual kindly titter.

'Mr Rowsley, is Mrs Baylham all right?'

'Mrs Baylham?' said Colin.

'Debbie Robson was really upset yesterday. Miss Waldridge had to take her home.'

Colin took his feet off the desk and lowered them to the floor.

'I'm sorry — can you tell me what you're talking about?'

For a second or two after she had told him, he went on handing back their marked essays on *The Franklin's Tale*. The most coherent parts of the essays were the bits they had parroted from him. No one like Deborah in this group...

'Girls,' he said. 'I think I'd better find out a bit more about this. I'm only the Head of Department around here: no one tells me anything. Can you get on with ... yes, do me a translation and comprehension passage. The end section, from *Aurelius, that his cost hath al forlorn* as far as *Which was the mooste fre, as thynketh yow*? Turn that into modern English, and then write me some context notes — you know the sort of thing.'

'Can you just remind us, sir?'

Desperately Colin said, 'Look — the whole passage is full of words from courtly love and chivalry: *grace, curteisye, gentillesse, trouthe* ... even *fre*, here at the very end. I've been going on about it for the last four terms, for Heaven's sake ... if by any chance I can't get back before the bell goes, can you just get on with it for homework? Sorry.'

He was not going to use the telephone in the main hall. Though the journey took him straight past the windows of the Headmaster's study, he went up to the telephone boxes on the main road. He could not really run these days, but he managed something fairly close to it. Three separate fully-formulated sentences went through his head: repeatedly, but in different sequences. *It's not your child. No one dies of a miscarriage these days.* And finally, damningly, *If she loses the baby, that'll make it easier for us.*

The ringing noise at the other end of the line went on for a long time. Then a sleepy-sounding Richard gave the number.

'Richard. It's Colin. I've only just this minute heard.

How is she?' Steady on — you're her friend and boss asking, that's all. For the moment.

'Oh — Colin. Sorry — I'm only half awake. They think it's probably going to be all right. But it still seems to be very painful, so they're keeping her in for a bit.'

'No one thought to tell me anything about it,' said Colin. 'I had to hear about it from the sixth form ten minutes ago.'

'Oh ... sorry. I was a bit preoccupied last night.'

'Christ, Richard, I didn't mean *you*. Someone at school should have told me. The girls said it happened in the lunch hour yesterday.'

'She was teaching little what's-her-name, the Oxford girl, and then she realised there was something wrong. That other female, the trendy-lefty one, took charge and got her to hospital.'

'Janet Waldridge?'

'Apparently she was a tower of strength. Mind you, so was Clare. She was alone for hours and hours before I got there, in pain and thinking she was going to lose the baby, but she wasn't a bit hysterical, or weepy, or anything.' Richard for a moment sounded distinctly weepy himself. 'Sorry, Colin. I didn't have much sleep. It was good of you to ring.'

'I'm sorry to have brought you to the phone — thoughtless of me.' Colin heard his own tone of calm concern. 'But I'm very relieved, of course. May I ring up again later to hear if there's any more news?'

Richard said 'Of course'. Then after a moment his voice came back, awkwardly. 'There's still a bit of a risk — they told me not to worry, but ... Colin, you go in for prayers and things, don't you? I know it's a bit much coming from a heathen like me, but you might say one for her, if you would.'

'Yes, of course. Goodbye, Richard. Sorry again to have woken you up.'

And give her my love? He leant back against the inside wall of the kiosk and shut his eyes. People with nothing better to do could look in and see him if they wanted to. The hair at the back of his neck was soaked in sweat. An adolescent voice outside the kiosk said 'Ee, it's Mr Rowsley — quick!' He opened his eyes, but whoever it was had gone already, leaving an echo of running feet. As though he could spare any thought for chasing a truant ...

Janet was standing in front of her class and talking to them. Like any other teacher in front of any other class. When Colin came in, some of the children even made a half-hearted effort to get up.

'Miss Waldridge,' he said. 'Can you spare me a few minutes, please?'

Janet looked at her watch. 'We'll leave it there' she said to her class. 'Just talk amongst yourselves till the bell goes, then get along to your next class.'

It was no different from what he or anyone else would have said to them. Outside in the hall they moved to one side, out of range of the glass panels in the classroom doors.

'Janet,' said Colin. 'Would you like to tell me, before I start shouting at you, your version of what happened yesterday?'

Janet was wearing a grey wool jumper and skirt. It made her body look square and vigorous.

'About Clare, you mean?' she said. 'How is she, by the way — do you know?'

'Yes, I do — no thanks to you. She's had a bad time, but she hasn't lost the baby, and it seems that there's a good chance she won't. *Now*' — his voice began to shoot up and down, out of his control — 'will you please explain how it was that you apparently took charge of the whole thing and never saw fit to let me know at any point?'

Janet looked puzzled but surprisingly patient. Perhaps that was what she was like with difficult pupils. 'Well, I could hardly have come down to Tenter Street and told you in person, could I? The main thing on my mind at the time was getting Clare to that hospital without making things worse. Did the secretaries get my message buggered up somehow?'

'Message? Janet, all this happened nearly twenty-four hours ago. The first I heard of it was at the beginning of this lesson, from my sixth-form group. *From my sixth-form group!*'

'I sent Deborah to ring for an ambulance' she said slowly. 'You do agree that was the most important thing, I hope? Then after that I told her to find Wendy Sykes, or the Headmaster, and let them know. I suppose I just assumed ... but Deborah's a sensible girl, I'm sure she did it. I couldn't have left her with Clare, though — she's only a kid, and I know enough ... well, let's just say a miscarriage isn't something you want a seventeen-year-old to see if you can help it. And Clare wasn't making any fuss, but she said she was frightened — which wasn't exactly surprising, but it seemed such an admission coming from her. So I stayed with her. It seemed the only thing to do at the time, and then later I —'

'Janet,' said Colin. 'Please stop.'

Janet stopped.

'I'm sorry,' said Colin. 'It obviously wasn't your fault at all, and I should have known it wouldn't be. In fact you come out of it with more credit than anyone.' He found he was shaking: probably had been for some time. Anyone coming into the hall would have had an interesting tale to report. 'Deborah won't have found Wendy Sykes, because she was over in Tenter Street. She must have been talking to me just when ... so presumably the person Deborah found and told was the Headmaster.'

'Oh, bloody hell,' said Janet. 'And he never passed it on to you.'

'No. I ought to be used to his malevolence by now ... no, I don't suppose it was even that. He just never thought it mattered to let me know.'

'I'm so sorry I didn't think to ring you up later. But when I got back here, I found myself having to cope with Deborah, who was in a frightful state; and by the time that was all over, to be honest, I was feeling pretty shaken up myself.'

'Of course you were. You'd every right to,' said Colin mechanically. 'Is the girl all right now?'

'Oh, I think so. I've seen her around this morning, anyway, and she didn't look any the worse for it. I think she's pretty tough really, in a reasonable sort of way. Are *you* all right, though?'

Colin took his spectacles off, rubbed his hand shakily over his face, put the spectacles back on again. Janet stared at him. He owed her some kind of explanation, certainly, but not the one that came out.

'It's not my child, you know.'

'Good God, Colin, I never for a moment supposed it was.'

Clare had been in pain, and afraid, wanting someone with her, while he had been talking to Wendy Sykes, and teaching 3T and 4F, and through the evening while he was marking exercise books and trying to make his sums come out as he wanted them to. He had slept peacefully and dreamlessly while she lay alone. He should have been with her, and had not been, and she had not asked for him. I'm no good to her. I can't support her, not financially nor in any other way. Perhaps she doesn't even really want me: she was trying to make amends, hand me back to Judith with my self-esteem restored.

He knew it was nonsense even as he thought it. He knew perfectly well why she had gone through it alone rather than ask for him. *It's not fair, it's not fair* . . . like the kids. He would have done the same for her. Only in the nature of things there was nothing he could do.

The stretch of grass between Middle and Upper School seemed to extend for miles. Of course he was late for his next class, and of course Kettleby was there before him. 'On another occasion, Mr Rowsley, if you are unable to arrive in time for a class, perhaps you would send word?'

'I've been speaking to Miss Waldridge, Headmaster. She was concerned about Mrs Baylham.'

There was no change of expression at all on the Headmaster's face. Only yesterday, Colin would have gone on and on trying to produce some reaction of guilt. He could hear in his own voice no anger or outrage, merely apology and self-justification.

When Kettleby had gone he handed out the exercise books. He noticed that he was leaving damp fingerprints on the covers.

Clare woke up to the bright cold sunshine of November. It

took the still dragging pain in her back and abdomen to remind her of where she was and what had happened; and what, inexplicably, had not happened.

She would still have a child: instead of the fulfilment, it was the disappointment which had been snatched away. She had done nothing, had been prevented from doing anything, to save it, and it had been saved for her, after all.

She wanted to imagine what Colin must be feeling and thinking; but whenever she tried to think of him he seemed tiny and far away — belonging to the time before yesterday. I love you, she said experimentally to herself, to him: I love you. And there was no doubt that it was true, but it did not bring him any nearer.

She dozed, was woken again and propped up. 'Yer'll need ter make yerself a bit smart for visiting time.' Richard had apparently driven home last night, brought back her hairbrush and make-up bag and one of her own night-dresses, and gone home a second time. A double trip of over sixty miles in the small hours of the morning. Could Richard really have supposed she had strong feelings about nightdresses or hairbrushes? All the same, it was a touching attempt to be imaginative.

'Now that's reely pretty,' said the nurse approvingly. 'We're very pleased with you, yer know.'

'Oh, I meant to tell you,' said Richard. He was sitting on the edge of the bed, holding her hand. He might feel she was not responding enough, so she traced patterns with her thumb on his palm. 'I meant to tell you, Colin rang up. To ask how you were.'

'Oh . . . that was nice of him.'

'He sounded very concerned. Good of him to take the trouble, I thought.'

'Well, we've all known one another a long time, haven't we? Still, he *is* good about that sort of thing.'

'He said no one at that wretched place of yours had taken the trouble to tell him what had happened, until this morning.'

Last night, whilst she had been lying here, eyes tightly shut, hands pressed against her belly, he had not known:

had gone home and marked exercise books and slept. They had sent out no thought messages to one another. Colin, I want to know what to do.

Richard said, 'I wanted to ask that Indian doctor what he thought about things, but they said he was off duty. Does it still hurt?'

'Quite a lot. They've given me some painkillers, though. It's not as bad as it was.'

'You look marvellous, when I remember last night,' said Richard.

'Poor love. It must have been awful.'

'Not much fun for you either, I imagine. I should never have gone away.'

'Don't be silly ... You are eating properly, aren't you?' Was this a guilty concern because she would not be coming back, or a prudent concern because she would be? She shut her eyes again: it seemed to be her way out of everything at the moment.

'Are you all right?' said Richard, panic in his voice.

'Yes. Really. Just wilting for a moment. I don't know when they'll let me out of here.'

'Even when they do, you certainly won't be rushing round cooking meals and carrying shopping bags for a long time. You're going to rest and do what you're told. And you certainly won't be going back to that damned school for a bit. Not at all, if I can help it.'

'Richard, even if everything else went by the board, there's Deborah to think of. The exam's only a fortnight away.'

'Love, you're just going to have to leave her to finish that for herself. If she's not going to produce the goods after all the effort you've put into it so far, another two weeks won't make any difference.' Richard was relieved at this turn in the conversation. Practical considerations made the night before seem unreal.

'That doesn't follow at all ...' said Clare.

'In that case old Colin will have to see to her, won't he? Don't tell me you don't think he's capable of it.'

'Of course he's capable. He can do it as well or better. But she's scared of him.'

'Scared of *Colin*? I took her for a girl of more spirit than that.'

Deborah's confession that she was afraid of Colin did seem, now, to have come from another girl, though it could only have been six weeks ago. The thought of all that time, of all that had happened in it, sent a great tide of exhaustion over her. She lay back weakly, and Richard said again, 'Are you all right? Shall I get the nurse?'

Clare shook her head. 'No — really. I just feel terribly *tired*.'

'You're worn out. That's probably what brought it on. I've been reading your baby books back at home.'

For some reason she felt a sudden temptation to cry.

'Richard, I was so *stupid*. I shouldn't have let myself get like that. I'm so sorry.'

'Not your fault.' If the child had been lost, he would have had to make a prodigious effort to forgive her; but the consequences of an action have a great deal to do with how the action is judged. Nothing disastrous had happened in the end; and you could hardly make a grievance of the fact that your wife had done her job too conscientiously. 'Poor old Clare' he said. 'But you do see, don't you, we've had a warning? We might not be so lucky next time.'

Eyes still shut, she nodded. 'I was beginning to see, anyway. You've got to be about three hundred per cent fit to cope with the way the job is now. And I couldn't do anything useful with Deborah in this state. It will have to be Colin.'

'He's going to ring up tonight anyway,' said Richard. 'I'll let him know. He can make some arrangement with Deborah without bothering you about it.'

Nothing was within her control at the moment. Colin would have to make the next move.

'Well, look,' she said, 'when you do speak to him, will you ask him to find out as soon as he can how she is? I don't suppose anyone's given the poor girl a thought since all this happened.'

Richard paused at the traffic lights on his way home, and saw a stream of children in what he recognised as the

Alderman Cassop uniform. He made a double loop out of the traffic and turned down into Tenter Street to look out for Colin. There was no sign, though, of that distinctively beat-up car: he must have gone already. Probably couldn't wait to get out of the building these days, poor bloke. He'd sounded a bit distraught on the telephone this morning... Richard shut off that recollection. He had betrayed more emotion himself than he would have wanted to.

He pushed away the thought that occurred to him next, more rapidly than he had ever pushed away an unwelcome thought before. Steady *on* — remember all the dreadful things you were thinking last night? None of this is anyone's *fault*. Get a grip on yourself.

He found himself back on the main road, the lights in his favour. For Heaven's sake, Colin's middle-aged. And married, and a Holy Roman to boot... And anyway, even if he — well, she wouldn't. She's not really very keen on that side of things, is she; even though we got over that bit of trouble she used to have? I'd never have thought of that if I'd had a proper night's sleep.

But though the idea was dismissed, the mark it made stayed with him all the way home: like a damp thumbprint drying very slowly off a page.

Colin sat on for nearly half an hour in the Tenter Street staffroom before he could summon up the energy to move. When he got downstairs he found the cleaners washing the floor; the effort either of apologising for walking over it, or of sitting down and taking his shoes off, seemed so enormous that he felt tempted to turn round and go back upstairs. 'Sorry,' he said tiredly. 'Sorry.'

'That's all right, pet. Good night.'

'Good night.' Even that made sweat start breaking out on his hands again.

It was nearly dark. He walked slowly to the hospital: if he hurried, he could not get his breath.

'Are you a relation?' asked the girl at the desk.

'No, just a friend.'

'I'm sorry, she's only to have visits from her family for

the next day or two. She's still very tired. Would you like to leave a message?'

'Please.'

He wrote 'Darling Clare' and then waited for inspiration. He was half relieved that they would not let him in. He wanted to see her, of course he did; but what was he going to say to her? He had said 'It'll be all right, Clare, I promise'. He could not look to her for strength now.

'Darling Clare' ... if only he could find the right form of words it would work. But nothing would come. There was no form of words that did not give some dishonest assurance. He screwed up the paper and said to the receptionist, 'It's all right, I won't bother. How long do you think she'll be in here?'

'Dr Patel says at least another three days.'

'I'll come back, then' said Colin. 'I'm sorry to have bothered you.'

Judith and the boys were due back on Sunday. *How all occasions do inform against me.*

Around four in the morning, he gave up the attempt to sleep. He came downstairs and tried to read, found he was too cold — at least that was one excuse — to concentrate, went back to bed and found that was no better. He switched off the light, tried once more to sleep, and found his heart thumping as though with fear. She's all right, he told himself yet again: Richard said so. In a couple of weeks' time it'll be as though it had never happened.

It's that I can't bear to think of her in pain ... no, don't lie. Shame. And guilt, and fear. Whatever I do now is going to be wrong. I love Clare: I didn't want to associate her with all this. *Which way I fly is Hell, myself am Hell ...*

He sat up, switched on the light for the last time. Come on, have a bit of sense. No one going to pieces could quote Milton to himself at four in the morning.

What you're afraid of isn't of doing evil: it's a primitive fear of being punished for it. Which puts you about on the moral level of Andy Reid, doesn't it?

On Sunday morning the hospital chaplain came round.

Clare said, 'It's only fair to tell you that I'm not a Christian.'

After that of course he had to stay: not to convert her, but to show her it was all the same these days. Clare said, 'I was at a funeral in your church last week.'

'I was sure I'd seen you before,' said the clergyman politely. 'It didn't upset you too much, I hope?'

'That isn't why I'm here now, if that's what you mean: but obviously it was a sad occasion. I was very glad you used the proper burial service, though as I'm not a believer I suppose that's beside the point.'

'Your colleague said something about that: the one who talked me into using the 1662 prayer book. He said the Church was for sinners, not for committees of the righteous. It was an odd way of putting it, but I felt he had a point.'

Colin, unmistakably.

'I didn't realise that was his doing,' she said. 'Mrs Auton thanked him for something — it must have been that.'

'He's very persuasive, your friend.'

'He's good with words, yes.'

But he's left no word for me. There was something she should understand and did not. She lay with her hands resting protectively over the place where the baby was, and tried to work it out.

On Sunday evening, just before it was dark, Judith and the boys arrived home. Edmund, on his way in towards the television set, said cheerfully 'Hello, Dad — had any orgies while we've been away?' Francis, eyes downcast, a bag in each hand, passed him on the garden path and said 'Dad'. With Francis that could mean anything or nothing.

Judith was locking the driver's door. She did not look up. 'I might as well leave this outside, mightn't I?' she said. 'You'll need it tomorrow morning.'

Colin said, 'Judith?'

She turned and looked at him. After three nights without sleep he probably did look pretty much like her idea of a true penitent. She put her hands up on his shoulders and gave him a small formal kiss. When his arms went round her, her body gave a small frightened quiver, and then was still.

There was no refusing that kind of offering. It would have been better for him to have had a millstone tied round his neck and to have been drowned in the depths of the sea.

Colin's handwriting was neat and schoolmasterly by habit and discipline. Even so, the first paragraph looked unnaturally tidy, as though he had been practising it. After that the writing began to go all over the place:

> ... I don't think I can leave Judith. You'd have every right to say 'Why didn't you think of that before?', and I couldn't give you any answer that wouldn't make you hate me even more than you're going to already. You said to me once that you loved Richard too 'in a way', and that it was Richard you were married to. I didn't understand at the time, but I suppose that's what I mean about Judith.
>
> I wish I could say 'Can you wait for me?' Some things, like money, would be easier a couple of years from now: but the most important things wouldn't be any different, and I can only manage to go on with this if I know there's no hope. And if I said 'Let's go on with it as an affair, since we can't have anything else', there wouldn't be much in it for you, would there? If we could have been together I could have tried to make it up to you that you got nothing from my lovemaking. But furtive trips to your house, fitted in before Richard got home, with the baby in the next room — that would be worse than losing you altogether. Or perhaps it wouldn't be, and I'd go on trying to snatch at what I could, until sooner or later Richard or Judith found out.
>
> I keep talking about you, and about Judith and Richard, and the only person I'm thinking about is myself. I haven't given you any chance to say whatever you might want to say. And if you asked me to change my mind I'd probably do it in about thirty seconds;

but you wouldn't ask me. I know that, and I'm exploiting you by knowing it. At least this way of doing things hurts me too. I don't know whether you can believe me or not. It wouldn't help anyway.

I'm not making sense, and I can't write any more. Try to think kindly of me when you can. But not too kindly: loving you was the only good thing about me. Even that last sentence is a way of manipulating you.
                                    Colin

She lay back on the pillows. The light hurt her eyes. 'Donna!' she called in a small polite voice.

After a few minutes Donna came. Clare said 'Could you please pull my curtains right round again for a bit?'

'Yer not reelly meant to have them round now, yer know. It upsets the other patients.'

'Please. If anyone's worried, just tell them I've got a headache. That's true, actually. Just for a bit, Donna, please.'

'Reelly ...'

'*Please.*'

'Well ... they'll have ter go back soon, mind.'

Of course she could not sob in that place, even if she had been able to. She lay with an arm over her eyes to keep out the searching light that came through. It was a completely crushing, inarticulate pain, and she did not know whether it lasted for the hours it felt like, or for only a few minutes.

'Now what is this about a headache, Mrs Baylham? If your blood pressure is up we cannot let you go home.'

She found her voice. It sounded a bit weak, but recognisable.

'I'm all right, I think. I just had some news that upset me for a bit.'

The doctor took her pulse, then her blood pressure. She looked at the rubber gauntlet as they inflated it round her arm. No use in being melodramatic and thinking of it as a manacle.

'Everything seems to be normal. But if there is any more alarm, Mrs Baylham, we must keep you here for longer.

So you will be a good girl now, I hope, and give us no more trouble.'

'No. I'll try not to.'

I expected nothing, and I've had more than I expected. It's not just my pain. Someone else's, who was part of me.

Underneath the bedclothes her body started to shake. It would stop in time: it would have to, before Richard came.

That morning Richard had gone into work again. Since he would have to take more time off when Clare came home, it seemed only fair. But several times, as he ran his eye down the columns of figures, he was attacked by a particular thought. He had gone on pushing it back. She *couldn't*, not with the baby ... and the baby couldn't not be his when he felt so much for it. He was beneath contempt even to think such a thing. He had gone on thinking it.

But in the evening Clare seemed so glad to see him, almost hysterically glad, that he knew, finally, that what he thought and felt were beside the point.

If, when you were afraid, you started praying to a God you did not believe in, that did not mean that God existed after all: it meant that when you were afraid you wanted Him to exist and make the lion lie down with the lamb. If, when you wanted something, you started to imagine yourself losing it, that was your fear speaking. Once you realised that, it was all right — because a thing could not be true and not true at the same time, could it?

She couldn't write to Colin directly at home or at school: you never knew who saw letters and drew conclusions from their postmarks. She couldn't do it over the telephone: what would happen to her voice, and who would be overhearing at the other end? It was not entirely attractive to use Deborah as a go-between: but she was not a child, and it would only be once. Clare wrote on a single sheet of paper:

Deborah, would you pass this on to Colin R? There are all sorts of odds and ends of teaching that he ought to know about. Sorry to use you as a postal service, but this way at least I'm *sure* it will be delivered!

With luck, it would never occur to Deborah, as it would certainly occur to Janet, to question this.

She looked up and saw the daffodils that Richard had brought. ('Well, I had the idea there was some poem about them, or something.') She had not thought that daffodils in November were within the bounds of possibility. They were fragile-looking, rather beautiful. Kind, literal-minded Richard, who had led her away from madness before, and would do so again. She had to protect her baby. She loved Colin: probably always would, in some remote way without hope that would hurt no one — perhaps, in the end, not even herself. Being forgiven made it easier to understand how to forgive; forgiving an injury robbed it of what made it unbearable.

After the curtains were drawn and the ward lights dimmed, she went on writing, like a naughty schoolgirl. There were four versions of it by the end: the last one was much the shortest. If only she could put the right thing down it would help his pain as well as hers. You couldn't go on being bruised in the same spot for ever.

> I want to say something that you'll believe; but everything that's true sounds facile. In a stupid way I keep wanting to say it was all *my* fault. That feels like the truth, but I know it isn't really, and it would be insulting to pretend it was. But you mustn't see it that way either: guilt makes you see things from the wrong angle, like being drunk, or having a temperature.
>
> Now I've made it sound as though I could somehow claim to be seeing things more clearly than you can. I've left out all the contradictions and hesitations, so that perhaps you still won't believe me. Please let me see you again. Not to try to change your mind, or even ask you why. But if we've got to say goodbye, it would help me if we could do it properly. I don't know whether we could go on being friends: I wish we could, because I can see that in a way that was the best

part of it. Please don't let those words about catching the bus be the last words I ever say to you.

If it sounded too articulate, like some high-minded nineteenth-century novel, it was the nearest she could get to combining honesty and charity. She sealed the envelope and put it on her bedside table. It was addressed to Deborah. At that point, not much to her surprise, she felt her tears start. She lay down — curled up, as her child was — and let them go on till they stopped naturally. They made no sound, and they no longer hurt as they had always done before. She began to drift off to sleep. There is no way of not running out, sooner or later, on someone else's pain.

Driving very gently and carefully, Richard brought Clare home. As they passed the side street leading down to the Alderman Cassop buildings, she peered towards them, but did not ask him to stop.

It felt odd to be wearing ordinary clothes again. 'I must have put on even more weight' she said. 'This was the last skirt I felt comfortable in, and now I can't do it up properly. I'll have to start wearing smocks and things.'

'You'll look lovely.'

Last time I walked up this garden path it was with Colin. But it'll get easier each time I do it.

Janet, wearing a startling pink tracksuit, turned up at the cottage the same evening. She and Richard sat on the foot of Clare's bed and drank sherry. 'Richard can't keep his eyes off your outfit, Janet' said Clare.

'If my wife wasn't watching,' said Richard 'there'd be no holding me.'

'*Weren't*' said Clare. 'Not *wasn't*.'

'Would you like me to thump you?' said Richard.

Janet laughed politely. Richard got up. 'Excuse me, ladies' he said. 'I must go and do battle with the supper. Janet, can I interest you in a nice bit of plaice? I can cook anything so long as it's fried.'

'No thanks, Richard. I had something before I came out.' Politically, no doubt, Janet felt obliged to have a northern high tea at five o'clock. When Richard had gone she said, 'So you're not coming back at all?'

'No. They won't let me. I actually wanted to, that's the funny thing. I wanted to know I was seeing the place for the last time.'

'You could always come back for a look round when you're better.'

'With all the kids gazing at my tummy? I don't think so. Anyway, how are things? I can't imagine I'm very popular, with everyone having to cover for me.'

'Alan's managing to have it both ways, of course. Being NAS he *isn't* doing any cover, but he still grumbles about it, or he did until Betty shut him up.'

'I am sorry.'

'Clare, don't be a fool.'

They looked at each other, embarrassed. Clare said 'Have you seen Deborah?'

'Yes. She's fine . . . Colin seems in a bit of a state, though.'

That was a path that couldn't, mustn't be taken. 'I expect he's just harassed, isn't he? Being one teacher short.'

Janet looked at her. 'Even I know occasionally when to mind my own business' she said. 'But I suppose you do realise he's in love with you?'

It sounded like an obscenity, though she said it matter-of-factly enough. Clare's first impulse was to say 'Of course he isn't.' But Janet commanded honesty.

'Yes. And I love him.' The forbidden, unbelievable relief of telling. She thought of Richard downstairs, slicing potatoes, following her instructions. 'Janet, don't tell anyone else, please.'

Janet said, 'I wasn't sure whether you did or not. You hide your feelings bloody well, Clare, I must say.'

'I know.'

'Why?' said Janet. 'You're both adults. There's no law against it.'

'We're both married to other people.'

'There are things that can be done about that, you know. It doesn't take a private Act of Parliament any more.'

Clare said, 'That doesn't help. The state of the law hasn't got anything to do with it.'

'I take it Richard doesn't know anything about it? Or what's-her-name — Colin's wife?'

'Judith. No, they don't. At least not so far as I know. And since it's over, there's no need for either of them to know.'

'But you still love him. And presumably you did have sex — it wasn't *all* hearts and flowers and quoting the Sonnets at each other?'

Colin's arms round her, shaking her awake. His hands searching her body for a response. His head on her breast.

'We slept together, yes. We never shall again ... Janet, I don't mind your asking about it, oddly enough. But why are you *still* using that accusing tone with me? For once in my life I've managed to do something good — or at any rate, not to do something bad.'

Janet said, 'You poor bloody fools. The pair of you.'

'I didn't ask you to start this. I'm sorry, Janet, you've been kind to me and to Deborah, and I dare say you're a great help to Colin. But that doesn't give you the right ...'

Janet said 'If you'd seen him the other day, after he heard ... *you've* no right to deny that kind of experience. It's dishonest, and it's cowardly. You're insulting your husband and Colin's wife. Do you think they couldn't live without you?'

'No, of course not. But — well, we couldn't live with ... Richard wants this baby so much; and Judith's given up twenty years of her life to having children instead of a life of her own. We'd be taking the past away from them as well as the future.'

Colin asleep beside her; skin against skin, hair against hair. *I'll make it up to you somehow ...*

'They'd manage. People have to get hurt sometimes, you know that as well as I do. They survive. They'd make new lives if you gave them a chance.'

'Where Judith's concerned, she's married to Colin for as long as they're both alive.'

'If she still hangs on to all that religious stuff, it can only be because she wants to. *He's* obviously grown out of it, hasn't he?'

'I don't know that what you believe necessarily has much to do with what you want to believe.'

Janet looked at her. 'Clare, I just don't accept all this, I'm sorry. Perhaps you do. But to me it sounds like an excuse for something else.'

Janet. Don't make it be all my fault again. I can't bear it.

'There *were* other things,' she said. She looked down at her hands on the duvet cover. Small hands with short unvarnished nails: only the two rings of her marriage and her engagement. 'I can't talk about those. I don't know whether we'd have managed to get over them. I didn't think we could, anyway.'

'And so you ditched him?'

'No,' said Clare, turning her head aside. 'He ditched me.'

Janet got up clumsily. 'Oh, Christ,' she said. 'I thought I'd got the picture. *Colin* was the one who finished it?'

'Yes.' Clare looked Janet in the face. Turning her ahead aside had been the final reflex of her old self. She was not going to be ashamed of failure ever again. 'And if *I* don't blame him for that, there's no reason for anyone else to, is there?'

Janet said, 'I'm sorry I said what I did. It's all more complicated than I thought.' Downstairs, Richard could be heard to switch off the extractor fan; then there was the sound of plates and cutlery being piled together. 'I'd better go' said Janet. She stood undecidedly.

'I've said I'm sorry, and I am' she said. 'But I still think you're both wrong. You're refusing to give yourselves, and Richard and Judith, the chance to grow and change. You hide behind one kind of pain because you're frightened of the other kind. But I will say there's a sort of lunatic self-consistency about it. Goodbye, Clare — I'll keep an eye on Deborah for you.'

Richard came up a minute or two later. 'Funny girl,' he said, arranging the tray in front of Clare. 'I quite liked her. From the way you and Colin used to go on about her, I thought she must be the most frightful old bag.'

'We weren't fair to her,' said Clare. 'I do realise that. I think we were both a bit scared of her integrity. There aren't all that many people who actually believe what they say and live up to it the way she does.'

'You ought to have more faith in people,' said Richard. He sat down on the edge of the bed beside her.

'Don't give me a pep talk now, love, please: I'm not up to it. Let me have my scepticism.'

He put his hand up to her shoulder, let it trail down over the outline of her breast through the nightdress. *Oh, Colin!* Then he rested his hand on her arm.

'Poor old Clare. You can have anything you want, if I can give it to you. You know that.'

She moved the tray, carefully. Then she put her arms round his neck and pressed her face against his shoulder. He put his hand on her hair. The embrace was unexpected at that moment, but rather sweet.

XI

When Deborah explained, nervously, about the Hopkins essay Colin said, 'Yes, of course', thinking vaguely of Sprung Rhythm and the philosophy of Duns Scotus. He had forgotten, or blotted out, the last sonnets. *I wake and feel the fell of dark, not day ... I see The lost are like this, and their scourge to be, As I am mine, their sweating selves ...* So it took him several evenings to get through her essay.

Whilst the reader is unlikely to lose sight of the fact that these are in the first place religious poems, Deborah had written, *the fact is that much if not most of the imagery suggests an inability either to communicate or to reproduce. Hopkins refers to himself as 'Time's eunuch', failing to 'breed one work that wakes', while in another poem his prayers are like 'dead letters'. It is surely not a biographical fallacy but a legitimate aid to understanding to relate this state of mind to Hopkins' experience of teaching at University College, Dublin, in the last five years of his life.*

University College, Dublin, was John Henry Newman's foundation; but Newman, famous for his habit of collapsing under pressure, had never had to teach there. Hopkins' accent and manner marked him out as different from his students for every day of those five years. Some of the handful of bellicose Irish Nationalists who made his life a misery might well have been Colin's own forebears.

'This is excellent, Deborah' he said when at last he handed it back. 'Do as well as that in the exam and you must have a serious chance. I've written in a few comments, but my only real quibble is about your use of the word *despair*. It does have a specific theological meaning, as well as describing an emotional state — did you realise that? It means a wilful refusal to believe that God will forgive sin. I don't think that's quite what Hopkins is describing, but if you think it is, you need to justify yourself, and understand the meaning of the word as he would have used it.'

There was a momentary blankness in the girl's face. Clearly what he had said was registering nowhere but in the facts-and-figures part of her brain. Why should it? 'Yes, I see,' she said. 'I'll remember about that. I must try not to be so illiterate about religion.' Then she apparently remembered something else. Her face went red. 'Mr Rowsley, I'm *terribly* sorry. Clare sent me this to give to you. I forgot all about it.'

Shades of a Hardy plot, the vital letter going astray. Only it did not matter how long it was before this one was opened. He would have a lifetime in which to remember Clare's reproaches. He deserved them, but that did not make him any better equipped to deal with them. 'It's all right, Deborah,' he said, putting the envelope straight into his pocket. 'I can't think it was all that urgent. Don't worry about it. Now, you've got about a week to go, haven't you – – do you want to bring me any more work?'

'Could I bring you my Hardy notes after the weekend, sir?'

'By all means. And you really don't have to call me sir. Colin will do, in private at any rate.'

Deborah blushed. 'Thank you. I come out with these bits of childishness sometimes. I suppose I'll get over it.'

'You've got plenty of time for that.'

His heart went on banging drearily away. How was it that no one else could hear it?

It was another two days before he got round to opening

the letter. At the weekend he pretended to have some tinkering to do with the car. When he had finished reading he sat with the letter trailing from his hand.

He had once said to her, *God help anyone who comes within range of your kind of love.*

She wanted to see him to say goodbye, to give some grace and dignity to the end of it. The reparations chalked up against him were so great that nothing could pay them off; that did not let him off paying the small debts that were within his means.

Shakily, Clare got up on Sunday afternoon and spent the rest of the day out of bed. There was hardly any pain left now: just a vestigial sense of discomfort and insecurity, and an overpowering lassitude. 'It's because you've been out of bed so long' said Richard. 'Anyway, you've no need to rush round any more.'

She had not had a chance to have her hair cut since the beginning of term. She tied it back off her face with a scarf. It was difficult to find anything in the wardrobe that would fit, except for a long muslin dress, straight down from shoulder to hem, which she sometimes wore to parties in the summer. With a shawl over the top it was warm enough. It looked eccentric, but not without charm; and she would never have to worry again about dressing eccentrically, would she?

In the early evening the telephone rang.

'That was Colin' said Richard. 'He asked whether he could look in later to say hallo and check over some school things with you. I said I thought that would be all right — but say no if you're too tired.'

Her tongue seemed to be suddenly too large for her mouth. She heard herself say 'No, that's all right. I've probably left hundreds of loose ends behind me.'

Richard hesitated. Some half-rooted impulse made him say: 'If he's here for an hour or so, I could nip down to Teesside and back and bring some work home: then I could stay here tomorrow too. I'd feel easier if I had at least one more day keeping an eye on you.'

'That would be nice,' she said calmly. He regretted

almost immediately having made the offer: had he been testing his own faith in the normality of things? But it would have been embarrassing to retract now. Don't be morbid, he said to himself like an incantation as he moved around the kitchen; don't be uncivilised.

Colin stood in the doorway beside Richard. There were drops of November moisture on his hair and on his dark overcoat.

'Find a drink, Colin, won't you?' said Richard. 'You must know where everything is by now. Clare isn't allowed to, so don't let her talk you into it. I'll only be about an hour. I'm very grateful.'

Colin sat on the other side of the room, as far away from her as possible. He did not take his coat off, and he kept his arms tightly folded across his stomach: leaning forward, as though it hurt.

'Colin, you look awful.'

'I'm all right.'

Outside the noise of Richard's car engine receded and died away.

She was half-sitting and half-lying on the sofa: cushions behind her back. She had done something to her hair which made her face look younger and rounder. Under the thin dress, the pregnancy which two weeks ago had been undetectable was startlingly apparent. They had sat on that sofa with their arms round one another, and she had said *Colin, if you're not going to stay ...*

'I got your letter,' he said. 'Thank you.'

She said 'I wanted you to come. And now I don't know what to say.'

'I liked Richard's tactful exit.'

'I'm quite sure he doesn't know anything consciously. But I sometimes wonder whether he hasn't put two and two together underneath.'

'Janet's put two and two together quite consciously, I'm afraid' said Colin.

'I know.'

'Has she talked to you about it?'

'A bit. I let her. I shouldn't have done, I know, but I felt so ... I won't do it again.'

'Clare, do *anything* that'll help. It's not for me to complain. I might have come out with something the other day, to Bob Murray ... only luckily he made it abundantly clear he didn't want to know. If Ted had been alive it might have been different.'

'Men don't talk to each other, do they?' she said. 'Not really.'

'Bob said my religion must be a comfort to me.'

'Oh, Colin.'

'It has a certain irony, hasn't it?'

'I don't think Janet will spread it around' said Clare. 'She's one of the few people I'd really trust not to. Do you think anyone else at school has guessed?'

'I thought Dave Bowburn had. But it was just a shot in the dark. Part of the workings of Dave's unpleasant little mind.'

He had taken his spectacles off and was twisting them round and round by the shank.

'You're making it all sound so ugly' she said. 'It wasn't, was it?'

'No. Though you'd have a right to think so. Do you?'

'You know I don't.'

'Yes, you told me, didn't you? Clare — I came because you asked me to. I wanted to see how you were ... and I thought perhaps I could undo a little of the harm. But there's no end to it.'

'You can see how I am. I've got to be careful for a bit, but there's no harm done. Least of all by you.'

'You look well,' he said. 'You look lovely, in fact.'

She can't have loved me that much. Or else we don't mean the same thing by love.

'It was a mistake to come,' he said. 'Only I couldn't ... I didn't expect ever to hear from you again, after what I'd done.'

In a minute the spectacle frames were going to break. He had written to her, *If you asked me to change my mind, I'd probably do it in about thirty seconds.* It would only be a matter of a dozen steps across the room to where he sat. She could put her arms round him: please don't go. And then would he give way? Or would she then have lost even that new, fragile shoot of self-esteem which was her future?

But you wouldn't ask me. I know that, and I'm exploiting you by knowing it.

She said, 'I won't ask you to explain ... or to change your mind. I wanted you to see that I'm all right. It's not that I didn't love you enough. Everything which hapened before last week seems a bit unreal now, though, and that helps. Perhaps it's just my hormones playing games again, and it'll all suddenly hit me later. But if it does ... well, I know, more or less, what I can cope with and what I can't. I have got something to look forward to. I'm not unhappy, really. But you are.'

'Yes. But it's my own fault, and I've passed enough of it on to you and to Judith.'

'Does Judith know?'

'No, I'm sure she doesn't. I must be hell to live with at the moment, but she seems to be able to put it all down to the job.'

'If you told her, would she forgive you?'

He thought for a moment. 'I suppose so. Yes, I'm sure she would. She's not vindictive: that's the trouble ...'

'Do you want to tell her? Because if you do, then don't hold back because of me. I'll have to take the chance on her telling Richard.'

Before I made love to her I said *You're not just inventing another way of punishing yourself, are you?*, and she said *No, I promise.* Of course you are, Clare. Given a chance you'd start doing it all over again.

'I'm sure she wouldn't do that,' he said. 'But I'm not going to tell her anyway. I've done her enough harm.'

'No more than I've done to Richard.'

'*Far* more. You don't know.'

I wanted to violate you, I wanted to punish you and hurt you, and I did it to her instead. Then I came into your bed, into your body ... and all this happened because of it.

He watched her sitting up carefully, curling her feet underneath her. It used to make my heart turn over to look at you: the old cliché made flesh. But now when I look at you all I can feel is this endless shame. I've killed even the way I loved you.'

Clare said, 'You could get yourself a drink ... I know it's no real help, but ...'

'I'm all right, Clare, really. I know I'm drowning in self-pity at the moment, but I'll get over it. I don't much want to, but I shall. Your letter's made all the difference.'

It came out so neatly, though he had not planned it. What had he come for — comfort? Or in order to be reproached? There was one thing that could justify his coming. He could do the pretending for a change.

'Has it really?' she said.

Francis as a small child in the back of a car. Going over some small stone bridge; Judith turning round to him. 'That must be the bridge that Pigling Bland and Pig-Wig ran across, to get to freedom — don't you think?' Francis, already an anxious child, saying 'Did they really? Did they really indeed?'

'Yes. Really.'

She said, 'Can we still ... see each other, sometimes? I shouldn't ask; say no if ... I don't want to make you do anything you don't want to do.'

'Of course I *want* to. But seeing you keeps it all alive: which is also what I want, of course.'

He got up and drew the curtains across the window. The stiffness in his walk was more noticeable. Where the light from the standard lamp struck his face she saw the pattern of broken veins that was beginning above his cheekbones; the coarser texture of the hair where it was going grey.

'I don't know. Clare. It would be nice to think so. I'd like to see the baby. And it'll help me to think of you, here in this house, waiting for it to be born.'

Or alternatively, that might be the worst endurance test of all. How can I tell?

She said, 'I can't even ask you to be a godfather, can I?'

'I make a poor enough job of being the ordinary kind of father. No, it's all right, I know that's self-pity too. Clare, as soon as Richard gets back, I'll go. Is that all right?'

Poor obstinate brave Clare. What chance have I left her to say no?

She bent her head, and nodded. He looked down at her hair: reddish-brown, redder now than it had been: Judith's hair had changed with pregnancy too. The little strip of black chiffon that tied it at the nape of her neck.

He said, 'I will come back — really. But not for a bit, if you can bear with me. Not till I'm a bit more like something human. You are really all right, aren't you?'

She nodded again. He said: 'Please let's talk about something neutral now, until Richard gets back. Then we can say goodbye calmly. Can't we?'

She drew a deep breath. 'Yes. I'll start. How's Deborah?'

Richard had driven down to Teesside and collected a pile of post and administrative paperwork. The calm and detachment with which he did it made him feel proud. This was a cool, intelligent way to behave: pushing your irrational fears down where they belonged.

On the way back to Gatelaw the irrational fears began to resist being pushed down. He covered the last ten miles at well over the speed limit. Fool, he said to himself. In the circumstances they can't be *doing* anything, can they? Even if it had ever occurred to them. Colleagues and old friends coming to the end of a stage in their lives, that's all.

He drove up the gravel path, making as much noise as he could, sending two funnels of light up the front of the cottage with his headlamps. Then he took his foot off the clutch and there was a great calm.

Once, Colin had felt so strong an impulse — on a September morning in the book room, when the sunlight shone down on the nape of her neck — to kneel down and put his arms around her, that it was as though he had already done it; and yet he had not moved. In her pretty sitting room that would still, for a little while, be unmarked with spilled paint or sticky fingers, he felt the impulse to say 'Clare, I was wrong: let me stay.' But even as he felt the impulse his feet were carrying him to the door of the room. It was not an act of resolution: it was a reflex of something that had already been decided a long while ago. In the doorway it came to him to say, 'You're worth someone better than I am': the satisfying pain of self-flagellation. But what could she answer to that, poor Clare, except to comfort him or to say, 'But it was you I wanted'?

'Goodbye,' he said. 'I — I'll see you.'

She could not quite manage to say goodbye or to watch him go. At any moment Richard would come in and she would have to show her face to him. She got up from the sofa, still very carefully, and twiddled the knobs of the radio till she found some brisk, cerebral harpsichord music to beat back the accusing darkness.

Colin came face to face with Richard in the darkened hallway.

'Richard,' he said. 'Will you excuse me if I don't stay? Judith will be wondering where I've got to.'

'You haven't got time for a quick drink?' Richard was already feeling ashamed of himself. All the same, he felt nothing but relief that Colin was going at once.

'I won't, thanks, if you don't mind. It was good to have a chance to talk to Clare, though. She seems much better.'

'Yes, I think so too.'

Colin said, 'You must be looking forward to the baby.'

'I am. I was going to say "You don't know how much", but of course I suppose you do.'

'Are you going to stay with her when it's born?' said Colin. Making himself suffer: watching, as though through a window, himself squirm.

'I'm not sure,' said Richard. 'I'd like to, in a way. But I'm a bit squeamish about blood and things. Did you stay with Judith when she —?'

'Yes. It was quite a daring thing to do in those days.'

'You didn't pass out or anything at the critical moment?'

Colin surprised himself by producing a quite creditable laugh. 'No. I'm usually reasonably good in a practical crisis. Anyway, once things start to happen you'll find there isn't time for you to faint.'

Richard thought, It's a pity we've never really been friends. I've always liked him. I've been imagining things. I ought to be ashamed of myself. Aloud he said 'You look distinctly knocked out at the moment,

Colin. I gather things are pretty frightful at that school now.'

It was almost the nearest to an intimacy that Richard had ever addressed to another man. Guilt and relief put an unexpected warmth into his voice. Colin's eyes filled suddenly with embarrassing tears.

'Pure hell, I'm afraid. Look, Richard, I really must be off. See you.'

Richard, standing in the doorway like a good host, saw Colin's blind fumbling with the keys, and the jolt with which he started the car. It was the mention of the school, not of Clare, that had set that off. Poor old Colin, he thought, watching the taillights vanish round the corner. But though his sympathy was perfectly real, it was not without a degree of self-congratulation. Professional disappointment was a grim thing, of course, but to let it get to you in *that* way ... The middle-aged crisis, thought Richard, feeling himself to be far from any such state.

Colin, too appalled even to swear at himself, turned out of the lane and on to the main road, and almost straight into the path of a lorry. He missed collision only by accelerating so hard as to send the car skidding three-quarters of the way across the road. One part of his instinct told him to stop and calm down; the more powerful part told him to keep on. Shock and momentary terror had put paid to the intrusive hiccup of grief, more effectively than any amount of resolution could have done. No death-wish there, you notice, Kevin Colin Rowsley. It ought to have been some kind of consolation.

On the Pelworth Road, in the shaky quietness, he switched on the radio. Some panel game: educated voices interspersed with gusts of manic laughter. Somewhere outside, beyond that glowing dashboard, people talked and laughed, without standing back and watching themselves, lonely scarecrows; without knowing that they had been totally abandoned.

Deborah pinned out the pattern for the dress, and started to cut it out on her bedroom floor. It was tempting providence, she knew that, to start making something to wear for an interview, but she knew she could not do any more work. Inside her head it felt as though a disc was spinning, whirling away every fact she had ever learnt and every idea she had ever had. She looked at the pattern pieces, and wondered whether black wool, however 'slimming', had been altogether a good idea.

It was the first time in her life that she had ever skipped her homework. And tomorrow would be the first time in her life that she had ever stayed away from school for any reason other than being ill.

She tailor-tacked and pinned the pieces of material. At that point she was called down to lay the table for supper, so she left the pieces on the floor. As she paused in the doorway to turn off the light, she thought, If I don't get a place, this room will remind me of failure for the rest of my life.

Judith was irritated to discover, when her washing-machine refused to work, that it was still psychologically important to her to have the washing done by the middle of Monday morning. The necessity of doing it by hand would have irritated her even more if she had let it. She rubbed and squeezed and rinsed. Edmund's rugger clothes were in such a repellent condition that she would have to leave them to soak. He was growing out of them as well, but that was just too bad. It would be enough of a problem finding the money to get the washing-machine repaired.

She knew she was not neurotic about money: it was only money, valuable simply for what it could buy: it did not represent moral worth, or achievement, or love. But the lack of it meant a house where the light-coloured walls were becoming grubby beyond the point where washing them down would make any difference, and where the warp-threads of the carpets seemed to show more clearly every time the light fell on them. The boys probably did not notice at all; Colin only vaguely; but she had to live all day with the evidence.

She ran another sinkful of water and shook in the soap powder. This would have to be the last lot until the water had had time to heat up again. She picked up a bundle of her own blouses. She was not a pretty woman, she knew that; she never had been. But she had been, and still could have been, 'good-looking'. Only now that she was in her forties, it was an enterprise that needed money. Her tall, broad-shouldered figure could look handsome, but not in the kind of clothes she could make for herself, or in skimpy chain-store things meant for young girls. For that, you needed small bones and delicate colouring like Clare Baylham's, and *she* could afford to buy good clothes anyway. Probably Richard earned enough of a salary for them hardly to notice the loss of hers ... oh, well, that physical type didn't wear so well: it depended on looking girlish rather than matronly. Judith Rowsley, you're being remarkably bitchy. Get a grip on yourself.

She ran cold water on to the lingering suds. Portrait of a graduate wife. How will our Clare take to it, I ask myself? Well, presumably people like that don't have children if they don't want them. Quite surprising she's giving up her job altogether, though: she always seemed so independent. Still, lucky to have the choice, unlike poor old Col. He's going to be completely on his own in that place now ...

Colin and Clare. How long had that thought been there, waiting to crawl out of the plug hole as the last of the suds went down it?

All this term, Colin had been aware of a temporary sense of relief every time the lights were against him on the way to school, or if a pedestrian chose to dither on one of the crossings. Even ten seconds' respite was something. This afternoon there were half a dozen children spinning out the journey back from lunch. Colin stopped to let them cross, and promptly stalled the engine. Even the car has psychosomatic symptoms, he thought: and then, between one jarring heartbeat and the next — I can't manage this much longer.

'Sir, are yer married?' shouted Melanie Turner.

'Yes,' said Colin shortly. He always answered personal questions up to a point. It did no harm to let them know you had a life apart from them.

'Sir, have yer got any children?'

'Two boys.'

The questions you did not answer were those that set out to expose where you were vulnerable. The kind of class he used to teach almost always knew where to stop; but the Melanie Turners of the world had no cutoff, no brakes.

'Sir, is yer wife on the Pill?'

'Open your books,' said Colin. 'Page thirty-two.' His hands were trembling again. *It always was the occupational disease of teachers, wasn't it?*

The minute Wendy Sykes came into the room, the sense of impending anarchy vanished. She must wonder whether I've always been as inept as this, and they've only just found out.

'Mr Rowsley,' said Wendy cheerfully 'I've come to take this little lot off your hands. The Headmaster would like a quick word right away. So if you can just tell me what we should be doing ...' She took the book from him and said out of the side of her mouth 'Relax. He's in a chastened mood.'

'Sir,' yelled Melanie, 'are yer being sacked?'

Wendy said calmly, 'If you'd like to see me at the end of the lesson, you and I will have a little talk about people getting sacked, Melanie.'

'Miss, I can't. I've got ter do some shopping!'

Colin left them to it. He went down the stairs and out of the building, then by way of the short cut over the matted grass of the playing fields. He had left his overcoat in the staffroom, and the cold wind cut through his jacket and shirt, driving him from behind. Nature had no cutoff or brakes either.

He went up the steps to Middle School. *Abbott, J.F., Durham Light Infantry; Adamson, W.R., Royal Flying Corps ...* no one would ever call *them* to account again.

Colin had not come face to face with Kettleby since that day after Clare ... He no longer cared what knowledge there was on the Headmaster's face.

'You have a right to know, Mr Rowsley, what I plan to do about the teaching in your Department, now that Mrs Baylham will not be returning to us.'

Colin found it in himself to stare back. All right: say it if you're going to.

'As you know,' said Kettleby, 'the whole future of sixth-form teaching in this area is under consideration at the moment. Last summer, I felt it was in the interests of the school for you to have experience of teaching the less-able classes. I make no apology for that, but the situation has now changed. With the falling pupil numbers I have known for some time that we should have our staff quota reduced; and it seems that we are not to be allowed to replace Mrs Baylham at all. In those circumstances I must obviously take steps to make it clear that the sixth-form and academic teaching in this school is still second to none.'

However sluggish Colin's reactions might have become, he was well used to reading the sub-text of Kettleby's speeches. Suddenly, the Headmaster was saying, there's more propaganda value in having you around, Cambridge degree and all. All the better if your experiences have tamed you a bit.

Kettleby said, 'All the timetables for your Department have had to be recast to absorb Mrs Baylham's teaching. I shall be asking you, with effect from this afternoon, to take over her sixth-form group and a number of the other top-band classes. I think you may take it that in future years your timetable will continue to be of that kind. This has all been a most sad and difficult business.'

The Headmaster's face said, Thank me. Put yourself on my side. I know all about you.

Standing in the doorway, compromising between dignity and self-preservation, Colin said: 'Naturally I'm pleased on my own account. But it's a pity any of this was ever necessary in the first place.' At the same moment, his hands stopped shaking.

He went up to the computer unit, picked up the copy of his new timetable and glanced over it. Once, he would have spared a thought for the junior members of his Department who would be getting the bad classes instead of him. They would just have to manage for themselves from now on.

He would need to go back to Tenter Street to collect his overcoat and briefcase and see that the textbooks were left in order. He set off again across the playing fields, the wind against him. In all that waste expanse of grass and mud, with the wind making his eyes water behind his spectacles, who would be able to tell that, for a second or two, he wept because it all came so much too late?

Deborah had had enough of sewing by the end of the morning. She thought that she could always do the hem and the cuffs and the zip-fastener next week, while she was waiting to see whether or not she got an interview. She wandered down into the centre of Stanburn, allowed herself the mild excitement of a hamburger, and then got on a bus. For a while it trundled through the depressed fringes of industry, and she wished she had brought something to read after all. Then the bus began to climb steadily up the Wear valley, rocking from side to side on the road in the wind. Up through stone one-row villages, above the tree-line, looking down into the mauve-green and slate-coloured folds of the river bed below, and at last over the watershed and into the remoter valley of the Tees. She assumed that there would be buses that would get her back somehow. She realised that she had never explored, never even noticed, her own countryside before, until now, when, as she hoped and supposed, she was just about to leave it.

As soon as Judith heard the car backing up into the garage she was overcome by shyness and apprehension. She fled upstairs before he could open the door, and called down when she heard him:

'Col — I've just started washing my hair. I'll be down in a few minutes.'

She looked at herself in the bathroom glass. Her flushed, startled face stared back at her. For the sake of verisimilitude she began to take the clips out of her hair.

Even if it's true, she told herself, it's not the end of the world. You're not a baby. Things like that happen.

If only it hadn't got to be Clare, who already had so much of everything.

So long as it's over, she thought, I can cope. And so long as it's not his child.

She's probably slept with dozens of men. She could have left him for me.

Judith swallowed sternly and reached for the shampoo bottle. All she could do for the moment was to keep things as natural as possible, and wait for the moment to break through. She only hoped she would know if it was ever the right time.

Sounds of a choir and orchestra were floating out from the sitting room. Colin was the musical illiterate of the family, but even he could recognise *Gerontius*. At least Francis's tastes seemed to be getting quieter.

Francis started nervously when he came in. A tall awkward boy with Colin's own face of twenty-five years ago. 'Shall I turn this down?' he asked.

'Not on my account.'

The sopranos, at once plangent and hopeful, soaring: *By Thy rising from the tomb, by Thy mounting up above*... Of course you can breathe: don't be more of a fool than you've got to be. He shut the door between himself and the music. *Spare me in the day of doom: be merciful: be gracious.* Who in his right mind would listen to *Gerontius* for the words, to Newman rather than Elgar? In the kitchen he cupped tap-water in his hands and drank it, tasting the chlorine.

Deborah refused her mother's offer of a sleeping pill. 'They make you woozy in the mornings, don't they?' she said. 'It's all right, I'll sleep.' But it was a long time before she did. She lay in the dark with her hands behind her head. On the whole, she thought, the banging of her heart was not so much fear as excitement.

The curled-up position was still the only one Clare could adopt lying down. She lay with her cheek against Richard's shoulder: she thought that he would like that too. They were not allowed to make love again yet — perhaps not for the whole of the pregnancy — but he seemed to accept that readily enough as the price to pay; and of course she did not mind.

'Deborah does the exam tomorrow,' she said into the darkness.

Richard put his arm under her neck and curved his hand round to her shoulder. There would be years, she supposed, of reminders like that: Richard innocently doing things which Colin had done. So long as that happened, there was no danger of forgetting. She put her fingers up and laced them through his. It wasn't betrayal.

'How do you think she'll get on?' said Richard.

'She *must* stand a good chance. She's developed such a lot. She was still a little girl, in some ways, when we started.'

'How soon will she know whether she's got a place or not?'

'Depends. But if anyone wants to interview her, it'll probably be in the next four or five weeks.'

'Well, it's all up to her now.'

'Yes. There's nothing more I can do ... Richard?'

'Mm?'

'Next autumn, when the new academic year begins, I was thinking of registering with Durham or Newcastle to do a part-time PhD.'

'What about the baby?'

'I'd only need a couple of afternoons a week. I could do the rest at weekends and in the evenings. It could all be very flexible. Pauline said she could help with baby-minding; and there must be someone in the village who'd be glad to be paid for a few hours ... there'll be tax rebates and things, won't there? It wouldn't really cost all that much.'

Richard wanted to say, I don't want anyone else looking after our child. But he knew that was not fair, not reasonable. Other people's children came to no harm by it.

'It's not the money,' he said. 'We'll have to be more careful now, of course, but I'm sure we could manage that.'

'You don't mind, do you? I think I've really got to have something like that. I can't live *just* for the baby, not after all this time.'

'No,' said Richard. 'I know you can't. You do need something else, I can see that. Do whatever you like.'

It was funny that she did not feel more elated, but that would come.

'Clare?' said Richard.

'Yes?'

'Why have you been *so* keen for Deborah to get to Oxford? You weren't really all that happy there yourself.'

'I was to start with. After that it was my own fault.'

'You don't think the same thing might happen to her?'

'It could. If it does I can't stop it. But I think she's tougher than that, somehow. She likes to please people, but ... she doesn't seem to feel the need to rise to other people's expectations of her the whole time.'

'Is that what you were like?'

'I think I still am.'

People think they want you to be open with them, to share yourself: but they don't, of course. They want only what they can cope with. But there must be some level between everything and nothing.

'In spite of everything,' she said 'it wasn't a time I'd have missed. It's like being in love: you'd rather be miserable that way, than happy any other way.'

To have been able to let love go, instead of snatching at it and watching it die, was something: a sign, perhaps, of having grown up at last.

Richard thought, She's trying to tell me something. Or perhaps there's nothing to tell. I don't understand things that aren't open: something can't be true and not true at the same time, can it?

But she's still here, after all, isn't she? And the baby will be here soon.

'I love you,' he said 'and it doesn't make me miserable.' That small doubt or fear, if it would not quite go away, would have to be lived with.

She touched his cheek. *And the thing we freely forfeit is kept with fonder a care* ... 'Nor me,' she said.

In time, stripped of all that she had carried with her for so long, she might even experience that adult pleasure she had never yet tasted. It did no harm to have hopes, provided you did not build your whole life up on them.

So long as you knew you must manage alone you could do so. Provided you did not have to believe there was any celestial puppet master mocking your jerky, ungraceful movements before you had even made them; no demented father-figure calling *Childe*.

On Wednesday morning in the book-room Deborah, her long hair scooped back into a rubber band, sat at a desk under the resentful eye of a conscripted PE teacher. The soccer field outside was a waste of frozen mud.

Instead of wasting time reading through the whole paper, she tracked down the three questions that invited her to write about all the reading and thinking she had done on Hopkins, and Larkin, and Chaucer. She decided Hardy was a little too obvious: she would save him for the general paper.

The questions were all open-ended, designed to accommodate themselves to ideas thought out in advance, instead of on the spur of the moment: not testing one's ability to bluff, or to think on one's feet, or to make information look like understanding. It was not the object of the exercise to fool anyone. She hoped for at least three years of her life in which this would not be the object of any exercise she undertook.

Everything hurt: daylight, the bare trees, chalk dust, his own footsteps along the corridors. All day Colin had been making his pupils read aloud in rotation throughout the lesson; letting them go without homework. If they stuck over a word, and he could find enough motive power to open his mouth, he prompted them: otherwise he let them work it out for themselves, or flounder. He could not have done that with his previous classes: the new ones, puzzled and surprised, could at least be run on automatic pilot for a while.

He was having trouble in swallowing. At mid-morning break he had to abandon his coffee: which was embarrassing, or would have been if anyone had noticed. 'Cheer up, Col' said Bob: 'Death can't be so far off.'

At the beginning of the lunch hour he went up to see how Deborah had got on. She was, after all, officially his pupil now. And his only remaining link with Clare. When she had gone he sat on in the book-room, turning over the pages of exercise-books, for an hour and a quarter. One thing about that was that it made the bell for afternoon school quite welcome.

The last period of the day was with what had been Clare's sixth-form group. It was in one of the worst of the temporary classrooms: chunks of the inside plaster-board had crumbled away; there was a large damp stain on the back wall; and most of the desk lids were broken. She sat here, where I am, and listened to them read ... he looked out at the darkness coming down outside; and then, since a Head of Department must not break down in front of his pupils, looked hard at anything: the holes in the desks where the china inkwells had been; Diane Hall's polished fingernails and Princess-of-Wales haircut.

In Deborah's absence, Diane was reading the closing stanzas of *Troilus and Criseyde*. She read quite prettily, in a local-drama-school kind of way; she had picked up from Clare some sort of modified Chaucerian pronunciation which allowed the verse its proper shape. Colin hardly had to move, or use his voice; and it was something to keep the upper area of his mind occupied.

> *Thorugh which I se that clene out of your mynde*
> *Ye han me cast; and I ne kan ne may,*
> *For al this world, withinne myn herte fynde*
> *To unloven yow a quarter of a day!*
> *In corsed tyme I born was, weilaway,*
> *That yow, that doon me al this wo endure*
> *Yet love I best of any creature!*

Outside, someone was banging a door, again and again. For a moment, Colin was convinced that he was going to be sick: which would, at any rate, have ensured that they never forgot that stanza. He must have moved, because Diane looked up. He nodded to her to go on; and found that he could, after all, swallow the bitter fluid that had filled his throat.

He had known that stanza before, of course. Only he had always read it in context, as he told his pupils to do: such-and-such a reaction is appropriate to such-and-such a climate of ideas. But Troilus's misery was no less real for being the product of an emotional fashion. Our ways of thinking and feeling choose us as much as we choose them; and words exist not to falsify feelings, but to make them bearable by giving them shape.

'Just a minute, Diane,' he said. 'Sorry to break in — can we go forward for a moment? Five stanzas from the end.'

Relieved at the shift back to teacherly authority, they all counted.

'Look,' said Colin, 'this stanza is the counterweight to the other one: it even has some of the same rhythmic patterns, reversed — we can look at that in a minute. It sets out an alternative way of feeling. In the part Diane read, we felt all Troilus's pain. He's lost Criseyde, yet he can't stop loving her, or find any way of living with it. I think you all found that bit convincing, didn't you?'

A cooperative murmur from someone. This way, not battling all the time, you could get back to sanity, back to doing what you could do well and usefully, without shame.

'But here, at the end, Chaucer gets accused of backing down from what he's written — of copping out to the priests.'

Mr Rowsley back on his religious hobbyhorse again — all's right with the world. What would Diane with her Scripture Union button say if I told her, Troilus is damned, Troilus will suffer for all eternity?

'But if you read the two stanzas together,' he said, 'you'll see that they go together. Chaucer's writing for an audience he can *see:* they're sitting round him, listening. He knows they'll protest, he knows they'll say Troilus's love was the best thing about him.

'He isn't saying "Do without romantic love": he's saying "Look at romantic love and what it does — and then put it behind you thankfully: come home from it." Let me read you this piece:

> *O yonge, fresshe folkes, he or she,*
> *In which that love up groweth with youre age,*
> *Repeyreth hom fro worldly vanyte,*
> *And of youre hertes up casteth the visage*
> *To thilke God that after his ymage*
> *Yow made, and thynketh al nys but a faire*
> *This world, that passeth soone as floures faire.*

'Beverley, what does Chaucer mean by calling the world a "fair"?'

'Um ... kind of like a circus, sir?'

'Lynne?'

'Something pretty, sir?'

'You're both right, in a way. It's a wordplay, isn't it? — "fair" means "beautiful", but it also means a passing show, something that ends at nightfall. I suspect that for a mediaeval poet the word "fair" had the idea of transience built into it from the start — do you know what transience is? God is a parent waiting up for his children, who have stayed out too late. The children resent it, in the way that we do resent our parents, and in the same way that we as readers resent what Chaucer is doing with our emotions. But it's the better kind of love, all the same.'

Deborah would have got the point, intellectually at least. The rest of them, with a bit of luck, understood the words. Their polite faces looked back at him.

Yonge, fresshe folkes could hardly be addressed to him, could it? And it was he who had done the casting out. She had loved him, not merely clung to him. Whatever potential consolation was offered by the poem must at some point be weighed up; and if bought, then paid for. All the same, it was at least a voice that he could bear to listen to.

Deborah sat and waited for her paper to be collected in. She was tired and rather stiff, but not in the least drained, either emotionally or intellectually. She thought Mr Rowsley (it was no use, she couldn't think of him as Colin) would probably quite like it if she found him and showed him the question paper before she went home. On Friday, after the last paper was finished, she would go up to Gatelaw on the bus and show them to Clare.

Carefully, so as not to break the ends of her hair, she took the rubber band off; she picked up her watch from the desk and strapped it back on her wrist. She thought that, so far, she had probably done rather well.